The Unveiling

The Unveiling

by
Leah Rae Lambert

iUniverse, Inc.
New York Bloomington

The Unveiling

This is a work of fiction. All of the characters, names, incidents, organizations, and dialogue in this novel are either the products of the author's imagination or are used fictitiously.

iUniverse books may be ordered through booksellers or by contacting:

iUniverse
1663 Liberty Drive
Bloomington, IN 47403
www.iuniverse.com
1-800-Authors (1-800-288-4677)

ISBN: 978-0-595-50597-5 (pbk)
ISBN: 978-0-595-61575-9 (ebk)

Printed in the United States of America

iUniverse rev. date: 8/26/2009

Permissions for Use of Excerpts from Song Lyrics and Poetry

"LET YOURSELF GO" by Irving Berlin
© Copyright 1935 by Irving Berlin
© Copyright Renewed, International Copyright Secured
All Rights Reserved. Reprinted by Permission
Excerpt appears on page 133.

IT HAD TO BE YOU
Words by GUS KAHN Music by ISHAM JONES
© 1924 (Renewed) WARNER BROS. INC. Rights for the Extended Term in the U.S. controlled by GILBERT KEYES MUSIC and THE BANTAM MUSIC PUBLISHING CO.
All Rights Administered by WB MUSIC CORP
All Rights Reserved Used by Permission of ALFRED PUBLISHING CO. INC.
Excerpt appears on 157.

BYE BYE BLACKBIRD
By Mort Dixon/Ray Henderson
Used by Permission of Publisher: Redwood Music Ltd.
Excerpt appears on page 287.

WHO AM I?
Excerpt from "Who Am I?" from *Chicago Poems* by Carl Sandburg,
© 1916 by Holt, Rinehart and Winston, © renewed 1944 by Carl Sandburg
Reprinted by permission of Houghton Mifflin Harcourt Publishing Company
Excerpt appears on page 1.

THE UNHINGING OF WINGS by Margo Button
Excerpt reprinted by permission of Margo Button, © 1996
Excerpt appears on page 237.

In Memory of My Mother

Acknowledgements

This book could not have been written without the input and encouragement of a number of people, including Yetta Rubin, Corrine Harris, Allen Rubin, Abe Rubin, Jack Rubin, Bess Tucker, and Larry Tucker.

Special thanks for additional assistance to Lisa Lambert, Philip Schein, Ray Ferris, Carol Swartz, and Nancy Merenstein.

Foreword

In this fascinating novel of multiple traumas—of forced migration, severe mental illness, and the destructive weight of family secrets—fiction mirrors the fractures in many real lives. *The Unveiling* is moving and knowledgeable writing. It helps us understand how a major psychiatric disorder is experienced, its impact on families, and how an unveiling, both literally and figuratively, can reinforce resilience and hope.

—Harriet P. Lefley, Ph.D., Professor of Psychiatry & Behavioral Sciences, University of Miami Miller School of Medicine

---

This marvelous book offers deep insights into the immigrant experience, tracing life in the shetl in Europe to the inner city of Pittsburgh. It gives a brilliant portrayal of the life of a family as it attempts to adjust to the transition into the American culture. It describes the impact of mental illness on the family and the stigma and fear that led to keeping secrets that, when revealed, liberated the family. The engrossing novel provides an important case study that shows the effects of social attitudes toward mental illness on the health of a family.

— Morton Coleman, Ph.D., Board Member, Southwest Pennsylvania Chapter, National Alliance for the Mentally Ill; Professor, Director Emeritus, University of Pittsburgh School of Social Work

---

I sat down to read a few pages of *The Unveiling*, but could not put the book down until I had read it from start to finish. This riveting account of a family's struggle with stigma, shame, economic hardship, derision, loss, and grief should be read by everyone who knows a person suffering from mental illness. Interwoven with these challenges, there are times of fun, laughter, and music in this vibrant family. The book conveys a wealth of important insights into the kinds of help persons with mental illness and their families need, and the enduring admiration and respect that they deserve.

As a lifetime mental health professional and relative of a person with mental illness, I've seen and read numerous personal accounts, all of them powerful. This distinguished book is unsurpassed among them. It provides a skillful and gripping portrayal of family life in the context of Jewish heritage: escape from oppression in Europe to grinding poverty in the America of the Great Depression; psychological and spiritual development in the midst of multiple adversities; and profound love, caring, and courage.

The context for the narrative is a reunion of family members at the time of Morton's death. Progressively through each of the seven days of sitting shiva, reminiscences by family guide readers to know each of them. Their secrets of grief, shame, and love are "unveiled."

The heroism and devotion of family members for each other and for Morton shine through the accounts of the long, tragic illness and its impact on so many near and dear. Ettie emerges as the star who unfailingly nurtured and guided her three children as a single parent. She tenaciously overcame seemingly insurmountable obstacles to make it possible for all three children to thrive and become highly successful adults.

Only at the end of Morton Burin's life did those who loved him recognize the many strengths and sources of pride he and they had shown throughout their lives. The book's title, designating an event that often occurs a year after a person dies, is also a metaphor for tearing off the shrouds of secrecy maintained by the beleaguered Burin family.

—Harriette C. Johnson, M.S.W., Ph.D., Professor, University of Connecticut School of Social Work

---

What a dramatic novel of a valiant woman, who in spite of her husband's serious mental illness, accomplished so much through the success of her children. Sadly, although the psychopharmacologic treatment of such illness has progressed so much in the past sixty years, the stigma still remains. I could not put this book down; I recommend it enthusiastically to families bearing the burden and stigma of mental illness and to mental health professionals who work with them.

— Emil S. Trellis, M.D., Distinguished Life Fellow, American Psychiatric Association

---

To read the moving story about the experiences of a Jewish family in the twentieth century evokes many layers of emotion. I can touch on only a few here.

Throughout the novel the healing effect of caring and compassion is striking. Shtetl life in the early years of the twentieth century must have been almost unbearable given the virulent anti-semitism of the surrounding peasants, the harsh economic times and the unprovoked violence. Life for a fatherless immigrant family in Pittsburgh was no picnic either. In both cases the support of family and friends made all the difference.

The theme of strong women is convincing . Ettie's mother Sarah was a single mother for eight very difficult and eventful years. Ettie's husband was absent for nearly fifty years. One must admire these characters. Both these women seem to have passed on an inner strength to their children…

Of particular interest to me was the theme of mental illness. The flashbacks to Morton's care in the state hospital were all too familiar. I started in Psychiatry just as the major tranquillizers were being introduced. Insulin coma and electroconvulsive therapy were still in common use. It is not easy to reconstruct the spirit of that time. In retrospect the ideal asylum would protect patients from themselves, provide occupation and as congenial an atmosphere as possible in hopes that they would recover, and some did. Because of the poor prognosis of schizophrenia, clinicians, and families, were willing to try anything that seemed to have a rationale. Indeed, in Ontario *families* urged the

Minister of Health to introduce lobotomy. After sending physicians to the US to look at results he agreed. One must remember that evaluation of medicines and other treatments in the'40's and '50's was still very primitive and often based on the clinician's impression…

This work leaves one with a sense of authenticity. At no point did I feel the need to suspend disbelief. Reading *The Unveiling* evokes a complex set of strong feelings: indignation, guilt, sadness and eventually a sense of joy.

— A. S. Macpherson MD, MSc., FRCPC, Professor Emeritus, Psychiatry, McMaster University

Preface

The Unveiling is about the power of a family secret and the struggle to reveal the truth. An immigrant Jewish girl and her family—after surviving destitution, religious persecution, and a harrowing escape to 1920s America—fight a decades-long battle to overcome fears about society's reaction to mental illness.

Although *The Unveiling* is fiction, real people provided the inspiration for most of its characters. Many of the events in the book actually happened or grew out of stories and experiences my family members shared with me. In writing the story, I filled in gaps in personal accounts by creating some fictional characters and experiences.

Extensive research and personal interviews provided rich source material for life in the shtetls of Czarist Russia, the struggles of new immigrants to Pittsburgh, Pennsylvania, and the particular challenges for families coping with the stigma of mental illness in the mid-twentieth century. I also drew upon my own memories of my father's struggle with schizophrenia, the impact his mental illness had on the family, the generosity and love of my immediate and extended family, and my mother's courage and determination.

—Leah Rae Lambert, 2008

PART ONE

A DIGNIFIED FUNERAL

My name is Truth and I am the most elusive captive in the universe.

—"Who Am I" by Carl Sandburg

The Arrangements

"Why are you doing this? What are you trying to prove?" Ettie Burin asked, twisting her napkin with both hands. That, and the sarcasm in her voice betrayed the depth of her fear. "I thought it would be a private funeral. I don't see why you need to get the whole world involved."

She sat staring at her two daughters across the table from her in a booth at Eat'n'Park, a family style chain restaurant in Pittsburgh. It was already 9:00 PM, and the waitresses were hovering near the tables not yet vacated. One waitress began to rattle dishes in an attempt to communicate to the few patrons still lingering that they should move on and let the staff finish their work for the day. Someone in the next room began vacuuming the carpet.

Ettie took a sip of her tea, plunked the cup back down carelessly enough that some of its contents spilled into the saucer, then pushed the saucer to the middle of the table to emphasize her disbelief at what she was hearing. She lifted her trembling right hand to the puff of white hair on one side of her face. The hair on the other side was flattened against her head where she had slept on it the night before. She wore no makeup and the deep creases in her forehead reflected the strain of her eighty-four years as she leaned forward on her elbow.

Collette, her elder daughter, began to cry softly. "He's my father, and I love him very much. He deserves a dignified funeral with a full religious service. I want this done properly."

They sat in silence for several moments before the waitress approached the table. "Is everything all right, ladies? Can I get you anything else?"

Ettie's middle child, Rachel, looked up, her frown fading into gratitude for the interruption. "Nothing else. Everything's fine, thank you."

Ettie didn't know what her daughters and her son-in-law, Stanley, had talked about before they picked her up at her Forward-Shady apartment building for senior citizens. She didn't even know where they were going until Stanley announced that he would drop them off at the restaurant, where they could talk and have a bite to eat while he ran a few errands to prepare for tomorrow's funeral. He'd be back for them in about an hour. Her youngest, David, was scheduled to arrive later, so she wouldn't see him until just before the funeral.

As soon as they had settled in the restaurant, Rachel revealed that she had not taken the time to pack properly. "When I received Collette's call at work, I assumed that David and I should arrive as quickly as possible to help you and Collette make the funeral arrangements." She'd arranged her flight from Toronto to Pittsburgh and left voice mail messages for her son and daughter, encouraging them to attend. Rachel sighed at that, and added, "I just hope I included enough specifics so they'll be able to arrange flights to show up on time for the funeral."

She looked across the table as her mother repeated that she expected this to be a quiet, private funeral.

Collette jumped in. "Everything is already arranged. Anyone who wants to come is welcome. Mother, I've already called your cousin Bea, and she agreed to call the others to let them know. An announcement has already gone to the *Jewish Chronicle*."

Stunned, Ettie stared from Collette to Rachel. "It just isn't necessary, and it doesn't make sense," she said, her tone both aggressive and pleading.

Collette cleared her throat and looked into her mother's eyes. "I don't understand why you don't realize this is the way it should be. Why would you want anything different?" Her oldest was usually mild-mannered and conciliatory, but now Collette was making no attempt to hide her irritation. "You know this is the way it's always done. To do it any other way would dishonor Dad's memory." She blinked back tears as her mouth tightened, clearly to stifle a sob.

Ettie looked at the ceiling. "Honor, shmoner," she mumbled. "I thought it would be private. If you only admitted how much trouble he always caused, you would feel differently."

"Mother, that's not fair," Collette said softly.

Ettie shrugged. "Collette, you're too sick. I don't want to upset you. I don't agree with this, but I guess I have no choice." She looked in sympathy at her oldest child, who had suffered for the past ten years from a disease of the immune system that had a long, confusing name. Nobody knew what caused it, and the best the doctors could do was treat the changing symptoms and try to keep it under control. Sometimes she functioned reasonably well, but it didn't take much for her to experience a flare-up and develop a myriad of illnesses.

Although Collette had been managing as well as could be expected, her symptoms had become more pronounced during the past year, with more fevers and congestion. The steroids prescribed by her doctor made her appear bloated, her face overly round—a far cry from the exuberant, bright-eyed young woman Ettie still pictured during their telephone conversations.

Ettie glanced at Rachel, then back to Collette, and finally gave in to a sense of resignation and dread. She realized it would not be fair, nor would it serve any purpose, to keep arguing. "So, what do you expect me to do at the funeral? What do you expect me to say to people? I hope you don't expect me to put on a show."

Rachel responded with an expression that convinced Ettie that they both held the same opinion. Then Rachel cleared her throat and assumed a professional tone, the same tone that never failed to irritate Ettie when she had dealings with people in various social agencies or government offices. "Well, Collette, what are the options? What types of services might we have? What can we arrange with the rabbi to help everyone feel better about this?"

"There are no options," Collette snapped. "Dad will be buried with the respect he is entitled to. It wasn't easy, making these arrangements today. Stanley and I have been on the go for hours. Now it's all arranged. We had to fit in half an hour with the rabbi at the only time he had available." The tears began to flow down her cheeks. She reached into her purse for tissue, then rose shakily, saying that she had to use the ladies' room.

Ettie watched Collette leave, then leaned forward and whispered to Rachel, "I don't understand her, why is she making such a hero out of her father? Dignity, respect, honor—heh! You'd think she doesn't remember what he was really like, what we went through, all those years with that man. If it weren't for her, I might have made different decisions years ago. Maybe you don't remember, but he caused her a lot of suffering too."

Rachel's mouth twisted as she rubbed her forehead. "How could I forget what went on? There is no way Collette has forgotten anything either, but she's always loved him. I've never seen her as assertive as this. It's quite shocking, actually." She took a deep breath. "I think we'd better go along with her wishes. You can't deny that she and Stanley were the ones who kept a relationship going with him all these years. Besides, we all know it wasn't really Dad's fault, what happened."

Ettie was hurt. "I suppose all those years that I *schlepped* shopping bags full of food to visit him when you kids were in school, wore myself out only to have him ignore me while he gulped down the food—I guess all of that doesn't count."

"I didn't mean that the way it sounded, Mother." Rachel reached over to pat her mother's hand. "I guess I was thinking about myself. Who am I to comment? I never got involved! For me, it was as if he died when I was a little girl. I guess that's why she figures my opinion isn't important now. You have to give her credit, she and Stanley took a real interest in him." Rachel leaned back, her eyes straying to the ladies' room door. "Obviously this means a lot to Collette. I've never seen her so insistent about anything."

As Ettie became more agitated, her voice became louder and sharper. "Does she think this can change anything?" Rachel put her finger to her lips, and Ettie lowered her voice, but continued. "Why do I need to go through this now? Didn't I suffer enough already? What will people think—they don't know the whole story! My neighbors thought I was already a widow."

There, it was out. So many years of embarrassment, of knowing she was living a lie, now out on the table! Ettie's hands shook as she lifted the cup of tea to her lips. "I guess it's too late now. I'm not going to cause Collette more aggravation and make her sick. I'll just have to go along with her. So what if everybody finds out that I've been lying!"

Rachel motioned for her mother to stop talking by nodding toward her sister as she made her way back to the table. When Collette sat down, Rachel said, "Will there be any further discussions with the rabbi? Will we all meet him and explain our feelings about the service, Collette?"

Ettie resigned herself to the reality that she would have to endure a public funeral.

"Of course," Collette answered, her tone tentative. "Anyone can talk to the rabbi and share their feelings. It's just a matter of whether he has any time."

Rachel pushed on. "I'll tell you what I think should happen, now that this is going to be public. I hope we can finally end the silence, the secrecy we forced on ourselves for almost fifty years. It's 1995 and about time to be open about what happened to Dad, to all of us. If the rabbi is uncomfortable with it, maybe I can write something and read it. Enough of this embarrassment and shame!"

Collette began to cry again, her face crumpling into a pained, almost desperate expression. She spoke quickly, not trying to hide her resolve. "Rachel, this is not the time to express public fury about the past and the mistakes people made. I don't want you to make any speeches about your anger. This is not about you and your feelings. You can't come here and write an essay about how you feel and make this about your feelings. This is Dad's funeral, and it's going to be done properly. I don't understand what you're trying to do."

"I'm not trying to make this about me," Rachel interrupted. "How can you say that?"

"No one can stop this from being dignified," Collette said firmly. "It's already arranged. If you want to call the rabbi and express your feelings to him privately, I won't stop you. He even said you should feel free to do so. Maybe tomorrow before the service you and David can meet with him." She swung teary eyed to Ettie. "Mother, if you want to meet him too, you should do so. But no public displays of bitterness, anger, or lectures about the system's failures, please. This is a time for the family to speak with one voice."

Ettie stopped herself from putting voice to the words in her mind: *Yeah, one voice, but it's never my voice.*

Collette opened her purse again and pulled out a small sheet of paper. "Here's what we sent to all the papers for the obituary." She began to read: "Morton Burin, beloved husband of Enta Burin, father of Collette, Rachel, and David, brother of Solomon and Daniel, seven grandchildren, two great-grandchildren, died at age ninety-one after a long illness."

Ettie felt the blood drain from her face. "Oh my God, oh no," she whispered.

"What's wrong, Mother?" Rachel gasped.

Ettie just sighed, "I guess it's too late . . . '*Beloved* husband'—really!"

The Service

On the day of the funeral, as Rachel rode with her brother to collect their mother from her apartment and take her to the funeral home, Rachel commented, "It's sad that we're burying our father on your birthday, instead of you celebrating with your family." David had not brought his young family with him. "I hope you have a good year ahead, despite how it's beginning."

"Yeah, the irony is precious. The father I never knew but always wished for, being buried on my birthday. It figures."

Rachel glanced at him. "David, I never asked you, but do you remember anything at all about him?" She couldn't remember ever speaking at length with David about their father and was embarrassed to ask, after all the lies she'd been party to. She knew the situation was more painful for David than for the rest of the family. He had never experienced any happy or hopeful times with his father.

David's laugh was short and bitter. "All I remember is the big lie! How could Mother lie to me for all those years? How could I have been so gullible, to believe her?" His tone grew accusing. "And how come you never told me the truth? Why did I have to find out the way I did?"

So he was not going to let her off the hook. She didn't know how to respond, except to explain that their mother had always insisted that she was not ready to tell him, that the truth was too awful for a little boy to know. Rachel had always feared the consequences, should she be the one to reveal the ugly truth.

When they pulled into the driveway of Ettie's apartment building on Forward Avenue, David said, "I'll wait in the car. You go get Mother."

Three white-haired women were coming out the front door as Rachel approached. One of them grabbed Rachel's arm as she passed. Rachel recognized her from her visit with her mother a few months earlier. "I'm very sorry for your loss," the woman whispered. "Is the funeral today?"

"Thank you. Yes, I'm on my way to get my mother now."

The woman smiled. "A wonderful person, your mother. You're very lucky to have such a mother," she said as she walked away with her friends toward the street.

As soon as Rachel pushed the buzzer for her mother to let her in, Ettie's voice came through the intercom as if she'd been standing beside it, waiting. "You don't have to come up. I'll be right down."

* * *

It was just a short ride from the apartment building to Hirsch's Funeral Home on Murray Avenue. When David pulled the car into the small, triangular parking lot at the side door, panic made Ettie feel light-headed. She waited for David to help her out of the car, then grabbed his hand and walked toward the entrance, feeling as if she were in a strange dream, about to enter a haunted house from which there was no escape.

She'd been here before—first for the funeral of Collette's first child, a beautiful little girl who was the victim of an unexplainable crib death at the age of ten weeks. Seven years later came the shocking death of Rachel's kind-hearted and talented first husband who, without explanation, took his own life, leaving Rachel a young widow with two small children. Ettie's heartbreak on those occasions had been overwhelming. *Not like now,* she thought. Now all she could think about was what others might think of her. And she realized that this had always been the case in her relationship with Morton. Her primary concern had always been the perceptions of others.

Ettie walked along the long, narrow hallway just beyond the funeral home's entrance, its lighting subdued to achieve a suitably somber atmosphere. Two rooms opened into the hallway, each with a removable black placard beside the door, announcing the name of the deceased person whose funeral would be held within. She felt a sharp pain in her stomach when she saw the name *Morton Burin* beside the second door. Drawing a steadying breath, she stepped inside.

The room resembled an old-fashioned parlor, its floor scattered with a variety of chairs upholstered in floral fabrics and occasional tables holding small lamps. An anteroom at the back was reserved for the immediate family. Ettie saw Collette and her family near the entrance to the small room that held the closed casket.

As soon as they saw her enter, Collette's son and daughter walked over and hugged Ettie, then escorted her to a small sofa in the anteroom. Following behind her, Rachel and David each patted Ettie on the head and kissed her as soon as she took her seat, then moved to embrace Collette. As Rachel took a seat near her mother, David went to the back of the room to join Stanley.

Collette, her face mirroring the deep sadness she felt, nodded toward Morton's two surviving brothers, the youngest of Morton's family, who were pacing along the back of the room. "They were the first to arrive," she whispered. "They were here even before we were."

Ettie followed Collette's gaze and saw the two men walk over to Stanley and David. For a moment, gazing at her son from this distant perspective, she was amazed at how tall and handsome he was, with a finely tuned body well over six feet tall. He looked much younger than his fifty-two years. After a few moments of whispered conversation, Morton's brothers approached Ettie and the others. They exchanged some stiff hugs and kisses, self-conscious shrugs, and quiet words of comfort. Then everyone except David found chairs to await the friends and family who would come to pay their respects and express their condolences. David continued to pace, dark head lowered, at times turning his back to everyone to stare out the window.

Within half an hour Ettie's nephew and a few cousins who still lived in Pittsburgh wandered in and made the rounds to say some comforting words to Ettie and her children. Whispered conversations were broken periodically by louder voices that made the room sound more like friends gathered at a social event than at a funeral. Finally Rachel's son Steve and daughter Laurie arrived. Most of the latecomers were friends of either Ettie or Collette, and didn't recognize Rachel or David or even realize it was their father who had died.

Watching Collette, who seemed to be wiping her eyes after every few sentences, Ettie whispered to Laurie, "I can't take much more of this; I can't wail and weep, pretending I'm the heartbroken widow." She sighed, shaking her head. "I guess everyone will talk about me now."

Laurie just patted her grandmother's hand. "Oh Grandma, it's okay, stop worrying."

A short, wiry man with bushy white eyebrows suddenly appeared and approached Ettie. He was almost bald, with only a rim of white hair that circled the back of his head from above one ear to the other ear. He leaned forward. "Ettie, it's a sad time. Such a pity! I was reading the *Jewish Chronicle*, and I saw that Mort passed away, so I came to pay my respects. Remember back then, we were all such good friends?"

Ettie looked blankly at the face before her, trying not to stare at the brownish-yellow tobacco stains that discolored his teeth and fingernails while she searched her memory for a name. Suddenly a glimmer of recognition swept away her confusion, and she relaxed. "Natie Gordon, is that you? Well, I'll be darned. You used to have all that red hair." He put his arms on Ettie's shoulders and with that, Ettie began to cry. She caught her breath and said softly, "*Oy*, I thought the tears were all gone years ago. It's nice of you to come.

"Natie, here are my granddaughters." She motioned for them to come closer, then pointed. "See those two guys over there? They're my grandsons. And I have three more grandchildren back in Kentucky—my son's kids." Ettie looked up at Natie. "Boy oh boy, it's been a lot of years since I last saw you."

Natie smiled wistfully, then said to Ettie's granddaughters, "Would you believe it, I knew your *bubbe* before she met Morton . . . Such a fun-loving girl she was, always dancing—loved to do the Charleston." He tapped Ettie on the arm. "Remember, Ettie, how our gang used to get together in that room on Wylie Avenue? It was part of the Hebrew Institute back then."

"Yeah," Ettie replied, grinning, "you would bring your harmonica and ukulele, play the music, and everyone would dance. Who worried about anything? Young and stupid, I guess that's what we all were."

Natie looked at Ettie's granddaughters and continued as if Ettie had not made the last statement. "The others, they all got tired out fast, but not your bubbe. I'll tell you, this girl could really dance! It was a beautiful sight. I remember how much we all enjoyed. Lots of times, the gang would make a circle around her to watch her go at it. So much rhythm and energy! She never ran out of steam. Wonderful person!" He smiled at Ettie. "She used to come to all the dances with her sister, Libby."

He nudged Laurie's arm. "You know, I used to wish I could have your bubbe for my wife. But she was hooked on Mort. He couldn't even dance, just liked to stand and watch." He looked at Ettie. "How many years has it been that I haven't seen you, Ettie?"

Before Ettie could respond, two women from her apartment building stepped into their circle and reached down to embrace her, telling her how sorry they were. One was Ettie's apartment building director, who turned to Rachel and said, "I've always considered Ettie a role model, someone who found the strength and spirit to live through pain and adversity."

Ettie offered a smile and expressed her appreciation, then turned her attention back to Natie Gordon, still speaking to her granddaughters. "You know, your grandfather was smarter'n anyone, the smartest of them all. *Vay is mir*, such a pity, so much suffering he brought Ettie!" He tilted his head and shook it, puckered his face and clucked his regret, then shrugged. "*Nu*, what can you do? Wonderful woman, your bubbe. You live near here, you visit her often?"

Laurie opened her mouth to respond, but before she could say anything, Stanley walked over.

"The rabbi is ready to begin the service," he told them. "We should all take our seats in the next room." He nodded toward the larger room, where the closed casket had been moved to the front.

This is exactly what Collette wanted, Ettie reflected during the service. The rabbi concentrated on the first half of Morton's life, how he came from a small village in Lithuania and as a young man studied in a yeshiva, how he and all his family had struggled so hard to survive during and after the First World War, how hard it was for him as an immigrant in the United States. He mentioned that Morton loved his children, that there had been hard times for Morton and his family, but did not elaborate, instead concluding with, "But this is not the time to dwell on those.

"It is hard to lose a loved one," he intoned, as if this death would have the same impact on Morton's family as would the death of an elderly father and husband in any family. He did not acknowledge that the significant loss had taken place fifty years earlier.

"Collette, Rachel, and David shared their memories of their father with me," the rabbi added. "They are grateful for the love and support of everyone."

The prayers and sermon helped most people in attendance to feel more comfortable. Nothing in it comforted Ettie. This was one more ordeal that she had to endure. She looked around at her cousins and friends in the room and wondered how many of them even remembered Mort. Nobody ever talked about him with her. Her brother Ben always had kind words of comfort about what had happened to Mort, if the subject came up, but Ben was a quiet man and did not like to discuss serious problems. If her sister Libby were still alive, that would be another story—*then* there would really be something to worry about! Libby would probably say something sarcastic about Mort and all the trouble he caused. Still, Ettie wished Libby could be here to share the early memories.

The Procession

The headache and nausea she felt during the slow ride to the cemetery did not surprise Ettie, with eight family members crowded into the stuffy limo. In addition to Morton's two brothers, Collette and Stanley, Rachel, David, and Ettie herself, Rachel had asked her daughter, Laurie, to take the last space, which was fine with Ettie.

"There's no air in here," Rachel said, fanning the air before leaning forward. "Could we have the window lowered?"

Ettie was freezing. "Please, leave it shut." She would put up with the headache.

Their vehicle led a line of eight cars, each with a little black flag waving from its antenna to signal to other vehicles that it was part of a funeral procession. They drove slowly through the narrow, hilly streets of Squirrel Hill. Some, like Beechwood Boulevard, were filled with older, stately houses built high off the street, their front doors reached by steep stone stairs. The lots were wide, the well-groomed shrubbery and grassy front lawns possessed of a storybook quality in summer. At this time in March, though, the branches were bare and the lawns still winter-brown. Indeed, the gray sky and bleak landscape seemed to match everyone's mood, and the ride began largely in silence.

Other streets in Squirrel Hill were filled with cramped and deteriorating semidetached houses, their yards containing only a few scraggly bushes, the atmosphere one of decay. "Some areas have become really run-down," Rachel commented. "I don't understand why I thought everyone who lived in this neighborhood was rich when I was a child."

"Well, they had more money than the rest of us did, you can be sure of that," Ettie answered.

The procession entered a less residential area. Not much had changed over the last thirty years. They drove along potholed streets lined with shabby apartment buildings and boarded-up stores, the broken sidewalks littered with debris. The people they passed seemed listless, as if unable to separate their bleak lives from the run-down landscape. In contrast, the colorful structures dotting the hillsides on the other side of the river could have appeared in a postcard from a picturesque, old-world city, at least from this distance.

Rachel spoke again. "This city obviously needs to be spruced up. It could be so beautiful, with the hills and rivers, the winding streets. Why don't they do something to fix it up, or at least keep it clean?"

"What do you expect? You're spoiled, living in Toronto," her mother scolded. "Pittsburgh is a poor, old city. It's a lot cleaner now than it used to be. You should have seen it when we first got here from the old country."

Ettie couldn't hide her annoyance. Rachel had always made it clear how anxious she was to leave Pittsburgh. It hadn't been so bad when she moved to Washington, D.C. shortly after she'd married. When that ended so tragically, Ettie knew the anguish her daughter felt. It seemed only natural for Rachel to return to Pittsburgh with her children. Ettie hadn't hesitated to give up her apartment and move into a larger place to help raise the kids while Rachel attended graduate school.

Those three years had been exhausting, but Ettie loved being so close with her grandchildren and had begun to think of them almost as her own. Despite Rachel's frequent reminders that she planned to leave Pittsburgh again, Ettie always expected the four of them would stay together until the children were at least teenagers. But Rachel had to go and fall in love with her boss, Cal, and she'd taken Steve and Laurie with her when they moved to Toronto. Rachel's promised visits a few times a year provided no consolation to Ettie.

She was not surprised that Rachel's loving relationship with Toronto turned out to be more enduring than her ill-advised second marriage. Ettie couldn't blame her for liking Toronto, but she never completely forgave her for leaving and taking her kids to another city.

David didn't share his sister's negative reaction to Pittsburgh. "What do you have against this city, anyway?" he challenged her. "I would move back here without thinking twice, if I had a good offer. It's a great city to live in—the people are so friendly, and there's as much to do here as anywhere else."

"I know, I know, you and the rest of the family love it here," Rachel sighed. "I just never felt happy living here. It isn't the city's fault. I guess I can't separate the city from all the things that happened when I was a kid."

Morton's brothers began talking, ignoring what Rachel and David were saying, as if they could shut out the real reason they were all in the car together. One of them mentioned that a famous boxer had come from one of the neighborhoods they were passing through. He couldn't remember his name. Then the other began talking about the first time he'd driven through the area, and got lost. Collette and Stanley remained unusually quiet.

David surprised everyone when he asked his two uncles to tell him what his father was like as a boy. After an awkward silence, Sol tried a joke: "Do you know how hard it is, at my age, to remember back that far?" David's expression made it clear that he would not be brushed off, and Uncle Sol got serious and began telling a story about their early years in the retail clothing business. "Morton had an idea for a big sale to improve revenues, but we all disregarded him—it seemed such a radical departure from what we were used to." He paused, shook his head. "Your father was ahead of his time, I guess."

David pushed for more, prompting them with, "What about the time he fell out of the back of a truck and bumped his head when he was a teenager?"

His uncles looked at one another, then back at David, and shook their heads. "Heard about that but don't really remember the details," Daniel said, then added, "We were both young boys back then."

The limousine descended a steep hill and crossed a bridge over the Allegheny River to meander for about fifteen minutes along an unfamiliar winding road. They drove around an S-shaped curve, up another steep hill, and into a rural area, with leafless trees bordering brown fields scattered with patches of melted snow and dirty ice. "Look, there's some blue sky peeking through the clouds," Rachel announced, "and the sun is trying to come out."

"Oh boy, life can be so sweet, on the sunny side of the street," Ettie sang sarcastically.

"Here we are," the driver finally announced, and they got out and walked to the graveside, where a few people were already standing.

The six male relatives invited to be pallbearers carried the casket slowly over the soggy, muddy ground. Ettie wondered if there had ever been a funeral where the casket was dropped and the body came tumbling out. *That would definitely spoil the dignity Collette had insisted upon,* she thought wryly.

It was much colder out here in the countryside. The dampness seemed to seep through her boots and send a chill up her legs. Ettie began to shiver, and Rachel put her arm around her mother and grabbed her hand.

Graveside

Once everyone was standing under the canopy covering the gravesite, the rabbi began chanting the Hebrew prayer for the dead. The family quickly joined in.

Yit-gadal v'yit-kadash sh'mey raba,
B'alma di v'ra hirutey, v'yam-lih mal hutey
B'ha-yey-hon uv-yomey-hon uv-ha-yey d'hol beyt yisrael
Ba-agala u-vizman kariv, v'imru. Amen.

As David took hold of his mother's free hand, Ettie's mind raced to other funerals, where she had felt so much personal grief. She thought of her father's death in 1954 when she, her sister Libby, and her mother screamed hysterically, as if they were back in their shtetl in Ukraine. She wondered what her mother would do if she were here now, especially considering how anxious her mother had been for her to marry Morton. No, this funeral was something else. It was lucky that her mother didn't have to participate in this. This was no cause for wailing.

When the mourner's *kaddish* was over, the rabbi and most in attendance continued:

The Lord is my shepherd, I shall not want.
He makes me lie down in green pastures,
He leads me beside still waters,
He revives my spirit . . .

***

Still holding onto Ettie's hand, Rachel began to wonder what her mother was thinking. Was she remembering any good times? Had she ever felt giddy with love? Rachel realized she never really knew what the attraction had been, or if Ettie married Morton only to please *her mother*. What Rachel did know was that Ettie had been only fifteen when they met; Morton was eight years older. She knew that their first meeting took place about five years from the time Ettie's family arrived in North America after surviving the hardships of war and a harrowing escape.

Morton had been in the United States about the same length of time. His family had not had it so easy either, even though his father was a rabbi. His mother had died in childbirth in Lithuania when he was thirteen. After her death, his malnourished older sister struggled to take care of the family as if she were the mother, but she'd been too sickly, and died herself a few years later. Morton had two older half-brothers whose mother had also died young. Those two had left for America several years before Morton and the rest of the family did, and only one of them, Isaac, survived those early years in the new land. It was Isaac who helped their father, Morton, and his three younger brothers make their way to America after they had endured hunger and war. The photograph taken before they left Lithuania, showing Morton, his father, and his brothers at the grave of Morton's mother, was one of the saddest pictures Rachel remembered from the box Ettie kept in her chest of drawers.

She returned to the present as the rabbi continued the funeral service.

Exalted, compassionate God,
Grant infinite rest
In Your sheltering Presence,
Among the holy and pure to the soul of
Morton Burin
Who has gone to his eternal home.
Merciful One, we ask that our loved one
Find perfect peace
In your embrace.
May his soul be bound up
In the bond of life.
May he rest in peace.
And let us say: Amen.

Rachel was surprised to see tears in her mother's eyes. Ettie wiped her face, blew her nose, and muttered, "Rest in peace, Morton. It's about time we both find some peace." Then she grabbed her son's arm and quickly turned to leave.

Memories

After the funeral the limousine carried them back to Collette's home, where a few cousins had prepared a light lunch for the mourners who attended the graveside service. Now the immediate family would begin to sit *shiva,* a time for family and friends to console the bereaved, to share memories of the deceased, and to pray.

Before opening the limo door, Morton's youngest brother asked Collette how many days of the traditional seven they would be observing the shiva. Collette didn't hesitate. "I don't know about everyone else, but I plan to sit the full week."

Ettie tried to keep her growing agitation from her face. Halfway out of the car when she heard this, she crooked her finger at Rachel to come closer, then shielded her mouth with one hand so no one else would hear. "I can't believe Collette is doing this to herself and to the rest of us," she whispered. "She's too sick, and it isn't necessary. She's trying to rewrite the past."

The trays of food helped lift the tension. Rachel fixed a plate for Ettie and one for herself. "The pastries are good," Ettie admitted in a whisper, "but nobody can bake like my mother did."

When they finished eating, Rachel, her brows pinched in concern, leaned close and studied Ettie's face. "You look pale, Mother," she observed. "Would you like me to help you up the stairs to take a nap?"

"No, no, it isn't necessary," Ettie insisted but finally, after some coaxing and further comments from her daughter about how drawn she looked, she agreed.

As soon as she stretched out on the bed, Ettie took Rachel's hand to keep her there. "You know, it's funny, but today I was thinking about my mother, wondering how she would have reacted to your father's funeral. She was the one who was so anxious for me to marry Morton.

She was excited about what a wonderful family I would be getting into—he was the son of a rabbi. That was really something."

Rachel had heard this before, how Ettie regretted marrying Morton but did it because she wanted to please her mother. "I still don't understand it, Mother. You must have liked something about him. You wouldn't have married him just to please Bubbe Sarah."

"Oh . . ." Ettie sighed. "Well, what's the use of talking about it now? You know my mother went through a lot before we got to this country. Did you know that her family was so poor, she had to help them by baking for another family when she was just a girl? She baked breads to keep us alive during the Russian Revolution. We'd have all been dead if she didn't know how to bake. What a rough life she had. Did I ever tell you the story of what happened back then?"

"You've told me some of it, Mother, but it's always interesting. It must have been terrible for Bubbe. She was a tough lady."

"One thing's for sure, Rachel, all the women had it bad in those days. We lived in Skvira, near Kiev in Ukraine. But it was all considered Russia back then. Let me tell you about Bubbe Sarah and what her life was like. I know the story because my mother told me parts of it, and my Aunt Golda—may they both rest in peace—liked to tell me the rest over and over again."

The door cracked open and Laurie peeked into the room. Ettie called out to her granddaughter, "Come in, Laurie; I want you to hear this too. I want you to hear about my mother."

PART TWO

THE SHTETL

The whole world is an exceedingly narrow bridge,
And the important thing—
The most important thing is not to be afraid at all.

—Brestlover Chasidim

The Narrow Bridge

Rachel settled on the bed next to her mother, and Laurie pulled up a chair. Ettie closed her eyes, trying to gather her thoughts. Then she cleared her throat and began.

"My mother's name was Sarah Burchinsky—they changed it to Burin when we arrived at Ellis Island. I guess they were lazy and didn't want to take the time to write out Burchinsky, or maybe they were just stupid and couldn't spell." Ettie curled her lip to show her disdain for the impersonal clerks she remembered. "It's funny, though—my last name didn't change when I got married because your father's name got changed from Burinovitz to Burin. My first name used to be Enta, but they misspelled it and wrote Etta. Later when we got to Pittsburgh, people started calling me Ettie. Aunt Libby's real name was Leiba Chana. She decided to change her own name when mine got changed. We liked our new names. They made us feel less like greenhorns." Ettie laughed.

"But that name business is getting ahead of the story." Ettie touched her forehead, then continued. "Libby almost died when she was an infant. Your Bubbe Sarah suffered a lot, taking care of her. She was a sickly baby, and then with me coming along so soon after that, just a little over a year later, it was hard on my mother."

Ettie described to her daughter and granddaughter an old way of life that had disappeared with the pogroms of the early twentieth century. "We didn't have much of a house, I'll tell you that. The most valuable thing in the room was that large oval picture of *Zayde* Moishe, my mother's grandfather, hanging on the wall near the big feather bed. My mother always said Zayde Moishe looked after us. I always thought he had soft, loving eyes that could follow us everywhere in the room. His gentle smile made me feel safe."

Rachel nodded, remembering earlier stories.

Ettie sighed. "The other special thing was what we could see from the two windows. One view looked down over the rooftops and beyond the trees, to the foot of the hill where the Ros River flowed." Ettie frowned, trying to remember. "I think that river flowed off the Dneipr River, but I'm not sure."

Laurie narrowed her eyes, as if trying to visualize the geography of her grandmother's childhood. "Grandma, were there other houses on the hillside? What were they like?"

Ettie thought for a while, then shook her head. "You wouldn't have been impressed, honey, if you looked at the outside of our house or any of those other houses on the hillside. They were a junky hodgepodge of old wood and patched-over roofs. The grounds were all scruffy, littered with a mish-mash of wooden boards, broken barrels, old water buckets thrown all over the place . . . what a mess. But my mother always told us it didn't matter what the outside of the houses looked like, it was the inside that counted. If it was neat and clean inside, you showed respect to God and did your duty to family. That's what she cared about.

"I can still remember the bottom of the hill, beyond the houses, the two rows of tall trees, rising above the roofs. I used to think they were like guards, protecting us all. They sheltered us from some of the wind in winter and gave us shade in summer. And I always think about that river." Ettie's voice trailed off and her gaze grew distant as she focused inward, on that faraway place of long ago.

"Your Aunt Libby loved that river too, and we had fun going there with your Bubbe Sarah. I remember my mother hurrying on warm, breezy days to join the other women of Skvira at the spot near the rocks where they washed their clothes. It was hard work, but I think they liked sharing news and gossip while they all scrubbed and rinsed their laundry. They spread the clean clothes on the large, flat rocks to dry, and fussed over us children while we played games nearby. Those are a few pleasant memories of Skvira and, believe me, there weren't too many of those."

Ettie had never shared these memories before. Rachel couldn't remember her mother ever describing anything pretty or happy about life in Skvira. She was surprised that she could still discover something new about her mother, especially the fact that her mother remembered natural beauty in a place she had always described as if it were hell on earth.

After a few seconds Ettie resumed, describing what could be seen from the second window of her house. "I liked looking at the river, but your Bubbe Sarah liked looking out the other window more. She could see the *Bes Medresh,* the place where all those young men studied the Torah. My mother was in awe of them, thought they all looked so scholarly as they stood on the steps and leaned on the railing in front of the building with their long, black coats blowing in the wind, looking so mystical. I remember those wide-brimmed hats covering their unruly hair and their *payes*, the forelocks curling at their cheeks . . ."

Ettie giggled and shrugged. "They were always discussing and debating, and my mother was convinced they were pious and brilliant, that any special prayers they might make would surely reach the ears of the Almighty. 'I wish I could get one of them to say a special blessing for all of us,' she always said. She believed that having them nearby would keep us safe." Ettie squeezed her lips together and frowned. "Yeah, sure!"

After a short silence she continued. "It must have been so hard for my mother . . . she was only four years old when her own mother died. She often told me about that funeral, always wiped the tears from her eyes when she spoke of her mother's death in childbirth. That was when her brother Shmulek was born." Ettie slowly shook her head. "I heard the story so often, it was almost as if I had witnessed it myself."

She looked at Rachel and Laurie. "I'll tell you the story," she said firmly, "so you understand the history of the family, and know about the suffering they experienced."

***

Sarah had just turned four when *Zayde* Moishe, her grandfather on her mother's side, took her to stay with him while her mother awaited the birth of her fourth child. Several days passed, and nobody mentioned her mother. Then Zayde Moishe called her to his side and lifted her onto his knee. He pulled her head to his chest, and she could feel him trembling.

"Sarah, my child, you are blessed with a new brother, Shmulek. He is a strong boy. Now you have to be strong too, and help look after

Shmulek. Your mama is with us no longer. She has gone on a long journey." He drew a deep breath. "Such a wonderful and pure woman . . . she took care of your father and her children, she cooked and kept the Sabbath . . ." He paused for a long time, and Sarah saw the tears well up in her grandfather's eyes as he looked at her. "God has made a place for her in the Kingdom of Heaven."

Sarah frowned, trying to figure out what this meant. "Zayde, when will Mama return from her journey?"

"Once she is in the Kingdom of Heaven, only her spirit will remain with us. But she will watch over us and speak to God on our behalf," he replied softly, as if in another world himself. Sarah did not understand. Why hadn't her mother taken her on the journey with her? She thought to ask Zayde Moishe, but he was sad, and she knew she must not add to his pain.

When Sarah returned to her house, curious to see her new brother, the first thing she saw was her mother lying still on the floor, wrapped in white linen, with a candle burning near her head. *How can she be in the Kingdom of Heaven if she is here, lying so still?* she wondered. "Has Mama come back from her journey already?" she called out.

Her Aunt Yetta put her arms around Sarah and swayed back and forth, crying. "Poor babies, poor babies," she sobbed.

Some neighbor women stayed there all night, guarding her mother's still body.

Sarah woke the next morning to the sobs and shrieks of the women as her mother's body was carried out of the house. Her terror mounted with each bewildering image, every frightful sound of that day, a feeling that would haunt her for the rest of her life, whenever she thought of the comforting embrace of her mother. What was happening? Why were they taking her mother anywhere, if she was already in the Kingdom of Heaven?

"Why is everyone so sad if she is with God?" she finally found the courage to ask her father. He just stared wordlessly at her, looking dazed and numb.

She never understood why God had taken her mother away from her. "Did I do something evil?" she questioned herself over and over, replaying in her own mind every thoughtless comment that might have provoked God's punishment, thinking about every missed opportunity to do something helpful that might have eased her mother's burden. Once she started to tell Zayde Moishe that she blamed herself, but he put his finger over her lips.

"*Shah*, be quiet, my child. Your mother had a pure soul when she returned to God, and her soul will protect us."

Sarah accepted this and believed it, all her life.

***

In the days just after his wife's death, Sarah's father, Fischel, was overwhelmed with trying to make a living, feeding the children, and somehow keeping the household running. Rarely was he able to join the other men in the usual prayers. A woman in the town who also had a small baby accepted the role of wet-nurse for Shmulek, so at least he flourished during the first year.

Sarah's older sister, Gitl, almost in her teens, tried to fill her mother's shoes, cooking and caring for the younger children, but it was too hard. Fischel would hear Gitl scolding Sarah, telling her to do chores, run errands, look after the baby, and he realized that Gitl was bullying Sarah. He often saw Sarah staring at him, but he didn't know what she expected him to do or say. She looked more and more like his dead wife, and that made him feel even more uncomfortable with this tiny, quiet girl, so obedient and so obviously unhappy.

At the end of the year, Fischel invited the town matchmaker to their home. "So, what can you expect? You have nothing to offer," she said during their whispered conversation, mindful of the children nearby.

"Nu," she added when Fischel hesitated later in their conversation, "she's no beauty and has some strange ways, but she is kind and gentle."

Fischel nodded, telling himself, *It will relieve the hardship.*

Not long afterward, Fischel told his family that he was bringing them a new mother, Fraydel, who would cook and look after them. But he saw Gitl's eyes fill with tears as she walked away from the table. Sarah just sat there staring at him.

"Well, what can you do with daughters?" he later asked his brother. "I try to get them a new mother to relieve their burdens, and they look at me like I am committing a sin."

"Give them time, Fischel. When the wedding takes place and Fraydel is here looking after the household, then they will be grateful."

But it wasn't long after the wedding that Fischel discovered that his new wife was not only strange, but also weak. She knew practically nothing about managing a household and, though kind, she was not at all comfortable with children. She was totally incapable of baking extra bread or producing other items to sell at the market to add to the family income.

Fischel traveled from rural village to village, peddling dry goods and kitchenware. He was hardly ever home during the week, and his efforts earned him so little, he could barely provide enough for his family to eat. Many meals were no more than bread and potatoes. Each time he arrived home, he found the household in disarray. Gitl no longer took responsibility for the chores, and Fraydel simply ignored them. *It's a blessing, at least, that she's a good person and does not shout or bully anyone,* Fischel tried to console himself.

Surprisingly, his new wife did make a strange contribution to the well-being of others in the town, and eventually helped her family in an unusual way. She enjoyed talking with her neighbors, many of whom believed that her strangeness was due to her ability to communicate with dead people. Women in the town would drop by to tell Fraydel about dreams they had of their departed relatives, seeking her interpretation, convinced the dead relatives were warning them or advising them about the future. Impressed with Fraydel's gift, people were willing to overlook the fact that she focused more time on dead people in dreams than on her children and household.

Sometimes, if she delivered a message that someone wanted to hear, the woman would give her a few eggs or, if she was able, some pickled herring or cabbage. But often the women were too poor, or too frightened about the dream, to think about offering anything. When Fraydel gave birth to her own first son, Nachum, she was unable to concentrate on the dreams people told her about, and she did not receive extra food. This meant, more often than not, that the family had to go back to meals of bread and potatoes.

* * *

When Sarah was six years old, Zayde Moishe took her and two-year-old Shmulek into his home to relieve his son-in-law of the extra burden. Sarah's eight-year-old brother, Henoch, spent the day at *cheder*, the religious school for boys. Her older sister was now making a contribution by laundering and pressing clothes for richer families in the town.

Zayde Moishe, a widower himself since before Sarah was born, had taken a second wife, a widow who had no children of her own. Her maternal instincts finally unleashed, she welcomed Sarah and Shmulek into her home and delighted in preparing them meals. She knew how to maintain a comfortable household with the meager earnings she got at the market, selling the aprons and smocks she was so good at sewing.

Zayde Moishe was not a scholar, but he had heard the stories of the Hasidic *rebbeh*, Nahman of Bratzlav, and fervently believed that at the end of all tribulations, people will understand the meaning of their hardships, and that nothing is truly evil. He believed not only in the miracles that religious leaders could perform, but also in the value of friendship and the importance of celebrating life.

A kind man to everyone, Zayde Moishe was particularly fond of his granddaughter Sarah, whose small round face, straight nose, and rosebud lips looked so much like those of his dead daughter. He loved to tell her tales of the Hasidic masters, and when she returned after spending *Shabbas* with her father and stepmother, he would always have something special for her to eat. "When you say special prayers, Sarah, miracles will follow," he liked to reassure her.

It was easy splitting time between her father's house and Zayde Moishe's because the two houses were just around the turn in the road from each other. During the afternoons Sarah often took Shmulek with her back to her father's home, where she enjoyed telling him stories and watching him crawl around on the floor with their half-brother, Nachum. This relieved her stepmother, and gave Fraydel time to once again help people understand what their dreams meant.

Sarah was fascinated by Fraydel's intricate interpretations of what appeared on the surface to be very simple dreams. A dream of a smiling dead aunt standing near a bed might mean the dreamer would soon have a baby and that God would smile on the infant. Or an unknown man in a wide-brimmed hat would indicate that the dreamer's son should be sent to the yeshiva to study, and someone from the synagogue would look after the boy.

Sarah believed her stepmother had mystical powers, a connection with the life beyond this one. Fraydel was pleased with Sarah's growing admiration, especially when the young girl was looking after Nachum so she could put more food on their table, thereby keeping Fischel calmer.

Sarah often had dreams about her own mother. She could still hear her soft voice, smell her milky aroma, and feel the warmth of her embrace, her hands and arms covered with flour from the bread she was baking. At night when Shmulek was afraid of the dark in the loft where Sarah and he slept at Zayde Moishe's, Sarah would comfort him, saying, "One day we will have banquets of food and a house with many rooms. I know this because I talked with our mother in my dream, and she assured me there will truly be a miracle. But first we have to prove we are worthy by doing good deeds."

Sarah and Shmulek split their time between Zayde Moishe's home and their father's for five years, spending many daytime hours and Sabbaths with their father and his new family, and weekdays sleeping and eating in their zayde's home. This satisfied Sarah, mostly because of her zayde's kindness.

* * *

When Sarah was eleven years old her zayde became ill, and she and her brother had to return to live with their father and stepmother full-time. By then Fraydel had three more children of her own and was expecting a fourth. Sarah's father was still working as a peddler, without much success. How there would be enough food for all of them was a mystery not even Fraydel could unravel as she tried to interpret her own dreams.

Then, one of the better-off women in the village, Bessie Kovitsky, wife of the wheat dealer, offered a solution. Bessie often visited Fraydel after dreaming of her dead mother. She had observed what an unselfish girl Sarah was and how much she tried to help. She waited until Sarah took Shmulek outside for a walk, checked the window to be sure no one was near the house to hear, and motioned for Fraydel to lean closer. She cupped her hand near her mouth for further privacy. "Don't take this wrong, Fraydel," she whispered, "but I think Sarah is old enough to help put food on your table."

Fraydel lifted her eyebrows and pulled back a few inches. "What do you mean? She is just a child. What could she do besides help with the little ones and the chores, which she already does?"

"Well, my husband is worried about how much work I do running such a big household, with so many rooms to keep clean. He told me to arrange to have someone help with the cooking and the baking. I can teach her how to bake, and we can give your family extra flour and other food as payment. I know I can trust Sarah. She would not steal from me, God forbid, and I would like her to be the one to help in my home." She leaned back, folded her arms, and smiled confidently. "So, nu, what do you say?"

Hiding her pleasure, Fraydel shook her head slowly, looking heavenward. "I don't know what my husband would say. Sarah is such a young girl." In truth she was relieved with the opportunity, but she needed a strong argument so she could convince Fischel. She knew he would be embarrassed at the idea of his daughter working in someone else's home.

Bessie met the challenge with a smile. "I wouldn't be satisfied with anyone else. Tell him I need her, and it will prepare her to be a good wife. It will make it easier to find her a husband, since you won't be able to offer much of a dowry." Bessie looked around at the disarray of Fraydel's household and her lips thinned for a moment. "And after she learns how to do what I need, who knows? There may be earnings she can use to add to what you and Fischel are able to save for her dowry." Bessie pointed to the low wooden chest sitting in the room, assuming that was where any dowry items might be stored.

Fraydel moved her head from side to side and assumed a quizzical expression, as if considering her husband's response. She looked at the window and then at the door. "I'll see what I can do. Tomorrow, stop by—I'll give you a final answer."

They both knew the decision was already made, that Sarah's father would only need to be reassured that no one would harm Sarah.

* * *

The next day Fischel called Sarah to the table and told her, "Bessie Kovitsky has paid you an honor. She has chosen you of all the girls in town to join her in her home. She will teach you about cooking and baking. She will also give you food for our family while you learn."

Sarah sat silently for a few minutes, blinking in shock. "Father, that is no honor. It is a shame. I will be a servant." She began to cry.

Fischel sat back, caught off guard by Sarah's boldness. Then he drew his brows down, leaned forward, and said firmly, "No, Sarah, it is an honorable way for you to help the family, and it has already been decided. Gitl has been helping by doing laundry for people who can afford to pay a little. You have to help too."

Sarah glanced at Fraydel, who looked down at her hands, saying nothing. Fischel got up from the table and walked to the window, keeping his back to Sarah and Fraydel. It was clear there would be no further discussion, and Sarah didn't dare question her father more than she already had.

Each morning except on the Sabbath, after the boys went to cheder, Sarah left for the Kovitsky home, returning in the early evening, after Bessie's kitchen was clean. She always brought some bread and potatoes and sometimes eggs or herring. Her family ate better, she learned how to bake *challah* and cinnamon cakes, and Bessie Kovitsky even managed to give her a few *kopeks* each week. Sarah gave some to her father and kept some for her dowry. By the time she was fourteen, she had managed to save many kopeks.

Then her sister announced that she intended to marry a distant cousin whose family lived in a nearby town. Her future husband was immigrating to a small town in western Canada where families were being encouraged to settle, and he wanted a wife to go with him. He had asked one of the families Gitl worked for if they thought she would be willing. He knew she was already well past twenty, but he would marry her with her meager dowry if she could get the money for a ticket to Canada. The matchmaker would be arriving the next day to see Fischel, but it all had to happen very soon—before the end of the month.

At first Fischel was shocked that he was the last to be contacted. But he realized that it might well be his daughter's last chance at marriage, given her age and their poverty. It would also make life simpler, if his eldest daughter no longer took up space in their house—although they would miss the contribution she made from her laundry work.

"Well, Gitl, you have been keeping some of your earnings for a dowry," he said calmly, though his voice held a brittle edge. "How much do you have?"

Gitl dropped her head. "I only have half, Papa." Her head swung up, eyes beseeching. "Can't we find someone we can borrow it from? It may be my last chance, Papa—please help me."

Her father ran his fingers through his hair, his mouth puckered in anguish. "Gitl, I wish I could help you. But how could I get that kind of money in a short time? Even if I go to my brothers and ask for help, we could not get half the fare. They are all struggling too. And everyone knows that it would be hard for me to repay any loans."

Gitl looked at Sarah. "You have been saving something. You don't need your dowry yet. If you give me what you have, I will send it back, even something extra, before you need it." Her voice grew enthusiastic. "Things will be better in Canada. We will have land to farm. I will repay you, and by the time you need it, you will have a bigger dowry."

Sarah looked from Gitl to her father, hoping he would not encourage Gitl in this solution. He looked away, paced the floor, stared at the ceiling and then his hands. He cleared his throat. "Yes, Sarah, it is necessary for you to help your sister, just as everyone in the family must look after one another. I know she will not forget her family when she gets to her new home in Canada. She will repay the loan. And after she is married, a match can be made for you."

Fischel's brother gave them a loan, and that, added to Sarah's savings, covered the cost of Gitl's fare to Canada. Gitl was married without fanfare and went on her way. Sarah continued to work and help the family through hard times, her father became ill more often, and the savings barely grew. Months later, when they finally received a letter from Gitl, it described a harsh, cold country and loneliness, but made no mention of repaying any loans.

* * *

Ettie started to cough. "Mmm, I need a glass of water, please, Rachel." Laurie leaped up and returned a few moments later with a glass of cold water from the bathroom. Ettie accepted it with a grateful nod, drank deeply, then set the glass on the bed table. She shook her head. "Your Bubbe Sarah never got over that. Every time she had an argument with her sister, Gitl, even when they were both old women, she would always go back to those unpaid loans and how she had to give up her dowry."

She fell silent for a few minutes, musing on the past, then her eyelids drooped. "I feel sleepy now," she said, and Rachel and Laurie rose and left the room.

They returned to the living room, where family members who had attended Morton's funeral were eating and talking. With Laurie trailing her, Rachel joined Collette, who was deep in conversation with her mother's cousin, Bea.

"It was my father who got me on the right track in school," a smiling Collette was saying. "When I first started school, they had two semesters each year, and I began in February. That's when we lived in that house on Roberts Street, and my world consisted of all the relatives who lived together there, with me the center of attention."

"I remember those days," Bea said, nodding.

Collette continued. "We never had any books at home. I didn't know how to focus on what the teacher wanted me to do. She tried to teach me how to read, but all I did was look at the pictures and make up stories about the family. So the school decided to hold me back half a year, saying I could start fresh in September."

Rachel had often heard about this episode but didn't want to interrupt, so she stood a little apart as Collette continued. "My dad was horrified, determined that no daughter of his was going to fail at school. That summer he went to the library and borrowed all types of books, made word cards, and taught me how to read—he was great. I loved reading after that. The teacher was shocked when I returned to school and knew all the words. And from then on, I loved school and everything came easy."

Bea responded softly, "Well, I didn't know about the reading, but I do know that your father was too smart for all of them. They didn't understand him."

Stanley was listening too, and seemed agitated when he called out to Rachel, "How's your mother doing? I hope she gets some rest. She looks awful."

Rachel nodded in agreement. "She's talking about the old country, about her family. It's interesting, but I guess she's exhausted."

The Tuba

Ettie heard what they said, and was ashamed at the pleasure it brought her to know they were concerned about her. *Let them worry,* she thought. *I didn't need all of this. I wish I had my mother with me; she would understand what I've been through. Her life with my father was never easy either. I guess that's why she was so anxious for me to marry into a good family.*

Ettie thought about her father, Yitzhac, and how he came into her mother's life. It wasn't that Yitzhac turned out to be a bad husband to Sarah. Sure, he was poor and uneducated. And worse, from Sarah's point of view, he had little faith in the value of religious observance and even poked fun at it. The main difficulty was that his attempt to better their lot in life brought unbelievable danger and hardship to his family.

Ettie realized that's why her mother wanted her to marry a man who had some standing in the community, a man from a respected family, a man whose religious education was strong. Who could blame her? She thought Ettie would have a better life. How could she know that a man from such a good family could bring such anguish?

Ettie called out, "Rachel, can you come back in here? I need you."

Rachel looked surprised when she stepped into the room. "Everyone thought you were asleep," she said.

"I can't sleep," Ettie said. "I want to tell you more about my mother, and my father, too."

She waited while Rachel settled in the chair that Laurie had pulled up beside the bed earlier. Then she began. "You kids always saw Bubbe Sarah and Zayde Yitzhac bickering. But at the start of their marriage, it seemed like things would be better. Remember all the times when my father got angry or poked fun at my mother, how she liked to remind him that he'd picked her himself, that no matchmaker forced him to marry her?"

As Rachel nodded, Ettie patted her hand. "I'll tell you how my parents met."

* * *

Thank goodness the dowry wasn't so important to Yitzhac. But that wasn't the only reason why the match with him was a good one for Sarah. He was only seven years older than she was, not an old man like the husbands some poor girls had to accept. Everyone talked about the match made for her neighbor's daughter, a pretty girl who had to marry that teacher after his wife died and left him with five children all under ten years old. Her poor neighbor had grown old and stooped by the time she gave birth to her second son.

Another thing in Yitzhac's favor, from Sarah's viewpoint, was that he had already served in the czar's army when their match was arranged. She would never have to worry that he'd be taken away, leaving her to fend for herself for many years. She smiled when she thought what a clever person he was, managing to protect himself from the dangers of battle and hardships of war. It was all because of the tuba.

Yitzhac had been one of the strongest young men in Skvira. His broad shoulders and compact, muscular body served him well if anyone picked fights with him. Conscripted into the czar's army while still in his teens, he wasn't afraid of the army, unlike others who willingly injured or mutilated themselves before appearing for their physical examinations. "Look at those cowards," he mocked. "Idiots! I'm not stupid, and the czar isn't worth it."

Yitzhac's army experience eventually became a source of amazement to the townspeople of Skvira, even though only Yitzhac knew the full story of how it happened.

Just as he arrived at the army base, he saw the commander pacing back and forth. Yitzhac had no idea that the reason was because a tuba player had become ill, or that the commander was worried about how he would manage to pull off the parade for the visiting general in the town square the next day. So Yitzhac was startled when the commander looked him up and down, then called him to his quarters.

"Do you know music?" the commander asked.

"Of course I know music. What's the big deal?"

"Hold your tongue!" the commander bellowed, then pointed at a tuba resting in the corner. "Pick up this instrument and march!"

As soon as Yitzhac did so without any strain, the commander gave another order. "Blow into it with all your strength on every second step you take."

After about five minutes, the commander broke into a hearty laugh. "Always remember what I tell you now. If anyone asks you if you are the camp tuba player, you give one answer and nothing more. Just answer 'yes.' Do I make myself clear?"

"Yes, Commander," Yitzhac answered as respectfully as he could manage.

The commander thrust a bundle of clothing toward him. "Here, change into this uniform. We have work to do."

For the next three hours the commander ordered Yitzhac to march, holding the tuba, and blow into it when the commander pointed the baton at him. The next day Yitzhac managed to perform during the parade without drawing attention to himself.

By the time the commander who had "discovered" him was transferred two years later, Yitzhac appeared to be an accomplished tuba player to everyone who saw him in parades. So for the entire five years of his army service, Yitzhac played in the army band, ate well, and never experienced the miseries of fighting in the Russo-Japanese War, although he was witness to extreme brutality and many unspeakable horrors.

Years later, Yitzhac chuckled anytime people he met spoke of the hardships of army service. "*Ech!* If you're strong and have a clever head on your shoulders, it's no big deal. I never learned to read music, but what did they know? I could march straight, blow into that thing at the right time, and hold it on my shoulders for hours without stooping. Those thick-heads never knew the difference."

People who knew Yitzhac enjoyed telling the tuba story, enhancing it with each telling so that people eventually left out the role of the commander and believed it was entirely Yitzhac's idea. Despite enjoying the attention he got from the tuba story, Yitzhac invariably ended the story by focusing on the hardships of the present. "A lot of good that tuba does me now. These days, it's the horse's strength that makes the difference whether we have anything to eat."

The Bargain

"So that's the famous story of the tuba." Ettie laughed, and Rachel joined in.

When Ettie resumed, her tone was serious. "My father became a *droshky* driver—you know, like a stagecoach driver—after his discharge from the army in 1905. By then he had learned a lot about horses and enjoyed their company. He always seemed to like his horses more than he liked people.

"It seemed a promising business," she said. "He made his decision as soon as he learned that one of the older drivers had died of typhus, a few months before his discharge from the army. His sister Golda arranged for him to have the use of a house with a stable on the side, and scrubbed it clean before my father moved in."

Yitzhac liked being his own boss. He was proud of his ability to meet the physical demands of guiding the horses and navigating the rough roads. In summer he could often negotiate enough profitable fares to make a comfortable living, but in winter people were more reluctant to travel and life was tougher. Although horse-drawn wagons were the only means of travel from shtetl to shtetl in Ukraine in the early 1900s, other strong men offered their services, and competition was fierce. Travelers often based their decisions on who got their business on the comfort of the buggy, the health and speed of the horses, and the driver's reputation for bravery and driving skills.

"My mother and father met because he was in that business," Ettie said. "My father often drove people to Pogrebischte, where my mother was born and grew up. While working for Bessie Kovitsky, she heard the Kovitskys talking about the strong droshky driver Mr. Kovitsky had hired for a trip. He was impressed by this independent man who had been drafted at the age of eighteen, but didn't get injured because he'd taught himself to play the tuba." Ettie shook her head, smiling with pride.

Then she lowered her voice as if sharing an intimate secret. "Everyone knew my father was proud, honest, and outspoken. He never welcomed discussions about the fare or the carriage conditions. If people complained, he'd tell them to find another driver—that's the way he was. My father didn't go out of his way to be nice to anyone. He was pretty shrewd, I'll tell you that, and he could tell a lot about people after a brief meeting. If he didn't trust someone, that was that. He never gave people the benefit of the doubt." Ettie paused, staring into space. "Sad to say, he was usually right."

"He was not the sort any well-to-do family would want for a son-in-law, despite the fact that he was a strong and respected driver. It was clear that he would never be pious or rich, so a *shidech,* an agreement for marriage, with a girl from any well-to-do family was out of the question. Whenever he came into town, he might stay overnight at the local inn or he might just stop, have one drink of schnapps with a good friend, then check for any returning passengers before going on his way. One thing I have heard about him, no surprise for a man of his age at the time, he had an eye on all the young women.

"The story goes that, during one trip Mr. Kovitsky took with my father, just as they were getting ready to leave, Mrs. Kovitsky sent my mother to the inn with a parcel her husband had forgotten. That was the first time my father noticed my mother. He was about twenty-five years old and she was eighteen. She always liked to remind him how he stared at her whenever he saw her after that day, especially while she walked with the other girls, all of them carrying their baskets full of purchases from the market. My father never denied the story."

Again Ettie looked distant, as if trying to envision her mother. "My mother longed to have her own home and family, and not have to work in other people's kitchens. She was always ashamed that she was so poor. Her younger brothers and sisters were now old enough to get along without her, but coming from a poor family, what kind of bridegroom could she expect? She once told me that she liked a young man in her village, but she knew his family would be arranging for him to marry someone with a substantial dowry. So in later years it made her feel proud to remember that my father chose her himself."

Suddenly smiling, Ettie tilted her head. "Who could've blamed him for noticing my mother? From what I've been told, she was a pretty and delicate girl, very petite, with a round face and fine features, and thick black hair that she braided and tied on the top of her head. But I know what really impressed him was how strong she was for such a slight person. She could carry heavy baskets and still move more quickly than the others. She was good-hearted, too, always worrying about others when they tired, and even offering to carry things from their baskets. I think he decided she was different, that she would be a good wife and make him a comfortable home." Ettie smirked. "Who knows what kinds of women my father had met when he was in the army?"

"How did he approach Bubbe?" Rachel asked. "It's so hard to imagine their first conversation. What kind of opening remarks do you think he actually made?" Rachel deepened her voice, imitating a man using a common pickup line. "Well, hello there, gorgeous." She laughed.

"Get outta here. Are you kidding?" Ettie exclaimed. "No man approached a woman on his own in those days. It was a complicated process using go-betweens. He used his oldest sister. I've heard what happened from more than one person. Just try to picture it."

* * *

One day in late fall, Yitzhac reined in his horses near a group of young girls and whispered to his passenger, "There."

Yitzhac's sister Rissela, a big-boned woman with a squarish face, wide cheeks, and deep-set eyes, stepped out of the carriage. "Which one?"

Yitzhac climbed down to stand beside her, then pointed to the young women carrying baskets from the market. "The one with the braids tied on top of her head," he said impatiently.

Rissela shook her head and looked skyward. "Oy! So small, so fragile." She dropped her gaze to her brother. "Yitzhac, do you know what you are doing? Tch-tch-tch."

Sarah saw him pointing but did not realize that she was the subject of their critical analysis. She continued walking home, her basket on her hip. Still shaking her head, Rissela walked the other way, toward the house occupied by Sarah's uncle and aunt.

Several days earlier, Yitzhac had instructed his schnapps-drinking friend to tell Sarah's Aunt Yetta that his sister would be paying them a visit to discuss a *shidech* between Yitzhac and Sarah. The friend had explained to Yetta that Yitzhac noticed Sarah each time he drove his carriage into town, and she was the one he wanted to marry. Yitzhac, he told her, was seven years older than her niece and earned enough to put food on the table. More important, he didn't care about the size of the dowry. He wasn't getting any younger, and it was time he took a wife. Sarah's aunt agreed to meet with Rissela before arranging a meeting with Sarah's father.

Yetta was naturally hospitable to Rissela. "Sit down, I'll get you a glass of tea. You must be tired from your journey."

"Thank you. The journey was not hard. My brother, Yitzhac, is the best driver around," Rissela said, making it clear that her brother was special. If Sarah had a small dowry, they would have to agree to Yitzhac's wishes without any demands. "You know why I am here?"

Yetta nodded.

"My brother is ready to take a wife. He is a very independent person and would not agree to a match with anyone unless he was convinced she would be suitable. He has seen your niece, Sarah, and he believes she will keep a comfortable home for him. Once they marry, he will take her to Skvira. He already has a place for them to live and expects only that she cook and make a comfortable home for him."

Yetta lifted both hands in a shrug and said carefully, "You realize, of course, that this is not up to me. Sarah's father, my husband's brother, must give his approval. He loves Sarah dearly. It will be very hard for him to have her move away."

Rissela noticed that she made no mention of the contribution Sarah made to the family by working in the Kovitsky house. *Shrewd,* Rissela thought. Admitting Sarah was hired help in someone else's house would put her family at a disadvantage.

"Please try to arrange for me to meet with your brother this evening," Rissela said politely, playing along with the formality—though she had no doubt that Yetta had already shared the purpose of this meeting with Sarah's father. "If he agrees to a match, we can have the engagement ceremony before I leave tomorrow, and plan a wedding for late spring."

"I will arrange a meeting between you and my brother-in-law," Yetta promised, then said again, "Sarah is a lovely girl, and her family loves her. It will be hard for them to have her move away. Her father will want to meet Yitzhac himself, after he speaks to you, to make sure Yitzhac is worthy of her. Only then might he give the final okay."

* * *

Despite her cautionary words, Yetta felt a huge sense of relief. She also loved Sarah and often thought of the girl's kind and quiet mother. *The pain she must have felt after her mother's death!* Yetta thought, her heart going out to her gentle, hard-working niece, who only tried to do what she thought was expected of her. Fischel's second wife, Fraydel, had come to love Sarah, but she had been expressing her concern that, as Sarah approached twenty, she was getting to an age where a match might be harder to arrange. Each time one of the other young women became a bride-to-be, Fraydel would comment on the good fortune of their families, to see their daughters married off before they became old maids. She would pat Sarah on the shoulder and wish, "Next time, may it be you."

Yetta, of course, had already spoken with Fischel, who was delighted and only too happy to be freed from worry over his daughter's marital status. Yetta knew this was largely due to guilt that he had insisted she give her dowry money to Gitl. Fischel had affection for Sarah and appreciated her kind and gentle ways, but she always looked at him as if he were somehow to blame for everything bad that happened. He did not know how to respond to his daughter's needs.

This time, dear Sarah, Yetta thought, *it will be you.* She hoped Yitzhac would be good to her, despite his brusque exterior.

* * *

Everything went as Rissela had expected, and after a modest spring wedding, Sarah was living in Skvira, a center of Hasidim in Eastern Europe. She felt she had finally found her true home. Yitzhac made few demands of her and enjoyed her cooking. His family treated her with respect and kindness. And the presence of the zealous Hasidim made her feel closer to her grandfather, Zayde Moishe, who had died before seeing her at the *chupah,* the wedding canopy.

Skvira was different from other Jewish villages because the Hasidic ways were different from the more rational Orthodox interpretation of Judaism. The Hasidim mixed their religious observances with superstition and strongly adhered to customs not prescribed in the Torah. In some shtetls they were seen as a threat to traditional beliefs, even outlawed in some Jewish communities in Poland and Lithuania. To others they were merely an oddity. But in Skvira they were mainstream, and to Sarah these fervent Hasidim in their long black coats and wide-brimmed hats were the closest connection to the All-Powerful she could envision.

* * *

Ettie paused thoughtfully. "My mother never told me how she felt about her marriage. Nobody ever talked about marriage like they do today. I've often wondered what she expected—she was so naïve. I know she was grateful that my father didn't care about a dowry and didn't expect her family to take them into their home as newlyweds to help them get started. She was comforted by the fact that he had a way of earning a modest living and was his own boss. I also know that my father seldom had kind words for her except when she cooked the special foods he enjoyed."

Waving her hand, Ettie shrugged. "I'll tell you something else: nobody ever explained to me what happens when you go to bed with a man. All my mother told me was that it wouldn't take too long, he'll be happy, and then he'll fall asleep. She never warned me about the pain. She said the most important thing was for a husband to give his wife children. Then it was up to God." Ettie looked at Rachel. "That's what my mother honestly thought. Boy, was she in a dream world!"

She yawned. "Now I'm ready for a nap."

Rachel tucked a blanket around her mother, shut the bedroom door, and joined the rest of the family in the living room.

Collette looked up from her conversation with an old friend from high school who had stopped by to pay her respects. "Is Mother resting better now, Rachel?"

Rachel nodded, then added, "It seems to make her feel better to talk about the past, about Bubbe and Zayde."

Collette sighed. "I know this has been an ordeal for her. I'm glad that she feels she can talk with you, Rachel. She always looks forward to your visits and enjoys your company. When I try to talk with her, she finds it hard to relax. I guess she can't stop worrying about my health."

The rest of the day continued as if the family had somehow been transported back to the rituals of the shtetls. Eventually Ettie woke, freshened up, and joined the others in the living room. Relatives, friends, and neighbors dropped by with pastries or fruit, visited a while, then left. Stanley organized salads and cold cuts on trays so that when dinnertime arrived, whoever was hungry could help themselves. Other relatives offered to help, as is customary during the period of shiva. However, Stanley had taken on most of the responsibility of managing the kitchen when Collette had become ill, to ease the pressure on her, and he made it clear that it was easier for him to look after the kitchen and the food.

Sometimes the conversation during the visits focused on childhood memories, how Collette and Rachel would join their cousins for the Saturday movies at the Enright Theater in East Liberty, or how much fun they all had at the picnics in North Park. Some of the conversation was about grandchildren—Ettie's or Libby's. Nobody spoke further about Morton. The silence that had surrounded him for most of the past fifty years continued.

* * *

After all of the visitors left, Rachel, Steve, and Laurie rode with David when he drove Ettie home. When he pulled up in front of her apartment building, Ettie asked David as she opened the car door, "How long will you be staying?"

"As long as I'm needed. If I can help, then that's the only reason to be here."

There was so much Ettie wanted to say to her son—about the pain she knew she had caused him, the forgiveness she needed from him—so much that was impossible to express.

"And the rest of you, how long will you stay?" she asked.

Their responses were equally noncommittal.

The Prayers

They arrived at Collette's and Stanley's home the next morning to find Collette sitting in the living room in her bathrobe, combing her hair. The dark circles under her eyes seemed permanent. "I'm sorry, I'm a little slow today." She looked up and smiled apologetically. "I still have to take a bath. But come on in and get comfortable. There's food on the counter—help yourselves. I'll join you in a little while."

Ettie looked at Rachel and slowly shook her head, saddened by how ill her daughter appeared. "We'll be fine," Rachel assured her sister. "I don't think anyone will be here for a couple of hours."

After breakfast they all moved to the living room, where Steve urged, "Grandma Ettie, yesterday you told my mother and Laurie lots of stories about the shtetl, but the rest of us got cheated. That's not fair. We want to hear some stories too."

Her other grandchildren chimed in: "Yeah, Grandma Ettie, we like your stories too—please tell us about your childhood."

Ettie threw up her hands. "Phooey, some childhood! I didn't know what a childhood was, not like you kids. We never had any fun, just lots of trouble. But I'll tell you the story I heard from my Aunt Golda, about the snow and the midwife the night I was born. Do you want to hear that?"

"Yeah, Grandma!"

"I bet you guys heard all these stories a long time ago. They're so old, they have a beard." Her audience laughed. "Anyway, if you wanna hear them again, here goes . . . Nobody knows for sure what date I was born, they just know that my father had to carry the midwife on his shoulders through the snow. That's what he always liked to repeat. The family knew how old your Aunt Libby was, and how long it was after Chanukah, so they decided my birthday was February tenth.

"Before I was born my mother was very worried about being

pregnant with another baby because Libby—she was still called Leiba Chana then—was less than a year old. She was such a sickly baby, and those *yentas,* gossips, told my mother that Leiba Chana was sick because my mother was pregnant while she was still nursing. That was after they told her it wasn't possible for her to get pregnant because nursing prevents the start of a new baby. What did they know—just a lot of *bubbe maisses*, old wives' tales. They all had such ridiculous superstitions, my mother more than most, may she rest in peace." Ettie sighed. "She had such a hard life.

"You know there were no hospitals or doctors in Skvira, and it was lucky they had a midwife. My mother was alone with Libby when the labor pains started. She must have been very frightened. She always told me she thought she was going to die, that it was a good thing my father's sisters lived nearby. Can you imagine how scary that must have been?"

This conjured murmurs of agreement from her family. When Ettie continued, everyone fell silent as another world opened before them.

* * *

It was just after noon on a winter day in 1911 when Sarah Burchinsky felt the first pain announcing that her second child would soon arrive. As usual, the only person in the one-room house with her during weekdays was her year-old daughter, who began to whimper when she saw her mother grimace and grab hold of the chair.

"Shah, be still," Sarah whispered. "It's okay." As soon as the spasm passed, she began cuddling Leiba Chana to comfort her.

"Here, sweet child, you want some challah?" Brushing the curly black hair from her daughter's dark eyes, Sarah kissed her forehead and stroked it to ensure she had no fever. The soft skin felt cool. Sighing her relief, she placed the little girl on the blanket she'd spread on the bed and handed her some cloth scraps left over from the suits Golda's tailor husband, Yankle, had been making. "Mama will always be here to take care of you, my little Leibana."

She studied her sickly daughter, named for her own mother who died too young, and quickly muttered a prayer. "God protect us, my darling girl, you're only a baby yourself." When Sarah first realized another baby was on the way, Leiba Chana was still nursing and not yet eating any solid foods. Despite what others said, Sarah had no doubt a new baby was growing in her womb. But it was Leiba Chana she fretted about because her appetite began to disappear, and then one day she awoke feverish, with severe diarrhea. Sarah continued to nurse, but something was clearly wrong.

The baby continued to lose weight and none of the remedies or prayers that the townspeople came up with helped. Sarah feared that God was punishing her for something. Her guilt was partially relieved when their neighbor, Fagala, visited and offered the child tea. The baby accepted it with a grimace that slowly changed to a smile. The next day Leiba Chana ate a small bite of challah. Sarah no longer tried to nurse her, no matter how much she cried and reached for her mother's breast. But Sarah could not shake her guilt and annoyance, especially after Fagala began spreading rumors throughout the town that "the new baby turned Sarah's milk bad and made the child sick."

* * *

Ettie paused in her story. "See? Even before I was born, I was blamed for bringing trouble to my family. I heard that story all my life, how I made your Aunt Libby so sick."

Rachel took Ettie's hand. "Aw, Mother, you don't really believe that, do you? How could they blame you for that? C'mon, tell us more about your mother and what it was like back then."

"Okay, but don't tell me I'm making things up," Ettie scolded. "I've heard these things all my life.

"My mother thought that the whole experience with her milk making Leiba Chana sick was a bad omen. To be on the safe side, she secretly arranged to have a woman they all believed had special powers visit, and invoke a prayer to remove the evil eye from her babies." Ettie dropped her voice. "My mother didn't dare tell my father because he would have laughed and called her a fool for believing such nonsense. He laughed at a lot of things she believed in.

"People in the town thought that Leiba Chana was like a delicate flower. She had wide cheeks, a round face, and rosebud lips that could form a beautiful smile. But my mother said she didn't smile much when she was a baby. With all her illnesses, it's no mystery why she was so small and frail for a child her age. My mother told me that, not long after the bout of diarrhea, she caught cold and suffered through a month of coughing and congestion." Ettie sniffed. "Well, at least I don't think they blamed *that* on me."

After a pause, Ettie chuckled. "Oy, the old-world remedies people used when anyone in the household had a cough! Sometimes they would place a poultice of hot breadcrumbs wrapped in a large, warmed cabbage leaf onto the sick person's chest, and soon thereafter the congestion began to loosen. Whenever this worked, my mother was convinced that the recovery was due more to the prayer she muttered to get rid of the evil eye than the poultice, but you could never be sure."

"What did she mutter?" Laurie asked.

"First she would repeat, 'Tu, tu, tu,' as if she were spitting on the floor." Ettie laughed as she imitated her mother. "Then she would say, 'The evil eye should not darken my home ever again.' She would follow that with a prayer to God to give her the energy to look after her family."

Ettie sighed and became more serious. "When I was about to be born my mother was alone, worrying about my father getting home and the quickly approaching Sabbath. She was worrying about dying, too, because her mother died when she was having a baby."

* * *

Friday was the busiest day of the week for women in the shtetl, their hours filled with shopping for food and preparing their homes. Sarah usually started her preparations on Thursday at noon, when she began her baking. She had to have the challahs ready by dawn on Friday morning for those women who might buy her braided bread for the Sabbath. This was Sarah's way of adding to the meager income Yitzhac earned from transporting people with his horse and wagon.

People in Skvira praised Sarah Burchinsky for her cooking and baking skills, and even more for her spotless kitchen. They paid her the highest compliment any woman in the shtetl could get, saying she was so clean, "you could eat off her floor." That was quite a feat, since the floors were made of dried mud.

But to prepare for Sabbath, to show your respect for God, you had to do more than usual. Sabbath was the time each week, no matter how grim life might be, when ordinary mortals could have a glimpse of paradise. There was to be no work, and that included no cooking. Fires could not be lit. Enough food had to be prepared in advance, not only for the Friday evening meal, but to last until sundown Saturday. The table and candles had to be made ready. If only she could get everything in place before the labor started in earnest . . .

Sarah had been able to buy a little beef that week, and considered herself lucky. Yitzhac would enjoy the *flanken* she was preparing. Sabbath was the one time of the week Sarah could be sure Yitzhac would not be traveling and staying overnight at inns in the towns where he delivered his passengers. He always arranged his schedule to return to Skvira for Sabbath. Cynical as he was about the existence of God and the value of prayer, even Yitzhac appreciated the opportunity for a day of rest. Besides, no Jewish traveler would ride or do any work on the Sabbath. This was the time the community devoted to God and family. The peasants who sometimes hired Yitzhac to take them to other towns understood what Sabbath meant to Jewish drivers, so they planned their journeys accordingly. Yitzhac knew it was necessary for his good name to give the appearance of respecting the Sabbath.

* * *

Ettie paused, frowning. "I'm sure you know my father was not a religious man. He always told us that he never liked cheder, the Hebrew school all young boys attended. He couldn't stop squirming in his chair or falling asleep during the long afternoons in the uncomfortable room, cramped and stuffy in the summer and drafty in winter. My father liked to stare out the long, narrow window, trying to see the blue sky or approaching storms. Then the teacher would pinch his arm or give him a crack on his wrists to bring him back to reality."

"That's awful," Collette's son, Jeff, blurted.

Ettie flicked her hand in dismissal. "It sounds awful, but my father used to shrug when he talked about it. He'd say that it proved how foolish it was to trust in God to protect him. The most important thing was to hide his fear, not give in and show the teacher how upset he was, but of course that just irritated the teacher more, and led him to inflict more physical pain on my father. So, even though your zayde somehow managed to learn the basic prayers, he never developed any interest in Torah studies.

"I suppose his cynicism about religion was my mother's first big disappointment in her marriage." Ettie tipped her head back, thinking. "Who knows, maybe that's why she got so excited about me having a chance to marry a rabbi's son. She was so sure that good standing with mysterious supernatural forces counted for everything." Ettie dropped her head and looked around at her grandchildren. "Some religious things my father went along with, just to avoid criticism from her and from his sisters, but he thought it was all a lot of hooey." She chuckled. "Maybe I take after my father, the way I feel about religion."

Jeff crossed to where Ettie was sitting and settled on the floor beside her. He touched his grandmother's hand. "Keep going, Grandma, we want to hear what happened when you were born."

Ettie tapped him lovingly on the arm. "Okay, okay." She drew a deep breath.

"The labor pains continued for a while without becoming too intense. My mother was determined to have everything ready before my father got home. Can you imagine *that* being the main thing on her mind? At least by then my sister was distracted, playing quietly with the assortment of cloth scraps."

As if describing what she saw in her mind's eye, Ettie painted a picture in words, of one large room where all the cooking and eating took place, furnished only with a large wooden table and five mismatched wooden chairs, enough to accommodate any of Sarah's relatives who might visit from Pogrebischte. A curtain hung from the ceiling behind the table to separate the kitchen area from the place where Sarah and Yitzhac slept on a mattress and pillows made from goose feathers. "A wedding gift from Yitzhac's sister, Golda, and her husband, Yankle," she added. Two wooden cradles made from crates were in the same area. The floor was of hardened earth, painted over with yellow mud that dried immediately after being applied.

* * *

Some weeks before the birth was expected to take place, Sarah had arranged for Golda to take Leiba Chana to her house before Yitzhac went to fetch the midwife. His older sister, Rissela, would come to help the midwife with the birth.

"Come here, my *shaina maideleh*, my pretty girl," Sarah whispered, scooping up her firstborn. She began to pat Leiba Chana's head, singing in a very soft voice the Hasidic tune her Zayde Moishe had taught her about walking the narrow bridge and not being afraid.

Sarah knew that many pious people believed it was forbidden for women to sing if men could hear them. But Zayde Moishe believed that everyone should celebrate the Torah by celebrating life. And singing and dancing were the best way to celebrate life. Of course, girls did not attend cheder, study Torah, or voice their opinions on the meaning of the religious teachings. Zayde Moishe agreed with the warning a rabbi had once given, that "an educated female is a cinder in God's eye." But what could be the harm in teaching Sarah songs or telling her beautiful stories of the miracles of life? He'd wanted her to know that she should never feel useless or abandoned, that God would help her to help herself. And Sarah knew that what her grandfather taught her must be kept a secret between them.

She held Leiba Chana and looked up at her grandfather's picture. "So today, Zayde Moishe, speak to God for me. Ask him to give me the strength, and to stay with me, to deliver new life in good health." She glanced around her home for comfort, her eyes coming to rest on the large clay stove against the wall that dominated the room. They relied on that stove not just for cooking; it was their only source of heat. On the wall on either side of the stove were ledges broad enough for a small child to lie on.

* * *

Ettie smiled. "I remember feeling really safe and warm when I could rest on the ledges near that stove." Her voice cracked, and she took a deep breath. "My mother was grateful to have Golda for a sister-in-law. My father had a brother, too, named Layve. Their father died a year before my father went into the army, and their mother died of typhoid fever while he was in the army. My father's brother and sisters were all married by the time he got out, and they welcomed my mother into their family. I guess they were relieved that they didn't have to feel responsible for my father anymore.

"Rissela was the oldest. The smartest, too, and the tough one. She took charge when family problems had to be solved. When they were kids, she annoyed her father by always asking questions, wanting to know the reason for everything. Everyone thought it was strange that a girl should be so inquisitive. Once her father actually consulted the rabbi to find out how to deal with her." Ettie snorted. "The rabbi said it was a pity that with such a head, she had not been born a boy, so she could have a life of study. He said a girl with such a brain is like an ostrich, a bird that has wings but will never be able to use them to fly."

"I think a lot of people still felt that way when I was growing up," Rachel observed wryly. "They didn't put it that way, but I could tell they thought it. I'm sure glad you had different ideas, Mother."

Ettie laughed. "Well, as Rissela grew older, she showed them. She was the one who always made the best deals for the goods she sold. Her husband was a *schlemiel*, a jerk who couldn't make decisions and never made a good living. But they lived comfortably for a while, thanks to Rissela.

"Layve, my father's only brother, was an innkeeper. His wife's father ran the inn for many years, and after they got married, Layve got a job as an assistant, looking after the accounts. When his wife's father died, Layve became manager. He and his wife seemed to work day and night, slaving to keep the inn clean and feed the exhausted travelers who arrived in the carriages coming through Skvira. My father helped bring them business by encouraging his passengers to stop there."

Ettie looked around at them. "You all know that Golda was the special one. My mother loved her, said her character matched her name. I remember seeing my mother put her arms around Golda, saying, 'What would I do without you? You are more a sister to me than my own sister ever was.' But my Aunt Golda would push her away, laughing, and reply, 'What's so much that I am doing? Sarah, you would do the same for me, I'm sure, if I moved to Pogrebischte as a new bride and you were still living there.'"

"I remember some wonderful visits with Aunt Golda and her family when they lived in Newark," Collette added. "She was very kind-hearted."

Ettie nodded. "That's the truth. Not only was she a good person, but she was blessed with a good-natured and successful husband. Everyone said that Yankle made the best suits of any tailor in all the nearby towns. Even the Russians who sometimes came through the town would go out of their way to get Yankle to make their suits. They said his suits fit better than any they could get from other tailors, but I'm sure the real reason they used him was because they knew they could pay less than if they went to Kiev for the same work." Ettie curled her lips in disdain.

"Well, I'm getting off the subject. This is supposed to be about when I was born." She closed her eyes, as if trying to envision what it was like for her mother as she prepared to give birth. "My mother grew very frightened when the labor pains became more frequent. But she knew she could count on Golda, who always stopped by in the early afternoon before Shabbas with some of the food her cook made. Despite how busy Golda was, getting her own home ready for the Sabbath, she always managed to get out of the house for a few minutes each week to look in on her brother's family.

"Your Bubbe Sarah told me about her prayers that day. The first was 'Please God, help us to have a good life and good health so we can provide for our children.' I now know there were lots of things scaring my mother, that night I was born. We can only imagine what she was worrying about."

* * *

Sarah tried not to think of Yitzhac's comments about how life would be better in America. Everyone had been hearing stories of people who moved there, how they wore fine clothing, lived in big houses, and always had meat or chicken to eat. But Sarah knew there were other stories too . . . stories of people living in squalid apartments, working on the Sabbath just to have enough to eat, and Jewish people being forced to eat unkosher meat. Yitzhac was ignoring those stories.

It wasn't surprising that Yitzhac wanted a change. His last horse had broken its leg in the summer when it tripped in a ditch. If it weren't for Golda, he wouldn't have a second horse now. And if the horses didn't move fast enough to get the travelers from Skvira to surrounding villages, there would be no extra tips when the trip ended, no matter how helpful Yitzhac might be lifting bundles for the weary travelers.

And if there was no extra money, she didn't know how they would get the extra food they would need to care for a growing family.

Whenever her brother, Shmulek, came to visit, he and Yitzhac would talk about the bandits who sometimes robbed travelers and beat up the drivers. Yitzhac was fortunate that this had not happened to him yet, but he knew he had to be on the lookout for strangers along the way. Everyone knew the stories of peasant boys sneaking aboard carriages and suddenly demanding money or jewelry. There were other hazards too. What if a peasant accused him of stealing a horse? He would have to arrange many bribes to avoid going to jail. Sure, the fact that he had served in the czar's army, that he could speak both Ukrainian and Russian, that he knew some Ukrainian people might help, but you never could be certain.

Yitzhac never repeated the stories of people who were forced to leave their homes and towns because of some local decree forbidding them to stay. But Sarah heard all the rumors when she washed clothes with the other women along the river. Neighbors had relatives who lost all of their possessions because local residents attacked them and set fires . . . who knew why? There were always stories of Jewish shopkeepers forced to go to court because peasants accused them of shortchanging them, stories of old men and women being sent to jail after being accused of selling brandy without a license.

The latest rumors about men who had already served in the army being forced to serve again upset Yitzhac the most. Shmulek was determined he would do anything to escape being drafted. Sarah shared their fear and disappointment. *But,* she asked herself, *how do they know it won't be worse somewhere else?* When Yitzhac spoke of America, Sarah did not interrupt. She simply gave him a glass of tea and a cube of sugar, waited for a pause, then tried to change the subject.

For her, the only solution was to hope for good luck and the blessings of the Almighty. Each time she looked up the hill to the fenced-in yard where the religious students gathered, she was sure that a special prayer for her growing family would help . . . if only she could convince one of the scholars to say one. But she knew what Yitzhac thought about those scholars. "What food have they put on your table lately?" he asked her, his tone sarcastic.

Despite all the worries, Yitzhac was excited about the new baby about to be born. He had one close childhood friend whose wife was also expecting a baby. Yitzhac and his friend had agreed that if one of their wives had a girl and one a boy, they would make a shidech to arrange for the children's marriage. They even agreed to have a celebration—formally seal the engagement, sign the binding documents, and smash the plate—when the kids reached the age of two.

But Yitzhac wasn't home yet, and first Sarah had to deliver the baby. She said the most important prayer of all, one she would say many times that night and after. "Please God, give this baby strong enough shoulders to carry the burdens you will send."

Her eyes drifted to the other window, the one that looked down to the river. It had been bitterly cold for weeks. Her house was halfway up the hillside, and she could see the other small houses farther down the hill, as well as the few larger houses closest to the river. Some of those houses even had two rooms. In the summer the breeze from the river cooled them, but at this time of year Sarah thought it was better to live back a bit, where you received shelter from the harsh winds. The branches of the trees near the river glistened with the ice still clinging to them from the last storm. With each gust of wind the trees bent sideways, as if cowering in fear of a powerful demon.

Skvira had already lived through two months of winter, with snowstorms more than once a week. For a while it had been nearly impossible to open the front door of the house. Then last week there'd been a thaw, a few days above freezing when everything began to melt, and water and ice had gushed down the hillside, bringing pieces of wood and silt along with it.

Yitzhac had found it difficult to clear the debris away from the front of the house before he left on his latest journey. Walking was an effort. With each step, Sarah's feet would sink deep into slush and mud. Inside the house it had become very damp, even with a good fire in the oven. Sarah feared Leiba Chana would catch another cold from the dampness.

Then the weather changed again, and bitter cold returned. *Thank God it got cold again and froze,* Sarah thought, even though the melted snow and mud had turned to chunks of ice. Spreading the ashes from the charcoal she used to heat the oven helped make the icy ground passable, but the snow and howling winds of the past few days had made it dangerous for Sarah to even step outside, in her condition. The sheds they used for toilet needs were quite a distance from the house, and Sarah feared for her safety each time she had to walk outside to relieve herself.

Darkening clouds scudded across the sky, blocking the sun, and whitecaps dotted the steaming water of the churning river. She was sure that a fierce storm was coming. The shadows of the bending trees made the river's white banks seem alive. New snow would provide some protection. Fresh snow was clean—preferable, as far as Sarah was concerned, to the mud and slush. If only Yitzhac would get home first.

As the sky became darker and more menacing, she uttered a third prayer. "Please God, bring Yitzhac home before the storm."

She murmured another prayer, seeking a blessing to be strong and not afraid, to rid her home of any evil spirits and to keep bad thoughts out of her mind.

Finally she saw Golda coming up the hill, carrying a bag. Sarah opened the door for her, and Golda exclaimed, "Sarah, it's cold out here—what are you standing in the door for?" She handed Sarah the bag containing some freshly baked poppy seed cookies and coffee cake as she stepped into the house.

Sarah replied calmly, "Now you are here, the baby can come, please God."

Arrivals

Ettie swept her eyes around the room and asked her family, "You must remember hearing Zayde talk about this many times. Do you want me to go on?"

Her grandchildren were quick to respond: "Please, Grandma, tell us the whole story," and "C'mon, Grandma, we enjoy hearing it."

Ettie looked at her son. "What about you, David? You're looking bored." David stood and stretched his arms. "I'm listenin', keep going."

Rachel and Collette both nodded when she looked at them. Stanley brought Ettie a glass of water and placed a bowl of fruit on the small table in front of the couch. Ettie smiled her thanks, then continued.

"Well, it wasn't so enjoyable for my mother. All she ever talked about was how scared she was. But my father told us about the trip he was making that night from Pliskov."

* * *

Yitzhac kept his eye on the darkening sky as he got closer to Skvira, knowing it would soon unleash a heavy snowfall. Already the horses were struggling to keep the pace in the wind-driven sleet that stung Yitzhac's face, but he was determined to complete the last few kilometers of his journey between Pliskov and Skvira without mishap.

The two boys he had picked up in Pliskov reminded him every few minutes how important it was for them to get to their aunt's home before the Sabbath, and how cold and hungry they were. The older one seemed barely past his *bar mitzvah*, the religious ceremony when a Jewish boy turns thirteen, and the younger one couldn't be more than ten. Their nagging was irritating, but Yitzhac couldn't help feeling sorry for them. He realized what a sad thing it was when a mother died and the sons had to move in with relatives.

"What else do you boys expect me to do?" he grumbled. "Why don't you just sit still and let me keep the horses calm? Don't you see how difficult it is for them?" Reaching into the sack on the seat beside him, Yitzhac pulled out the bread he had been saving from last night's dinner at the inn and handed it to them. "Here, maybe this will keep you both quiet while I try to keep the horses on the road."

The older boy thanked him and broke off a piece for his brother. They both ate so quickly, Yitzhac was sure it was their first bite of food in a long time. He too was getting hungry, but he knew a good meal would be waiting for him when he got home.

The younger boy began to cry. "I'm cold," he sobbed. "I'm tired. Will we ever see our home again?"

At that moment they rounded a treacherous curve and the wagon swerved. Yitzhac gasped, fearing the whole carriage was about to topple down the hillside.

"Oy, *Gevalt! Gevalt!* Heaven forbid!" the younger boy wailed. "Get me out of here! Save me!"

"Enough, already!" Yitzhac shouted. "Stop making commotion, like bandits. There is nowhere else for you to go. Can't you see the storm? Your aunt will make you warm and feed you if you let me get you there in one piece."

The sleet had turned to snow and was now falling so heavily that by the time they were approaching Skvira, not only was Yitzhac's hat fully covered in snow, but his eyebrows and eyelashes were as white as those of an old man. When he brought the carriage to a halt in the middle of town, he called out to the boys' cousin, waiting in a doorway out of the weather, "Here are your cousins—now *you* can listen to their *kvetching* for a while! They gave me such a headache. It's a miracle the horses didn't go lame." There was no need to be polite, he knew he would never get an extra tip from that family.

Yitzhac continued on through the driving snow to his home, where he disconnected the carriage and led the horses into the stable attached to his house. He fed them some hay, wiped them down, and patted their heads. Then he checked their legs, hoping he would not lose another one this winter. He would hate to have to ask Golda and Yankle for help again.

The aromas of the Sabbath meal reached him as he approached the door to the house, and his stomach rumbled. He had already decided he would not go to the *mikveh,* the ritual bath, today, but instead wash up as best he could using the basin and water he had fetched from the pump before he made the last trip. He hoped Sarah would have the table ready so he could eat quickly and rest, after all the trouble caused by the weather. *I hope she doesn't ask me for the tips I got this week,* he thought. *After I buy hay for the horses, there will be barely enough to keep us going.*

Golda opened the door. She was holding Leiba Chana, who was crying fitfully. "Thank God, you have arrived," she said as she stepped back to let him inside. "Now everything will be fine."

Yitzhac looked around the room. Sarah sat at the table, grasping its edge. Beyond her, sheets had been hung around the bed—they were preparing for the birth of the new baby!

"Soon it will be time to get Rissela and the midwife," Golda told him. "But for now, Sarah has your dinner waiting for you."

"Don't worry, Yitzhac, everything is as it should be," Sarah said, waving him forward. "Here, sit down. I made you something special for Shabbas. First we will light the candles."

No one seemed concerned that it wasn't yet sundown. Sarah poured a small glass of wine, and Yitzhac drank it in one gulp. Neither Sarah nor Golda reminded him to say the blessing. Sarah then put the challah in front of him, and he tore off a large piece and began eating while she put the flanken and potatoes on a plate. Yitzhac ate quickly, using the challah to sop up the meat's juices.

Golda sat across the table with Leiba Chana, handing small, bite-size pieces of challah to the one-year-old until she turned her face away, full. When Yitzhac finished what was on his plate, Golda said immediately, "Now, Yitzhac, it's time to tell Rissela to come, then fetch the midwife. The snow is getting worse, piling up against the houses." She looked to Sarah. "It's time for you to get into bed."

Yitzhac was relieved to get out of the house for a little while and let the women take over these things. He hoped it would not take as long for this baby to come as it had when Leiba Chana was born.

He'd been in the room, hearing Sarah scream, while the others rushed about for a full night and most of the next day. It had been a terrifying experience, especially since there was nothing he could do to help. Until that moment when he was a bystander at his daughter's birth, he had always thought nothing could frighten him.

He sighed as he pulled on his only pair of high boots—the ones left over from his army service—flung his heavy jacket over his shoulders, grabbed his hat and scarf, and opened the door. The icy wind slapped his face as his feet sank into the newly fallen snow piling up against the bottom of the front door.

When he reached Rissela's house, her family was just beginning the Sabbath meal. They were not surprised that Sarah's time to give birth had come, and Rissela assured Yitzhac she would meet him at his home shortly.

Sorel, the midwife, was a widow whose son sometimes helped Yitzhac's brother Layve in the stable at the inn, seeking food or clothing for any extra favors he might be asked to do. Sorel nodded curtly. "I will be ready quickly," she said, then added, her tone mildly wheedling, "but my boots have a hole in them, and there was no time to get them repaired this week."

Yitzhac sighed quietly. She would expect him to look after the boots after the baby was born. He also knew she would expect him to do something to protect her from the ice and snow this night. She was a small woman, not too much bigger than Sarah had been when he first saw her. "Put on your coat, Sorel, and I will stoop down. You climb on my shoulders and put your hands under my chin. Sit very still, and I will carry you to Sarah." Later in his life Yitzhac loved to describe his role that night, carrying the midwife on his shoulders. It became another story about the strong man who carried the tuba in the czar's army.

By the time Yitzhac arrived with the midwife on his shoulders, Rissela was already there. Sarah was lying behind the tent made of sheets, and the red ribbon to keep the evil eye away had been tied to the bedpost. The big pan of water was heating on the stove. Yitzhac noticed that Rissela had already put the coins in the water so that when the midwife was ready to clean the newborn, she would see the coins and take them as her payment. Golda had already taken Leiba Chana to stay with her family until the baby's birth.

Yitzhac looked around the room in growing anxiety, then called out to Rissela, "I need to check the horses. If you need me, I'll be in the stable."

Yitzhac always felt calm when he was with his horses. He loved the feel of their smooth coats and the way they seemed to respect his strength. Words were not necessary. These two had been easier to handle than most, right from the start. He hoped they would get him through the remaining weeks of winter without injury. With this stormy weather, all trips would take longer until after the spring thaws. He would have to seek passengers whose destinations took him over well-traveled roads. He hoped they would also be passengers who tipped enough so that he could feed his family. With a new child to look after, Sarah would not have as much time to bake goods to sell at the market.

He brushed the horses, trying not to think of what he'd heard in Pliskov last week. More rumors were circulating that the czar planned to force men who had already served their time in the army to return and serve again, maybe for twenty-five years. He'd heard stories of armed men breaking into homes and dragging off former soldiers with no regard for their new lives and families. *I will never let that happen to me.* More and more, people were talking about America. Could life be any better there? "Ach, people make up stories," Yitzhac scoffed, trying to calm his fears. "They don't know what they're talking about. I'll just wait and see." He gave the horse he was brushing a final slap, then piled up some straw in the corner of the stable and lay down. After the stresses of the day, it was not long before he fell into an exhausted doze.

A few hours passed before the creaking of the stable door startled him awake. "Come, Yitzhac," Rissela called. "Come to the house, quietly. Don't disturb Sarah. This one was easier for her than the last one, but she needs some rest." She fell in beside him as he passed her in the doorway. "Better start thinking about another dowry. It's another girl."

"This one will be named Enta, for our mother," Yitzhac announced to his sister as he looked at the baby, already clean and lying in Sarah's arms in the small blanket Golda had brought last week. He turned to the midwife, who was finishing a cup of tea, and offered to take her home on his shoulders, as he had brought her.

* * *

Sarah lay quietly, holding their new daughter and gazing at the picture of her grandfather, Zayde Moishe, hanging on the wall nearby. She smiled. *Thank you,* she thought, *and thank you, Mama, for protecting me and helping me to deliver a healthy baby. Thank you for making this one come faster.* Sarah looked down at the sleeping infant. *She looks stronger than Leiba Chana, too.* Sarah closed her eyes. *Please, God, keep us safe.*

After Yitzhac left with the midwife on his shoulders, Sarah whispered to Rissela, "I hope he's not too disappointed I didn't give him a son yet."

"Don't worry," Rissela assured her, patting Sarah's forehead. "This baby has our mother's name, Enta. That means more to him."

Ten days later the wife of Yitzhac's friend gave birth to a healthy boy, Ephriam. When Yitzhac heard the news, he lifted Enta out of her cradle, took her to the window, and looked down at the trees still glistening with icy crystals from the frost that had settled across the town. "We must soon put some bed linens into the chest to start Enta's dowry," he said to Sarah. "What a match this will be!" Then he looked down at his new daughter's wrist, staring at the red ribbon that would keep away the evil eye.

* * *

"So that's the story of my arrival," Ettie finished. She rose and walked toward the window, patting her granddaughter on the head as she passed. "My father always thought I was special because I had his mother's name. He always told me I was the strong one. Yeah, strong enough for all the surprises in my life," she sneered. Then she sighed. "Oh well, what's the use of complaining."

Collette joined her at the window and embraced her. "Life hasn't been easy for you, Mother. But you've been strong, just like your father said, and look at everything you've accomplished. We're all proud of you."

When Ettie saw the tears brimming in her daughter's eyes, her throat closed and she found herself fighting tears of her own—all in vain. Soon they were both crying. Rachel cleared her throat, then echoed her older sister, telling Ettie how much respect everyone had for her.

Laurie began to chant, and her other grandchildren joined in: "Grandma, Grandma, she's the best!"

When the room was quiet again, Collette's daughter, Andrea, asked, "Whatever became of that kid Ephriam you were supposed to marry, Grandma?"

Ettie turned and shrugged. "I don't know. His family left Skvira around the same time we did. I heard that they went to Chicago. When I was a little girl, I always expected to marry him." She smirked. "Once when we kids were playing around, we even had a mock wedding. It was your Aunt Libby's idea." Her smile faded. "I'll tell you the truth, if I saw him now, I wouldn't know who he was."

Departures

Stanley reminded the family that several people might drop by that afternoon, during the first full day of shiva. Sure enough, within the next half-hour, Ettie's brother Bennie arrived with his daughter and son-in-law. Next Libby's son Danny arrived with his wife, Ettie's nephew calling as they stepped through the door, "How's everyone doin' today?"

David was first to answer. "We've been listening to lots of stories about Skvira. It's like a whole different world coming to life, the way my mother talks about Bubbe and Zayde and your mother, and all their relatives."

Danny came over and kissed Ettie on the forehead. "You all had a rough childhood, didn't you, Aunt Ettie?"

Bennie shook his head sadly. "Nobody should know from such troubles. I was just a little boy when we left, but I still remember that river in Skvira."

Ettie jumped in. "Did anyone ever tell you that my mother had another daughter before Bennie was born? She was about a year younger than I was—Terzl was her name. She got very sick, maybe typhoid fever, I don't know. My mother once told me that Uncle Yankle arranged for my mother to see the Skvira rebbeh for a blessing and to find out what to do. The rebbeh told her that she should not question God's will, that God would help her to know what to do. He gave her a blessed coin, telling her it would always remind her not to be afraid." Ettie flung up her arms in exasperation. "A lot of good that did!"

Then she sobered. "She never wanted to talk much about it, but she told me how hard it was for her. Then not too long after Terzl died, she knew you were coming along, Bennie. She wanted a son for Papa, but this time she waited to tell him. He had been working harder than usual."

Bennie nodded, and Ettie began the story that she had been told.

* * *

After dropping passengers in Pogrebischte, Yitzhac found his friend for a drink of schnapps at the inn. His friend leaned across the small table and motioned for Yitzhac to do the same, then he whispered, "Mr. Kovitsky, whose family Sarah used to work for—the police chief has spoken to him. The chief says that more men will soon be drafted into the army. No one will be out of danger, even those who have already served."

Yitzhac tried to keep a brave front. "I already gave my five years. What are you telling me, that they will expect more than that from me?"

His friend's eyes widened and he nodded furtively. "It may be. The rumor is, they will be drafting the men who already served *first*. That way they will have battalions ready if needed. And you won't be able to stay in the band with the tuba this time. They need men to fight. Talk to Sarah's brother, Shmulek—he also heard this news. He is planning to go to America as soon as he can arrange the money for his fare. He hasn't told you or Sarah because you have been suffering enough with your other troubles."

Yitzhac waved his fears away. "Ach. You people, you believe every rumor you hear. Shmulek wants to go to America to pick up the gold from the streets. Since he was a little boy, he's been dreaming big dreams—of making his fortune, of miracles. But I hear there are people coming back from America already. I hear stories of bandits there too. Such a golden land, it's not."

His friend wagged a finger at him. "This is not a silly rumor! I too am thinking about leaving. Don't wait too long, Yitzhac. Talk to Shmulek before you go home."

Yitzhac laughed and shrugged. But later, when he was alone, he thought about his years in the army, remembering the soldiers he saw returning from battles with ugly wounds, some missing legs or arms. He could still hear the anti-Semitic curses hurled at him, especially when the soldiers got drunk.

I don't know, maybe he's right, maybe they will try to make me go back, he thought. *Who will question the czar? Besides, who knows how long I can make a living driving people around with my horses and wagon, on these roads full of mud or rocks. It takes so much to keep the horses healthy, and people always complain I don't go fast enough. They don't pay me the extra kopeks anymore when I help with heavy baggage. Maybe in America there is a better life. Who knows?*

But what about his family? Where would he get enough money to take them with him? And would Sarah go willingly? She sometimes repeated news she heard from Golda about their cousin Chaim, who'd gone to New York in America two years ago, and how he always had enough food, even an extra suit with a vest to wear on Shabbas. But Sarah changed the subject whenever he suggested that life in America might be better for them. *Still, this might be a good time. Leiba Chana isn't so sickly anymore, and Enta is a quiet, strong girl. Thank God!* Surely his mother in heaven is looking after Enta, who has her name. The more he thought about it, the more he thought the time might soon be good, and it might even get Sarah's mind off the dead baby.

When Yitzhac saw Shmulek later that evening in Sarah's father's home, he greeted him more warmly than usual. "So, brother-in-law" Yitzhac whispered, "I hear you have news."

Shmulek put his finger to his lips and shook his head. "Shah, be quiet here—I can't talk in front of the others yet."

Later, as Shmulek walked Yitzhac to the inn, he repeated the same rumors about more men soon to be drafted. He had been saving a long time to make the trip, that was no secret, but now it was getting dangerous, and he had to leave quickly before they could force him into the army. He was trying to arrange for his half-brother, Nachum, to accompany him. "In a few weeks we'll be ready. We'll set out for the Austrian town of Brody, travel by train through Germany, then into Antwerp in Belgium. There, we will embark on a ship for America."

Shmulek grew ebullient as he described his plans. He put his arm around Yitzhac's shoulders and stared at him. "Well, Yitzhac, why don't you come too? What's here for you? Just misery and bandits. Who needs the czar and his army?"

Yitzhac shrugged. "Just let those fools try to attack me. I've shown them before who is tougher, and I will do it again." Yitzhac shook his fist in the air and dismissed the threat of bandits with a flick of his wrist. But then he said quietly, rubbing his chin, "Yes, but the draft—that's another matter." He changed the subject. "Sarah will be upset to hear you are leaving so soon, and taking Nachum too. Will you come to Skvira before you go, to say goodbye to her and tell her you hope we will all soon join you?"

"Of course. Will you have room for me in your droshky tomorrow when you return?"

Afterward, Yitzhac thought about the hard life he would always have in this land. Still, he wasn't convinced that leaving for the unknown was what he wanted to do. His horses—what of them? Could he get a good horse in America? Would they need someone to drive a carriage there? He wouldn't know the roads—how could he get people from one town to another? And most people speak English in America, except for the Jewish immigrants still speaking Yiddish. Could he learn the new language? How would he get enough kopeks to pay for tickets for all of them? He didn't have the answers. He tried not to think of more questions.

* * *

The next day Sarah smiled her pleasure when Shmulek walked in with Yitzhac. "My brother, what a great surprise!" She laughed as she hurried to set another place at the table and pull up one of the old chairs. Then she put her arms around him. "You are well? And our older brother Henoch and his family—they are well, too?"

Shmulek laughed. " Sister, your greeting is as warm and welcoming as what I smell coming from that large pot you've got cooking on the stove! Yes, I am well, as is Henoch and his family, and all our other relatives in Pogrebischte."

Lucky I decided to show Yitzhac that I would push the sadness away and do what was right, Sarah thought. *And good thing I made a big pot of barley soup and some extra bread!* She looked up at Yitzhac and wondered why he looked so gloomy. Then her mind raced ahead. *With Shmulek's company, there will be laughing and stories. He always brings light into the room. Maybe tonight will be a good time to tell Yitzhac about the new baby on the way, and how my mother came to me last night to tell me this one will be a son.*

Sarah was proud that Shmulek had grown into a fun-loving, confident man. Everyone liked having Shmulek around. She was sure this was because she had always been there to protect and comfort him when he was a baby, and always tried to make sure he wasn't afraid as he grew up. Now he was learning how to run a shop and be a butcher. He would have a good life, and maybe—please God—there would be a good wife to make him happy.

Shmulek swung around and held his arms out. "Come here, Leibana," he called to Leiba Chana, "give your Uncle Shmulek a big hug." She ran to him, and he lifted her in the air and swung her around. Leiba Chana giggled and asked for more. "Beautiful flower with my mother's name, you make me feel like I have my mother with me."

Enta watched from the corner, then lowered her eyes, disappointed that he hadn't noticed her. Then he called out to her, "You too, special little girl—come here and give your uncle a kiss." Enta rose and slowly walked over, then reached up to kiss him lightly on the cheek, a little frightened by his loud voice, even though she knew her mother loved him. He patted her head, saying, "Pretty little Entala."

He walked over to Sarah and took her hands in his. "Sister, I'm glad to see the color back in your cheeks." He added in a whisper loud enough for Yitzhac to hear, "Yitzhac must be treating you well after all."

Feeling her cheeks heat, Sarah waved him away.

Yitzhac cleared his throat, then took out the cloth he used as a handkerchief and blew his nose. "Enough carrying on, already—it's time to eat."

"I have it ready," Sarah said, irritated that he would not join in their happy mood. She put the bread on the table and quickly served the men and the children. When they had finished their second bowls of soup and she was sure that everyone was full, she filled a bowl for herself and sat down. They talked about their stepmother, Fraydel, and how much faith the people in Pogrebischte still had that she could talk with the dead about the future. Her four children born after Nachum were growing taller, Schmulek told her, and at least now they all helped keep their home clean.

After Sarah poured the tea, Shmulek cleared his throat and grasped his sister's hand. "Well Sarah, I have important news. I leave with Nachum next month for America. My friend Abie Molofsky—remember him? He's the one we all saw off when he left for America last year. He sent me a letter, says he has a room and we can stay there with him."

Sarah felt her smile fade. She widened her eyes, although she was not surprised—Shmulek had been talking about America for years. "God in heaven, give us all strength. But . . . why so soon, my brother?"

"Don't you hear the stories, here in Skvira? In Uman the bandits, the rotten pigs, came in and stole whatever they could find. They beat people in their houses and then set many of them on fire. Your old boss, Bessie Kovitsky, she lost some cousins. They found them the next day, lying in the street with burns and broken skulls." Schmulek snorted. "Who needs this country? Who needs the czar? There are rumors now that soon they will be forcing more Jews into the army. Even Yitzhac should be careful. There are stories that they will call back everyone who served before because they are already trained."

Finally she knew the reason for Yitzhac's gloomy expression. She looked at him. "You heard these stories too, my husband?" She'd heard of the attacks on Jewish villages, but prayed it would not happen in Skvira. She felt confident that the holy men and students she saw through her window would keep the town safe. *God would not let anything terrible happen here.* But the czar's army and the draft . . . that was something else.

Yitzhac nodded. "Who doesn't hear rumors? Who knows anything? They keep us down with their rumors. I'll stay ahead of them, those scum, those stinking animals! I will not go back into the army." He set his glass of tea on the table. "Don't worry, they won't get me."

"Well, at least think about following me to America soon," Shmulek interjected, glancing at Sarah.

"How will Fraydel manage without you and Nachum?" Sarah asked Shmulek.

"She'll be glad to get rid of us," Shmulek joked. "Of course she'll miss the money I bring into the household, but with two less mouths to feed, she won't need so much."

They talked about their Aunt Yetta, who was getting older but was still strong. Sarah shook her head in sympathy as she spoke of how much Yetta suffered, taking care of their uncle after his illness, which had left him incapable of getting around on his own.

Yitzhac was very quiet through the entire meal. When Sarah got up to clear the table, he asked Shmulek to come into the stable while he brushed and fed his horses.

Sarah knew he was more worried than he pretended. She wondered what they were talking about out there. "God will give us strength. He will help us through this too," she said, trying to convince herself. She would wait for another day to tell Yitzhac that he would soon have a son, please God.

A week later, after the Shabbas dinner, Sarah studied Yitzhac's face. He seemed less worried. It had been a good week. He'd had more passengers than usual, and some even gave him extra kopeks. As well, Sarah had sold more challahs than she had in a year.

Yitzhac pushed his bowl toward the center of the table to make way for the tea. "Nu, Sarah, I saw my friend and his son Ephriam when I stopped to let the travelers off the wagon. The boy looks strong. It is a lucky thing for Enta that we have such a good match for her."

Sarah smiled. "We need to give thanks for another blessing, Yitzhac. God is also blessing us with a child again, and my mother came to me to tell me this time it will be a boy. There will be a name for your father."

"Only pray to God that this one should be strong like Enta, whether it is a boy or a girl," was Yitzhac's only reply.

Shmulek and Nachum both came to visit one more time before leaving. Samuel, Rissela's oldest son, had become a photographer's assistant, and he took a picture of Shmulek standing behind Yitzhac, who was seated in a big chair in Rissela's house.

"When you get the picture, it is to remind you that we all belong together in America," Shmulek told Sarah as they embraced before he left. "I will not say goodbye because we will soon be together. Stay strong, my sister. Have a healthy son." Shmulek twirled Leiba Chana, bent and kissed Enta on the cheek, and told them, "I will see you beautiful girls in America."

"Go in good health, brother. You should live and be well, and please send us a letter," Sarah whispered through her tears.

* * *

For a few months things remained calm. Leiba Chana was almost four years old by now, still sickly but talkative and playful. Enta had grown into a quiet child, always wanting to please her mother. Yitzhac had not spoken to Sarah about leaving for America since Shmulek's departure, but she was sure he was considering it, especially when he remained totally silent for long stretches of time.

Her fears became reality one day during the early summer of 1913. Over an hour after he left on the day's journey, Yitzhac burst back into his house, moaning and cursing. "*Oy vay*, damn those c*hazars*, those pigs, they tried to kill me! Those bandits, they almost injured the horses, they took all my money, they beat me—look how my head bleeds. A plague upon them! May the evil eye never leave any of their homes."

Enta ran over to her mother and grabbed her skirt. Leiba Chana began to cry. Golda, who had stopped by a few minutes earlier, stared at her brother in alarm. "Yitzhac, where did this happen?" she exclaimed.

"Not far out of town. They robbed my passengers too. People will think I've grown weak, that I can't protect them. What will happen now? How will I make a living? Gevalt, what will I do?"

"*Vay is mir*, woe is me, Almighty help us, take pity," Sarah moaned, tears welling in her eyes as she fetched a clean cloth, dipped it in a basin of water, and moved to examine her husband's head. "Please, husband, sit still," she admonished him as she pulled his hair back and began cleaning the wound. "We will find a way. Pray for God to protect us," she pleaded.

Yitzhac didn't answer immediately, but stared into space. Suddenly he looked up. The fear was gone from his eyes and he wore his usual tough expression, only it had hardened. "No, Sarah, God does not answer your prayers. Don't you know that? Enough already!" he shouted. Then his voice got very calm and he spoke slowly. "It must be done; it's time. Listen to me, wife—it's time! After the new baby comes, it's time. Enough of your begging God to protect us. It's time already for us to act for ourselves. I will join Shmulek in America after the baby comes."

Sarah stared at him in stunned silence. New tears began to flow. He did not look at her, but continued as if she had voiced arguments. "Don't ask how I will do it. We already had a letter that Shmulek wants us to come, and he has a place I can share until you and the babies can join me. I will go first, after the new baby arrives. When I get there, it won't take long . . . I'll make enough money to send for you. By the time the new baby is weaned, you will have the money to buy tickets for yourself and the children. And by then I will have a place for us to live. Don't argue, I won't listen—it must be done."

Golda looked at them both, eyes wide with alarm at the fear she saw in their faces. She knew as well as Sarah that when her brother made up his mind so emphatically about anything, there was no use discussing it. She jumped in before Sarah had a chance to say anything. "Sarah, maybe Yitzhac is right. Yankle hears stories every day from the Russians who come to him for suits. Bad times are coming, maybe war."

The fear threatened to overwhelm her, and Sarah swayed on her feet, feeling the blood drain from her face. Then Golda's arms were around her, helping her to a chair. "You are never alone," Golda murmured to her. "We will always be here to help you until Yitzhac can send you the money to join him. The only important thing now is to not be afraid. Stay strong, and prepare for the new baby . . . please God, a son for Yitzhac."

And that was that. Sarah accepted that it was meant to be. If her brother was making a life for himself in America, then they could too. Besides, what was the use of arguing when she knew it would only make Yitzhac angrier without changing his mind?

Enta ran over to climb onto her mother's lap. Her small round face creased in concern, she put her arms around Sarah's neck, then tried to wipe away the tears glistening on Sarah's cheeks. Leiba Chana jumped up to join them, bumped her head on the table, and began to scream. Yitzhac went into the stable.

The time remaining went quickly. Sarah gave birth to Benjamin, always known as Bennie, in September. It was not an easy birth, but it ended with much celebration in Skvira when people heard it was a boy to be named for Yitzhac's father. Bennie was a rosy, happy baby, strong and calm, like Enta. Sarah tried not to think of the future while they celebrated the *bris*, the ritual circumcision. When she held Bennie in her arms to comfort him, she wondered how long she would have to be both father and mother to her only son. "I hope your life will not be filled with more pain, my son," she whispered. "May you live to be one hundred and twenty years."

Less than a month after the bris, Yitzhac had his bag packed and his ticket ready. The hardest part of the preparation for him had been selling his horses. Golda and Yankle added to the money he got for the horses so he would have enough to live on while waiting for the ship's departure in Antwerp. When Bennie was six weeks old, Yitzhac told Sarah he was ready. Rosh Hashana and Yom Kippur were over. The sooner he could get started, the sooner he could send for them. In the meantime, his sisters and brother were there to help.

Sarah could barely sleep the night before Yitzhac's departure. She dozed off a few times, only to relive the sense of abandonment she had experienced as a child after her mother's death. She would wake with a start, and realize with dread that it wasn't just a dream, it was in fact happening again. Her final dream comforted her. In it a Hasidic scholar with reddish-gold sidelocks smiled at her, pointed to a large ship, and nodded happily.

In the morning she fed the children and filled a sack with bread, a boiled egg, an apple, and some hard cookies for Yitzhac to eat on the first part of his journey. Golda, Yankle, and their children appeared at the door. Golda and the children would stay with Sarah while Yankle accompanied Yitzhac to the carriage waiting at the inn. The rest of the family would say goodbye there.

Yitzhac took Sarah aside and whispered to her, "Remember, you are the one who talks with God. I hope He hears you and will keep you strong for all of us. Don't forget me. Someday life will be easier. For now, you know I must struggle for a new life. I will send a letter as soon as I am together with Shmulek. In a little while, when I've saved the money, you can be sure I will send enough for all of you to join me. Take care of our children."

It was the first time Sarah could remember that he did not poke fun at her belief in the Almighty.

As he embraced her, Sarah realized she had never before seen tears in his eyes. "May God watch over you, my husband," was all she could say.

He turned quickly and held each of his children in his arms, one by one, running his hands through their hair and over their cheeks. First he kissed Leiba Chana, then he hugged Enta close to his face, then bent to rub the back of his son, asleep in his rough cradle. He turned away, hurriedly kissed his niece and nephew, embraced his sister without speaking, and then walked out the door.

Golda came to her, and Sarah began to cry quietly on her shoulder. She quickly realized that her children were watching, all crying themselves. "Shah, shah, *kinderleh,* be quiet, children," she called to them. "Everything is okay. See? Mama's fine."

That night she took the three children into her bed, held them very close, and let them stay with her until morning. She could not drift off for a long time, instead staring into the darkness, asking herself over and over, *How will I manage? Why am I always the one left behind?* Then she saw moonlight from the full moon shining through her window, and thought, *Maybe this is a good omen, that the heavens will light the way for Yitzhac's journey.* She prayed to God to bless Yitzhac and give him safe passage. "Don't take him from me like you took my mother. Please let us join him soon," she pleaded.

* * *

"We didn't see him again for close to eight years," Ettie said.

Waving his hands for emphasis, Bennie stood. "Try to understand. Sure, Papa's timing made it hard for everyone, but I know he intended to build a better life for all of us. Who knew what would come next, with the war and all the misery?"

Ettie added with an air of finality, "I guess it never would've been a good time for him to go."

Conversation for the rest of the evening turned to the weather, jobs, and children. People began to leave around nine-thirty, all expressing the hope that their next get-together would be for a happier occasion. As Bennie prepared to leave, he motioned for David to join him in the other room.

Bennie cleared his throat, uncomfortable about what he wanted to say. "You don't remember much about your father, do you?"

David grimaced in annoyance and shrugged. "Nah—how could I?"

"I understand how you must have felt all your life," Bennie said. "You know, I didn't have any memory of my father until I was eight years old." He put his hand on David's shoulder and stared into his eyes. "A lot of people didn't get along with your father, but I never had any problems with him. I know your mother had a hard life because of him. But you should realize that she did the best she could, and she shouldn't have anything to regret."

David shrugged again. "Yeah, maybe you're right." He didn't sound convinced.

Bennie left David and returned to the other room. He embraced Ettie and whispered, "I hope you're getting some sleep."

"Who can sleep?" she answered. "It feels like a book is ending, even though I put it on the shelf years ago. I keep thinking about the past—but more about what went on when we were kids, not so much about Morton." Bennie squeezed her shoulder, and she smiled at him. "Thanks, Bennie; I'm glad you were here tonight."

PART THREE

THE SEPARATION

We beseech Thee, O Lord Our God,
Let us not be in need either of gifts of mortals, or of their loans,
But only of Thy helping hand which is full, open, holy and ample,
So that we may not be ashamed, and may we not be in need of people.

—Prayer after meals

So That We May Not Be Ashamed

When Yitzhac left for America, Ettie was only two and a half years old. She had no clear memory of what happened in the next months, but Sarah often repeated how much Yitzhac's family helped them manage during those first few months.

Yitzhac's brother Layve asked her to bake bread that he could use to feed the travelers who stayed at his inn. In return he would give her and the children a portion of the other food he served his overnight guests. Sarah was grateful for this *mitzvah*, his good deed in offering her some way of earning the help he wanted to give so she would not suffer the shame of taking charity. But she was determined to find other townspeople with whom to trade her baked goods. She didn't doubt that Layve needed the bread, and it was no secret that she could bake better than most. But Layve's wife had always done the baking for the inn. Sarah's baking might help his family for a short time, freeing his wife to spend more time on her other chores, but later in the winter, on days when no overnight travelers arrived, it would be a hardship for Layve's family.

She never forgot to say the prayer after meals, beseeching God to "let us not be in need either of gifts of mortals, or of their loans . . . so that we may not be ashamed."

Two days after Yitzhac's departure, not long after Sarah finished her baking and the newly baked breads were cool enough for delivery, she looked out the window that faced the river, checking to see if the ground was muddy. Then she opened the door and put her arm out. It was still relatively warm for mid-October, although the trees had been shedding their leaves for days now. In the bright sunlight, the light wind made the shadows from the branches dance across the paths. The vivid colors of early fall had faded, a gloomy reminder that the embracing beauty of autumn would soon be replaced by the bleak dangers of winter. Sarah shivered. At least the ground seemed dry, and they would have no trouble walking to the inn.

She called Leiba Chana and Enta to get ready, kissing their foreheads as she helped them pull on the sweaters she had knitted for them. Next she wrapped Bennie in a blanket and put him into a sack she had made to fit over her shoulders and around her neck. That way he could rest on her bosom, and she could look down and make sure he was comfortable. "Come, kinderleh, we have a job to do. Leibana, you hold one of Enta's hands while I take the other." With her free hand, Sarah carried the sack that held her loaves of bread.

They were on their way home after delivering the bread to Layve when Sarah's neighbor, Fagala, joined them. She carried a bucket of water that she had just filled from the well. Smiling, Fagala urged, "Sarah, come join me, we will have a glass of tea together." She waved her hand for Sarah to follow her.

Sarah hesitated, nodding toward the girls. She knew Fagala was a yenta, a gossip who would try to pry information from her about the kind of help she was getting from Yitzhac's family. Then she would pass this information on to everyone in the town. Still, if you were careful, Fagala was enjoyable to talk with. Besides, it would be good to have company in the coming months. Sarah capitulated with a sigh. "I have to get the children home, but maybe just for a short visit."

Before Sarah was seated, Fagala began, in her less than subtle way, to probe for as much information as she could. "At least it's good weather for Yitzhac to be traveling to America. God should grant him an easy journey. I hope your brothers have a big enough room so Yitzhac can have his own bed. I hear some of the men have to share a bed as well as a room." Sarah didn't know so she just shrugged. "You should be well, please God, and hear from him soon, Sarah. Let's hope he will send enough money for you and your children to have an easy journey when you join him."

"Amen," Sarah agreed, "it should be so."

Over tea, Fagala talked nonstop about how difficult it was for people in nearby towns to make ends meet. She repeated stories of peasants getting drunk and destroying homes and shops in neighboring villages. "You know, Sarah, many families are leaving—some for New York, some for Chicago, some for Canada, some even for Argentina."

Fagala looked over at Sarah, who was feeling more and more dejected. Without waiting for Sarah to react, she blurted, "What about your sister in Canada? Do you ever hear from her?"

Sarah couldn't avoid reacting now. "Sure, we hear from her. She has three sons and two daughters already. It seems life is hard in Canada, too." The last thing Sarah wanted was to be reminded of her disappointment with her sister, Gitl, but Fagala had managed to reopen that wound. Sarah had been trying so hard to dispel her anger over having to give Gitl the money from her dowry. That money had ensured that Gitl was not left behind by *her* husband.

Fagala sighed dramatically. "Nu, what can you do, it's not easy to be a Jew. We were not meant to have easy lives, in Skvira, America, Canada—I don't know."

Sarah looked around for Enta and Leiba Chana, hoping to get away before her annoyance became too obvious. She heard them giggling in the corner, but before she could make her move to leave, Fagala lowered her voice as if someone would hear and shared her next bit of gossip.

"You know, Sarah, I heard that Masha Walchinsky went into Kiev and sold some whiskey. In one trip she made enough money to feed her children for weeks. Maybe you could look after your family that way. Of course, if they catch you, that's another matter. Ach, remember those people who were put in jail for ten months because they didn't have enough to pay the bribes?"

Sarah nodded and added, "Everybody has a sack of troubles, Fagala. If we would all put our sacks in the middle of the room and see everybody else's, we would take our own sack back."

Fagala gazed at the ceiling and commented nonchalantly, "Well, I suppose you will now be selling more cakes and challahs."

Sarah knew Fagala was looking for confirmation of what she would hear about soon enough, that Layve was buying her bread. "I'll do what I can," she said firmly, then decided to take the initiative. "Tell me, Fagala, what word from your brother and his wife in America?"

In response Fagala rose, opened a drawer, felt around under the folded linens, and produced a photograph. "He just opened his own dry goods shop there, and is doing very well. Look at this picture—the fine suit he is wearing, with a vest, yet! He looks rich."

"Beautiful," Sarah agreed. "*Kaynahora*—may the evil eye stay far away from him."

Fagala frowned at the photo. "But I don't know, he looks like a *goy*. I hope he doesn't eat *treyf*, unkosher meat." She sighed. "Who knows, maybe one day our families will all be together again in America."

Sarah nodded. "It should be so, please God." Before Fagala could say more, she called the girls to get ready to go home, slung the sack holding the still sleeping Bennie around her neck, thanked Fagala for the tea, wished her good health, and left.

* * *

The first snowfall arrived, and still no word from Yitzhac. Sarah consoled herself with the knowledge that he would first have to find someone to help him write a letter. Even if he managed to do that during the first week after his arrival, it would take several more weeks for mail to make the return trip across the ocean and overland back to Skvira—just as long as it had taken Yitzhac to get to Pittsburgh in America, where Shmulek was. She hoped her husband was well and was thinking of her. *Who will take care of him if he gets sick?* she wondered. She knew her brothers Shmulek and Nachum would not know what to do.

Sarah was grateful to Yitzhac's family for their many kindnesses. In addition to the baking Layve arranged for her to do, Golda invited them to her house for Shabbas dinners, and Rissela sent her oldest daughter to take Leiba Chana and Enta for a walk on the days when Sarah went to the market to sell her breads and cakes. With the extra earnings, she and the children were not doing so badly. So what if there was no meat most weeks, just a piece of herring now and then? She was especially happy that the peasant lady who delivered fresh milk liked her bread so they could make an exchange, and some days she could even get an egg or two. Some weeks they got a bit of chicken or fish at Golda's on Shabbas, and the potatoes, carrots, beets, and cabbage she kept in a cold spot in the stable would last a while. Bennie was still nursing, and the girls didn't need very much.

Finally, when the snow had already been on the ground four weeks, Sarah saw Layve's son walking briskly up the hill. He called when he saw her, "Aunt Sarah, Aunt Sarah! My father says you should come fast—a letter has come from Uncle Yitzhac. I will stay here with the children," he told her when he reached her door. "He's waiting to read you the letter. Please hurry."

"Thank God, he arrived safe and sound," she said, kissing her nephew before glancing out the side window toward the Bes Medresh.

By the time she got to the inn, she was totally out of breath, and her heart was pounding. Layve had not yet opened the envelope, waiting until Sarah arrived. Now he tore open the envelope and pulled out a single piece of paper. He cleared his throat, and read:

Dear wife and family,

The journey was not easy, but I made it. Shmulek is well and working hard. We have enough to eat and a place to sleep. Everybody is in a hurry in America, and it is a hard life. There is no gold on the streets here, but there are many bandits. It takes too much money to buy a horse and wagon, so I carry crates of potatoes on my back to the carts other men have, and I help them sell to families in the neighborhood. This way I earn enough money so I have something to eat. As soon as I get enough for a ticket, I will return to Skvira.

Remember me to our children and to the rest of the family.

Your husband,
Yitzhac

When Layve finished reading, he and Sarah just stared at each other. They had all heard stories about men returning when they could no longer endure the harsh conditions facing immigrants in America.

At first Sarah felt relieved that Yitzhac was alive and well, and that she would not have to face the heartache of leaving the people she loved, nor expose her children to the dangers of such a long and arduous journey. But she had been mentally preparing for a change, even looking forward to starting fresh, maybe having a better life, and now a cold knot of panic formed behind her breastbone. The dangers facing them here were getting worse. If Yitzhac returned, what of the bandits who beat and robbed him? Surely there could be no characters as evil in America. And there were still fearful rumors that the czar was forcing people back into the army. Could Yitzhac pick up again, driving people from town to town to make a living? Travelers who at one time preferred Yitzhac as their driver had since found others who were still in business. How hard would it be for Yitzhac to win back their confidence?

His return would be embarrassing. Yitzhac would be ashamed. *And,* Sarah wondered sadly, *if Yitzhac returns, will I ever see Shmulek again?* She curled her fingers into her palms. *Why is he putting me through this?*

Layve saw the worry and disappointment in Sarah's eyes. "Well, Sarah, it is no secret that Yitzhac has a mind of his own, he is a stubborn man. But who knows? By the time he's managed to save for a return ticket, maybe he will change his mind and send for you instead." He shrugged and tried, "If he does return, we won't all have to say goodbye."

Sarah took his hand in hers, but did not look at him. "God bless you, Layve, you understand much. Whatever God wishes, we will do." She composed herself and asked, "Will you send Yitzhac an answer, letting him know that I am concerned for his good health, and that I and the children are managing well with help from his family? And . . . tell him that we hope to see him soon. Whether it is meant for him to return to Skvira or for him to change his mind again and stay in America, his family will follow his wishes."

"I will," Layve replied.

Sarah nodded. "I will pray for the best, what else can I do?" Then she added, "Tell him his son is a fine boy."

Sarah knew that it would take months for Yitzhac to save enough to return. *By that time, summer will also have returned, and his trip home might not be so dangerous,* she consoled herself. *Or maybe he will change his mind again.* She thought of their children. Leiba Chana was already four years old and Enta almost three. Bennie was growing into a chubby, contented little boy. *But he needs his father.*

Enjoy Life in Spite of Life

At the end of the second day of shiva, Ettie sat in the front seat of the car with David as he drove slowly out of Collette's driveway.

"Mother, do you remember any happy times when you were a kid?" Rachel asked from the backseat, where she sat with Laurie and Steve. "Did you ever have fun?"

"What kind of fun could we have? Everything was so difficult."

They drove in silence for a few minutes. Then, as they approached the traffic lights at the main road leading from the suburban area into the city, Ettie surprised them when she said, "You know what? I do remember a special day, when the winter had barely passed. I'm not sure how long my father had been gone by then. My mother's older brother, Henoch, arrived from Pogrebischte to do business in Skvira. He was always serious, never much laughter—not exuberant like my Uncle Shmulek, that's for sure. But this time he called for me to come over to give him a hug. It's all coming back to me now . . . "

* * *

"Come here, *shaina maideleh*, pretty girl," Henoch coaxed. "Your uncle will teach you something real nice."

When Enta came to him, her uncle took her hand and motioned toward the empty, unused stable. "It's time for you to learn to dance the *kazutski*, so when there's a wedding in the town, you'll know what to do."

Enta looked uncertainly at her mother, then lowered her head.

Sarah smiled. "Go, my precious daughter, have a good time."

Uncle Henoch lifted Enta as they entered the stable, keeping one arm around her waist and holding her other hand in the air. Hay still lay scattered on the floor, and the smell of horses made Enta sneeze.

Humming the same music she had often heard her mother hum when she was baking, Uncle Henoch began dancing slowly, swaying back and forth, then faster, whirling around the room, all while holding her in the air.

He stopped and put her down. "Now extend your arms," he told her, and held his hands straight out in front. When she obeyed, he clasped her hands, and showed her step by step what to do. "Now you try it by yourself, my *maideleh*."

With each move she made, he clapped and told her she was so smart. "Quite a dancer, my little one."

Enta didn't want to stop, she wanted to go faster and faster. "More, uncle, more," she pleaded, holding out her arms for him to join her again.

He complied, and they danced until finally he groaned, "Oy, your Uncle Henoch is out of breath. Next time I visit, we'll dance again."

They returned to the house, with Enta jumping up and down in glee. "Mama, Mama, I can dance!" she shouted excitedly. She reached for Uncle Henoch's hands and tugged on them. "Please, uncle, let's show Mama."

He circled the floor with her, humming, and Sarah began to clap in rhythm, humming along. Leiba Chana held out her hands and Sarah grasped them, making the foursome required for the dance. They went in and out once and circled once, then laughed and sat down. Leiba Chana clapped her hands happily. Enta began circling the room alone, repeating some of the dance steps.

Sarah smiled. "Thank you, brother. I have never seen her so happy."

* * *

"Wow, so that's how the dancing all started," Rachel said, her voice tinged with admiration. "I can picture you at the family celebrations dancing the kazutski, the fox trot, the Charleston, to whatever music was playing. People always said nobody was as light on their feet as you, that they used to stand around and watch you, because you were the best."

Ettie felt her face relax. "Aw, go on, there are lots of good dancers.

But that's my earliest happy memory." She smiled, looking out the windshield but focused on the past. "I always loved to dance."

Later, when Ettie was alone in her apartment trying to sleep, she was still unable to pull herself out of the past. She lay in bed, familiar images and Yiddish voices from her childhood playing through her mind, bringing her comfort. Her mind conjured fuzzy memories of some other happy times. These mingled with the stories her mother had often repeated through the years, and she pictured herself back in Skvira in 1914, when spring came with its melting snow and the resulting mud. Her mother had always been trying to keep the hardened floor clean, scrubbing everything she could reach in the one-room house.

* * *

"Soon it will be *Pesach,* Passover, and we have to make the kitchen ready," Sarah explained. "We will go to your Aunt Rissela's for the *seder.* It will be different from the Shabbas dinner, with more food and more prayers, all about Moses leading the Jewish people out of Egypt. Golda's family and Layve's family will be there too. I'll make new dresses for both my girls. Your uncle Yankle sent some pretty cloth."

Before Passover another letter came from Yitzhac. Sarah took the children with her when word came from Layve. There was great excitement about this letter because it included a photograph of Yitzhac standing beside a chair, wearing a Western-style gray suit with a vest and tie. He looked proud, almost prosperous, and still strong, but there was a brooding sadness in his eyes. Gone was the defiant expression that once was enough to keep people from challenging him. Sarah wondered what other things had changed.

The letter made no mention of his plans to return. He reported that he was recovering from a cough he'd had for the past month, that Shmulek and Nachum had helped him as much as they could. When Sarah heard this part of the letter, she shook her head, eyes closed, trying to picture his situation. She could imagine Yitzhac lying in a dirty bed in a strange room while her brothers stumbled around trying to care for this big-boned, grumbling husband of hers. *It's not right. My brothers should not have to look after him—it's my responsibility,* she thought. And then she shuddered in sudden fear, wondering, *What will happen to me if he dies over there?*

The next part of the letter was more cheerful, reporting that Shmulek was seeing a girl who lived two streets away—her name was Franya, and her family had come from Pliskov. She was a lively one, and a wedding was likely before the end of summer.

Yitzhac and Nachum will be his only family at the wedding, Sarah thought, disappointed that she would miss this happy event. She had never imagined Shmulek would be married without her being there to dance at his wedding. *Well, if Shmulek has a wife, at least there will be someone to cook for those men. If Franya is lively, she will have energy to run a household for them.*

Yitzhac ended his letter by saying he missed his wife and family and prayed they would soon be together. Sarah could tell by the way the last thoughts were expressed that they were the words of the letter-writer, not Yitzhac's, but still she was comforted that the letter expressed concern for her.

When they were back in their home, Sarah wrapped the photograph of Yitzhac in a cloth and put it on the shelf with the one taken before Shmulek left for America. The next day when Enta was resting on the ledge near the fireplace, she watched her mother carry the cloth to the table, where she took out the two photographs and laid them side by side. She held one up to the light by the window, then the other. Then she walked over to the photograph of Zayde Moishe on the wall and shook her head. "Zayde, you told me not to be afraid, but what do I do now? When will I see my husband again?"

Unbuttoning her blouse, Sarah pulled out the handkerchief she kept there and untied the knot. The few coins earned from selling her breads and cakes tumbled onto the table. She shuddered. Then, holding the handkerchief over her eyes, Sarah moved the coins around until she felt the one the rebbeh had given her when she sought his intervention before her third child died. She kissed it, then gathered the coins back into the handkerchief and returned it to the place inside her blouse.

A week after Passover ended, when green shoots were peeking through the patchy snow, heralding the blooms to follow, and tiny green buds had emerged on many trees, Sarah sat quietly nursing Bennie, enjoying the sunshine streaming through the window. She jumped when the door flew open, and Golda burst into the room to share news of an upcoming wedding in town.

"The first week in August," Golda answered when Sarah asked when it would take place. She smiled proudly. "Yankle has the great honor of making the groom's wedding suit, so it will also be a profitable arrangement for us. The groom is from Tureni—not much of a scholar, but from a well-to-do family."

"And the bride?" Sarah asked impatiently.

"The oldest of the miller's three daughters. Her uncle arranged the match last fall while doing some business in Tureni."

"Such a match, Golda!" Sarah exclaimed. "We should live to see it for *your* daughter someday."

Golda was not so enthusiastic. "Plenty of time for that," she replied, gathering Enta and Leiba Chana into her arms and kissing each on the cheek. "She's just a child."

Leiba followed Golda to the door, where she tugged on her aunt's arm. "Please, aunt, please—take me to your house! Please." Sarah nodded to Golda, and they both left.

Enta, still sensing her mother's excitement, jumped up and down. "Mama, when I marry Ephriam, will there be a big celebration too? Will we dance? Did you have a big feast at your wedding, Mama?"

Sarah looked away, unsmiling, which sobered Enta. She stopped bouncing and watched her mother with large eyes. "It is God's will to celebrate a wedding," Sarah said carefully. "A woman is nobody if she doesn't have a husband and children. After she is married, she must pray to God to give her strength to look after her family. Only if a woman has a husband will she ever get into the Kingdom of Heaven."

* * *

In her mind's eye, Ettie pictured that wedding from the past as if she were walking with the other townspeople behind the bride and groom, all of the adults carrying lit candles in their hands as the procession slowly wound its way to the synagogue. She could see the embroidered cloth chupah, or canopy, held up on poles by people from the town. She saw the huge synagogue door opened wide in welcome, watched again the bride and groom sipping wine from a cup and the groom stomping on a glass, heard the shouts of "mazel tov."

She smiled in remembrance of a feast that would never be matched, with its seemingly endless platters of food and cakes. Best of all had been the dancing. The men danced together on one side of the room, the women on the other, not mixing with the men. Her mother, Golda, Rissela, and Layve's wife had danced together. She had partnered with Leiba Chana, and they joined a circle with other cousins, all dancing until her mother told them they had to leave.

And she remembered the walk home, when she asked with a sense of urgency, "Mama, when can I marry Ephriam so I can dance again?"

Sarah brushed the hair away from her daughter's eyes. "Sweet daughter, who knows what will happen with that, where we'll all be? We'll have to see what God wills."

* * *

The feeling of euphoria ended the week after the wedding. The summer was almost over, and the women of the shtetl were gathered at the river, washing their clothes. Some of their children helped while others scampered about, playing little games. A third letter had arrived from Enta's father the week before, in which he mentioned that he still planned to return to Skvira, as soon as he could arrange things.

Enta took Ephriam's hand and offered to tell him a story. They found a flat rock high on the hillside near the river, where they could still see their mothers, but her sister was out of earshot. Enta's story was about what would happen after they got married, how they would live in a big house and ride in a golden carriage.

"You'll never go to America alone and leave me, will you, Ephriam?" she asked in a pleading tone, thinking how sad her mother appeared while looking at her father's photograph.

Ephriam shook his head. "Of course not! But tell me more about the golden carriage. Will it have ten horses? Will they go like this?" He jumped up and began prancing about in imitation of a horse.

Just then a stone hit the spot where Ephriam had been sitting, and three others landed near Enta, one grazing her leg. She looked around and saw some peasant children running past. Another stone hit her arm.

"*Bei Zhidov.* Smash the Jews. Dirty Jews, dirty Jews!" the children shouted. They ran, then stopped and threw more stones that landed near Enta and Ephriam. "Smash the Jews!"

When Sarah and Ephriam's mother heard the children's shouts, they left their baskets of clothes on the rocks and ran to scoop up Enta and Ephriam, then ran back to their baskets holding the two children. Sarah put Enta down, lifted Bennie into her arms, and called to Leiba Chana, "Come—hurry! It is time to return to our homes."

Her mother bolted the door shut when they were all safely inside, then put her arms around them and rocked on her feet.

* * *

Ettie's mind jumped to another scene, sometime at the end of a winter and close to the celebration of *Purim*. As difficult as times were for everyone, families looked forward to the celebrations at the shul, the holiday when children dressed to celebrate the ancient time when Queen Esther helped to save the Jewish subjects from annihilation at the hands of the wicked Haman. Golda had a long dress her daughter had worn a few years ago, and if it fit Leiba Chana or Enta, one of them could be Queen Esther.

While Sarah began baking the *humentashen*, the three-cornered pastries filled with poppy seeds, Leiba Chana suggested, "Enta, why don't we play another game and pretend you and Ephriam are getting married?"

Enta hesitated, glancing uncertainly at her mother. Enta was sure she would have some reason why it would be forbidden, some superstition about tempting fate.

"We can get the other children to carry candles and pretend they are lit," Leiba Chana continued, her enthusiasm fueled by the festive atmosphere, "and we can use the fallen branches near the barn to hang some cloth on for the others to carry like a chupah. I'll be the mother, and we'll see which cousin wants to be the father, and who wants to be the rabbi. Look—I have this white cloth I got from Uncle Yankle. You can put it on your head like a veil. We can dance the kazutski."

The prospect of dancing convinced Enta. She decided to plead with her mother to let them do this just once.

When they asked, Sarah said thoughtfully, "Zayde Moishe used to tell me, 'To praise God, one must live, and to live, one must enjoy life; one must enjoy life in spite of life.'" To Enta's complete surprise, Sarah smiled at her and said, "Yes, kinderleh, go and enjoy, have a good time. Who knows what the future holds?" She sighed, and her smile turned sad.

About ten children living in the houses on the hillside nearby joined in their game. They marched over the road from Ephriam's house to the side of Enta's house in view of the Bes Medresh. They used a cup of water to signify the glass of wine and wrapped some dried leaves and acorns in a piece of cloth for Ephriam to stomp on instead of breaking a glass. It made a crunching noise that resembled that part of a real ceremony. Almost immediately, the children rushed giggling into the empty stable, where they sang and danced until dinnertime.

* * *

And that's definitely the last happy event I remember ever happening in Skvira, Ettie thought the next morning, when the family gathered at Collette and Stanley's house for the third day of shiva. *How different my life would have been if I had been able to marry Ephriam.*

As she wondered if her grandchildren wanted to hear more about the hardships everyone in Skvira endured after that, David suggested to his two nephews that the three of them go out for a walk. Andrea and Laurie decided to join them, leaving only Ettie, Rachel, Collette, and Stanley sitting in the quiet house.

Collette began to talk about her own childhood and how proud she'd been when her father led their Passover seder for some of their friends. "I'll tell you this," she said solemnly, "I've never been to a better seder. He explained what all the symbols stood for and what every prayer meant, and he tried to include everybody. Do you remember, Rachel, when you found the a*fikomen*, the *matzos* hidden for the children to hunt for before the second half of the seder could begin?"

Rachel nodded and smiled, enjoying the chance to reminisce about the past, Ettie knew. Both her girls recalled familiar stories whenever they were together.

"You said you wanted a baby doll as your reward for returning the afikomen," Collette continued. "Dad was so excited and eager to please you, he took me with him during the week to buy one for you. I helped him pick out just the right one. He was such a good father."

Ettie looked down to hide her smirk. She saw Rachel looking at her, her brows pinched in concern, hoping that her mother would not say anything to upset Collette again.

"I was so thrilled," Rachel added, turning back to her sister. "I loved that doll, with its overalls and long blond braids. What a shame things didn't stay that happy for our family."

An uncomfortable moment was broken when the doorbell rang. Collette jumped up to admit Morton's brother Sol and his son, Lenny.

"We don't have a lot of time," Sol said, "but we wanted to stop by and see how everyone is." He looked around. "Where are the others?"

"They went for a walk," Collette answered, sounding apologetic.

Clearly disappointed, Sol and Lenny sat for a while making small talk about family members whom Ettie rarely saw. Sol tried to shift the subject to Morton, saying, "You know, Lenny and I visited Morton regularly during the past ten years. I really enjoyed talking with him about the old days in Lithuania. I think it made him feel good, that he remembered everything in such detail about those times."

Again the moment was broken when a few of Ettie's cousins and Collette's friends arrived, and Sol and his son left soon after. Collette commented more than once how close she'd been to her father, and how much she would miss him. Each time, everyone else became very quiet and had nothing to add. The morning drifted by slowly, the polite conversation not masking anyone's discomfort.

War

After lunch, before any other visitors arrived, Ettie asked her son, who wore a faraway expression, "Hey, David, whatsa matter? You look upset, do you feel okay? Did you talk to Sandy and the kids? Are they okay?"

David dropped his eyes. "It's hard for Sandy to look after the kids alone. Sari's behavior's been erratic, and it's a big worry." He glimpsed Collette and Stanley exchanging a worried glance, and stopped talking about his teenage daughter.

Rachel's son Steve broke the silence. "Grandma, I'm disappointed. You haven't told the scariest part of your story, what happened with the police, and when all those soldiers started to attack the villages."

Glad for the distraction, Ettie replied, "Okay, are you sure you want to hear more, that I won't put you all to sleep?" When her grandchildren laughed and promised to stay awake, she began with, "I don't know the details of how the war got started and who entered on each side. I just know that the townspeople began to talk about a new war after someone killed the Austrian archduke and his wife in Sarajevo in June."

Stanley cleared his throat, then said, "I've read a lot about the history of that time. By August, Austria had declared war on Serbia, and Germany was getting into it, siding with Austria. Then Russia decided to defend Serbia, and Austria and Germany declared war on Russia. Eventually it became Turkey, Austria, and Germany on one side fighting against France, Belgium, Britain, Serbia, and Russia."

Ettie shrugged her shoulders. "All I know is that people in Skvira realized nobody would be able to travel safely to European ports to sail to America. And of course this alarmed my mother."

* * *

Golda tried to calm Sarah's fears, assuring her that Yankle heard things from his customers that suggested this war would end quickly—the Russians outnumbered the Germans, and the winters were so cold that the others would give up before winter's end. Most people in Skvira were not too worried about the outcome. They didn't care if the czar's army was beaten, since the czar did nothing to protect them from bandits and killers, perhaps even encouraged the rampages.

Still, Sarah was not convinced. "I hope Yankle's informers know what they're talking about," she replied. "We all know what happens to Jews when the peasants have a bad year."

From then on Sarah insisted that her daughters stay beside her when they accompanied her on her chores. She didn't want them to go out of the house unless she could see them from the window. Golda dropped by more often to take Enta or Leiba Chana to her house.

Winter and the first snowfall surprised them in mid-November. Sarah, her hair and eyelashes dusted with flour from her baking, her eyes full of tears from chopping onions for the pot of soup simmering on the stove, looked up impatiently when the door opened. "Hurry, come in already," she scolded her daughters, who had been playing in the snow in front of the house. "Close the door, you're letting the cold in!" Then she saw Layve step inside with them, and her tone changed. "Layve, what brings you here today?"

Leiba Chana tugged on Layve's sleeve. "Uncle, I want to see the surprise."

He smiled and handed her the bag of treats he'd brought. For a moment he watched her spread the treats on the table and begin nibbling at them. Then he looked at Sarah. "Come, pour two glasses of tea and sit down with me for a minute."

When she'd complied, he leaned his elbows on the table and said, "Sarah, I hear stories from people stopping at the inn. The war in the west is getting worse. It's not safe to travel. They're blocking the water and the trains. I don't know when Yitzhac will be able to return home, or if you'll be able to join him if he decides to stay in America. I don't even know if his letters will get through. God willing, everyone says the trouble will be over quickly. They say it can't last long, not with these cold winters."

Sarah began to cry. "Oy, I should have known. My mother came to me last night in my sleep. She held a bloody shirt in her hand. She told me I have a long wait, that I will not see my husband for many years. She was trying to warn me, Layve."

It was at this point that Sarah lost all hope that she would soon be reunited with her husband, either in America or in Skvira. She dared not think beyond the next year. She looked at her three children. Bennie was past his first birthday, healthy and happy, no trouble. *But,* she thought, *a boy needs a father.* Enta, almost four, was strong and helpful, but she was fearful and almost never smiled. Still, Sarah knew her little Enta would do the right thing. Even her eldest, Leiba Chana, sickly little Leiba, was stronger than she used to be and was trying to learn how to help with the baking. She never seemed afraid of anything. Grateful to be blessed with these beautiful children, Sarah vowed she would never let anything happen to them. She would protect them with her life.

Rumors of the war continued through that winter. Despite the sub-zero temperatures, the Germans had cut through the Russian lines into Poland, taking huge numbers of Russian prisoners. Some were Jewish boys drafted during the last year. Families wept, not knowing if their sons were dead or prisoners.

Many young men and even some women began to meet secretly. They blamed their harsh life on the czar and could not understand why anyone would want to fight for him. Some talked about going to Jerusalem. Many believed that the Socialists or even the Bolsheviks offered the only alternative to the poverty and fear the Jewish people had always experienced under the czar. Families tried to forbid their children from attending such meetings, meetings that they all knew could prove disastrous, but many young people were convinced that the piety and scholarship of their elders had not secured anything except more hardship. They felt they had nothing to lose, and it was well worth the risk to seek change.

As winter drew to a close in 1915, a letter from Yitzhac somehow got through. He expressed deep concern for the safety of his family, admitted to some loneliness, but indicated that he was adapting to the new land. He had written other letters, he said, and wondered if any had found their way to Skvira. He longed for news of home, but had resigned himself to staying in America. There were no alternatives. Even if he could get passage across the ocean, a journey through Europe to return to Skvira was impossible.

Shmulek is well, Yitzhac's letter reported. *He already has a daughter, also called Leiba Chana for his and Sarah's mother. I still carry crates of potatoes and help load them onto carts for men to sell in local neighborhoods. Soon I hope I will be able to buy a horse and buggy, and that will make life better when we can all be together again.*

Sarah was grateful that he had not forgotten her and the children. Even though she understood the danger, she couldn't stop her disappointment that he would be spending the money he had saved to buy a horse and buggy instead of saving it for the day she could join him. *It's too dangerous to think about leaving now anyway,* she told herself, *and with most mail not getting through, it would be too risky for him to send money.* Still, she wished he had found a way to use the money to help her. *Even if he sent something to make it easier for me to feed the children, that would at least make life easier,* she thought, then felt her cheeks flush in embarrassment at feeling sorry for herself instead of being concerned for Yitzhac. *Don't be foolish!* she admonished herself. *The mail would most likely fall into the hands of enemy soldiers, who would just take the money for themselves.*

Police

Ettie stopped and shook her head in disbelief. "Years later, my Aunt Golda told me more about what happened during those years. It's hard to believe we all survived."

Stanley filled in some more historical details on the First World War, telling them that, by the end of 1915, Germany occupied all of Poland. Hundreds of soldiers were killed in battles fought on fields frozen by sub-freezing winds. The war dragged on, and with Russia cut off from its allies, hunger spread throughout the lands held by the czar. Peasants with food to sell from their fields could now demand higher payments. With fighting men often going hungry, the people of the shtetls had to resign themselves to stretching the little they had to last longer than ever.

Rachel asked Ettie, "Mother, what did you do to keep from starving, do you remember? I read somewhere that women always knew how to make an entire pot of soup using one small piece of chicken or meat, and that they could make it last several days. But almost nobody had meat or fish, except for a little bit of pickled herring sitting in a barrel of brine. Is it true that several families would share the brine, taking a cupful and dipping their bread in it to give it the taste of fish?"

Ettie thought about Rachel's question before responding. "Yeah, I remember that going on. It was a hard time, and things kept getting worse. I heard that young scholars who, in the past could count on a different family every night to provide a meal, had to manage with only three or four meatless meals a week, sometimes with only a chunk of bread to tide them over on days with no meals. I remember eating some meals with my Aunt Golda and Uncle Yankle, but I overheard them say that they were worried that the cabbage, pickled beets, and potatoes stored for the winter might not last till spring. I remember them wondering where they would find food in spring, if most of the peasants' crops had to supply the czar's army. My mother always said how grateful she was that Yitzhac's family shared with us what they could so we wouldn't starve. But everyone was hungry, even Golda and Yankle."

* * *

Yankle had more work than ever, but when he was commissioned to sew uniforms for some of the officers in the czar's army, he and Golda could no longer count on receiving enough money or goods in exchange to enable them to replenish their food supplies. The last time, when he'd completed the winter uniforms, his payment had been a speech by the commandant, telling him it was everyone's duty to contribute to the war effort, and how thankful he should be to have this opportunity to honor his czar.

When soldiers used Layve's inn, they would drink too much and often destroy furniture, kitchenware, and bedding without paying for their lodgings or food. Many times Sarah and Rissela joined Layve's wife in cleaning the inn and trying to make repairs after the soldiers left. Layve knew there would be great trouble if he complained, that he would be accused of shortchanging customers, and as a Jew he might even be sent to jail without a trial. So he held his tongue.

The times when Sarah was able to get flour, she kept her family from starving by baking enough bread to exchange for milk from the peasant family that had a cow. It frightened her when she saw Enta chipping away at the lime-based plaster on the walls of their house and biting or sucking on it to ease the gnawing hunger in her stomach. "Entala, my baby, that will make you sick. Come, let Mama make you a bit of tea." The warm, bitter liquid was comforting, even if there was no cube of sugar for it. Enta obeyed, as always wanting to please her mother, but she often seemed listless, and swayed on her feet as if light-headed.

Sarah was determined to find a way to get through the winter without her children falling ill, convinced that if they could make it till spring, the war would end. She believed what everyone said, that the armies could not last much longer. And, she hoped, perhaps then she would hear from Yitzhac, and he would tell her about joining him in America.

Her thoughts frequently turned to the rumor Fagala had shared with her just after Yitzhac left for America, about people who made money by selling whiskey in Kiev. Back then she'd thought those who tried it were fools, to put themselves in such danger. But now it was the only possibility she could think of, and it seemed a risk worth taking, a way to get them through this rough time.

She had never been to Kiev, but Yankle had told her what it was like—how busy the marketplace was, how people came there from everywhere, how there were so many people and so much activity that anyone looking for you wouldn't be able to find you. *I will discuss it with Layve,* she decided. *He will know what people are saying about the current situation in Kiev.* She hoped he would offer to provide the whiskey for her to sell.

"No, Sarah, no, it is too dangerous," Layve protested, trying to stay calm when she told him her plan. "We cannot let you take that chance." He too had been trying to think of a plan, he admitted; some way of getting more supplies. He assured her that he had enough food for her children, but his face was tight with concern, and Sarah knew he was worried about how long he could keep the inn functioning, with the food dwindling the way it was. His own children had grown thin, and his wife didn't seem to have the strength anymore to cope with the children, the house, and her chores at the inn.

Sarah straightened her slender shoulders, tilted her head back, and stared into Layve's eyes with the same pleading expression that had always unsettled her father. "Layve, God gives me strength, I must try this. Please, I need your help."

Her brother-in-law sighed. "I'll think about it," he said. "But we must come up with a plan that will work." He waved a hand toward some broken chairs waiting for repair. "I have work to do now, but later I will visit Rissela and Golda, and see what they think. Maybe Yankle will have some advice. We'll sleep on it. It can wait for tomorrow," he assured her.

The next day when Sarah dropped by the inn carrying Bennie, with Leiba Chana running ahead and Enta holding onto her skirts, Layve called her into a corner and whispered, "We'll all help. Golda will explain later."

Sarah nodded, face solemn. She was pleased that things were moving forward, but well aware of the dangers.

They gathered at Yankle and Golda's house that evening. A scowling Rissela began by warning them all about the dangers. "And what about Sarah? She could be thrown in jail. It's not only the whiskey—Jews from the shtetls aren't supposed to travel to Kiev without permission."

Yankle tried to downplay her fears. "Ach, Rissela, you think only of problems. Sarah's kind face and innocent manner will not raise suspicions. She can make it work. The market in Kiev is always buzzing with activity. People buy and sell everything there. As long as she appears to be selling goods that are not illegal, no one will question her."

Layve would be supplying the whiskey, as Sarah had hoped. He had been saving some that he'd made the year before for special travelers staying at the inn. The bottles were hidden in a huge box behind the extra blankets in his bedroom. "It used to give comfort to some of my regulars," he said, "but lately I seldom bring it out, because it just adds to the soldiers' unruly behavior."

There was a huge demand for whiskey in Kiev. If Sarah could pull this plan off, they could make enough to pay the high prices the peasants now expected for food. "I can almost taste the food we'll be able to get with Sarah's profits!" Layve exclaimed.

"If Sarah comes back safely with profits from selling the whiskey," Rissela warned, "it is important that the officials never find out about her activities. Even a rumor that Sarah sold whiskey in Kiev would exact a costly price." Jews were not permitted to sell whiskey anywhere without paying bribes to officials. Sometimes they were accused of selling it illegally even when they had obtained permits, and if the bribes to the police and judges were not high enough, they could be thrown in jail for months without a trial.

Yankle showed Sarah how to sew a special band of heavy cloth around the waist inside her thick gray skirt and attach little pockets of cloth to the band to hold the small bottles of whiskey against her underwear. "You'll have to be careful not to brush too close to anyone, or bump into anything," he warned her.

Golda added, "Just be yourself, Sarah, and no one will suspect anything. You will be there selling the aprons and smocks Yankle will provide. You will keep your bag of money in your blouse where you always do. When you are holding the apron or smock in your hand, you can unbutton your coat and reach into your skirt to get the whiskey out. Just remember to keep your hand covered by the apron. No one will see."

* * *

Tuesday morning did not begin as usual. Enta's mother was usually dressed and working in the kitchen before she, her sister, and her brother were even out of bed, but now her aunts, Golda and Rissela, were there to help Sarah dress. She could not remember anyone ever being there to help her mother dress. She overheard them talking, their voices low and urgent, about what time she must meet the train, and Enta wondered what all the excitement was about.

Her mother's heavy skirt seemed different somehow. Enta frowned as the women held the skirt up and inserted small bottles into pockets inside the waistband. This was strange indeed!

"Mama, why are you putting those bottles in there?" Leiba Chana asked. "Can I play with one?"

"Be still," Aunt Rissela said firmly. "You must not talk about this. It's nothing. Your mama is busy. You and your sister, go play with your brother!"

Rissela's voice softened as she turned back and patted Sarah on the shoulders. "Well, Sarah, at least the cold weather will make these layers of material less conspicuous." She handed Sarah an extra sweater to pull on over the blouse and the first sweater she already wore.

Sarah donned that, then put on the heavy black coat that fell almost to her ankles. She arranged her brown scarf to cover her hair, braided and pinned across the top of her head. Then she pulled on the only boots she had, and stuffed some extra cloth inside to cover the holes. Straightening, she told Enta and the other two children, "I am taking the morning train to Kiev. There, God willing, I will sell enough aprons and smocks to be able to buy more food. After today, my kinderleh, you won't have to eat junk off the walls to keep your bellies full."

Enta was heartened until her mother turned and stared at the picture of Zayde Moishe. She looked frightened! Was there something bad in Kiev? Enta's fears escalated when Sarah came over to kiss them goodbye. She held each of them against her longer than usual. It conjured a vague memory, mostly forgotten, of her father kissing them all goodbye. The images vanished as Sarah walked quickly to the door, and Enta's fear surged again.

As the door closed behind her mother, Enta ran to the window and watched Sarah walk down the hill with Rissela, watched her getting smaller and smaller as the distance between them grew, watched her mother look back one last time before she turned the corner and disappeared. Something was wrong, terribly wrong. Enta began to cry. "Where is my mama going and when will she come home?" she sobbed.

Leiba Chana wagged her finger at her and shouted, "Stop that, you silly crybaby! Can't you see that Mama went to Kiev to sell the little bottles of whiskey? That's how she will get money to buy food."

Golda, eyes wide with alarm, grabbed Leiba Chana and lifted her into the air. "Shah, Leiba, don't ever say that. Your mama went to sell aprons and smocks. The bottles are water in case she gets thirsty." Then she looked at the ceiling and moaned, "Oy vay, what's wrong with us? We should have been more careful around these children."

Enta pursued her with more questions. "Why does my mama have to go to Kiev? Why can't she sell those things here? We don't know anybody there; what if she gets sick? Why didn't she take us with her?"

"Entala, be still. Your mama will tell you all about it when she returns. Now let's get ready. We'll spend the day at my house. Your cousins are waiting for you. Maybe you can all tell stories. Come Leiba, help get Bennie ready."

The day dragged for Enta. Her heart was not in the games her cousins initiated to distract her. Golda served them warm cabbage soup and bread, but fear that her mother might vanish drove Enta's hunger away, and she could only finish a few spoonfuls. When Enta announced she could eat no more, Leiba Chana slid the unfinished bowl of soup across the table, lifted it to her mouth to drink what was left, then wiped out the bowl with her last chunk of bread. Enta went to the window to watch for their mother's return.

When the sky began to darken, Golda whispered to Yankle, and he left. Enta watched him walking toward the inn. She knew her fears had substance when her uncle returned alone and shrugged. "No one knows," she heard him whisper to her aunt. "Maybe she missed the train."

"Where's my mama?" Enta murmured. "Where's my mama?" She began to cry softly. Bennie soon joined in.

Leiba Chana looked at their aunt and uncle, who remained quiet, then scolded Enta and Bennie, "Stop that, you two, do you hear, or I'll tell Mama when she gets home how much trouble you both made. Stop that, now! Behave like I do. Stop making trouble for Aunt Golda."

Enta looked at Golda, realized that her aunt had nothing comforting to say, and ran to sit by herself on the floor in the corner of the room, holding her hair against her cheek and rocking back and forth.

"Business must have been better than we all expected," Yankle said with false optimism. "Your mother must have been making so much money, she lost track of the time. She's probably sitting in the train station now, waiting for the morning train. She will return tomorrow."

Golda nodded briskly and, after a grateful glance at Yankle, said, "Come help, we will arrange everything so you can all sleep here with us tonight." She called to her daughter to bring out some extra blankets. They made one place for Leiba Chana next to her bigger cousin, another for Bennie next to her. Golda put Enta on the mattress bed where she and Yankle slept.

Enta would never forget the fear and sense of foreboding of that night, her panic that she had lost the most important person in her life. Lying in bed with her aunt and uncle, she tried to remember her father, who had left for America two years earlier. She couldn't remember his face, except for the images in the two photographs her mother had. But in those he didn't look like a real person, sitting in a chair wearing clothes that were different from any she had ever seen, except in photographs. Everyone told her he was a big man and that she "had his face." When she tried to picture the man in the photograph who had shoulders big enough to carry the midwife through the snow with her face, the image became frightening.

She shuddered. *What if Mama disappears? What if I can't remember her face?* she thought. *No, I must not start to cry again and wake everyone. They'll get mad at me. Why can't I be brave like Leiba Chana?*

The strange sounds Enta heard throughout the night unsettled her more. Beneath her uncle's snoring, she heard scratching against the walls, as if animals were trying to get in. Even when she realized it was the wind blowing through the trees, making the branches brush against the house, the creaking and grunting sound that accompanied it reminded her of the story her mother liked to tell, about the bear that tried to steal food left to cool on a windowsill. Although no one had ever seen a bear in town, and the story ended with the housewife tricking the bear into giving back the food, Enta couldn't stop thinking about the story. She didn't think she could trick a bear, and she wondered what she would do if a bear came into the house.

Animals howled in the distance, and the shadows of the swaying branches floated across the wall, looking like waving arms. Enta shivered. Were these animals coming into town at night, looking for food? Or worse, were they the long, ghostly arms of the spirits who rose at night from the cemetery? Maybe they were her dead sister's arms, and the howling not animals, but her baby sister calling to her. Where would those arms take her if she drifted into them? Her mother talked about her own mother or Zayde Moishe coming to her in dreams. But this was no dream! Maybe Zayde Moishe was really here, calling to her. If she answered, would she finally get to meet him? His kind smile soothed her fear, and she longed to be sitting with him so he could comfort her, the way he'd comforted her mother and made her feel safe when she was a young girl.

Enta drifted into a fitful sleep. The shadows turned into drunken peasants riding large horses, waving knives at her mother and shouting, "Those whiskey bottles, lady, give us those whiskey bottles!" They reached for her mother's skirt as her mother floated into the air, her face gradually disintegrating into wavering shadows.

One large shadow became her father, still wearing his American suit and vest, riding his horse out of the distance. When he got closer she realized it was her own face she saw, and her father became her, and she was riding a horse toward her mother. But her mother kept floating farther away, and she could do nothing to help. "Entala, Entala," her mother kept calling, "you know what to do, you know what to do."

Enta woke with a start and relaxed for a minute when she realized that her mother was not calling to her, but her panic soon returned. She was at her Aunt Golda's and Uncle Yankle's, and her mother was still missing. Unfortunately, her hunger also returned, and her head ached. As her stomach grumbled, she remembered watching Leiba Chana finish her soup. *Stay still!* she scolded herself. *Don't wake aunt and uncle, who always try so hard to help.*

She looked out the window, and through the frost thickening there saw that the sky was getting lighter. Snow had been falling, but it was warm here in the bed with her aunt and uncle. The shadows had disappeared from the walls. Looking at them, Enta noticed the framed oval photograph above the chest of drawers. There was something vaguely familiar in the faces of the stern man and woman looking out at her. She had never noticed them before.

Finally her aunt woke and saw her staring at the photograph. She put her arm around Enta and whispered, "That is my mama and papa. You have my mama's name." She sat up and swung her feet to the floor. "Come quietly, let the others sleep."

Enta was pleased that the outdoor stalls her aunt and uncle used to relieve themselves did not smell as bad and were not as far away from the house as were the ones her family shared with other houses nearby on the hillside. After returning to the house and splashing cold water on her face, she felt a little energy returning. By now rays of sunlight were descending from between the dark clouds, and the wind had calmed. Even though there was a chill in the house that the bright blue sky did nothing to warm, it gave Enta more hope than she'd felt the day before.

It was mid-afternoon when Layve ran up to the front door, hollering breathlessly for everyone to hurry. When the door opened, Enta saw her mother walking slowly in the distance. Sarah's braids were totally undone, her dark wavy hair hanging down her back and partly covering her face. Her coat was unbuttoned and her scarf gone. She carried nothing in her arms or on her back. When she got closer, Enta saw how dirty her face was, how the buttons were torn from her coat. "Mama, Mama, you're back, you came home!" she shrieked through her tears.

"Of course I came home, what did you think, I wouldn't return to you?" Sarah chided.

Leiba Chana began to cry as she tugged on her mother's arm. Bennie ran to his mother, and she lifted him, showering his face with kisses and tears. Then she put him down and kissed her daughters. "It's okay, sweet kinderleh; Zayde Moishe watched over me."

"Come, let your mother rest," Golda scolded. "Can't you see how tired she is?" She took the coat from Sarah and helped her to a chair. "Here, let me make you a little tea."

Once Sarah was sipping the hot liquid, Golda prompted, "So, tell us—what happened? Can you talk? Are you okay?"

Enta always wondered if the story her mother told included all the details of her ordeal, or if it had actually been much worse than she was willing to admit to anyone.

Sarah clicked her tongue against the roof of her mouth. "Tch, tch. What happened to me shouldn't happen to my worst enemy. Such an innocent face I guess I don't have after all. Do you really want to hear?"

"Go on, Sarah, tell us. If you get it out, you'll feel better," Golda urged.

Sarah nodded and after a moment to gather her thoughts, said, "Well, you were right, Kiev was crowded and noisy. So many people coming and going, such commotion! At first I thought it was all working out for the good. I had already sold a lot of whiskey and several smocks. The bag of money was almost full. Oy, why didn't I stop then? I should have been satisfied. But no, I still had three more bottles and a few smocks, how many I can't remember. I thought I should sell it all before returning. It would get all of us through the winter." She shook her head. "Only three bottles left, can you believe it?"

Sarah lowered her head, then sipped more of the tea. "Nobody's ears should have to hear what happened to me next. Out of nowhere someone came up behind me, grabbed my arm, pulled open my coat so that buttons flew off. Then he began grabbing me around the waist, laughing, and calling me such names! I can't repeat those names. He told me to come with him. I started screaming for help, but then I looked at him and realized that he was a policeman . . . Such a person—his teeth should fall out of his mouth and onions should grow from his head! I pleaded with him to let me go, that I had to get back to my children before dark, but he just laughed. Another one was sitting on a horse at the edge of the market. He looked meaner. He told the other one that they'd better teach the Jew a lesson. They asked my name and where I was from, then held my arm and forced me to go with them."

Sarah sighed. "The next thing I knew, they'd pushed me into a building and locked me in a room with two other women and three men. One of the men was a drunken peasant who kept spitting at my feet. The other man kept rocking back and forth, mumbling and slobbering. I think he was a *meshuganer*, a crazy man. He never said anything. One of the women couldn't stop crying; she told me that her cousin had bribed these officers last week; that was the only way she had been let go. She didn't have any money for bribes. When I asked her what she'd done, she said she hadn't done anything wrong, had just been standing in the market with her husband. The third woman said she knew of an old lady who spent six months in jail, supposedly for selling whiskey, even though she didn't even have any." Sarah dragged a trembling hand over her forehead. "Believe me, when I heard that, my heart almost fell out of my body."

She began to cry, but went on. "They left us in that locked room all night—no chairs, one blanket on the floor, no food or water, one pot to relieve ourselves— can you believe it? Right there in front of each other. Oy, the shame!" Sarah covered her eyes, then pushed her hair back from her face. Her face was red, as if she were reliving the embarrassment and humiliation.

Enta went over to her and kissed her hand. Golda and Layve looked at each other, then at the children. "Let them be," Golda said firmly. "They have been worried. It won't hurt for them to know about these no-good *shtiks drek*, pieces of shit, they should all rot in hell. The children need to know how their mother suffered to get food for her family and for all of us." Golda rose and went over to take Sarah into her arms. "Can you talk about the rest?" she asked gently. "How did you manage to get home?"

Sarah blew her nose and spoke again in a softer voice. "After what seemed like ten nights, the policeman who had been sitting on the horse came into the room and pointed to me. He called me worse names than the first one had, names I won't ever repeat, heaven forbid, and shoved me out the door. I thought they would beat me, that I would never see any of you again. It was terrible, terrible." She rubbed her hands up and down over her face, then rested her forehead on the table. A long time passed before she continued.

"I was pushed into another room where a huge man with a round, red face was sitting behind a desk. He asked, 'What is this stinking Jew bitch in here for?' and the officer from the horse said I'd been selling whiskey. 'We never saw her there before,' he said, 'but there might still be some around her waist. She was selling smocks and aprons too.' Then I realized I still had some smocks tied to my back."

Sarah hesitated, took a deep breath, and pressed on despite the tears streaming down her cheeks. "I began to sob and beg. I told them I have three little children, that my husband is gone to America, that it had been two years since I'd seen him. 'We are hungry,' I said. 'Please don't make my kids orphans. I only came to Kiev so I would be able to get food for my family.'

"They hollered that I should know Jews are forbidden to sell whiskey, even to come into Kiev. They laughed and pulled my braids apart. The one who was on the horse—in hell he should rot!—he began running his hands through my hair. The one behind the desk coughed, reminding him to get back to the business at hand.

"Then they asked me to show them what I didn't sell and to give them the money I had collected all day. They didn't give me any privacy, and I had to reach into my skirt in front of them to get the three bottles still around my waist. I reached into my blouse to get the small pouch of money. They spilled the moneybag onto their table and counted it. They asked me to show them what was left on my back. Four smocks were all I had left. They put their hands all over the smocks and said they knew some peasant women who would enjoy them. They rubbed them against their bodies, between their legs, and laughed." Sarah began to sob. Golda brought another glass of tea and put it in front of her.

"Next thing I knew they were waving their fingers at me, warning me that for this offense they could put me in jail for years, but they would be kind to my children and let me go. They said if they ever caught me again, it would be jail for sure, that I should stay away from Kiev forever. Then they pushed me against the door, it opened, and I fell out. As I stood up, I could hear them laughing.

"I walked out the front door and hurried to the train station to wait for the next train. I sat in the corner, so nobody would recognize me. I am shamed. It's a good thing they didn't steal my fare, but I suppose they wanted me out of Kiev." She shrugged. "That's all. It was too dangerous. I should have known better. Now God has punished me for wanting too much."

Sarah finished her tea, rose, and walked over to each of her children, touching their cheeks and their heads. "Don't worry, kinderleh, your mama will never do anything so crazy again. Forgive me. We will find other ways to survive. We won't be separated again."

Enta had never seen her mother so disheveled and embarrassed. She wanted to do something to make her mother proud, so she could hold her head high. She knew the best thing she could do at that moment was to be obedient and helpful. But she vowed to herself that she would be careful to never again bring shame to her mother.

Sarah looked at her brother-in-law. "Layve, I will make it up to you, losing your whiskey for you like that."

Layve responded without hesitation, "You got out of there without them harming you. You should live and be well, that's all that matters. We did not use all the whiskey I have stored, and we can always make more. By the time winter is over and Purim comes, the war will be over, there will be more food. We will be able to celebrate your good fortune that you didn't go to jail. For now, let's say a prayer to give thanks to God for our health."

Reds and Whites

Ettie fell quiet, exhausted by the pain of that memory.

Collette was shaking her head. "You never told us that story before, Mother. Poor Bubbe, what a horrible thing she had to go through."

"I'll bet every family who lived through those times has some horror stories, probably worse ones than ours," Ettie responded.

Rachel mentioned the scenes she remembered from the movie version of *Doctor Zhivago.* "So much of the land was devastated. Increasing numbers of young men got forced into the czar's armies, and those who returned often had parts of their bodies blown away or their minds lost to what was happening around them." She shivered and shook her head.

"That was a terrible time," Stanley agreed. "But, reading history books about the events of that period, I was surprised to learn that a large number of Jewish boys and men stepped forward to fight to defend the czar and the country."

* * *

Not only did the war outlast the frigid winter, but during the summer of 1916 close to two million soldiers died in France. The Russians were advancing by September, with hundreds of thousands of Austrian soldiers being taken prisoner. Life all across Eastern Europe continued to be arduous, unpredictable, and at times terrifying. Large numbers perished—the elderly, frail children, even once-strong men now wracked with hunger became ill and died. A sense of hopelessness pervaded communities as another winter approached with no change in sight.

Many Ukrainians vented the centuries-old, virulent hatred for Jews who had been bred among them. Branded as "Christ-killers" and "blood-suckers," Jews were seen as the real enemy. The army was told not to buy goods from "traitor" Jewish merchants. But the Jews were not the only recipients of this mass anger. This was something they shared with the czar, who many believed was the main cause of their misery.

Young people and workers organized into groups in the larger cities to speak out against poor working conditions and to seek improvements. Many were convinced that more power in the hands of the workers and the poor would lead to greater freedom and prosperity for everyone. Small numbers of Jewish youths defied their elders and joined these groups. Religious scholars warned against putting faith in such false ideals. In their minds, only the Torah could show the way.

Other idealistic Jewish youths turned to Zionism as a different way out. These young people were convinced that only life in Jerusalem could be more meaningful and sought ways to return to the Promised Land. But the religious scholars branded this kind of thinking an outrage, a deviation from practicing God's commandments and laws. To them it meant looking away from God's word and the kingdom of heaven for satisfaction.

Because so many young, vibrant men from shtetls all across Eastern Europe had already departed for America or were in the war, the people who carried on in the villages in accordance with the traditional Jewish customs were largely the elderly, the very pious, the women and children. The harsh life of the past at least offered the comfort of knowing what was expected of you in different situations. But now situations occurred that had no precedent.

* * *

Sarah's spirits remained low after her humiliation in Kiev. She scrubbed her home more vigorously than ever, as if she could wipe away the shame of the experience. Her children irritated her more often, especially Leiba Chana, who argued about how to do the menial chores and began to cry for more food than the small share Sarah could manage. Sarah knew she was becoming irritable with her children, but at times she was so exhausted and hungry, she had little patience. When she could get enough flour, she kneaded the dough and baked her challahs with added attention to detail, trying to atone to those who would eat it for her failure to provide more food by selling the whiskey. She awoke earlier each day and found time to help Layve at the inn, to make up for the lost whiskey. She knew his wife had cried bitterly about their losses, even after hearing about Sarah's cruel treatment.

Another winter began without word from Yitzhac. No letters were getting through to anyone from their families in America, so she received no word about him from others either. The railroad system throughout the land was in a shambles, there was no firewood or coal for warmth, and increasing numbers of soldiers were deserting, roaming the countryside in tattered uniforms, looking for food and shelter. Messages that got through from other shtetls brought stories of relatives who were starving, people who had become ill and died from lack of food or proper care. A typhus epidemic spread across the land.

Grief began striking closer to home. First Fagala's youngest daughter developed a high fever and died. Next Yitzhac's cousin who lived in the neighboring shtetl died after giving birth to a daughter without the help of the midwife, who herself was in bed with a high fever. Sarah's children were beginning to associate illness with automatic death. The shrieking and wailing, the grief-stricken families sitting shiva, were becoming all too familiar.

Whatever hope Sarah tried to muster about the future was soon dashed by tumultuous events outside of Skvira. In 1917, any semblance of order that had existed in their shtetl, despite the suffering they were all enduring, was disrupted forever.

Russian soldiers were deserting in droves. People blamed the czar for the two million deaths, the widespread misery. On the fifteenth of March the czar was forced to give up the throne. The following month Lenin and the Bolsheviks gained control of the government. People passing through Skvira reported the news that America had entered the war. Surely this meant an end was in sight.

Yet it was not to be. Fighting continued through another summer. As the Russian people faced their fourth harsh winter, Lenin seized the palace and the Bolshevik government signed an armistice with Germany with a new slogan: "Peace, Freedom, Bread." But there would be no peace within Russia. Instead this Russian Revolution would set in motion a civil war, unthinkable bloodshed, and the slaughter of innocent people.

During the summer of 1918 Bolsheviks killed the czar and his family. In the fall, after a German collapse, an armistice was signed. But no peace was on the horizon within Ukraine. As the Bolsheviks, or Reds, fought over control of the Russian Empire with the anti-Bolsheviks, or Whites, Ukraine declared itself independent of Russia and formed its own government.

This was seen as a time for fulfillment of Ukrainian dreams, a time to get rid of the historic domination by other nations, be they Russians, Germans, Poles, or any other people. The peasants saw an opportunity to gain the upper hand over the landowners and the townsfolk. Anarchists were against all efforts to impose state order. Kiev changed hands sixteen times in thirty-six months. Rumors about disasters were reinforced by the spreading of counterfeit money, the plummeting value of the currency, increasing inflation, rising food costs, and fuel shortages. It all amounted to chaos.

Attempts by the Bolsheviks to take food from the peasants led to new conflicts, particularly when they placed Jews in top positions within these disrupted communities. It was not difficult for the enemies of Bolshevism to equate their misery with the Jews. Although Russia stirred special hatred among the Ukrainians, the Jews were even more despised. Pogroms turned into mass butchery, and random atrocities were fanned by governments and a press that used anti-Semitism as a way of uniting Ukrainians against Bolshevism. No city or town in Ukraine was spared.

There are frightening events in people's lives that signal the deterioration of everything they have been familiar with, even if the familiar has been characterized by misery and deprivation. Up to that time the people of Skvira knew how to get through the hardships that were commonplace: hunger, cold, illness, premature death of loved ones, loneliness. Periodically there had been pogroms where damage was done to their town. They had lost relatives who lived in other towns where the pogroms were more vicious. But for the next two years devastating horrors and terror became so overwhelming that Sarah no longer reassured her children that God could hear her prayers.

* * *

Her mother's desolation at that time had filled Enta with a sense of gloom that would later cloud all memories of her childhood. Now, as Ettie's family discussed the history of those times, repeating what they had read in textbooks or had seen reenacted on film, she realized that her life before 1918 was a series of blurred images when compared with the suffering, stark brutality, and terror dominating everything for the two years that followed.

"I remember what happened in our village after the murder of the czar and his family," she said suddenly, interrupting the historical discussion. "My mother and Aunt Golda were sitting at the table drinking tea, talking about the trouble in the land, when a commotion that had started in the distance suddenly got closer, and we couldn't ignore it. I ran to the window and saw a boy, not more than eleven or twelve years old, running up the road, wildly waving his arms, screaming, 'Run and hide, run and hide! Soldiers on horseback—burning houses! They have swords!'

"Aunt Golda rushed out the door, waved him over, then grabbed his shoulders and tried to calm him down. She offered him water, asked how he knew. He explained that he hadn't seen them. As soon as his town was warned, his father had told him to run ahead to Skvira.

"Golda grabbed his hand so they could hurry to Layve's inn, get someone to warn the townspeople and, at the same time, send someone ahead to warn the people of the next town. After she began to run, she turned and called back, 'Get the children, fast, Sarah, and come to my house. We'll hide in my cellar.'"

* * *

As they rushed out of the house on their way to hide in Golda's cellar, Sarah kept repeating, "Mama mine in heaven, Zayde Moishe, help us."

Rissela was already there with her family when they arrived, and she instructed them not to make a sound, saying they must keep everything totally dark until they heard the soldiers leave. For a long time—it seemed like hours—nothing happened. Sarah thought maybe the warning was a false one, maybe no soldiers would come.

When Bennie started to whimper, she put her fingers over his lips, whispering, "Shah, shah, my child." Just when Leiba Chana began to whine that she was hungry, a noise like distant thunder began outside. Sarah squeezed her hand over her daughter's mouth. As the sound got louder, Sarah recognized it as the hooves of galloping horses, getting closer.

Loud voices rang through the streets: "*Bei Zhidov*, smash the Jews, the murderers of the czar! Kill the Bolsheviks." Agonizing screams followed, and Sarah and the other two women murmured fervent prayers for God's intervention as her family crouched in the damp cellar near the barrels of pickles.

They remained in the cellar all night, no one speaking. The children dozed off leaning against the adults and woke when Layve rose and said he would crawl out first, to see whether the bandits were gone. "No one else move until I return," he cautioned.

They were all wet and cold. Sarah noticed Enta, cheeks red with embarrassment, pulling a fold of her skirt over a wet spot on the front—she'd urinated during the night. The other children looked wet too, but she kept quiet, and nobody else said a word about it. A few minutes later Layve called to them, and they all emerged as if into a different world.

The wails of women and children filled the streets. Three of the young scholars, still wearing their long black caftans, lay in the street in pools of blood, their heads and chests an unrecognizable, bloody mass. Their black hats had blown away. One's arm had been chopped off. Sarah gasped at the outrages that had been done to the bodies of the gentle young men she saw so often from her window. Trying to shield her children from the horror, she grabbed their cheeks and turned their faces away, then extended her skirt to block the view. "You don't need to look on such things, my babies. Come with me, come home."

But there was another ugly surprise when they got home. Their windows had been smashed and their feather mattresses cut open, leaving a blizzard of feathers drifting all over the room and floating out the windows. Two chairs had been smashed, and shattered dishes and cups were scattered across the floor. Sarah quickly looked to the wall, and cried, "Thank God, it's a miracle! Zayde Moishe, you are still with us." *Maybe God does still protect us,* she thought.

Men on horses again arrived in Skvira a week later, and their family had no warning this time. Enta was in the empty stable, trying to teach Bennie to dance. Leiba Chana was helping Sarah bake challahs. Suddenly the door banged open and two ragged-looking men burst inside, brandishing long knives. Sarah screamed and cowered back against the stove as they advanced, one of them shouting, "Your money or your life, Jew whore."

"I am a poor woman, how would I have money?" she sobbed. "Don't harm my family, please, I beg you."

The men laughed, and one used his knife to skewer a cooling challah. He held it in the air for a second, then tore off a chunk and began eating it. The other copied him. They placed what remained of the two challahs inside their shirts. "We will kill you, whore, if you don't give us your money," one hissed as they moved closer. Sarah closed her eyes as he held the knife to her throat.

"Leave my mother alone, you bandits!" Leiba Chana screamed at them from the other side of the room. She whirled as Enta and Bennie tumbled in from the stable, then turned to again shout at the bandits to leave her mother alone.

They ignored her. "Your money or your life," one threatened. "We're warning you!"

Enta stared, face pale with terror. Suddenly Bennie lunged away from her, ran across the room, and jumped first onto a chair, then from there onto his mother's back. Sarah felt his arms circle her neck, then his hand reached into her blouse, grasped the little pouch of coins, pulled it out, and threw it across the room.

The man holding the knife at Sarah's throat turned quickly, saw his partner picking up the bag, and hurried across the room to be sure he got his share of what was inside. They threw back the one coin Sarah had received from the rebbeh she visited before her daughter Terzel died. "Smart little boy you have there," one shouted as they ran out the front door. "We won't kill you now. Next time don't be such a fool."

Leiba Chana and Enta ran forward as Bennie slid off Sarah's back, and began kissing their brother. "You saved Mama's life," Enta exclaimed, "you saved her!"

Sarah hugged each of them, tears streaming down her cheeks. "Yitzhac," she sobbed, "why did you leave us to this life?

She looked around the room. "What else do they want from us? We have nothing left, nothing." After the last attack on Skvira,

Golda had managed to get some glass that Layve and his son used to repair the windows, and Rissela had given them two of her older feather mattresses. The two broken chairs and the dishes had not been replaced. *It doesn't matter,* Sarah had thought; *Yitzhac isn't home, and no one drops by anymore to eat with us.* If they did, the only thing she could offer anyone was tea and challah anyway, so they didn't need the broken dishes.

She looked at her children and opened her arms. "My children, come here. You're all that matters." And she began rocking back and forth, trying to hold them all in her arms at once.

Rissela's oldest son, Samuel, found them like that when he came pounding on the door to tell them that he and a group of other young men had found two bandits just outside of town, sitting by the river eating challah.

"They were laughing about how they got the money from the 'stupid Jew family,' how the little boy had saved the day," he said. "My friends and I snuck up from behind and bashed their heads with rocks, knocking them out. That's when I found this." He held up the pouch of coins Sarah kept under her blouse, and Sarah cried out in recognition. Samuel grinned. "I thought I recognized it as the one my mother gave you after your narrow escape in Kiev."

Sarah kissed him, but warned that he should not be putting himself at risk. "It will only bring more trouble if you fight back. They blame the Jews for everything."

Her nephew shrugged and looked around the room, his eyes stopping on the photograph on the wall. His gaze grew distant, and he said slowly, "They already blame us for everything, Aunt Sarah. The old ways don't serve us any longer." He looked back at her. "We must fight for the right thing. We must protect ourselves. What good has come from meekly letting them have their way with us while we pray for God's blessing? Aunt Sarah, it's too late to hope that our silence will protect us from those who blame us for their own misfortune. We must make our own fate."

In the weeks that followed, every time the bands of fighters and robbers made their way to Skvira, there was enough warning for most people to get to their hiding places. Soon after the incident with the coins, a band of Reds rode into town, shouting for people to join the

Bolsheviks. "We will make sure everyone has land and food. Come out and help give power to the people." They waited, but no one emerged from hiding. Before riding out of town, they set fire to two homes near the bottom of the hill, forcing the families to run to their neighbors' homes.

Two days later a group of soldiers—this time Whites—arrived, shouting for revenge on the Jews who had murdered the czar and were now helping the Bolsheviks. They set fire to a large house not far from Golda's and Yankle's, where three families were hiding. All of Sarah's family hiding in Golda's cellar heard the screams. Sarah held her children close to her chest, trying to cover their ears with her hands and skirt. No one dared look through the crack in the window.

The next day the details of what had happened spread quickly through the town. Smoke had billowed from the windows of the burning house, eventually forcing three women, many children, and two elderly men out. They ran from the house, waving their arms in terror, pleading for their lives. Three of the soldiers jumped down from their horses, grabbed the women, one holding an infant in her arms, tore their clothes off, and began raping them there in the street. The soldiers still on horseback shouted, "Show the filthy traitors who is in charge. This is to punish you for what you did to the czar."

One of the elderly men rushed forward, crying, "Oh no, no! My daughter, my daughter, keep your filthy hands off my daughter."

As he lunged forward to protect his daughter, a soldier still on horseback rode toward him, knocked him down with his horse, and rode over his head and chest several times. When the soldiers finally left town, the old man was barely breathing, his chest crushed and his skull fractured. It took him hours to die.

* * *

Years later, looking back on this time, Ettie Burin could not remember how many times their shtetl was overrun by armed bands, or how many terrorizing months or years passed. What she did remember was a prolonged nightmare where her family hid in cellars time and again, emerging only when things got quiet to search through the wounded or dead. Between each episode, people prayed that the worst was over, only to become convinced that something even more devastating was about to happen.

Something worse did arrive, and its name was Petliura—the only individual Ukrainian name Ettie would remember of all those connected with the tumultuous events of the civil war.

Word spread quickly that Petliura was a bandit far worse than any others they had seen, a Ukrainian nationalist who had amassed a large band of followers from among the peasants. He and his troops roved from town to town, engaging in mass killings, burnings, and rapes, all far more disastrous than anything experienced before.

Warning came to Skvira in April, 1919, from one of Yankle's former customers from Kiev, who was passing through. "Petliura is marching this way. He and his people destroy anyone and anything standing in their way. Warn the townspeople to leave this village. You only have a few days to get away from his murderous rampage." He told Yankle the direction in which they were headed and suggested how best the villagers might avoid them.

Yankle suspected the man bringing the warning was working for the Bolsheviks, and that his reason for warning them of Petliura's advance toward Skvira was not out of concern for their well-being. Whatever his motives, his message could not be ignored. Yankle spoke to Layve and together they managed to convince the townspeople to leave Skvira and hide in a neighboring town until they could be sure the danger was past.

Samuel and his friends stubbornly refused to abandon the town to troublemakers. Rissela cried to Sarah, "*Vay is mir*! My dearest son, how can he do this to me? These are murderous pigs, we are nothing to them, and my Samuel thinks it is time to be brave."

Sarah took Rissela in her arms but could only say, "You are right, Rissela, you must convince him to leave with us."

The more Rissela pleaded with Samuel and cried that he would be in danger, the more resolute he became that he would not be a coward and run away. To placate his mother, he promised that he would stay hidden in Skvira, notify the others when the gang left, and tell them what direction Petliura was heading.

Telling the story of this part of her childhood three-quarters of a century later brought Ettie to tears. She could remember vividly how she trembled while helping her mother pack a sack with challah and raisins, blankets and sweaters. Leiba Chana helped tie it around her mother's shoulders so she could carry it on her back. There were smaller sacks for Leiba Chana and Enta to carry on their backs.

Who knew how long they would have to stay away? Enta's mind raced with fears. *Will we be thrown in jail like Mama was in Kiev? Will horses stomp on us? Will we get stabbed to death?* She didn't dare let her mother know she was thinking such thoughts. She could see how worried her mother was already.

"Why can't I stay and hide with Samuel and his friends?" Leiba Chana suddenly asked. When Enta nudged her and frowned, Leiba Chana whispered to her, "It makes no sense to have to walk all day or even longer. Who knows what kind of bandits will be waiting for us on the road?"

When Enta heard that, it was too much. She began to sob. Bennie crawled under the table and put his hands over his eyes.

"Now you've done it, look at the trouble you've caused," Sarah scolded Leiba Chana. "What am I going to do with you? Tell me." When Leiba Chana opened her mouth to protest, Sarah shook her head and waved a hand. "There's no time to talk now. Someday when you have your own children, I hope you'll understand how much I suffer for you."

She took Bennie into her arms and kissed him. "Come, Entala, I know I can count on you to do what I ask without stirring up trouble. Everyone has to go. Leiba Chana, get ready and come along. There are people in the other town to help us hide."

Almost everyone in the town had gathered at Layve's inn. A few people had horses hitched up to carts, but most were on foot.

When Enta got older, she would not remember how far they walked over the dusty roads. But she would remember babies crying, some of the boys running ahead, mothers scolding, and her sister asking for food, saying she wanted to rest, then letting go of her hand and running ahead to walk with the older children. She would remember seeing Ephriam, the boy she expected to marry someday, walking ahead with his father, holding tightly to his hand and never looking around. He seemed tiny. She wondered if he was strong enough to make this journey.

Finally they arrived at a small village where Fagala's cousin lived. All the villagers tried to help, making space for the refugees from Skvira to hide with them. As Ettie retold the story, she could not remember if they stayed overnight or if what seemed an eternity to a small child was really just a few hours. The hiding ended when she heard her Uncle Layve announce that they could return to Skvira. Her cousin's friend had arrived to tell everyone that Petliura's army had been in Skvira and then headed in the opposite direction, just as Yankle had been warned by his customer.

The walk home did not seem as long, now that they were retracing a familiar path, but Enta was exhausted, dirty, thirsty, and hungry. The blisters on her feet made each step torture, though shock made her forget the pain as she approached Skvira. Why were people screaming? Hadn't her cousin's friend said the soldiers were gone?

People who had been shuffling along a few minutes earlier ran past them. "Enta, take your sister's hand," her mother ordered, her face tight with fear. "Come!" She lifted Bennie into her arms and ran.

Why are people hurrying to the river? Enta wondered as she and Leiba Chana ran after their mother. Terror wrapped her heart, blocking out the discomforts that had seemed so all-consuming only moments ago, when she saw the smoke rising from the charred husks of houses near the water.

Sarah stopped abruptly, and Enta and Leiba Chana stumbled to a halt beside her. Enta followed her mother's gaze. There was her Aunt Rissela, sitting on the flat rocks by the water, holding the limp body of her son, Samuel. Moaning in wordless pain, she kissed him and stroked his head. All along the path, other mothers cradled their sons and wept.

The only survivor of the group of friends that had remained behind in Skvira was the one who had come on horseback to tell them to return. He had hidden behind some trees beyond the town. They had all tried to hide when Petliura rode into town, he told the townsfolk later, but the bandits searched everywhere, and had found the rest of them. They'd tried to resist, but the gang killed them on sight.

Enta would forever carry the image of her weeping aunt, holding the body of her dead son in her arms.

The funerals for the slain youths were followed by days of calm, until a new scourge spread across the world, inflicting a punishment that had no political or military affiliations. The flu epidemic of 1919 gave every family someone to bury.

Uncle Layve was one of the first in Skvira to be stricken, probably because he came into contact with so many travelers at his inn. After a week of high fever, he was gone. Each of his five children became ill; only his wife and two of her children survived.

The day after they buried Uncle Layve, Enta fell ill. Sarah wrapped her in extra blankets and settled her on the warm ledge beside the fireplace so she would not get chilled. She brought her warm tea, rubbed her head with a cool cloth, and administered all the remedies the town knew.

The tightness in her chest made each breath Enta took a struggle. Her mother's face drifted before her as if on a cloud, while the room swayed behind her, every detail out of focus. She heard her mother crying, then singing to her. She tried to answer, to assure her mother that everything would be fine, but she wasn't sure if any words ever came out. She lost track of how many days passed.

Then she saw Zayde Moishe walk out of the picture frame, stride across the room toward her, and smile. She felt him touch her forehead and heard him whisper, "Entala, my child, you have strong shoulders. Your mama needs you. You will stay with her for a long time. You will make her proud." He turned and walked back into the picture frame.

And everything came into focus.

Enta called out to her mother for more tea, and Sarah began to cry. "My baby girl—a miracle! You will now get better."

"Mama, it was Zayde Moishe," Enta told her mother. "He spoke to me and touched my head. He's the one who made me feel better."

Sarah nodded, smiling through her tears. "It has happened again—my grandfather is still protecting us." She went to the window to look at the Bes Medresh. "Thank you," she murmured in prayer; "now I know you have not deserted us."

Escape

Just after Passover in 1919, in Enta's ninth year, new events began to unfold, but she would not know the results for another year.

An astonishing letter addressed to Uncle Yankle arrived from their cousin Chaim, in New York. It was the first letter anyone in the family had received from America in two years. Chaim expressed concern about everyone's well-being, inquiring about who had survived the war and the epidemic. Some word had gotten out about the murders and deaths and the ongoing civil strife, and family members in America worried about the fates of their loved ones. Chaim included special messages to many individuals, including one from Yitzhac to Sarah saying how much he longed to have his family with him and how much he hoped she and the children had come through the mayhem in good health.

Now that the Great War was over and travel was again becoming possible, Chaim explained, many more Jewish families were trying to leave the shtetls of Eastern Europe to make a new life in America. What he did not reveal in the letter was that traveling was still treacherous. People needed huge sums of money, proper papers, and planned travel arrangements to cross borders. Crossing from one country to another on the way to Belgium to board ships across the ocean was hazardous, and there was always the danger of attack, robbery, and murder for Jews leaving those areas where the civil war continued.

Luckily, some Jewish people living in America were trying to help those who wanted to emigrate from Europe. Chaim said that he would do what he could to get that help and provide assistance for all the family members from Skvira who wanted to come to America. He could not provide more details yet, but looked forward to word about who had survived. He closed by warning that it was best to be very cautious.

"That means people should not discuss the possibility of leaving for America with anyone outside the family," Yankle added when he read that. "Safe passage will depend on keeping secret any plans made."

The only clue Enta had about the remarkable journey she would soon begin was the more cheerful look on her mother's face and the occasional lilt in her voice, even though the fears of armed bandits had not dissipated. She seemed to be doing more cleaning in their house, even rearranging their few belongings. She mentioned Yitzhac more often, hoping aloud that he would be proud of his children when they were all together again.

Imitating their mother, Leiba Chana began to warn whenever Enta did something that she didn't like, "Just wait, Papa will not be proud of you. He'll scold you when he finds out."

Enta tried to remember what her papa looked like, but her memory was blank. She wondered when he would be returning to Skvira.

* * *

In early summer Golda rushed into their home, waved for everyone to come close, and whispered, "Good news! Cousin Chaim has arrived from New York. He is here. We have to be ready at sunup tomorrow. You must not tell anyone."

Sarah kissed Golda. "A blessing from the Lord, Golda. May He guide our way." Then she turned to her three children and explained, "We will be making a long journey in the morning, so we have to work very hard to get ready." Her voice grew stern. "Above all else, you three must be very quiet."

"Oh no," Leiba Chana groaned, "another journey to hide from soldiers!"

"Shah, daughter—this is a happy journey," Sarah whispered, "but there are dangers."

Several families gathered at the meeting place just as the sky began to lighten. They brought with them only the belongings they could carry on their backs or drag along the ground. The most important belonging Sarah brought was her picture of Zayde Moishe, packed carefully in the large cloth bag in which she had stuffed pillows, blankets, other small photographs, eating utensils, and whatever warm clothing she could fit.

She and her three children were told to get into a wagon where a family of five waited along with Golda, Yankle, and their son and daughter. Sarah had also agreed to help two orphan children making the journey to join their aunt and uncle in New York, a boy a year older than Leiba Chana and a girl who was younger than Enta. No country would be willing to accept two orphans who had no family accompanying them, so she would pretend they were her children to enable them to cross borders and get into America.

Rissela and her family chose to remain in Skvira. She could not bear to leave the grave of her beloved son. Layve's wife and two surviving children also remained behind. She hoped to continue to manage the inn, with help from her children. (More than twenty years later they would all be forced to leave their homes, and would be murdered by the Nazis.)

Sarah never had a chance to say goodbye to any of her family in Pogrebischte, to visit the cemetery to bid her mother, father, or Zayde Moishe farewell. Her brother Henoch visited once more before they left, and Sarah sensed they would never again be together. Only months after she left Skvira, she later learned, Henoch was stabbed to death by a gang of soldiers hacking at people in Pogrebischte.

Cousin Chaim went to each of the wagons before the trip began. "We will ride until sundown, stopping from time to time for life's necessities," he said when he reached their wagon. He pointed to a pile of large blankets stacked in the wagon bed. "Cover yourselves with those, and stay covered, not talking or making noise of any kind. People passing by must have no idea how many people are traveling in this group, or it will be very dangerous."

All in all there were close to eighty people leaving the area in six wagons, but they could not travel too close together or appear to represent movement of a large number of people. They could all be killed if detected. "I will be nearby," Chaim promised. "I will answer any questions if we are stopped by the authorities."

He patted Leiba Chana and Enta on their heads. "You will be good girls and help your mother, won't you?"

The girls nodded solemnly, not realizing that they were leaving behind all that was familiar to travel to a strange land. Enta looked fearful, and Sarah realized that she probably thought this trip was like the last one, that they were running away to hide from danger for a short while. Sarah smiled at her daughter and stroked her dark hair. "We will not be returning to find anyone hurt this time, Entala," she soothed.

They moved quickly for the first part of the trip. There was enough bread to eat, people dozed off when they were sleepy, and everyone remained silent. Aside from the rough and bumpy ride, nothing terrifying happened. Enta sat quietly between her mother and Golda, and the orphan children also remained quiet, their eyes round with fear. Leiba Chana kept asking why everyone had to be so quiet, why she couldn't get out and walk around. Sarah rolled her eyes and pleaded, "Shah, dear daughter, don't cause trouble. Please, do as you are told."

The other family in the wagon included an older father with his young second wife, two older daughters from his first marriage, and one baby less than a year old. Each time the baby began to cry, the terrified mother put it to her breast and let it nurse until it fell asleep. Her breast milk was clearly drying up, because the baby would awaken a short time later, crying again. "Shah, shah," the mother whispered. "They must not hear."

Just after sunset the wagon pulled into a small town, and they glimpsed the shadows of waiting people. "Remember, stay hidden. Let Cousin Chaim do the talking," Sarah whispered. "These are friends who will give us a place to stay until the horses are fed and rested. You must be quiet, and don't ask questions."

Chaim beckoned to the family with the baby and told them to follow a waiting boy. "He will show you where to go." He turned to Sarah as she helped her children and the orphans out of the wagon and indicated a woman whose head was covered by a kerchief. "Follow her."

The woman took them to a large house, where she told them to wait in a room behind the kitchen. It had no windows and smelled musty, with cobwebs filling every corner. Sarah looked around in dismay, thinking of the tidy house she'd left behind, but settled the children and gave them each a piece of challah, and they soon drifted off to sleep.

It was still dark when the same woman returned and told them the wagons were ready. After putting the five children on the wagon, Sarah embraced the woman. "God will bless you," she murmured gratefully.

"When can we go home?" Bennie whined. "I'm tired of this wagon. I want to go home now."

Yankle looked at Sarah with concern in his eyes, and they and Golda grimaced, shaking their heads. "Keep still and don't ask, don't make trouble," Sarah scolded Bennie. "You must be patient. This journey is necessary, and we cannot turn back now." There was no point in telling the children the purpose of their trip. If soldiers or bandits stopped them and learned their destination, they would be in far more danger.

"Do as you're told," Leiba Chana scolded Bennie. But then she looked at her Aunt Golda. "I don't understand why you can't tell us why we are making such a long trip."

It was totally dark when they arrived at the edge of the Dniester River. Cousin Chaim was waiting for them. "This is the most important part of the trip," he said. "There are guard boats in the water, looking for people trying to cross. The Romanian government does not welcome all the refugees from the civil war. If they catch you, they will send you back. They have even thrown some people into the water and watched while they drowned. Once you get across, we have contacts who will help us. Things will get better when we all get across."

Sarah clambered into the rocking boat with the other people from their wagon, and the pilot guided the boat out into the choppy water. Enta grabbed her skirt and her sister's arm in alarm, and Sarah noticed how pale the motion of the small craft made her, but somehow her younger daughter managed to remain still. She glanced up into the black sky and saw only a few specks of distant stars. There was no moonlight to guide them, but the darkness sheltered them from roving boatmen who, Chaim had whispered in warning, tried to capture escaping Jews to rob them, beat them, or kill them. She turned her gaze to the blackness where she imagined the far shore lay, and felt the wind blowing over her face, like a mysterious force trying to push them back.

Then she swung her face around in near-panic when the baby began to scream. "Shah, be still," its mother murmured urgently, rocking it as she looked around at the watching faces. Sarah saw the whites of her terrified eyes.

"We will all be killed if that baby doesn't stop crying," the man rowing the boat growled.

Sarah heard the woman sob, and then the silence became eerie. It wasn't until they were met by strangers on the Romanian shore that the woman let go of her baby's limp body. Sarah stared in horror at the anguished face of the woman who had killed her own child with the force of her hands, trying to keep him quiet. Her expression was worse even than Rissela's when she'd been holding Samuel's dead body, but nobody was permitted to take time to mourn outwardly. Golda put an arm around the woman's trembling shoulders and guided her away as they tossed the baby's body into the black waters of the river.

"Quickly," the Romanians urged. "We have shelters arranged where you can hide."

Time passed slowly in Romania while they waited for the processing of papers that would allow them to move legally across Europe to Antwerp, and the ship that would take them from Belgium to America. They were kept safe in dark rooms that blurred the passage of time. It was winter again before they were able to continue on the next stage of the journey, but they left in daylight and boarded the train in full view of anyone who cared to notice.

Sarah, unable to accept the legitimacy the new official papers bestowed upon her, warned her children to be quiet and not attract attention. Leiba Chana did not share her mother's fears and started conversations with fellow travelers, who were charmed by her friendly face and petite features. They gave her extra pieces of food from the supplies they had packed for themselves. "What am I going to do with that girl?" Sarah sighed, holding more tightly to Enta and Bennie. "She has a mind of her own."

Chaim had arranged everything for their arrival in Antwerp. The ship would be sailing in two weeks. They had lost three travelers since leaving Skvira—the baby who died in the boat when his mother tried to keep him quiet, an elderly cousin whose heart gave way before the crossing into Romania, and a cousin who died in childbirth during the months in Romania, waiting for the official papers that would enable them to obtain passage to America. The survivors from all the wagons came to a total of seventy-seven people: twenty women, ten men, twenty-two teenagers, and twenty-five younger children. Chaim arranged for all of those he was leading to America to come together for a photograph two days before the ship was scheduled to sail.

"This photograph is for me," he told them. "You will scatter across many cities after reaching New York. This will give me assurance that I served my family and community." He paused, then added in a quieter voice, "Perhaps when my wife and children see your faces—see the pain, the fear, the exhaustion etched there—they will understand why it was necessary for me to risk doing this."

But the nightmare was not yet over. The journey across the ocean in the cramped quarters in the lower sections of the ship, with its continuous tossing and swaying, left many constantly seasick—Enta among them. Nauseated by the smells of not only vomit but the closeness of so many bodies, Sarah struggled to care for her five young charges. When they finally arrived at Ellis Island, they were all too sick and too dirty to feel any joy or any concern about the next hurdles awaiting them.

PART FOUR

THE GOLDENE MEDINA

If you step out on the floor
You'll forget your trouble
If you go into your dance
You'll forget your woe.

—"Let Yourself Go" by Irving Berlin

Reunited

Ettie looked at her watch and was surprised that they had been talking, with few interruptions, for close to two hours. "I don't know why I keep talking about all of this now. I must be goofy or something. Nothing can change the past. I was afraid of my own shadow—a big, terrified dummy!"

No one had warned her, all those years ago, that she would never see Skvira again, that she would never again lie on the ledge by the fireplace, or look out the windows at the Bes Medresh or at the river and trees at the foot of the hill. More importantly, she'd thought she would see Ephriam again, that he would still be the one she married. Later her mother would tell her that he and his family had escaped and joined their relatives in Chicago, but not then . . .

Rachel glanced at Collette, who leaned forward, smiling gently. "Mother, I thought you wanted to talk about your family and how you all managed to survive. You should feel proud that you came through so much and are still a strong person, but if it's upsetting for you to relive all those bad memories, we can talk more another time, if you want. I think we should get ready for more visitors now, anyway."

Ettie stared out the window at the trees while she collected herself, then looked around the room. Her eyes fell on a notebook and pencils lying on top of a side table, and her mind journeyed back to Ellis Island, and all the papers she'd seen on the inspector's desk while she waited in front of him. She never did know what the clerks were writing, but it was in the very first room that her name changed from Enta to Etta. *Probably just a careless spelling mistake or sloppy handwriting,* she thought, and smiled inwardly at the further permutations of her birth name—when everyone started calling her Ettie, the name Enta disappeared.

Leiba Chana had changed her own name, deciding that everyone should forget about her middle name and just call her Libby, though she remained Leiba Chana to her mother. It was easy for the rest of the family to get used to the new names, Ettie and Libby, and it made them feel a little closer to the new, foreign language they heard around them.

Ettie shuddered as more memories of Ellis Island came to the forefront—how they'd cut all the girls' hair so short, they all looked like boys. *At least they didn't shave our heads, like they did the boys',* she thought. They were told this was necessary to get rid of lice. Ettie couldn't remember any of them ever having lice. It was all so degrading—the haircuts, being told to strip so they could be examined. *At least the girls were separated from the boys for that.*

Last came questions, and more clerks writing on papers. She couldn't understand what they were saying, but there'd been enough interpreters present that her mother had managed to struggle through the answers. Her mother had been concerned about the two orphan children she was pretending were her own. *We all wondered what would happen if anyone said something to cast suspicion on them. We worried that we would all have to return to Skvira!* But nobody had become suspicious, and almost everything unfolded as they'd hoped.

Well, except that they found ringworm on Bennie's head. The officials wouldn't permit him to leave the island with the rest of his family until it cleared up. *Poor Bennie! He must have been so frightened, in this strange place away from his mother and sisters for two weeks. But they found it on Golda's son, too, so at least Bennie wasn't completely alone.* Ettie felt a twinge of old guilt, remembering how relieved she'd been that it hadn't happened to her, that she and Libby were allowed to leave with their mother.

Through the years, people had asked Ettie about her reactions when she finally reached America. One of her most vivid memories was standing behind a huge, locked gate, and her shock when her mother suddenly pointed to a strange man on the other side and began crying. "See that man over there?" she'd exclaimed to Ettie and Libby. "That's your papa!"

The man did not look like the father Ettie had envisioned. She had seen the photograph he sent after his arrival, but she had no memory of what her father actually looked like, and her first thought was, *How can that man be my father? He has such good clothes on.*

No matter how hard Ettie tried, she could never remember what had happened between her first sighting of her father and when they began walking away from the ship.

She did remember seeing the first black person she had ever seen in her life, a fat woman sitting on a bench near the docks, nursing a baby. The blackness of the woman's skin terrified Ettie, and she began to cry, fearing that they would have to run and hide. She smiled at another lasting memory—seeing somebody eating a banana and wondering what that strange-looking thing was.

Somehow, with Cousin Chaim's help, they managed to get the belongings they'd brought from Skvira, including the picture of Zayde Moishe that remained with Sarah for the rest of her life, and got out of New York City and onto a train to Chaim's home in Newark, New Jersey. It was a surprise to discover that Chaim and his family did not actually live in New York, as they had always believed when they spoke of him in Skvira.

After a few weeks Bennie was released, and Sarah, Yitzhac, and the three children left on a train for Pittsburgh, to share rooms with Shmulek and his family. Those first weeks in America remained fuzzy in Ettie's mind. Her father seemed like a stranger to her, with his gruff ways and temperamental outbursts. When she or Libby or Bennie giggled or spoke too loud, he shouted for quiet. If they got too noisy, he threatened, "You see this belt? If you keep it up, I'm going to use it on you." He didn't use it, but Ettie was never convinced that he wouldn't, and she never fully trusted him.

When they decided to move into some rooms of their own, Ettie often heard him scolding her mother for not cooking his food exactly how he wanted it, or for not looking after his clothes properly. Sarah usually responded with sarcasm: "So, what do you do all day? You don't know what we went through while you were here, enjoying America. And what for, so you could take care of your horse and sit around with your friends? Even now, you don't make a good living, and I have to struggle so we have enough to eat with what little money you bring home."

Her father would wave his arm as if he intended to slap her, then end the discussion by leaving the room, muttering, "This is the thanks I get for giving Chaim all the money I had, so he could get you out of Skvira. I could have let you stay there."

Yitzhac earned money using his horse-drawn cart, at times collecting junk and scraps, other times driving it around the local neighborhood, selling potatoes. If he could sell out his load of potatoes, he might make a dollar or two, unless it was already mid-afternoon, when the customers would insist on paying less. Not wanting to be stuck with the potatoes, he often sold them for much less than they were worth. He had no patience for the housewives who argued with him over the price of a few potatoes, or complained that the potatoes did not look fresh. Ettie often heard him complaining to Sarah, "I know they're fresh! They are just trying to get me to lower the price." He would say this with one hand absently bracing his sore back that seemed to get worse every day because of the heavy bushels of potatoes he had to lift onto the cart at the loading area in the Strip District.

He had no great ambition, and after he sold his cartload of potatoes, even if it was still early afternoon, he would come home. When Sarah chided him that other men would get a second load and earn extra for their family, he responded by waving his arm out toward Sarah and asking an imaginary person in the room, "What does that woman want from me?"

The only time Ettie saw pleasure on his face was when he was looking after his horse, brushing him and getting him water and hay. His big concern, often expressed, was keeping his horse healthy for at least another season.

* * *

Sarah was not surprised that Yitzhac avoided communicating with her, or that he was so stubborn. He had been that way in Skvira. What had changed was the pride that once made people respect him. Back in Skvira, he had been determined to show people that the weather or bandits would not deter him from completing his journey. The years since he'd left Skvira had broken his spirit, and he was now content to live from day to day, earning enough to help pay for essentials, even going hungry occasionally when his back hurt too much. She knew that, before his family joined him, his needs had been minimal; he had lived as a boarder, eating whatever his landlady gave him. Now he had five people to house and feed, and the burden seemed almost too much for him to bear. They rented rooms that they could afford and, if the property owner raised the rent, they moved somewhere cheaper. Sarah managed to squeeze in boarders, men who were on their own as Yitzhac had been before her arrival; otherwise they would not have been able to make ends meet.

Several months after Sarah and the children arrived, Yitzhac moved them to a small town called Apollo, thirty miles outside of Pittsburgh, where he could use his horse and cart to collect and sell junk. He made a better living there than he had in the city. And it was there that Libby and Ettie learned English, and with that, the meaning of the taunts of the other children who called them "Christ-killers."

Sarah felt isolated, longing for the friendship of neighbors who spoke Yiddish. After a year she convinced Yitzhac that they should return to the city by repeatedly warning that if their children didn't grow up around other Jewish people, they might end up marrying non-Jews.

On their return to Pittsburgh they settled into a rented house on Roberts Street in the Hill District, and remained there for over fifteen years. Sarah continued to make a major contribution toward the family's expenses by renting two of the rooms to men who had no families with them. They loved her cooking, and spread the word to single men living in the area that the food was always good and the place clean.

Sarah's days were filled with scrubbing floors, dusting furniture, washing sheets and towels, and the one thing she enjoyed, cooking. She took pride in how well she could stretch whatever ingredients she could afford. She discovered that she could buy eggs cheaper if she bought them slightly cracked and used them before they could spoil. She had learned long ago how to stretch a few vegetables into a large pot of soup or borscht. Her true joy came from baking her delicious challahs and coffee cakes. Every week she prepared gefilte fish for the Sabbath, and when they could afford a chicken, that became a feast.

Ettie loved to join her mother on Thursdays, when she went shopping on Center Avenue to prepare for the Sabbath. It made Ettie feel good to look at all the food. The neighborhood offered a choice of kosher butcher shops, although Sarah could rarely afford meat. The shopkeepers in Young's Dairy Store and Yossel Markowitz's Fruit Market always praised Ettie for being so helpful to her mother by carrying some of the bags. Sometimes Sarah bought an extra piece of fruit for a penny or a bunch of carrots for a few cents, as a treat when they got home. Once in a while she bought her a lollipop, called a sucker, for a penny. The one place Ettie was hesitant to enter was Mrs. Sommerman's Chicken Store, where the live chickens were on display until someone chose one and waited for it to be slaughtered.

For Sarah, shopping day was her social life. She enjoyed it for the gossip the other women shared, the news from Skvira or the towns surrounding it. They talked about who was getting married, who was having a baby, who had recently arrived in the Hill District from their part of the "old country."

The lives of those in Pittsburgh's Hill District were a far cry from those of Jewish people who had settled in Pittsburgh years or decades earlier, people who were already living in nicer sections of the city, like Oakland, East End, or Squirrel Hill. While Sarah and her neighbors worried about having enough money to buy eggs or a few vegetables, some of these earlier immigrants, now successful businessmen or professionals, were buying automobiles for over six hundred dollars. Their wives were wearing high fashion dresses that cost close to eighty dollars. Those with enough money attended the Nixon Theater, made annual trips to Atlantic City or even Miami Beach, and paid to have their names and addresses inserted in the *Criterion*, the local Jewish paper, to extend greetings to their friends and families before the High Holy Days.

Yitzhac spent his spare time drinking tea at a neighborhood café, talking with friends and playing cards. Anyone who dropped by their home could see that Yitzhac and Sarah were disappointed with each other. Their constant bickering sometimes resulted in shouting matches and threats. During their eight-year separation, Yitzhac had longed for the compliant woman who had put his needs above all else. When his family finally arrived, Sarah didn't hide that she was more concerned about the children than him. He grumbled that his family didn't appreciate how hard it had been for him to adjust to a new country without his loved ones, how lonely he had been, how many temptations he had tried to resist. He stopped trying to explain how hard it had been to get other work, how quickly he had learned about the impossible situation facing immigrants with no skills and no English, even those who were not Jewish.

Sarah, forced to survive during the eight years of separation through her own ingenuity and courage, became self-reliant while fantasizing about an easier life in America. She was grateful that their lives were no longer in constant danger, but her husband did not appreciate what an ordeal she had endured. He had become negative about everything, had lost the self-confidence that people in Skvira admired, and was now a bitter man. They were tolerant of each other and grateful for the relationship, but their main pleasure came from the family and friends from the old country who dropped in for tea, gossip, advice, and friendship.

They remained closest with Sarah's brother Shmulek and his wife Franya, and Sarah's half-brother Nachum, who visited often and periodically helped them when they had trouble making ends meet. Before Sarah and her family arrived, Shmulek had saved enough money to buy a grocery store with a small butcher shop at the back. Franya and Nachum helped run the store. It had been a struggle to make a living until Prohibition was enacted, but once liquor was no longer legal, they supplemented their income by making whiskey in the bathtub upstairs. The police knew that they and many other shopkeepers had these side ventures brewing whiskey, so the local cops stopped by every Monday to get paid their share of the profits in return for keeping quiet.

Often, when Yitzhac had a bad week and brought home very little money, Sarah bought her groceries from Shmulek, who charged her practically nothing. With that help her family never went hungry. However, in return, Sarah felt obliged to help with the whiskey making.

"It will lead to trouble," Yitzhac warned her.

She used that as an opening to remind him, "I wouldn't have to do it if you earned enough for the family to get along." That always stopped his bullying. She was grateful that nobody had ever told him that she'd been arrested in Kiev for selling whiskey, and subsequently mistreated by the police. If he had known about that, Yitzhac would have been even more aggressive in his opposition.

Greenhorns

Thursday night marked the end of the third day of shiva. To give people time to prepare for the Sabbath—sundown Friday until sundown Saturday—shiva would end early Friday afternoon and begin again Saturday night. Ettie's four grandchildren decided to return to their homes before the weekend began. Andrea would be driving back to her home in Maryland, Jeff to Philadelphia, and Laurie and Steve would fly to Toronto Friday afternoon. David and Rachel decided to remain with their mother and sister until Tuesday morning, the official end of the week of shiva.

Ettie gazed sadly at her grandchildren. "Who knows when I'll get to see you guys again? I'm gonna miss every one of you. Next time we're together, it should be for a happy occasion."

Andrea giggled. "Oh Grandma, we'll be coming again soon. Don't be sad."

Jeff went into his childhood bedroom and found some old photo albums. "Look, Grandma, here's a picture of you holding me when I was a baby. I liked it when you visited—we always had fun playing games. We loved it when you came to babysit, even though Andrea and I would tease each other when you left the room, and you got very upset."

"Yeah, and those trips you made to Toronto were great," Laurie added. "You liked to play store with us, remember? You would pretend you had so many things to sell, and it all seemed real. My friends were always amazed that I had such a fun grandma."

Steve nodded. "I remember looking forward to seeing you at the Toronto bus terminal, waiting for you to come down the bus steps with shopping bags full of chocolate chip cookies." He grinned and winked. "Those bus drivers were always laughing with relief. You must've been talking about how long the trip was taking."

Ettie laughed and nodded. She looked around at them. "All my grandchildren give me so much *nachis*, so much pleasure."

When the time came for Ettie to say goodbye to her grandchildren late Friday morning, it unleashed a storm of tears and anguish. She held each one close to whisper something personal that made each of them smile. Once they were gone, an uncomfortable quiet settled in the room.

Stanley prepared a light lunch, but Ettie just picked at her food. Rachel and David convinced her to join them in the family room, and they watched the end of the news, then flipped channels without finding anything else of interest. Rachel looked at Ettie, wondering how she could get her mother to feel better about herself, and finally asked, "You liked school after you came to America, didn't you, Mother?"

The topic seemed to irritate Ettie. "Yeah, I liked it, but a lot of good that did me! In those days, girls weren't supposed to go to school—at least, not in my family. My father didn't care about school, he just wanted me to go to work and make money to help the family pay for things. It was because of your Aunt Libby—my mother and father thought that if Libby could go to work and make money to help out, why shouldn't I? Things might have been different if they had let me stay in school."

Rachel quickly realized this was not the subject that would cheer her mother—Ettie had to drop out of school after finishing the eighth grade. She believed that was the reason her mother had always pushed them to get high marks and a good education, why she insisted education was the most important thing. *How different would Mother's life have been, if she had continued her education?* "Mother," she said, "tell me this: if you had stayed in school, what kind of career would you have pursued?"

Ettie thought a moment, then replied, "At that time I wanted to be a bookkeeper. Anyway, it's all over and done with—why go over all that now?" She waved the question away, then lowered her head and sat thinking for a few minutes. When she looked up, her expression was wistful.

"That first day of school, after we arrived in Pittsburgh, I was so scared. I didn't know what I was supposed to do, where to sit. The seats were so small. Libby and I were older and bigger than the others, and I felt ridiculous."

* * *

In April, 1921, Ettie and Libby began school for the first time in their lives. Shmulek's wife, Franya, took them to the office to register them. Ettie had just turned ten; Libby was past eleven. Neither had ever read a book, and the only English they understood were the words they had picked up from Shmulek and his family in the few weeks since their arrival in Pittsburgh. Everyone at home spoke Yiddish. Most of the children in the neighborhood spoke a mixture of Yiddish and English. Some of the immigrants who had arrived in their neighborhood a little earlier than the others spoke more English, and laughed at the newcomers, imitating them and pointing at them, calling them "greenhorns." Ettie was desperate to learn the new language and the new ways so she could escape the taunts and insults.

When Ettie and Libby walked into the stuffy third grade classroom, the other children were sitting in five rows of seven wooden desks with attached seats. The teacher waved them toward three empty desks in the row closest to the large windows. Ettie passed several children whom she recognized from her street, but she was too terrified to even smile. Libby waved to one girl, then one of the boys giggled. The teacher tapped her ruler on the desk and glared.

Ettie noticed dusty writing on the black slate walls but had no idea what any of it meant. Along the top of each wall were the neatly printed letters that her Aunt Franya had prepared her to recognize as the ABCs, each capital letter of the alphabet followed by its lowercase form.

Ettie could make out a little of what the teacher was saying: ". . . *work hard . . . pay attention . . . put up your hand."* Then the teacher read out names, and children answered "here" while raising their hands. Ettie's heart pounded when she heard her name, but she raised her hand and whispered, "Here."

The teacher pulled out a book and said something about the Bible. Ettie could not understand the words. They all folded their hands and recited a prayer, then stood and saluted the little flag hanging from the wall. Ettie heard everyone say in unison, "I pledge allegiance." None of it made any sense to her, but she imitated what the others were doing and moved her lips, pretending to be reciting with them.

Next the teacher handed out books to the students and returned to the front of the classroom. She called out a name and pointed to the girl sitting in the first seat in the row next to Ettie's. The girl stood up and began reading from the open book she held. Ettie looked around and noticed that the other children were following along, some using their fingers to trace the lines on the page. She looked down at her open book, but had no idea where to place her finger.

The teacher called on a boy in the back of the room to read next. He stumbled over each word, then repeated what the teacher said when she corrected him. Some of the other children giggled. Ettie went cold. What if the teacher pointed to her? She didn't want them to laugh at her!

As if she'd read Ettie's mind, the teacher swung her finger toward Ettie and called her name. Ettie stared at the teacher, then down at the book, in rising panic. When the teacher repeated her name, she pushed herself to her feet, gripping the edges of the desk. The book felt like a lead weight when she lifted it from her desktop. She blinked at the page, swallowed, and suddenly the room began to spin.

The next thing she saw was Libby, standing beside the girl she had waved to when they'd entered the room. Both of them were looking down at her. The girl was sprinkling drops of water on Ettie's head, while Libby was scolding in Yiddish, "Ettie, you silly fool, why did you pass out? Mama's gonna be so upset."

At the end of the morning, the children lined up to leave the building to go home for lunch. Some of the girls whispered and pointed at Ettie, laughing and pushing each other. Libby grabbed her hand and said, "Come on, let's get out of here."

A little girl named Tilly stepped forward and took Ettie's other hand. "Don't worry," she whispered in Yiddish, "you will soon learn to read and to talk like they do here."

Then Libby promised, " I won't tell Mama and Papa what happened," and Ettie nearly sagged in relief.

That afternoon, shortly after school resumed, a young woman wearing a light blue suit, her hair pulled into a bun, entered their classroom and pointed to Ettie and Libby. "Come with me."

She led them into a small room beside the principal's office. Pointing first to one, then the other, she said, "Your name is Ettie; your name is Libby." She pointed to herself. "And I am Miss Pokovsky." For the next half-hour she held up pictures of dogs, cats, dresses, books, dishes, boats, and children, saying the name of each and then showing them how the word looked when printed.

Excitement surged through Ettie when she realized the woman was teaching them to read and identify words in English. She wanted more! "When will this happen again?" she asked in Yiddish.

They met several times a week, usually in groups of three or four children, with the special teacher assigned to help immigrant children learn enough of the language to participate in the regular classes. After a few months, Ettie could read most of the lines in the book the teacher distributed. Libby was learning too, but she laughed at how serious Ettie got when they met with Miss Pokovsky, and teased her about reading those baby books.

Libby was too restless to concentrate on what she thought were useless activities. She could not understand why the teacher expected them to be so quiet and still. When she wanted to say something to one of the other pupils, she would turn around and speak. The teacher was always scolding her, "Okay, Libby Burin, stop that whispering and look up here at what I am writing on the board."

Sometimes Libby would whisper in Yiddish, "Who cares about that?"

By 1924, when Libby was close to fifteen and Ettie thirteen, they'd progressed to the seventh grade and could now speak English with very little Yiddish accent. School was the happiest time of the day for Ettie. Her teachers often complimented her on work well done, and that led to admiration from the other girls. Ettie took learning seriously, trying to remember every new word she learned, to grasp what each story was about. She usually knew the answers to the teacher's questions after the oral reading concluded each day, although she was reluctant to raise her hand to answer them. She liked arithmetic best, and enjoyed surprising the teacher with how fast she could add and subtract, even multiply.

Miss Parish, the seventh grade teacher, had no patience with the young people who were too mature for the classes they were in, who did not pay enough attention to learn how to read their history books or to do the arithmetic assignments. Some of them were too independent. It didn't take her long to recognize that Ettie would always have the correct answer, whereas Libby would likely say that she didn't know and sometimes add sassily, "Who cares, anyhow? It doesn't matter." The teacher tried to avoid conflict and misbehavior by directing questions to the "Burin girls"; Ettie was always the one to stand up and answer.

Libby had absolutely no interest in the books they were assigned or in learning how to do the long division. Her marks were always near the bottom of the group. What Libby excelled in was interacting with the other girls. She always remembered to ask them about their families, to remember their birthdays, and to compliment them when she liked their hair or the dresses they wore. She enjoyed the attention she got in return. Naturally, the other girls liked to sit next to her and to walk home with her.

One of the girls invited Libby to stop by her home after school. While there, Libby related excitedly to her family afterward, she overheard the girl's father talking with a friend about the man's business, and how hard it was to find people who could roll the tobacco carefully without creating a lot of waste. "I walked over to the man and introduced myself and told him, 'If you need part-time help, I can work after school. I'll be very careful and do a good job.'"

The businessman liked the fact that Libby showed initiative, and besides, what was there to lose? He could pay her low wages, and if she didn't work out, he could fire her. So Libby began to work a few hours after school and during part of the weekend. After a few months, she arranged for Ettie to join her when things got busy.

Now school seemed even less important to Libby. Often when she thought the teacher wasn't looking, she tapped one of the girls on the arm and made whispered plans for the weekend. The teacher reacted by slapping her desk with a ruler, glaring in exasperation across the room at Libby. Libby just laughed and picked up a book. These episodes embarrassed Ettie, but she assumed nothing more serious would come of them.

Finally the teacher exploded. Ettie hadn't noticed what Libby was doing that was unusual enough to draw the teacher's ire, but suddenly she was red-faced and shouting in a shrill voice, "Libby Burin, what are you up to now? I insist that you stop carrying on this way, stop disturbing the class. You should be ashamed of yourself!"

Libby seemed to forget where she was and shouted back, "Ashamed of what? You don't know what you're talking about. I'm not doing anything to be ashamed about, and you can't talk to me like that!"

The teacher's face flushed crimson. Slamming her book onto the desk, she strode over to Libby, lifted her by the arm, and slapped her across the cheek.

A hush fell over the room. Libby blinked back tears and yelled, "You won't get away with treating me like that!" She stalked out of the room and out of the building and never returned to that school again.

Later, Ettie arrived home to find Libby seated at the kitchen table, drinking tea. Sarah stood behind her, shaking her head and motioning to the ceiling as she moaned, "Now what am I going to do? *Tsores*! Troubles! Always *tsores*! Do I need this now?"

"I don't care what anyone says, I am not going into that place again," Libby said in a tone that suggested this wasn't the first time she'd voiced this opinion. "That teacher doesn't know what she is doing. She'll never lay a hand on me again."

The next day Sarah and their Aunt Franya went to the school to inform them that Libby would not be returning. They had decided not to mention the slap in the face, not to make trouble. The principal explained that the law required that Libby stay in school for another year, until she turned sixteen. However, she could attend part-time classes in another building if the family needed her to get a job.

Ettie felt guilty at the relief she felt when she realized that her sister would no longer embarrass her. The teacher would never scold *her*—she sat quietly, did her work, answered the questions when asked, and was pleased when the teacher asked her to help collect books or distribute papers.

Working Girls

"School was where I felt most comfortable and safe," Ettie concluded.

She glanced over at David, remembering all the worries she'd had when he was a boy, especially when the teachers told her he was misbehaving in school or not achieving up to his potential. She marveled at the fact that he had become such a respected scholar.

She caught the sadness in his eyes, and he stretched and said as if to distract her, "So, go on—what kind of job did Aunt Libby get when she left school?"

Ettie pretended to be unhappy talking about the past. "Why are you guys dredging up all this old stuff? Talking isn't going to change anything, I'll tell you that. It's all water over the dam."

"C'mon," David pleaded, his imploring expression exaggerated, as if he were a little boy asking her for a piece of candy. "I'd like to know more about what it was like, back when you were a teenager."

Ettie played along, sighing, "Well, I'll tell you what I remember." She closed her eyes, pursed her lips, and sat in quiet thought for a moment. Then she described how Libby's dropping out of school changed all of their lives.

* * *

Libby knew some of the older girls, who told her about their jobs at a candy factory, where she could make as much as fifteen dollars a week as a candy wrapper. They told her how hard it was, working in the cold room, standing in one place, their hands moving quickly to get the paper around each piece of candy while supervisors watched to make sure they kept working. There were quotas, and girls who didn't wrap enough pieces of candy got fired. But for those who were fast, the pay was better than what they could make at other jobs. The hardest part was working in rooms that were kept cold so the chocolate wouldn't melt. "Sometimes your hands get so stiff, it's hard to move your fingers," they told Libby.

Still, she thought it would be worth a try, to make extra money. She caught on quickly and enjoyed trying to exceed her quota. Even more, she enjoyed the friendships she established with the other girls. The supervisors were impressed with her output and occasionally gave her a few extra pieces of candy to take home at the end of the week. When she received her weekly wages, sometimes a few dollars more than fifteen, she gave most of it to her mother to help with household expenses, and kept a little for her own needs and some fun.

Thus Libby assumed a role typical of the children in some immigrant families struggling for a better existence in America. She became the main wage earner. Other families were convinced that education was the way for children to better themselves. Those families sacrificed to ensure that their children obtained the education and skills to improve their lives. But many immigrant families thought that it was a waste of time for girls to get an education, and if girls started school when they were almost grown and expected no tangible benefit from a few years of schooling, it was not easy to motivate them.

* * *

Ettie continued to talk about Libby's work, unable to separate her admiration from some jealousy and anger. "Your Aunt Libby had enough money to go to the silent movies on the weekends, especially if her favorite stars were in them, and sometimes to attend the live shows at the Stanley Theatre." She paused, frowning in concentration. "What did they call those shows anyhow?"

"Vaudeville?" Rachel suggested.

Ettie nodded. "That's right. Well, she bought a lot of things that made our home nicer, and that made her the big boss of the house. She tried to tell everyone what to do. My mother listened to Libby because she was the one bringing in the money. I even heard my father bragging to the neighbors that Libby knew what was important, knew that family should always come first."

"Aunt Libby was always such a generous person, and so good to us," Collette said. "I'll bet that was hard for her, to work all day, then give the money to your parents."

Ettie rolled her eyes in silent disagreement with the interpretation her oldest child had of Libby's behavior. "Well, I'll tell you a really good thing Libby did with her money, something I loved. She bought a Victrola. That was when our house became the most popular place in the neighborhood. All of our friends liked to dance, especially the Charleston. Oh boy, how we all loved that music! I guess I have to hand it to Libby, she used her money to bring us a lot of pleasure."

Collette smiled. "I remember when you taught me how to dance. You've always been such a good dancer, Mother. You have great rhythm."

Ettie's smile faded. "My father didn't like it. He liked the money Libby brought home, but he didn't like the Victrola and the gang coming to our house to dance. He couldn't tolerate the noise. And he always thought the guys were up to something nasty. I'll never forget the time he came in to check up on us, and saw one of the boys standing with an arm around a girl's shoulders. They weren't kissing or anything, but my father rushed in shouting, 'Bums, get out of here! All of you bums, out, out!' It was so embarrassing. And they had to leave."

Collette winced while Rachel and David both laughed. "That's like a comedy routine, the mental image of our grandfather chasing everyone from the house for no good reason," David said, chuckling.

Ettie pursed her lips. "Go ahead, laugh if you think it's so funny. It wasn't funny at all to Libby and me. My father could sure spoil everything."

"I'm sorry, Mother," Rachel said, trying unsuccessfully to stop laughing. " It's so outrageous, that's all."

Ettie scowled. "It was worse than outrageous. My father never trusted us. When we went to dances at the Irene Kaufmann Settlement House on Center Avenue—we all called it the Ikes then—we would see him hiding behind a tree, watching us, making sure we didn't let any boy take liberties with us. Can you believe that?"

Ettie took a moment to pull her sweater up over her shoulders as she calmed her anger. "And one time it was worse. One Sunday afternoon a bunch of us went on a picnic to Schenley Park. I went in a rowboat with a boy—I can't even remember his name now—and by the time we got the boat back to the shore, all the others had started for home. We began walking as fast as we could, but when we got to the bottom of my street, one of my friends came running to tell me that my father was furious and was waiting for me with his belt. I began running, and dashed right by him screaming that I didn't do anything wrong. I ran up the stairs to my bedroom, crawled under the bed, and stayed there all night." Ettie dropped her voice. "He was screaming and threatening me, but I felt good because I got away from him, and he didn't lay a finger on me."

"That must have been awful," Rachel exclaimed. "Were you still in school when this was going on?"

Ettie nodded. "Yeah, I was in the eighth grade, a big year in my life. Some of my older friends went on to a program in a two-year business school instead of high school. With that training they could expect to get jobs working in offices as typists or bookkeepers." She smiled in sad remembrance. "I liked to watch one of my neighbors coming home from work, all dressed up, looking sophisticated, like a real somebody. I was sure you could get respect if you had that kind of job."

Ettie sighed. "Still, I knew that it would cost money and probably would not work out for me to go. Whenever Libby talked about her job, I would tell her that I hoped to work in an office, not in a freezing candy factory. Libby kept reminding me that it would cost the family too much to send me to business school, that our parents had barely enough for necessities. She'd tell me that I was wishing for crazy things. Boy, was she right." Ettie shrugged. "I don't know what got into my head, thinking they would let me go to school.

"One day in April my teacher asked me to stay after school and help her wash the chalkboards. She told me that I was doing very well in my classes, and that my family and I should decide whether I would go on to high school or to business school. I told her I would have to discuss it with my family. I was hoping that somehow my mother could manage to scrape together the money to send me to business school, at least for the first year. I can't remember, but I don't think it cost very much.

"That day when I got home from school, I told my mother that the teacher had asked me to discuss something important with her.

I explained what kind of job I could get if I graduated from business school, but it would take two years and a little money."

Ettie looked at her hands, clasped together in her lap. "My mother put her arms around me and began to cry. She asked me where I thought they could get extra money. She told me what I already knew, that my father barely made enough for us to get by each day. We would starve without the money Libby contributed and without the boarders who paid a little each week. She reminded me that sometimes she still had to get food from Uncle Shmulek's store and often couldn't pay him till later. They were counting on me going to work as soon as possible so I could contribute to the family too. 'You should realize that your father has to pay for food for his horse as well as for us,' she said. 'If he can't feed the horse, he won't make any money to help with expenses. Where do you expect us to find the money for you to go to business school?' she asked me."

Ettie hesitated, then added, "Whenever my mother got mad at my father, she would say that his horse meant more to him than the rest of us did."

"I don't think Bubbe Sarah really believed that," Collette interjected. "I'm sure you never believed that either, Mother, did you? Zayde had to struggle, and without the horse, he would never have made any money. Besides, his health was never good—remember how he used to cough? I always think how sad it must have been for people like Bubbe and Zayde, who had to work so hard just to make ends meet."

Ettie looked away, staring out the window for a few moments before continuing. "Well, you are right about how hard it was, but it didn't seem to worry my father, as long as he had a few coins in his pocket. It's true, by that time he wasn't too well because he smoked too much and developed asthma. Remember how he used to brag about how many years he smoked Camels?" They nodded. "So he had a good excuse not to work too hard." She couldn't keep the bitterness out of her voice. "Of course they couldn't find the money to send me to business school. But that wasn't all. They couldn't even afford to let me go to high school. I had to leave school and get a job so I could make money and help the family."

Ettie stopped, unsure if she should repeat the details of what had happened that day. *Yes, tell them,* she decided, even though remembering how her father had turned and glared at her as he shouted still upset her.

"My father was furious when my mother told him I wanted to go to business school," she said. "He slammed his fist on the table and screamed, 'If Libby can earn money and help us pay for food and other things we need, Ettie can, too! Besides, a girl doesn't need an education. You can diaper babies just the same with or without an education.' He told me he'd hear no more of it, told me, 'You have one thing to do—make money and help the family, just like your sister. I never expected you, my daughter with my mother's name, to be so selfish.'" Ettie stopped, blinking back tears, remembering what her father had muttered as he left the room: "Those quiet ones, they get strange ideas."

Rachel's face crumpled in confusion when Ettie finished, as she struggled to understand how her grandparents could have been so unenlightened. "I didn't know Zayde thought that way," she said. "I always believed that people, even back then, understood that education was the way to a better life." She thought a moment. "I remember the last conversation I had with Zayde after his heart attack, just before he died. It was a year before my high school graduation. He told me he hoped I would be able to go to college."

Ettie stifled a surge of anger. "Sure, I guess he'd learned his lesson by then. I guess he realized he should have let me go to school."

Rachel opened her mouth, then shut it without saying anything, not sure how to respond to the emotion in her mother's reply. Finally she asked, "Did you ever think of asking someone for a loan?"

Ettie threw up her hands. "Rachel, what are you talking about? Don't be ridiculous. Who could I go to for a loan?"

"What about your Uncle Shmulek? He had the grocery store, maybe he would have agreed to give you a loan. Or your Uncle Nachum, what about him?"

"Uncle Nachum? He didn't have anything. He worked in Shmulek's store. Shmulek had his own family, a wife and five kids. My mother wouldn't let me bother them or anyone for a loan to go to school, even if I wanted to ask. I do know that all of Shmulek's kids went to high school, and there weren't any arguments about it for them. No, my mother and father wanted me to forget about school and get a job and pitch in. And I wanted to make my mother happy, so I stopped complaining and got a job as a sales clerk at Woolworth's 5 & 10."

David looked first at his mother and then his sisters, as if trying to decide whether it was wise to ask a question. He cleared his throat once or twice, then jumped in. "Did you ever consider going to night school?"

"I did go to night school for a few months and did real well in English and math," Ettie replied, "but I had trouble with typing. After a while, it got too hard to work those long hours all day and go to school at night. I was tired—but that wasn't the main reason. I was missing all the fun. There were dances and parties I wanted to go to. I didn't think night school would get me anywhere. I tried again later, before I got married."

Ettie didn't mention all the sleepless nights she'd spent after returning exhausted from working ten hours and then worrying about how well she was doing in night school, how she lay in bed nights, reliving all the fearful moments of the years before their arrival in America. Up until the decision that she must get a full-time job instead of continuing with school, she had always expected her mother would protect her and look out for her best interests. When she left the eighth grade, she knew she was on her own. Her mother didn't speak up for her, and her father didn't care what was in her heart. Ettie felt defeated. She figured there was only one way she would ever have a brighter future . . . she would have to marry an educated man from a good family.

Stanley, who had been in another part of the house, walked into the room. "Whatcha all talkin' about?"

Ettie brushed her memories aside with the sweep of her hand. "Old *maisses*, all those old stories, they're all over and done with. What's the good of talking? You can go on from today till tomorrow, it won't change a damn thing!"

Stanley nodded toward the kitchen. "C'mon, let's have an early dinner, and we can all relax tonight, since there's no shiva. I'll put some food out on the table, and we can help ourselves."

PART FIVE

THE RABBI'S SON

I wandered around, and finally found—the somebody who
Could make me be true, could make me be blue.
And even be glad, just to be sad, thinking of you.

Some others I've seen, might never be mean,
Might never be cross, or try to be boss.
But they wouldn't do . . .

—"It Had To Be You" by Gus Kahn and Isham Jones

The Kiss

After dinner Collette brought out photographs she had taken during a visit with her father about thirty years earlier. Three-year-old Andrea sat on her grandpa Morton's lap, laughing. Jeff was in Collette's arms, leaning sideways, his arms reaching for his grandpa. Morton's clothes didn't fit properly and his hair was disheveled, but the photograph could have been taken at any family gathering in the 1960s.

David scanned the photos and quickly handed them back to Collette, saying after a few minutes, "I remember when you and Stanley took me to meet Dad a year or so before my bar mitzvah. I don't know what I expected him to be like. It was a weird thing. I was shocked when he started to gobble up his food as if he were starving, like he thought he would never get to eat again."

Clearly trying to put a positive spin on the conversation, Stanley said, "When I met your dad, the first thing he wanted to talk about was whether I was a Republican or a Democrat. Then he wanted to play checkers. He was so good at checkers, nobody could ever beat him. I remember giving him a book written in Hebrew. He didn't hesitate, began reading it immediately and never hesitated over a word. It was impressive."

"Dad didn't know who I was, the first time I visited the hospital," Rachel said, her voice subdued. "Eight years had gone by without any visits because at the time children my age weren't permitted to visit." She stopped and shook her head, then continued after a long pause. "The fact that he didn't know his own daughter convinced me that it wouldn't matter to him if I never took his grandchildren to visit him. How could he miss grandchildren he didn't know existed? They finally met him a few years before he died, because they asked to meet him."

As Ettie listened to their perceptions of Morton, it was hard for her to accept that they were talking about the same brilliant man from the highly respected family, the son of the rabbi, she'd met when she was only fifteen. How could this be the same man she thought would make her life better, the same man her mother thought would bring honor to the family?

She lifted her hands, waving them helplessly. "Well, I'll tell you something, he was a different person when I met him." She added wistfully, "Without him I wouldn't have my three wonderful children and all my grandchildren. I'll grant him that!"

"What was he like when you met him, Mother? How did you meet?"

Ettie smiled at Rachel, who had often spoken with her about what her father had been like as a young man. She knew what her daughter was doing, and agreed—perhaps it *would* be good to talk about it again, about what he'd been like when they'd first met. She sighed as her mind drifted back to that first meeting in March, 1926. "I was so young and naive. He was much older, you know. He was a boarder in the house of my mother's friend. We first met when he suddenly appeared in our friend's living room doorway. Your Aunt Libby and I were there with our friend Tilly, and we were all dancing. I thought I was hot stuff, and I guess after he saw me dancing, he fell in love."

* * *

Libby had not yet left school. One day on their way home from school, their friend Tilly Weiss, the girl Libby had befriended on the first day of school, invited her and Ettie to stop at her house to practice new dance steps—something they did often.

Tilly's mother, Sophie Weiss, was much more sophisticated than Ettie's mother, yet somehow Sophie and Sarah had met while they were both shopping for the Sabbath, and had become friends. Sophie was less concerned than Sarah about the reactions other people might have to her daughter's dancing, and she didn't mind the loud music either. In fact, she sometimes joined the girls for a few minutes, hoping to learn to dance the Charleston herself.

"We have a new boarder," Tilly said as they approached her house, "and it's funny, because he has the same last name as you. His name is Morton Burin."

"Our name was Burchinsky in the old country," Libby said. "They changed it at Ellis Island. The same thing probably happened to him."

Tilly nodded. "Yes—he said it had been Burinovitz in the old country. Anyway, he travels around selling dry goods to stores in the small towns around Pittsburgh—which suits me, because he's rarely home. Not like the last boarder." She grimaced. "*He* was in the house every night, sitting there in the living room, reading. He made me feel uncomfortable, as if I had nothing important or interesting to say."

Ettie first saw Morton while she, Libby, and Tilly were in the middle of a dance, each shaking her arms and shimmying her hips, clapping and whirling around. Suddenly he was there, standing in the doorway, staring at them with a big grin on his face. He was very thin; his blue suit seemed too big for him, and his tie, loosened around his neck, made his white shirt also appear ill-fitting. She almost giggled when she noticed how his straight black hair poked up in places and fell across his forehead, totally untamed despite the hair tonic. He had a handsome, angular face and dark, deep-set eyes with a hint of sadness that the grin couldn't hide.

He spoke with barely a trace of the Yiddish accent so many people had then. "Don't let me stop you, girls, you're good."

Libby spoke first. "We're not putting on a show for anyone, only practicing new steps before we go home. If you like dancing so much," she added with a sassy tilt of her head, "you should come to the dance at the IKS on Center Avenue tomorrow evening, at seven-thirty."

Morton wasn't to be brushed off so quickly. "Where do you live?" he asked, and looked pleased when Libby told him. "I have to go that way now, right past your home, in fact! I'm on my way to get some things I need from the drugstore down the block. I'll walk with you."

The walk took no more than five minutes, and he used the time to tell them he had moved into the neighborhood just last week from Vandergrift, a small mill town not too far from Pittsburgh. "I like it that so many Jewish families live in the Hill District," he said. "There are only a few Jewish families in the area around Vandergrift, but my brothers have a clothing business, and they have to stay where they can make a living." He shrugged his understanding. "Me, I want to be independent, become successful on my own, without having to do what my older brother tells me to do. I like the stores and activity here in this neighborhood, they remind me of the town in Lithuania where I was born."

When they reached Ettie and Libby's house on Roberts Street and paused to say goodbye, Libby reminded him, "I hope we'll see you at the dance tomorrow night. Remember, seven-thirty, okay?"

Their mother was waiting when they stepped inside their house. "Who is that young man?" she asked. When she heard his name, she nodded in approval, her expression animated. "Last week Sophie Weiss told me all about her new boarder. She's known Morton's family since the days when she and her husband also had a business in Vandergrift. She bragged to me about his respected family." Her tone became reverent. "He and his four brothers are the sons of a learned and devout rabbi, Mordecai Joshua—the most respected man in their town in Lithuania."

Ettie and Libby looked at one another. "He never told us that," Ettie said, wondering why he had not mentioned it. She did know that she was suddenly intrigued, and listened eagerly as Sarah shared with them all the details that Sophie had told her about the family.

There had been bad luck for the women of the family. The rabbi's first wife had died around the turn of the century after a lingering illness, leaving two sons. Morton's father then married his first wife's niece, who gave birth to a daughter and three sons, looked after a shop while her husband studied and prayed, then died shortly after the birth of her fourth son.

"Such a pity! Morton's older sister—Rachel, her name was—tried to take her mother's place, but she died herself, from consumption, when everyone was cold and hungry near the end of the war," Sarah reported, nodding in empathy as she related that last. She continued talking, trying to remember what Sophie had told her, explaining that even though the Lithuanian villages did not experience the same terror as the Ukranian shtetls, no one escaped the misery and suffering. "It was bad for all Jews," she repeated, shaking her head.

"The oldest brother, Isaac, made a big success," Sarah said, clearly impressed with the details she was repeating. "First he was a peddler, selling dry goods. But he worked hard and saved, until he could open his own clothing store." She opened her eyes wide in admiration. "He was such a *mensch*, a real person! As soon as he had enough saved, he sent for his father and four half-brothers."

Sarah paused in thought, putting her hand on the side of her head, as if that would help her remember the details of her conversation with Sophie. Then she brightened and resumed her report. "Morton's family arrived in the United States a little earlier than we did," she said. "His brother's store provided a good living, and his brother's wife made a pleasant home for them all." Sarah shook her head slowly, a look of admiration on her face, repeated what fine people they were, and then continued.

When Morton and his family first arrived, his father spent some time as a rabbi in small congregations in towns near Chicago, but he was now an assistant rabbi in Braddock, a community just outside of Pittsburgh. "Morton's youngest brother, Daniel, is still in school," Sarah added. "His other brothers, Sam and Sol, work in Isaac's clothing store."

"Morton worked there too, until recently," Libby said. "He left to try to make his own way."

"Well, Sophie says that Morton is the most learned of all the brothers in the family." Sarah nodded, touching her head. "Sophie said that, when he was a boy, the others in the family had to save food for him, even when they were hungry, to ensure that he had the energy to continue his studies. While his mother was still alive, she would find the time to take him from one town to another so Morton could read those Hebrew books for the different rabbis and discuss the meanings with them. They would tell her that he had a good head on his shoulders and would have a great future." She lowered her voice, as if imparting a secret. "Two years before his bar mitzvah, they sent him to the yeshiva in Vilna—you know, where all the scholars lived. Everyone expected him to be pious like his father." She clasped her hands on her breast as if sharing in the other woman's happiness as she finished, "Morton was his mother's pride and joy."

When Morton's mother died, he was devastated. "Sophie said he got in with the wrong crowd and stopped studying the way he should." He began to participate in youth groups that encouraged settlements in Palestine and prepared documents that criticized the religious scholars in nearby towns for not doing enough to help their people have a better life. They pinned a list of complaints to the wall of the synagogue in their town, a terrible embarrassment to Morton's father, but Sophie was convinced that Morton's only motivation was to try to help the Jewish people.

Sarah repeated what Morton had told Sophie about his boyhood dream, to be a pioneer in Palestine and help revive the Holy Land. But his family didn't want him to go alone into such a dangerous life. When Isaac sent tickets for the family to come to America, his father would not exchange Morton's ticket for another destination. So Morton came to America.

"Sophie is convinced that he not only has a good head and a kind heart, but that someday he will make a real contribution to help the Jewish people," Sarah finished breathlessly, looking from Ettie to Libby. Ettie returned her smile.

* * *

Ettie was not surprised to see Morton at the dance the next night, looking very uncomfortable as he leaned against the wall near the entrance. *That must be his favorite spot,* Ettie thought—*leaning near a doorway, ready for a fast getaway.* He was as out of place as he so obviously felt, much older than Ettie and the other teenagers. Libby motioned for him to come in and join their group, but he just waved and continued his leaning and observing.

Ettie and Libby danced with the boys they knew, the same ones who attended all the dances and parties. They tried all the new jazzy steps, one in particular called "black bottom," during which they kicked up their feet, slapped their hips, and shimmied.

When the music stopped after the last dance, Ettie looked up to find Morton suddenly standing between her and Libby, asking to walk them home.

"It's not necessary," Libby told him airily "We don't need an escort, we're here with our friends . . . but you can walk with us if you want."

Several others started to walk with them, dropping out as they reached their houses, closer to the settlement house than that of the Burin girls. Eventually only Ettie, Libby, and Morton were left.

As they approached their front porch, Morton reached for Libby and leaned forward, trying to kiss her. Libby swung her arm around and slapped him across his face, yelling, "Hey, you—look but don't touch!"

He laughed, rubbing his cheek. "You can't blame a guy for trying, can you?"

"We can be friends," Libby told him haughtily, "but only if you don't get fresh."

Morton stayed away until Sunday the following week. Libby had gone to the movies with her friends, and Ettie was sweeping their front porch when she noticed Morton walking very fast from the direction of his house. He seemed to be deep in thought, and almost walked past her, then swung around and stopped. "Oh, are you alone here?"

She explained that her parents were in the house, but her sister was out. Morton looked relieved. "You're a very pretty girl, you know. What other things do you like to do besides dancing and sweeping porches?"

Ettie felt her cheeks flush, and looked away. "Well, if you must know, I like to read a good story," she said.

Before Morton had a chance to answer, the front door swung open, and Ettie's mother stepped out, smiling. She introduced herself. "Would you like to come in and have a glass of tea?"

A thrill of excitement shivered up Ettie's spine when he accepted. She followed as Sarah led him into the kitchen, where the aroma of the cinnamon buns baking in the oven hung heavy in the air. Her mother smiled warmly as she pointed for Morton to sit down at the table. With a habitual dusting of her hands on her white bib apron, Sarah turned to fetch the tea and glasses. Ettie slipped into one of the chairs across the table from Morton.

Morton asked how they had survived the war as Sarah poured the tea. "And tell me how you escaped," he added.

Sarah seldom spoke to anyone about the suffering they had endured, except when she and Yitzhac were bickering and she was accusing him of neglect. But she opened up to Morton. She spoke Yiddish with a very different accent from Morton, who was a *Litvak,* Lithuanian. Ettie was not always sure what he was saying, but the three of them managed a reasonable conversation.

Morton told them that the League of Nations was trying to ensure that there would be no more wars. He spoke about the problems and possibilities in this new land and admitted that he would rather be with his cousins who were pioneers in Palestine. "I read the *Forward* newspaper in the local library, and as many books on the subject as I can," he explained. "That is how I know these things."

For Ettie it was as if Morton had turned on a light that enabled her to see beyond their little neighborhood. The only other person in her life who seemed to know anything about the world was her Uncle Nachum, but he never talked with her about anything like that. Her father said Nachum was a Trotskyite and dismissed everything he said as foolishness.

Ettie was fascinated by Morton, drawn to his intellect as well as to his dark, lean looks, sad eyes, and air of mystery. He was not like the familiar boys she and Libby hung around with, the boys who danced and joked most of the time. Morton was already a man of twenty-three. *That is the difference,* she decided, *he is mature.* Then she felt a twinge of disappointment. There was no way he would be interested in someone like her, someone so much younger, who couldn't begin to understand the world the way he did.

During the following days, each time Ettie opened her front door, she hoped she might see Morton. She'd look for him as she walked home from school, often making excuses to drop by Tilly's house on the way. She'd offer to go on errands in the hope that she would see him walking up the street. She'd stare at any man walking her way, thinking before he came close enough to be sure, that maybe he was Morton. But then she'd realize that that one was too fat, that one too tall.

Finally her mother mentioned that Sophie Weiss had stopped by for tea and had told her how easy it was now to look after her house, because her boarder Morton was away, selling his goods from town to town. He was sleeping in his brother's home in Vandergrift whenever possible and would not return for a few weeks.

Ettie and Libby continued to go to the dances at the IKS. Each time Ettie danced to the popular jazz tunes, she imagined being loved by a mysterious stranger, and it was as if she were hearing the music differently. She abandoned herself to the exciting rhythm of the Charleston, her friends stepping back to watch her shimmy and shake.

She wondered what it would be like to dance with Morton—until she remembered him telling her that he couldn't dance. *I could convince him to try,* she thought.

When Morton finally returned from his sales trip, Ettie glimpsed him through her window, looking exhausted and disheveled as he walked toward the drugstore. *Probably to buy some cigarettes,* she decided.

After a few days of silence, he suddenly appeared at their front door and asked her if she'd join him for a walk. He shared his frustration about trying to make a living by moving from town to town, sleeping in uncomfortable rooms, eating whatever was available wherever he was boarding, and having to return to his brother's home so often. "My brother's wife is a wonderful cook and homemaker," he clarified, "so that makes it bearable. And my brother is a good businessman, but he wants to have his own way in everything." Morton sighed. "He won't listen to anybody's ideas." He paused, then added that he longed for a home and family of his own.

For the next few months the pattern was the same. As summer approached, the stifling air inside the houses forced families out onto their small front porches, hoping to be cooled by a fresh breeze as they relaxed and watched what their neighbors were doing. Since the local drugstore was a block away from Ettie's home, friends and neighbors walking there often stopped to chat. Whenever Morton was in Pittsburgh, he timed his trips to the drugstore to coincide with the time he thought Ettie might be on the porch.

Despite the fact that Libby had told him they could be friends, she never got over her annoyance at his attempt to kiss her. The first time she saw him approach, she blurted loud enough for him to hear, "Oh, there he is again; what's he gonna try this time?" Each time she saw him after that, she marked his approach with a sarcastic comment or disapproving look. Ettie tried to stop her by changing the subject, but finally handled it by walking to the other side of the porch and pretending not to hear.

Yitzhac trusted Morton even less than he trusted the younger men he had chased from the house for dancing too close and touching the shoulders of the young girls. He wasn't impressed that Morton came from a good family. He was sure that this man, several years older than his Ettie, was up to no good. When he saw him coming, Yitzhac muttered, "There's that big shot who thinks he's so important."

Only Sarah greeted Morton warmly. She always asked him to come sit a while or to have some tea. But he never accepted the invitation. "I'm taking a walk," he'd reply, then turn to Ettie. "Care to join me, Ettie?"

"Be back before dark," a stern-faced Yitzhac called after them.

Ettie never got bored during the walks. Morton told her about the latest books he was reading or about what was happening in politics. He asked her what she thought about some of his ideas and responded with questions that indicated he was taking her opinions seriously. He told her about his frustrations with his work and his dream to someday become a teacher, even though he knew it was impossible without a formal American education. "My favorite experience was when I was tutoring boys learning Hebrew," he told her, smiling. "There is great joy in helping young people learn."

Morton fascinated Ettie, as he began to open up a larger world for her. He seemed interested in her life too, asking about what she was learning at school and her wish to go to business school. Later, when she knew this dream of hers would not be fulfilled, he was the only person who seemed to understand her disappointment. He put the idea of night school into her head. It was something he had done himself shortly after his arrival in the United States, and he never regretted it. Yet she wondered why he still seemed so sad, and sometimes very hurt or angry, particularly when he felt someone did not respect him.

Despite all the talk and encouragement, it was clear to Ettie that Morton was attracted to her for more than the walks and talks. Sometimes when she was answering his questions, she noticed him staring at her with the same expression she saw on the faces of male movie stars before they took the young heroines into their arms to kiss them. Pretending she didn't notice, Ettie changed the subject, turning focus away from her by asking him questions about the books he was reading.

As her final months of school approached, Ettie asked Morton to sign an autograph book, something all the students got as they finished what for many would be the last formal educational experience of their lives. Morton made it clear what was on his mind by writing, *To Ettie—Curiosity killed the cat.* He did not sign it.

Not long after the book signing, during one of their frequent walks together one early June evening, Morton put his arm around Ettie's waist for the first time. A thrill ran through her, quickly replaced by fear. "You know you're very special to me," he said. "I feel so relaxed when I'm with you. You're different from the other girls I've met."

She knew she had to resist Morton's advances, despite the excitement of feeling special to someone. At eight-thirty, daylight was quickly giving way to gray-orange dusk. They were standing near an unpaved alley, beside a parked truck that belonged to a local store that was already closed for the evening. Ettie looked around to see if anyone was nearby, half hoping to see someone approaching so she could use that as an excuse to push Morton away. But they were alone. "What's so different about me?" she blurted.

Without warning Morton leaned forward and kissed her hard on the mouth. Ettie wasn't sure if she liked it or not, she was so surprised and frightened. Nobody had ever discussed the kind of fluttering feeling she now had. Her mother had only warned her not to let boys touch her or she would be in trouble. "We'd better get back or my father will be in a rage, and out looking for me," she stammered when he drew back.

Morton put his finger over her lips, then cupped her cheek in his hand and looked into her eyes. "You mean a lot to me, you know. I've never felt this way about anyone, and nobody has made me feel this good."

They walked to her home, not touching, not speaking. As they turned the corner onto Roberts Street, they both saw Yitzhac standing on the bottom step of the porch with one hand on his hip, looking down the street. When he saw them coming, he turned and went into the house.

The Postcard

Times were better in the country in 1927 and 1928 than they had been when Ettie's family first arrived. New immigrants still had to work hard to make a living, but it was easier to find jobs. Many families were beginning to live more comfortably, now that their children had more permanent jobs. Ettie's family was not unusual, with Libby working in the candy factory and Ettie now holding a full-time job in the bargain basement of Frank & Seder's Department Store.

Yitzhac still didn't earn enough to make Sarah happy, and he was coughing and wheezing more and more. Somehow he managed to carry the heavy bags of potatoes from the market to the cart, and to ride around the neighborhood shouting for the housewives to come out and buy. He never stopped worrying about keeping his horse healthy, devoting much of his time to its well-being.

Sarah was happy that she no longer had to ask Shmulek to give her food on the promise of payment later. With the contributions of her two daughters and the money Bennie was now earning in his spare time carrying bushels of lemons to the horse-drawn carts, she never had to worry about paying the rent or buying food. They all shared the same sense of optimism that had spread throughout the country, with people buying and spending, feeling things could only get better.

Now that Ettie was contributing almost as much as Libby to the upkeep of the family, she felt less afraid of her father. She was pleased that she could manage to keep a little of the money she earned to buy makeup or even a dress now and then. Her relationship with Morton had clearly reached a new level. Sometimes he even accepted Sarah's invitations to sit with them on the porch, even if the conversation was mundane.

Sarah loved serving Morton whatever pastry she had baked that week. When he told her that her baked goods were the best he'd ever had, she glowed. She asked him about his family, especially his father, and then went on to ask about what was happening in the world and in local politics. She did not understand most of his answers, but she was convinced that he was brilliant and felt honored by his attention. Ettie enjoyed these talks with her mother and Morton, mostly because her mother seemed so happy and proud. And Libby was around less, spending more time with her friends. Yitzhac remained unfriendly, offering a gruff hello before abruptly leaving the room.

Ettie convinced herself that Morton was feeling less moody about his work prospects as he became more successful in selling his goods from town to town. He was able to invite her to go to movies with him occasionally, and he sometimes agreed to join Ettie at parties and picnics with her friends. A few times he brought along two of his brothers, asking Ettie to arrange dates for them with her friends. Ettie could tell that Morton's brothers were not at ease with her or her friends, and were joining in only to please him. They were polite, but reserved.

Then came a big surprise. Morton asked her to join him on a visit to his father. She knew from Sophie how respected his father was and what an honor meeting him would be. She wondered what this meant about her relationship with Morton, and the future. Her mother glowed when Ettie told her what she would be doing the following Sunday, but Ettie couldn't help being a little frightened at the prospect of the meeting.

As Morton drove the old jalopy he used when he went from town to town, he assured Ettie that although his father was devout, he was not old-fashioned. He dressed in a modern way and did not believe, as some rabbis did, that he should impose his way of worship on anybody.

When they entered the apartment, Ettie was surprised at how modest it was. She had been expecting something grand, for a man of such stature. The walls lined with books impressed her immediately, and when Morton introduced his father, she was again surprised, this time by how much older than her parents he seemed. White-haired, with a short, well trimmed beard, he stood very straight and carried himself with an air of confidence. He wore a perfectly pressed black suit.

It soon became clear that he was the gentlest person Ettie had ever met, humble and kind, asking how long the drive had taken, whether they were tired, and if they would like a glass of tea. He spoke Yiddish with the same Litvak accent as Morton, but by now she had grown accustomed to it and was able to communicate.

"What part of Europe does your family come from?" he asked her, then shook his head with a faraway look at the mention of Skvira. Ettie thought she detected just a hint of disapproval in his face, but it soon disappeared.

He directed most of his questions to Ettie, asking how her family managed during the war and nodding sadly when she told him about some of the horrific events they had lived through. "Your mother must be a very strong person, my dear, and your father very honorable, not to forget his family." He smiled kindly.

Near the end of the visit he asked Morton when he would be visiting his brothers next, and Morton simply shrugged and became visibly agitated.

His father gave him a quizzical look. "You shouldn't turn away from family," he said. "You can always count on family to fulfill their responsibilities, my son."

The rabbi stood, told Ettie how pleased he was to meet her, and put his arm on Morton's shoulder. "Look after yourself, son." He turned to Ettie. "I hope you will honor me with a visit again sometime soon."

Morton was so quiet on the drive back to the city, Ettie wondered whether she had done something to offend Morton or his father. When he dropped her off at her home, he told her, "I'll be away for a few days, maybe a little longer." It was two weeks before he dropped by again. They never talked about the visit to his father.

Morton was most comfortable when they took long walks together. He thrilled her by telling her how happy she made him, how pretty she was, and how much he enjoyed talking with her. She did not push away from the kisses, so long as his embrace didn't lead to his hand sliding under her blouse or skirt. Somehow they came to an unspoken understanding about how far he could go.

As much as she enjoyed his attention, Ettie remained concerned by the sadness that seemed always to lurk beneath the surface. He never seemed satisfied with himself. When he spoke of his brothers, it was in a bitter tone. At times when they were alone, enjoying a conversation, he would pause to stare at people walking across the street, then fall into a long silence. When they were in conversations with other people, he might suddenly erupt into fierce anger if someone disputed something he said. She often wondered where he was when he seemed to disappear for days at a time. He always replied that he'd been working.

During those absences, Ettie liked to join Libby and their other friends at the IKS dances. When there were not enough boys around for everyone to dance as couples, groups of girls would get up to try out the latest steps. The boys were all old friends and many were good dancers. They liked to tease and joke around. Ettie laughed a lot when she was with them, but she was beginning to feel that it was frivolous. These friends were considerably younger than Morton, more carefree and, in Ettie's opinion, definitely less intelligent. There was no air of mystery, no promise of a better world. When any of them hinted at the possibility of a romance, Ettie brushed them off with a joke.

One Saturday night in early March, 1929, as Libby and Ettie were approaching a street corner after leaving one of the dances at the settlement house, Morton joined them, out of breath. "I have some news," he said. "I've just returned from a meeting with my brothers this afternoon. Their store is doing very well, and they have a chance to buy a second one in a town near Vandergrift. They want me to help run it with my brother Sam." He hesitated. "I'll be moving to Vandergrift to live near the store."

"So this is the way you say goodbye?" Libby snapped. Ettie gave Libby an irritated glance and a nudge in the side, then looked at Morton. She was puzzled, wondering what this meant for their relationship. Finally she said without much conviction, "If this is what you want, Morton, if you think it is right for you, then I wish you the best."

The three of them walked the rest of the way in silence. When they reached the front porch of the house on Roberts Street, Morton held Ettie back at the bottom of the stairs and whispered in her ear, "Can we talk alone for a minute?"

Libby waved her hand. "Don't worry about me, I can take a hint." She ran up the stairs and went inside.

Morton stared at Ettie for a moment before he said, "This isn't what I want to do with my life, Ettie, you know that. But temporarily, it'll help my family and will give me a much better income. I know it will be harder for us to spend time together, and I'll miss you, believe me. But I'll come in to see you on my days off. As soon as the store is up and running smoothly, I want you to be my wife. I hope you will agree to that. You know I love you."

Ettie's heart lurched, then she began to cry. "I love you too, Morton," she murmured.

They embraced and kissed quickly. "I have to leave tomorrow," he told her, "but I'll try to come back to the city on Sundays, my day off. I hope you'll be home on Sundays."

Ettie agreed, but she was confused about what all of this meant. It was not the kind of proposal she'd always dreamed of—they'd set no date, made no real plans for a wedding. She wasn't even sure if they were actually engaged. Yet she told Morton she loved him, and he said he wanted to marry her. *Is this what love really is?* she wondered.

She ran into the house and found Sarah and Libby whispering at the kitchen table. Sarah looked fearful. "Nu, what happened?" As soon as Ettie explained what she and Morton had discussed, Sarah broke into a huge smile. "What a match that will be, marrying a rabbi's son! Such a good family, a good business, a smart man. Oh, sweet daughter." She rose and embraced Ettie.

Libby joined in, then broke away, saying, "I'm going to go and tell all our friends!"

The happy mood soured when they saw Yitzhac standing in the doorway. He had been listening to their conversation, unnoticed at first, and with no immediate reaction. Before he turned to leave, he shook his finger at Ettie, putting words to her uneasiness. "Such a proposal, it's not right. What kind of man is this? He leaves town and expects you to wait till he's ready to marry you. I don't care how good a family he comes from. Just because his father is a rabbi doesn't change anything—he's not treating you right! I don't like it one bit."

"You're always looking for trouble, never trusting anyone," Sarah shouted after him as he turned to leave. "You should try for once to make your family happy!" When they heard the front door shut behind him, she patted Ettie's cheek. "I pray for your happiness, my daughter."

"Well, I will need more than prayers, Mama, but I do know that Morton is very special, and I am honored that he loves me."

Morton dropped by the following day to say goodbye. Since it was Sunday, he would drive to Vandergrift, eat with his brother's family, and get a good night's rest before meeting with his brothers and their lawyer on Monday to get all the papers signed. "Then we can begin hiring the sales clerks and organizing the clothing displays. I will come to town as soon as I have a free Sunday," he assured Ettie, and they embraced self-consciously, aware that people on the street were staring.

When he walked over to Sarah to say goodbye, she quickly pulled him to her and kissed him on the cheek. Libby was out with her friends, and Yitzhac remained in the house.

Morton did show up, most Sundays. He usually wanted Ettie to go to Schenley Park with him. She would pack some sandwiches for a picnic on the grass, and they would spend the day walking along the paths, talking, and embracing. At first Morton would tell her about his ideas to make the store a success, particularly the marketing techniques he thought would be successful, the kind of displays they should have, the special sales.

"Sam likes the people who live in the town," he said of his younger brother. "He's more interested in getting to know the customers, in trying to build up their loyalty."

By the summer, though, it was clear that Morton and Sam were not working well together. Sam disagreed with Morton's competitive approach, and their older brother, Isaac, agreed with Sam. Morton told Ettie about their arguments, and how little they cared about his feelings. Ettie spent most of their time together consoling Morton, trying to help him find ways to try out his ideas without upsetting his younger brother. By the time he had to return to Vandergrift, he would seem more content.

"You mean so much to me," he told her. "You help me see things more clearly. I love you."

But there was no talk of setting a wedding date, and Ettie would not bring it up for fear that any pressure from her would cause Morton to become totally distraught. Each time she returned home from one of their outings, she had to disappoint her mother and sister when they asked if they could begin the wedding preparations.

Then three weeks went by with no word from Morton. Ettie wondered if something had happened to him, but she was too proud to tell anyone outside of her family that she had heard nothing. One day when she returned home from work, she saw a postcard sitting on the table in the hall. She picked it up, looked at the picture of a huge ship on the front, with a flag on its bow and smoke billowing from its stacks, then flipped it over. It was addressed to her, with a one cent stamp affixed to it postdated *Sep 27.29.* Then she read the pencilled note, which first startled, then shocked her:

> *Dear Ettie,*
> *We sail on this boat at 12 o'clock today. I want to say goodbye to you and the States. Take care of yourself and don't forget to write often. Mail can reach me at the address below. Morton Burin, F.A. Haw. , c/o commanding officer, Fort McDowell, Cal.*

It took a few minutes for the reality to sink in: Morton had joined the army.

Meant To Be

As Ettie stopped talking, she saw her children glance at each other, unsure what to say. They'd all seen that postcard in the box of photographs they had enjoyed ruffling through as they were growing up. It seemed out of place, but it was the only thing they had with their father's writing on it. *Now they know the story behind that,* she thought.

Ettie stared into space, into the past. "What a jerk I was, such a silly jerk. That was it—no forewarning, no explanation, no goodbye, nothing. Just a postcard and an address. I should've realized there was no future with him—the end."

Collette rose and sat down next to her. "It must have been a big shock for you, Mother," she said gently as she slipped her arms around Ettie's shoulders. "How did you handle it?"

Ettie threw up her hands. "He broke my heart, that's what he did! I couldn't eat, I couldn't sleep, and I didn't want to see anybody. It's a good thing I had a job I was good at, and that nobody I worked with cared about what Morton did to me. It allowed me to get away from my mother's sad stares, my sister's sarcastic remarks about Morton, and my father's 'I told you so's.' I didn't go to any dances for more than a month. I just sat around, listening to those sad songs all the time . . . " She began to sing:

There'll come a time—don't you forget it
There'll come a time—when you're gonna regret it
Someday when you get lonely
Your heart will break like mine—you'll want me only.

Ettie tilted her head to the side. "I can't believe I still remember so many of the words. And that other one, too—'It Had to Be You,'" she sneered.

After a long silence she released a self-deprecating laugh. "It had to be him, all right. A few weeks later I got a letter from him, begging me to write, telling me how lonely he was, asking me for a nice picture so he could show me off to the other guys and let them see what a beauty his girlfriend was. I went and had that picture taken—the one you always look at, where I'm standing with one hand on my hip, looking to the side, imitating a movie star. I guess I thought I was hot stuff. Such a beauty! Your father loved it."

"What was going on with your family in those days?" Rachel asked. "It must have been very hard for them, right after the stock market collapsed. How did you manage?"

"We were lucky," Ettie replied, feeling her shoulders relax as the subject shifted to something less emotional. "We couldn't afford new clothes very often, or movies, but we had enough to eat." She spoke about many of the men in their neighborhood who didn't have a place to sleep or food to eat. "If they came to the door when my mother was home, she tried to give them a bowl of soup or a slice of challah if she had any extra. People slept in the spare beds and paid her a dollar or two a week. There were always strangers in the house."

Ettie paused and pursed her lips in thought. "I wonder if maybe the Depression was easier at first for poor families who never had much to lose to begin with, families with no savings and no investments." She sighed, letting out a long, deep breath. "After all, we had been through war, disease, and near-starvation, had all suffered so much during our escape from the old country, that we knew we would find a way to survive through these hard times too. One thing I know for sure, we didn't have to worry about soldiers arriving on horseback to steal, slash, and kill.

"Libby and I both kept our jobs, and we were both good at what we did. To tell the truth, your Aunt Libby was amazing. She could wrap the candy faster than the other girls, despite the cold rooms and the pain in her fingers. Her boss explained that he could no longer pay her as much as she had been earning, and sometimes he didn't have enough to pay even those lower wages. Libby always worried when she saw him carrying a bag on payday—she knew he would be giving her candy because he didn't have enough money to pay her the full wages—but at least he never laid her off."

Ettie began to smile. "I was a real go-getter, selling clothes in Frank & Seder's bargain basement. My wages were peanuts, but the few cents commission I got for my sales could add up by the end of the week. Looking back . . . " she shook her head in wonder, "I don't know how I did it—taking care of several people at once, convincing them to go into a dressing room and then finding things for each of them to try on. I never forgot which dressing room each person was in, and I never allowed anyone else to ring up the sales for my customers. Some of the other girls who worked there called me The Grabber because I took on so many customers at once, but it didn't bother me—it wasn't a popularity contest, and I needed the money." She lowered her voice, as if the customers were in the house and might overhear her admit the tricks she used to make a sale. "You had to know when to compliment the customers about how good those $1.95 cotton housedresses looked on them. And I'll tell you what else, I was very fast getting the merchandise to the counter and writing up the sales so they wouldn't leave; I had to make sure that nobody else took my customer."

Ettie smiled her satisfaction, enjoying this memory. "They never found mistakes in my book at the end of the shift. And I was always ready to work overtime if they needed me, just to get the extra commission."

Smiling himself, David jumped to his feet and walked over to peer into his mother's face. "Wait a minute," he teased, "I thought you were sad that you had to leave school, but now you're telling us how much you enjoyed being good in the business world. How can that be?"

Ettie gently pushed him away, saying, "Oh, go on. What else could I do? You have to make the best of things. School wasn't meant to be. If I could make my family happy by bringing money home, then I wouldn't give them anything to complain about. But no matter how hard I worked, I never earned as much as Libby. So she was always the boss at home."

"What about Uncle Bennie, what was he doing all of this time?" Collette wondered.

"Oh, they wanted to send him to a trade school to be an electrician or something. Who knows what they were expecting from him, but he didn't even know how to screw in a lightbulb. Still, he was a boy, so I guess they figured he needed a trade. He wasn't the least bit interested, and it didn't last long. He was happy to leave school and get work as an assistant to my father's friend, some guy who had a horse and cart, selling lemons in the same neighborhood. Bennie was never tall, but he was strong as an ox, and it wasn't too hard for him to carry the heavy bushels of fruit from the warehouse to the cart, and he enjoyed helping the family too. His boss was a go-getter, always filling up with enough produce to cover twice the territory as my father did with his potatoes. Everybody liked Bennie; he was easygoing, never got into arguments with anyone."

Removing her glasses to clean them with a tissue, Ettie rubbed her eyes, before continuing. "To tell the truth, I think Bennie liked the atmosphere at the market down on the Strip, liked getting there at six in the morning every day and seeing people he knew. Do you have any idea what it was like at the market back in those days?" She smiled, seeing it all again in her mind's eye. "I remember going a few times. You could see all the guys scrambling, competing to see who could get their carts loaded faster, all of them calling out to each other. Lots of commotion." She nodded.

"That wasn't all Bennie liked. He enjoyed meeting the housewives who came to the cart to buy the fruit. They knew his name, and he was very helpful. He was good-looking, too. Some of them would pat his head or pinch his cheek, telling him what a nice husband he would make for some lucky girl." Ettie leaned forward and dropped her voice as though imparting a secret. "But you know what Bennie liked best? He couldn't wait to finish work so he could go to the ball field and play baseball. He was a good player too."

Rachel smiled. "I remember seeing Uncle Bennie playing baseball at the family picnics. He was always better than all the younger guys, and he seemed to be having fun, just like a kid."

Ettie nodded, then looked around at her family. Sometimes she couldn't believe how well they'd all turned out. She'd worried constantly about their futures, especially about David growing up without a father. Who would have imagined that two of her kids would have Ph.D.'s? She looked at David, so handsome and intelligent, a successful professor with many publications to his name, and a nice family.

There had been different fears with Rachel. She was such a sickly kid. But look at her now, with a successful career, in charge of other people in a government department, financially independent. Some bad luck in her personal life, but she has two terrific kids, and now a new man in her life, who seems to be treating her well.

Of course, Collette was the one who led the way for everyone, getting all those honors in high school and at Pitt, the first in the family to get a college degree, then a successful teaching career. Ettie was grateful that Collette had an attentive and caring husband in Stanley, and two wonderful children. And considering her health problems, her courage is amazing. She yawned.

Stanley was watching her. "It might be smart for all of us to get some extra rest," he suggested, looking around so the comment didn't seem directed at her alone. "Try to get a good night's sleep, Mum," he whispered in her ear when he walked them to the car.

She laughed. "Ha, that'll be the day!"

* * *

Sitting alone in her apartment later that evening, Ettie thought about how different her life could have been. What if they hadn't had to leave the shtetl and she had married Ephriam, the son of her father's friend? *I guess I should stop thinking about that,* she reminded herself. *We would've all been killed when the Nazis marched through; we'd be dead and buried.*

There were others she might have married. Some of the guys liked her a lot, even after she met Morton. *Natie Gordon was one, and a good guy, but I wasn't attracted to him. What was it I found so attractive about Morton? Was it his dark good looks, his intelligence, his worldliness? Or was it how proud my mother was about his family's status, about his father being a rabbi?* Ettie shook her head. Could she really have been so naïve, to think that through him she could bring happiness to her mother?

Even though Ettie thought that a lot of her mother's beliefs were *bubbe maisses*, old wives' tales, she couldn't help believing that she had been given the evil eye when she was born and that certain things were *beshert,* fated. Yet if that were truly so, she would have to stop blaming Morton for bringing her pain.

She continued to berate herself, angry that she hadn't had the good sense that Libby did, to resist his advances. *Why didn't I listen to that fortune-teller we all went to before Morton returned from the army?* The woman had told Ettie that someone was traveling over water to see her and that she should never marry him. It frightened her at the time, but she soon convinced herself it was all hocus-pocus.

As she thought of that, her mind drifted back to the winter of 1930.

* * *

The shock of Morton's army enlistment had become a dull, empty feeling in the pit of her stomach, most noticeable when she awoke each morning and suddenly realized she had nothing to look forward to. She received a letter from him once or twice a week, in which he described the beauty of Hawaii, explained the army routine, talked about some of the other men, and usually closed by mentioning that he missed her and hoped she was well. The letters brought to life what he was experiencing, but they were a far cry from love letters, and they left Ettie feeling more alone after the reading.

She responded in a similarly newsy manner, unable to resist mentioning friends who had become engaged and news about her family, hoping he would realize how much he had walked away from even though in her heart she was convinced that he was not the least bit interested. She filled one letter with news of the arrival of her cousin Jake from Saskatchewan, the rebellious son of her mother's sister. Unhappy with the poverty of life on the Canadian prairies, he had come to Pittsburgh to see the relatives he had met only once before. She commented about his good looks and friendly personality, about how Libby was introducing him to all her friends and showing him around town, and how she had laughed when he opened his suitcase and she saw only a few items of clothing and a pair of ice skates.

Morton responded that he was glad Libby, and not Ettie, was spending time with Jake, adding, *I hope you plan to wait for me.* Ettie was pleased at the hint of jealousy. The most romantic parts of Morton's letters were the lines telling her how he enjoyed looking at her photograph and that the other men kept asking him how he'd managed to get such a beauty as his girlfriend.

Ettie rarely smiled anymore, and her mother became worried about her despondency. She convinced Libby to try to get Ettie to the dances.

Ettie agreed only after Libby and Jake told her they wouldn't go without her.

When Ettie walked into the IKS dance, she imagined the eyes of her friends staring at her with pity. She shook off the feeling and joined in dancing the Charleston, but the music did not bring her the same exhilaration it had just a few months before. She looked around and realized that she was totally out of tune with the other people there. *The boys seem sillier than before,* she thought in dismay.

Then Natie Gordon approached her. "Why was Morton stupid enough to go off and leave you here?" he asked in a loud voice. "I wouldn't ever do that to you if you were my girlfriend."

She tipped up her chin. "There's plenty of fish in the ocean," she agreed, "who needs him!"

Natie smiled, grabbed her arm, and they began dancing. She danced with every boy who asked her that night. When she got home, she felt like crying. *I won't go again,* she decided.

Shortly afterward, Ettie decided to give night school another try. She had completed two courses after her graduation from the eighth grade—mathematics, in which she'd done well, and typing, in which she struggled. Maybe this was the time to try again to get a high school diploma, and not worry about excelling at typing. Her family tried to talk her out of it, using the same arguments they had used before: education was a waste of time for girls, she might get exhausted and not be able to work and contribute to the family's welfare, she still needed to find somebody to marry. In a rare show of determination, she told them her mind was made up and registered for English and Mathematics.

At first she felt like a misfit, returning to school after being away for two years. The lockers in the hallways, the strange smells, the blackboards and chalk, the ringing bells—all took her back to a time when she was less independent. She didn't know many of the other students, and feared being exposed if she made mistakes. The worst part was how exhausted she was after being on her feet all day as a sales clerk. But the teachers were more pleasant than she'd expected, more encouraging, and she got all of her assignments in on time and received high marks on her tests. She felt shy and uncomfortable when the teacher asked her questions, but she managed to give the correct answer most of the time.

After the first few weeks she met Harry. He had recently moved to Pittsburgh from Cleveland, but had been brought up in Toronto, Canada. He was a serious young man three years her senior, anxious to get his high school diploma so he could attend college to become a journalist. Ettie noticed him one day as she was walking to school, and then again as they both left. They headed in the same direction but did not speak until their next meeting. He began smiling at her while commenting, "We obviously both share the same evening activity." When they discovered that Harry was boarding in a house a few blocks away from her home, they began to walk together to class each evening, and after classes ended, Harry usually waited for Ettie at the front door of the high school.

Harry was tall and muscular, good-looking, well-mannered, and reserved. He had a positive outlook on his future and was optimistic about becoming a journalist. "I'd love to write books someday," he confessed.

Ettie told him about her family, her job, and her boyfriend in the army. He asked questions about her experiences escaping from the shtetl and what it was like when her family first arrived in Pittsburgh. She was flattered at how intently he listened. "Someday I'll write about the brave people who suffered so much to come to America, to take part in the new exodus," he told her. "I'll write about all of their contributions to this new land."

He often asked her about Morton, what she'd heard from him, how he was managing. He was particularly interested in the experiences Morton must be having. Years later, when Ettie read the book *From Here to Eternity*, about the hodgepodge of men who had volunteered for the army and were based in the same Schoefield Barracks in Hawaii as Morton was, she thought of Harry and wished he had been the one to write about it.

"My family still lives in Kensington Market—that's the Jewish area of Toronto," he added. "It's not very different from life here in the Hill District. I'm hoping my brothers and sisters will be able to join me here someday. There are more opportunities for Jewish people with an education to get a good job here, in America."

"I met a girl," Harry told Ettie on one of their walks to school. "I like her a lot. She's the second generation of her family to call Pittsburgh home. She's educated and sophisticated." A while later he confessed to Ettie, "I think I'm falling in love with her."

Her family discouraged the relationship, however, and took her to Miami Beach for several weeks. Later he told Ettie how heartbroken he was: "She's engaged to someone else, a lawyer."

Ettie listened and sympathized, sharing some of her own feelings of abandonment. She couldn't help feeling a pang of disappointment that Harry did not feel the same way about her as he did about the girl who broke his heart.

Her anticipation of the walks and conversations with Harry helped Ettie to forget how exhausted she was after standing on her feet all day in the bargain basement. Their conversations ranged from what was happening in their private lives to the problems everybody faced as they tried to make a living, and what their teachers were covering in the night school classes.

The term ended in early June. Ettie saw Harry once in a while during the summer when he walked past the house on Roberts Street. He usually stopped to talk for a few minutes, and once he invited her to join him for a lecture he was attending at the local library. He seemed to know most of the people in attendance and socialized easily, always smiling and offering encouragement. He wasn't silly and brash like the boys in her neighborhood, and he wasn't moody like Morton had been. Ettie often thought about how pleasant life would be, if she were married to Harry.

The contrast with Morton became more disturbing as the tone of his letters became increasingly troubled. The army was not offering the escape from life's pressures he had hoped to find. The other men constantly insulted him for being small in stature, and they made fun of what remained of his accent, calling him kike and yid and dirty Jew. Invariably he would end up in fistfights with them, and now his nose was broken. He sent her a photograph of himself standing in a garden in front of the hospital where he was recuperating after his nose had been re-set. A few other men stood nearby and a pretty nurse was in the background. Ettie wondered about the pretty nurse. She had heard that women were different in Hawaii. She couldn't help imagining how he must be carrying on.

Finally, close to a year after Morton left for the army, he sent Ettie a letter explaining that army life was intolerable and he had to get out. At that time, the army's policy permitted men to buy their way out before the end of their term of enlistment. He still needed one hundred dollars. He had cousins in New York who had promised him sixty-five, and he pleaded with her to help him get the remaining thirty-five. He explained how much he was suffering and how his life depended on her. When Ettie shared the letter with her mother, Sarah went to the shoebox she kept in her closet, pulled out thirty dollars, and handed it to Ettie. It was all she had.

Before Ettie could obtain a money order to mail it to Morton, his brothers Isaac and Sam appeared at the front door of her house one Sunday afternoon.

"Can we go somewhere, take a walk, and have a private conversation?" Isaac asked her.

"Yes, yes, of course," she agreed, once she'd recovered from her initial shock.

They walked half a block in silence before Isaac began. "We expect Morton will be writing to ask you for money for his buyout from the army," he said, watching her. When Ettie nodded, he continued. "He asked us for the money first, but we decided it was not a good idea." He paused. "We don't think it's a good idea for you to send money, either."

"Please understand how difficult it is to ask you not to send him the money," Sam pleaded when she turned wide eyes on them. "Believe us when we tell you that if we thought it would help him, we would send it. But he has to learn a lesson—it's really important that he finish something he starts. It will be bad for him to take the easy way out of this."

"But he sounded so distraught in the letter he sent me," Ettie protested. "It worries me. I think it would be cruel to make him stay." What she didn't tell them was that she thought they didn't want her to send him the money because they didn't want him to come back and marry her. She finally agreed to think about their request, and they parted in front of her house.

She discussed it with her mother, who told her it would be a shame to make a man stay where he was obviously being mistreated. The next day Ettie added an additional five dollars that she'd been saving for a new dress to what her mother had given her, purchased a money order at the post office, and sent it to Morton. She wondered when he would arrive home, and if this meant they would get married after all.

She had finished two more courses at night school. The new fall term had just begun, and the assignments seemed much more difficult. Fearing that she might not be able to keep up with the others in the class, she confided her concern to Harry.

"You'll do fine," he assured her. "You've handled the course work so far, haven't you?"

"Yes, but the homework takes longer, and the assignments are more difficult than last term's."

"You'll handle it," he assured her again, then peered at her face. "Really! Or is something else bothering you?"

Ettie didn't answer immediately. But Harry's reassurance concerning the school assignments *had* released some of the tension she seemed to always feel in her shoulders. "Well . . ." she finally admitted, "I am wondering what will happen when Morton returns."

"Hard to know," Harry replied. "But I think helping him was the right thing to do. It sounds as though he's in an impossible situation. And," he added, "would he ask for help from someone he didn't feel close to and trust?"

Ettie nodded, but this time the tightness in her shoulders didn't ease. She could only hope Harry was right.

In mid-October, 1930, nearly two months after she'd sent Morton the money, Ettie stepped out onto the front porch. The sky was a clear, bright blue and cloudless, and the air held just the slightest hint of crispness. This was always the saddest time of year for Ettie. The leaves were already fading after their glorious color, and bright and mild days would soon give way to darkness and the burden of heavy coats, boots, gloves, hats, and scarves.

She took a few deep breaths and swung her gaze absently along the street, then stopped, focusing on a familiar-looking figure approaching from up the street. Ettie squinted. It was a man, and he was hurrying, but she couldn't recognize him at first. There was a hitch in his step, and he walked slightly stooped. Then, as he came closer, she recognized him—Morton. *He's so thin, and he looks so much older,* she thought.

He began to wave, and as she ran down the steps to meet him on the sidewalk, his face broke into a broad smile, and he looked younger again. They embraced, not worrying about the neighbors who might see. "Thank you," he whispered in Ettie's ear. "You're my lifesaver."

Sarah had emerged from the house and stood at the top of the steps, smiling and waving. Yitzhac stepped out behind her and actually said hello as he shook Morton's hand. Bennie burst through the door last, then stopped and saluted. Ettie smiled, glad that Libby was out for the afternoon with their cousin Jake. Those were the best moments of Morton's homecoming.

"I can't stay," he said when Sarah invited him inside. "I've taken a room back with Sophie Weiss's family, and I have to get settled." He turned to Ettie. "I'll be in touch as soon as I find work." He didn't ask Ettie anything about herself. Even though she had written to him about night school, thinking he would be encouraging and proud, he never said a word about it. Instead he stepped back to look her up and down. "You're so grown up, a woman now." Then he leaned close and repeated, "You're my lifesaver."

Ettie's heart sank as she watched him limping briskly away.

Morton returned to the peddling job he'd had when she first met him, driving from town to town, selling goods to shopkeepers that they would try to sell in their stores. "I went to see my brothers," he told Ettie the first time he visited. "I wanted to seek their forgiveness for running off the way I did. We all agreed that it would not work out for me to return to the store. Sam's managing it very well, and the people in the town respect him." He shrugged. "There isn't enough business to require a co-manager. If I need any help, I should let them know. I'd much rather manage on my own. Besides, they never really like having me around."

Ettie had every intention of continuing with night school, but she soon found that she didn't have adequate time to concentrate on her assignments and also join Morton for walks when he showed up and expected her to be available. Her marks began to slip, and she was not always able to answer when the teacher directed a question to her.

One evening Morton dropped by just as she was preparing to leave for that evening's class. She saw Harry heading her way as she stood on the sidewalk talking to Morton. When Harry reached them, he stopped and nodded politely to Morton. "Hello," he said. "You must be Morton—Ettie's told me a lot about you. I'm Harry, I take night classes with Ettie."

Morton muttered a response, staring angrily at Ettie. "I can see I'm in the way here," he told her, as he turned and stalked away.

She looked at Harry in stunned silence. As they walked down the street and turned the corner, she began to cry. "I'm sorry," she said, "I've been so frustrated and tense and disappointed—I have to let some of it out." Harry handed her his handkerchief, and she took it with a grateful nod and wiped her eyes. "I know Morton needs my help, and he means a lot to me, but ever since he returned from the army, he hasn't been the same man. He's moodier and doesn't seem interested in what's happening around him."

Harry put an arm around her waist and guided her into an alcove formed by the inset entrance of a locked store. He drew her closer, one hand on her shoulder, and patted her back. She rested her head on his chest. "Morton's obviously been through a very difficult experience," he said. "You're showing strength of character by being so understanding." He drew back to look at her with so much understanding and respect, she reached up and hugged him.

"You're the kindest man I know," she said, suddenly wanting him to take her in his arms and tell her he loved her. *Tell me to break off with Morton,* she thought. *Tell me I should tell him that the relationship can't work. Let me tell him that I love another.*

Harry did not push her away. He kept her in a loose embrace, but said nothing until Ettie stepped back.

Ettie often thought about that moment, wishing her fantasy had become reality. As the years passed, she accepted that it had been *beshert,* her fate, that she would marry Morton. That didn't stop her from wondering why she had not heeded the warning signs and the gut feeling that Morton would not make her happy. *Was it really because it meant so much for her to please her mother by marrying the son of a rabbi? Was that truly why she went ahead, despite her misgivings that it would not be right? Or was there some other feeling inside of her? Might it have been because she felt that Morton needed her and she believed she could help him, that she could make a difference?* Her father had told her over and over to leave Morton, that he would only cause her heartache. But in the spring of 1931 she agreed to marry him, and they set a date for August.

Harry later married a young woman who was not an immigrant and whose family was well educated. Ettie realized how unrealistic her fantasy had been, but she still thought about what a different life she might have had.

Two Families

Morton was barely earning enough to pay for his expenses, but Ettie assured him that she would continue to work, and they could save money by sleeping in the third-floor room her mother now used for boarders. Sarah, thrilled with the idea of her daughter marrying into such a family, was eager to find ways to help the new couple. Of course Ettie could not continue with night school. She dropped out immediately, without completing any of the second term courses she had started. She did not discuss it with Morton, and he never questioned her about it.

Two months before the wedding was to take place, Libby began planning Ettie's bridal shower. Libby would be the maid of honor, and among their friends, the maid of honor always arranged a shower for the bride. They would invite all of their friends and relatives, who by tradition would bring their wedding gifts to show them off at the party.

When Morton heard about it, he was furious. "This is unheard-of in my family!" he exclaimed. "It's like begging for gifts, crude and embarrassing."

They argued bitterly about whose family traditions they should follow and ended by calling off the wedding. Morton left town, returning to his brother's home in Vandergrift.

It all happened so fast, Ettie was in a state of shock. She was embarrassed, afraid to tell anyone—until she realized that she had to confide in Libby, to stop her from continuing with plans for the shower. The next day she asked Libby to walk outside with her, but they were halfway to the corner before Libby finally blurted, "So why are we here? What is it?"

Ettie studied the sidewalk. "The wedding is off," she finally said.

"Oh no!" Libby gasped. "How could he do this to us? Who does

Morton think he is, disgracing us this way?" Then she dropped her voice and warned, "Everyone is going to talk about you being jilted again by the same man. Our family won't be able to hold their heads up! Does he think his family is too good for us, after all we've done for him?" Libby crossed her arms.

After Ettie explained what the disagreement was about, Libby continued. "And who will repay the thirty dollars Mama sent Morton?" she demanded. "All the money she had, to help him get out of the army. And I've already paid money for the hall above the Roosevelt Theater for the shower, already sent out the invitations." She waved her hand at Ettie. "You'd better do something about it fast, or the whole family will suffer badly from such a humiliation." She turned away, saying, "I'm going with Jake to the movies tonight, but you'd better get this straightened out soon."

Ettie cried all night.

The next day she wrote Morton a long letter, apologizing and pleading with him to return so they could try to work something out, saying they could forego the bridal shower if only he returned, and adding how much she loved him. He was back as soon as he received the letter. They agreed to cancel the shower, but since the room was already paid for, they would have their wedding on the day originally scheduled for the shower. It was just a few weeks off, June 28, 1931. People would be told that they were coming to the wedding instead of a shower.

When they signed the *ketubah,* the marriage contract, before the ceremony, Morton asked Ettie why she was crying. "Because I'm so happy," she lied.

Morton was standing under the *chupah,* the wedding canopy, when she entered the room with her mother and father on each side of her. He looked very handsome, his unruly black hair tumbling over his forehead despite all efforts with a comb. His deep-set eyes focused only on her, and his angular face broke into a wide smile. His brothers stood to his side, well dressed, visibly ill at ease, and unsmiling. His father, who would be officiating at the traditional ceremony, stood in the center. Libby and Bennie were on the other side of the chupah, smiling and nodding, seemingly unconcerned about the seriousness of the event.

Ettie wore a soft blue chiffon dress she'd bought at a sale in the bargain basement where she worked; there was not enough money or time for her to buy a wedding gown. There were no photographs. The refreshments consisted of tuna fish sandwiches, potato salad, and a cake Sarah baked for the reception. It was all they could afford. In fact, they had to get the tuna fish from Shmulek's store, promising to pay him for it as soon as they could save some money.

A few friends, including Natie Gordon, brought their instruments and provided music for the dancing. Morton actually tried to join in for one dance, though he did not know the steps. He stomped on Ettie's feet more than once, and thereafter remained on the sidelines, watching, for the rest of the evening. Ettie danced with almost everyone, whirling through the kazutski and other old-world dances, the Charleston and fox trot. She let the music dull her fear that she had made a terrible mistake. She danced with Uncle Shmulek, with Bennie, with her cousin Jake, with the women as well as the men. She kicked up her feet, shook her hips, waved her arms, all in complete syncopation with the music. She gave the appearance of being deliriously happy.

Morton's brothers and Isaac's wife remained on the sidelines, talking with each other, with Sophie Weiss and her husband, and with the few friends they had invited. They did not mingle with anyone from Ettie's family, other than responding with the proper handshakes and a few words with Bennie and Jake.

They prepared to leave well before the celebration was over, each shaking Ettie's hand, giving her a peck on the cheek, and telling her how glad they were that Morton had found someone he could feel comfortable with, someone he could trust. Morton's father smiled at her and said, "May you both be blessed with a full and happy life."

"We know you'll be good for him," they said, and she wondered if they meant it. *Or are they disappointed that Morton didn't marry someone from a more distinguished family?*

There was no honeymoon. They simply returned to the third-floor room at the house on Roberts Street. "It's important for you to do your duty for your husband," Sarah had told her, trying to prepare Ettie for the wedding night. "You give him your body for his pleasure."

Ettie was nervous, but not afraid. She had read stories about how romantic it was when a man loved a woman and they became one.

She had once enjoyed Morton's kisses and embraces, before he went into the army . . . and she remembered how she had felt when she was hoping Harry would return her embrace. So she was looking forward to being thrilled by Morton's closeness, and his touch. All of these longings were dashed as soon as Morton got into bed with her.

He immediately pulled her close. "I'm so glad you're now mine," he told her, before he lunged in to kiss her closed mouth, so quickly and so hard that her teeth were jammed against her lips. She wondered if they'd drawn blood.

Without warning he lifted her nightgown up to her waist, rolled on top of her, and tried to thrust his penis into her vagina. Ettie cried out at the burning pain, trying to push him away. "Please, you're hurting me!"

He ignored her pleas. "Relax and enjoy it," he told her. "This is what married people do."

The intense pain lasted for only a short time before he relaxed and pulled away. He rolled onto his side and fell asleep, and Ettie stared at the dark ceiling, wondering miserably what had just happened.

The next morning he had to leave on one of his selling trips. She heard him go, but pretended to be asleep until after he left the room. Then she rose, pulled the bloodstained sheets off the bed and washed them in the bathtub, then hung them on a chair to dry while she went downstairs to eat breakfast and go to work.

* * *

Through the years, when her daughters asked why she didn't have any photos of her wedding, Ettie told them that they'd been too poor. She made up stories about happy weddings and told her girls that she and Morton had a special song—"Always." But now, reliving the memories of the true events of her wedding upset Ettie, and she went home to another restless night.

She felt drained when she awoke on Saturday morning. *Maybe I should call David and tell him that I want to stay in my apartment for the day*, she thought. *Shiva won't begin until after sundown. But . . . what will the neighbors think, if they find out I was home by myself while my children were in town?*

She rose with a sigh, showered, dressed in black slacks and a black and white pullover, and combed her hair. She could not escape the past. *How did I get through all those years?*

When David and Rachel arrived to pick her up for the drive to Collette's, she embraced them, sighed deeply, and told them she needed more time to get ready.

"What's the matter, Mother?" Rachel asked in alarm. "Is this all getting you down?"

Ettie was grateful for the concern. "I did all I could for your father, you know; I tried to be the best wife I could, but it didn't help. Nothing helped. Nobody knows how hard it was. I thought it was all over and done with, that's all. But this week, I'm reliving it."

David shrugged. "You know, we're all uncomfortable, but we're doing this for Collette. It means so much to her, it's the least we can all do."

"Yeah, I know," Ettie sighed. "She loved that father of hers, no matter what happened."

She was saddened to see Collette's pale, puffy face and the dark circles under her eyes when they arrived at her house. *Has she been crying,* Ettie wondered, *or is it her illness making her look this way?* A tray containing eggs, cream cheese, herring, gefilte fish and lox, various cheeses, and fruit had been put out on the table for lunch, along with a basket of bagels and a plate of cookies. Ettie concentrated on the food, so her daughter wouldn't be upset by the concern on her face.

Rachel, beside her, nudged Ettie's elbow. "Hey Mum, remember when you used to go to Pechersky's on Mellon Street every Sunday morning and get all this stuff for us as a treat? I loved those rolls you bought there, and my favorite cookies. We'd sit around and talk and laugh while we ate them."

"Where was I when that was going on?" David asked.

"You were there too," Ettie told him. "Don't you remember?"

David shook his head. "Maybe I was out playing ball or something. I only remember that happening a couple of times."

Collette's mind was on earlier times than that. "Mother, I was just thinking about how many people from our family lived together in that house on Roberts Street. We were there with Bubbe and Zayde and Aunt Libby, before Rachel and David were born. There was always a lot of excitement."

"Too much, for some people," Ettie replied, puckering her lips in a grimace. "Your father couldn't stand it. He never liked my family, and he wanted to get away. We never had any privacy, but we were lucky to have a place to stay." She paused to select a few cheeses, then shook her head. "He never made a good living. After you were weaned, I had to return to work. It's a good thing it worked out that Aunt Libby was able to watch you." Ettie looked up and smiled at Collette. "It was very hard to leave you, but she loved you, and you made everybody so happy."

* * *

How can I be pregnant already? Ettie wondered, a cold knot forming in her stomach. *I know all it takes is one time, but still . . .* Morton had tried to be gentler with her after that first night. He was calmer and more affectionate, and although Ettie remained tense, satisfying him was not as painful as it had been the first time. There were even times when he caressed or tickled her first, and she relaxed a bit, although she never experienced the ecstasy suggested in the movies.

The baby was due in April, just ten months after the wedding. Even before the doctor confirmed the pregnancy, everyone in the family knew because she had terrible morning sickness. She felt the same way she'd felt on the boat coming over from the old country, when she could barely look at food. A few weeks after the nausea began, the bloody spots appeared, and the doctor told her to get off her feet. This she couldn't do, because she had to work as long as possible to make enough to pay for their share of the family expenses.

Morton was thrilled about the pregnancy, which relieved Ettie. He showed more interest in her well-being, even joined the family meals and conversations, despite his discomfort when sitting at a table where everyone talked at once, yelling when they wanted something and grabbing plates to be washed before he was finished with his food.

Motivated by his desire to make enough of a living to support his family and get them into their own apartment somewhere, he spent more and more time away, driving from town to town, trying to sell his goods to local merchants. By then the Depression was hitting all of the small towns very hard, and Morton was lucky if he earned enough to pay for his gasoline and other expenses. Not only was Ettie lonely and exhausted, but she was becoming more and more dependent on her family.

Then Libby announced that she and her cousin Jake were going to get married next spring, two months after Ettie's baby would arrive.

Since arriving penniless from Saskatchewan two years earlier, Jake had been living at their house, pitching in by helping Yitzhac sell his potatoes. He had no education or special skills and no interest in learning a trade, but he and Yitzhac together were able to double the money Yitzhac had been bringing home. At first Jake wore only the shabby clothes he'd brought with him and seemed confused about how to behave in social situations. But he had an exuberant personality and enjoyed spending time with Libby's friends. Soon he was one of the most popular boys in the group. Libby showed him how to dress more stylishly and took him to movies and dances, confiding to Ettie that she always enjoyed having him as her escort because he looked like one of the movie stars she had a crush on.

Everyone who met Jake liked him. Ettie appreciated his ability to make everyone in the family feel more relaxed, the way he showed an interest in everyone, laughed and joked, and always saw the bright side of life. He had no interest in books or world affairs, though, so Morton showed very little interest in him.

When news of the engagement reached Gitl, Jake's mother in Saskatchewan, she wrote that she did not approve of her son marrying her sister's daughter, but Jake's father intervened, and the wedding plans went ahead. The house was filled with excitement over Libby's wedding and Ettie's expected baby.

Collette was born in April, 1932, a week before Passover. Ettie felt the first labor pains when Morton was on one of his sales trips. She found her mother and Libby in the kitchen, cleaning in preparation for the holiday.

"I think the baby is on the way," she told them. "I'm leaving for the hospital."

She was alone when she walked down the street to board a streetcar, and nobody was with her when her daughter was born.

As soon as Morton learned of the birth, he hurried back to Pittsburgh, and bounded into the hospital, unshaven and travel-stained, to see his new daughter.

"Her Hebrew name will be Chaya, for my mother," he gushed, beaming.

They had not discussed a name before the birth, and Ettie had picked out a different name. Her mother had always told her that it was customary for the wife to choose the name of the first child for someone in her family. It was clear to Ettie that Morton would never be convinced to change his mind on this matter so she never challenged him. Instead she said, "Now we should also choose an English name for her"

Morton looked from her to his daughter and nodded enthusiastically. "Yes, a name that starts with a C." He thought for a moment, then brightened. "Collette. I really like that name," he said, referring to a movie actress he liked, and from that time forward he doted on his oldest daughter, Collette.

When Ettie arrived home with Collette the morning before the first Passover seder, her mother and sister were cooking the traditional holiday foods. Nobody in the household had thought of buying any of the supplies needed for a new baby, no clothing or even a small tub to use for bathing the baby. Libby agreed to look after Collette so Ettie could go to the drugstore on the corner to buy the most urgent items.

When the owner set her choices on the counter and began to total the bill, she could barely meet his eyes, and she felt her cheeks growing hot. "I need these for my new baby," she said. "I—I have no money right now, but I promise to pay as soon as I get some."

"I'm confident that you'll pay the bill," he told her kindly when he saw how distraught she was about asking. "You take them, and take good care of your baby."

Collette cried nonstop throughout the seder that night. Ettie's attempts to nurse her were futile. The incessant crying and fretting continued for two months, worse at night than during the day. The doctor said the baby was healthy and she was gaining weight, but she must be colicky. Morton stayed awake with her, walking with her during the night, singing to her, trying to calm her so she wouldn't wake the entire household. Ettie had never seen a man show so much love toward a baby. This tenderness, more than anything else about him, convinced her that she truly loved Morton despite his erratic behavior.

After a few months, Collette abruptly stopped crying. The way she smiled and responded to everyone in the household helped to change their constant complaining about the crying into eagerness to hold her on their laps and talk baby talk with her. Her curly black hair grew longer and thicker. Her round face, rosy cheeks, and full smile drew people to her, not only family who lived in the household, but relatives who came to visit and neighbors who saw her in her buggy.

Collette's close bond with her father intensified, and she broke into a big smile and held out her arms to him whenever he walked into the room, preferring his attention most of all. He proudly carried her in his arms as he walked around the block, and took her with him when he went upstairs to their room, where he could sing to her or make up fanciful stories that he accompanied with animal sounds and broad gestures. She delighted him with her giggles when he tickled her.

After Collette's arrival in April, the family focused on Libby's wedding. Libby had saved enough money from her job to buy a beautiful white satin dress with a train and a matching headpiece with a long veil. She not only arranged for a photographer and a reception for all their family and friends, but was also able to pay for refreshments, including chopped liver and cold cuts, in addition to the cakes Sarah baked. Several of her friends were bridesmaids. Ettie, as a new mother still nursing her baby, was not involved in the wedding party or even the dancing.

Ettie was sincerely happy for Libby, pleased that she was marrying a good person in Jake, someone who loved and needed her. At the same time she felt ashamed of her jealousy, because her own wedding had been such an embarrassment.

Libby and Jake went on a honeymoon, a weekend at a downtown hotel, and then returned to Roberts Street to live in a room on the second floor. Jake would continue to work with Yitzhac, selling produce from the horse and cart, together covering a much larger territory than Yitzhac had ever done alone. This arrangement continued until Jake found a job working for a local furniture store.

Ettie weaned Collette by the time she was fifteen months old, and returned to work, pleased that she could leave her baby with her sister. Jake was contributing enough money to the household that Libby could stop working, and she was happy to take care of Collette. Libby showered her with attention, took her along on her visits to all her friends, and enjoyed playing with her and combing her curly hair. Ettie returned home each day exhausted and depressed that she could not be the one taking care of her own daughter.

After a few months, Libby announced that she was pregnant, but assured Ettie that she would take care of Collette as long as she could. When Libby's son Danny was born, Ettie became even more upset that she had to continue working, but Morton's income was not adequate. With Libby and Sarah both at home, Collette received good care and grew to love her new cousin Danny as if he were her younger brother.

The knowledge that Collette was well cared for helped Ettie to remain reasonably content living in the house on Roberts Street, despite Morton's irritability about the situation. She hoped that somehow Morton would earn more money, so they could contribute their share without her having to go off to work each day. She enjoyed being part of the noisy family conversations, and she looked forward to the visits from other relatives, including Jake's brother and two sisters, who had also moved from Saskatchewan to Pittsburgh by this time. Nevertheless, her nerves were on edge each time Morton showed his displeasure with her relatives, especially when he got impatient with Sarah or showed disdain for an opinion someone expressed. She appreciated that Jake tried to overlook Morton's moods, but Libby couldn't resist reacting with sarcasm. And Morton and her father obviously avoided any contact with one another. The only person Morton remained totally calm with was Bennie.

* * *

"It was wonderful living in that house, with everyone treating me so well," Collette said wistfully. "I didn't realize that there was any tension. Everyone asked me to dance and sing, then they hugged and kissed me." She paused, her expression dreamy. Then she looked at Ettie. "I was a happy little girl, but I realize now that it must have been a hard way for you to start a marriage, Mother."

Rachel stared at her sister. "You sure have different childhood memories from mine. I guess by the time I was born, new babies weren't such a big deal in the family."

"My main memory, Collette," David interjected, "is that you were the one who gave me a lot of attention."

The rest of the afternoon was relaxed and quiet, with Collette first describing her happy memories of living with her relatives, then talking about her high school years and how she first met Stanley on a blind date. She talked about how much she loved attending the University of Pittsburgh and the new friends she made there, the other boys she dated and how happy she was that Stanley was persistent and their romance blossomed. These were all memories the family frequently shared during visits, memories Collette found comforting as her illness became a more dominant force in her life. Ettie dozed off every few minutes while Collette was talking, but each time she awoke, she would add her own interpretation to the last thing Collette was saying.

Saturday evening after sunset, shiva would begin again, and they prepared themselves for what they expected to be the busiest time for people to drop by to pay their respects.

Some of Collette's friends arrived first, bringing cookies and fruit. Conversation was polite and general; once again people seemed to avoid talking about Morton. Finally Ettie's cousin Bea arrived, and peered at Ettie with concerned eyes.

"You don't look well, Ettie," she said. "How do you feel?"

Gone was the pleasant, relaxed mood of the afternoon. Ettie felt dissipated and responded in a gloomy whisper, "How can I feel? I thought he couldn't cause me anymore pain."

Bea shook her head in sympathy, looking over at Rachel, who had also heard the remark. She said in an undertone to Rachel, "You know, they never understood him. He was too smart for all of them, that was the problem."

Ettie was immediately sorry that she'd blurted out such a bitter remark. She had never expressed such anger at Morton publicly, instead trying all these years to pretend that her sad life was just bad luck. *No one mentions anymore that awful day when things came to blows,* she thought.

But it was never far from Ettie's conscious memory.

Unraveling

Collette was almost three when the family celebrated the wedding of Shmulek's oldest daughter. Before walking to the synagogue a few blocks away for the ceremony and reception, everyone congregated outside the house on Roberts Street for a family picture. Ettie was dressed in a blue polka-dot dress, with an alluring white flower tucked into her wavy black hair. In the photo she saw later she was smiling demurely for the camera, but she realized she had not been able to hide the sadness in her eyes. Morton was still slim and handsome in his dark suit. Collette looked bubbly and sweet in a flowered cotton dress with full skirt. Ettie had pulled back her dark curls and caught them in a large bow.

The reception music was exciting and uplifting, helping Ettie put aside her worries about Morton's reaction to life in the crowded house, the fact that he did not make enough money to allow her to take care of her own daughter, and his bad moods. Morton stood watching as he always did when Ettie danced with her cousins, her uncles, and her friends. When they formed the circle to do the traditional dances her tension eased, and she laughed and called out to others to come join the celebration.

When the musicians began to play a fox trot, Jake came over and took Ettie's hand. "C'mon kiddo," he said, "you're gonna dance this one with me."

They moved onto the dance floor, he put his arm around her waist, and they began taking the first steps. Suddenly Ettie felt a hand fall heavily on her shoulder, and she nearly stumbled as it pulled her back. She turned to see Morton, his face dark with fury, yelling at Jake, "I'm not gonna let you break up my family."

Ettie gasped as his fist shot through the air and connected with Jake's face. Jake fell to the ground, and Ettie screamed, horrified at what was happening. Then she swayed, and everything went black.

She came to, sputtering and blinking, as someone sprinkled water on her face. Her fuzzy mind registered shouting, and the sound of running feet.

"What's going on?" a woman called.

A man's voice growled, "Get him out of here."

When her eyes focused, she saw a hysterical Libby standing before Morton, jabbing her finger at his face for emphasis and screaming, "You crazy man, get out of here! I don't ever want to see you again!" Two of Shmulek's sons were tugging at Morton, and finally pulled him away and guided him toward the door.

"He's ruining my life," Ettie moaned.

Jake staggered to his feet, blood pouring from his nose. "Okay—I'm okay. Settle down, everyone." Bennie grabbed his arm and went with him to the men's room.

"Is Jake okay?" Ettie asked the person who helped her up, her eyes following Jake and her brother.

Her father took her arm and whirled her to face him. "I told you not to marry that *meshuganer*," he shouted at her. "This is all your fault."

Sarah rushed over and put her arms around Ettie as she sobbed. Collette followed her grandmother to her mother's side and stood whimpering, tugging on her mother's dress. Sarah lifted her granddaughter and whispered to her, *"Shaina maideleh,* shah, shah, be quiet now." Ettie reached out to take her daughter into her arms.

Ettie walked home carrying her daughter, Collette crying for her daddy. When she reached their third-floor room, she found Morton sitting on the bed with a packed suitcase at his feet. She placed Collette on the floor, at first ignoring Morton, but then turned for him to see her look of desperation. After a short silence she lashed out.

"Now you've done it. Are you happy? Are you satisfied, now that you ruined my cousin's wedding, that you could have killed Jake? We were just dancing together. You never want to dance, so why did you care if I danced with him? I can't take this anymore. You're driving everyone away. How can I face my family after what you did?"

Collette started to cry, reaching for her father. He took her into his arms, brushing back her hair and kissing her forehead. "I can't take this anymore either, Ettie. I tried, but I can't live this way. You care more about your family than you do about me. They don't have any interest in me, and I always feel like an outsider, even when we're eating dinner.

"I know I just did something terrible, and I'm sorry. I won't blame you if you never forgive me. I lost my temper when I saw you dancing with all of them, happier than you ever are with me. I know you're always comparing me with Jake, wishing you could have what your sister has. Well, I am who I am, and I'm not Jake. You can't get used to that, Ettie. I want to talk about important things, to read, and try to learn what's going on in the world." He began to choke up, and could barely get his last sentence out. "I can't live like this anymore. I have to leave this place."

Morton handed Collette back to Ettie. At that moment he looked like a lost child, and despite her anger, Ettie understood how hurt he must be to have behaved the way he did. A part of her wanted to reach out to him and show some understanding, to forgive him, but what he did made no sense—it was brutal and humiliating, and he hurt someone who was kind and friendly to everyone. After all the suffering her family had endured, they didn't deserve him spoiling their *simcha,* this happy occasion.

She knew they would never be able to brush Morton's behavior under the rug. Her family would not accept him any longer. She could not leave with him—they had no place to go, and they could not afford to be independent. She tried not to think about what could possibly happen next. *If he could punch Jake for no reason . . .* No, it was better to let him go. *Maybe he'll think it over and come back and apologize to Jake, to my family. Maybe if he seems sincere, they'll let it go.* She doubted that. And she knew in her heart that she could never let this happen again.

Collette began sobbing, again reaching for her daddy. Morton's face crumpled in agony. "You know I can't live without my daughter," he said, "but I can't stand it here, and now they wouldn't let me stay if I wanted to." Ettie didn't contradict him. "I'll move away for now, and as soon as I'm settled, I hope you won't stop me from spending time with my daughter. I love her more than anything, Ettie, you know that, don't you? And I love you too, but I can't go on this way." He rose, kissed Collette, grabbed his suitcase, and left.

When the rest of the family returned they found Ettie sitting on the floor, rocking Collette in her arms, both of them crying.

"He's a troublemaker," Libby screamed. "I don't want him in this house!"

A Woman of Valor

It always caused Ettie pain to think about the weeks and months that followed. A foggy gloom had descended, and each morning she awoke thinking the nightmare would be over only to realize that it was closing in on her more and more. Lucky she still had her job. Before leaving for work, she would make sure that Collette had breakfast and was dressed, then she'd put her into Libby's arms and kiss her goodbye, dreading the long day ahead. When women dragged their crying children with them while they shopped, she heard in their voices Collette's cries, and envisioned her running to Libby for comfort, which depressed her even more.

People were becoming more hopeful, now that President Roosevelt was making progress helping the nation struggle through the Depression; but jobs remained scarce, and Ettie realized she was fortunate to have one, despite the meagre wages. She must not jeopardize that, although it was a big challenge for her to get through each day. The fun of serving several shoppers simultaneously was gone. Most people were "just looking." If they actually decided to remove garments from the rack to try them on in the dressing rooms, the clerks had to remember exactly what they took and ensure that they brought them all back to the racks. They had to make sure the "lookers" didn't get away wearing one of the garments under their street clothes or stuffed into another bag or large purse. In those days even the most honest-looking people had become desperate and could not be trusted. Ringing up a real sale was hard work, even for flimsy housedresses that cost $1.95.

Despite her sadness Ettie managed better than most of the clerks. She found herself becoming cynical, joking about being able to convince customers what a bargain a particular item was when she knew it was worth less than half of what they were paying. She felt sorry for the people who spent their last dollar on a *shmuta*, a rag, but she realized that if they didn't buy it, there would be less for her to contribute to the family.

Ettie's co-workers noticed the change in her. In the past Ettie had been the one to crack the jokes about their bosses or the funny people who sometimes walked through the aisles every day. She had been the one to keep them all laughing by pretending the items they were selling were lavish evening gowns meant for movie stars. Now the twinkle was gone from her dark eyes, replaced by a deep sadness. They didn't know why because she was too embarrassed to tell any of her coworkers that she and Morton were separated, pretending instead that he was on buying trips when their conversations drifted to anything personal.

When Ettie took the trolley home at the end of the workday, so exhausted that her feet and legs throbbed, she often let her imagination drift back to the excitement she felt when she first met Morton. She could never forget how brilliant he had seemed to her, how he shared his ideas about a better world, and how he made her feel that she was special. What had happened?

Maybe, just maybe, she thought, they could make a fresh start. Maybe there was something she could do to help him relax more, to enjoy good times, to be less suspicious of people and more confident in himself. If only he had a steady job and income, then he could have his wish to be independent of her family.

She was convinced that it was her responsibility to find a way, if only for Collette's sake. The love Collette and her daddy felt for each other was greater than anything Ettie had ever seen between father and daughter. It was heartbreaking for Ettie to welcome her daughter home each Sunday afternoon after she spent the day with Morton, only to have Collette run after him with outstretched arms, crying, "I want my daddy."

During one of these episodes, Morton did not simply turn back and give his daughter an extra hug, but walked up to Ettie, stared into her eyes, and pleaded, "I want my family back together!" Ettie felt a moment of hope, destroyed by his next terrifying words. "If I don't get my family back, I'll kill the person who made me lose my family."

Ettie stood frozen in stunned silence. Her mind raced, her eyes blurred, and she felt faint. But she told herself, *No, you can't pass out this time, Ettie. You have to continue to stand here and stop him from doing harm to anybody.* She looked into Morton's glaring eyes and began to cry. "Morton, what are you talking about? Who are you talking about? Nobody made you lose your family."

His face twitched with anger. "I know you're jealous that Libby's married to Jake. You wish he was your husband. He makes you laugh, and he likes to dance. You always told me you wanted to learn about the world, to read and discuss new ideas, to make a difference. But when I saw you in his arms on that dance floor, I could tell what you really wanted—a happy-go-lucky guy who enjoys things the way they are and lets others worry about what needs to change in the world. I could tell he was the one you loved."

Well, there's one thing he's right about, Ettie thought bitterly. *I do wish I had married someone else. But not Jake.* Sure, she enjoyed Jake's company because he was a fun cousin. But it was Harry she thought of . . . If only he had responded to her and not encouraged her to be loyal to Morton! Harry not only had the intellect and ambition she admired, but he was gentle and considerate too. She had only seen him once or twice since he'd moved to another neighborhood, and she had tried to forget about him. She knew he was happily married. *He never cared about me in any way beyond that of a friend,* she told herself. *The whole thing was just a fantasy.* She had gone through with the marriage to Morton, and that was that.

Ettie knew that she was stuck in this relationship, even if they were separated. What kind of life would she have if she got a divorce? It would only lead to more misery. Divorce was a disgrace, and she might be shunned. No, Collette deserved a chance for a normal home life. And with this threat, she realized that it was up to her to try to placate Morton, to protect her family and to keep him from doing harm to anyone.

"Oh my God, Morton, you know you're the only person I ever loved," she lied. "Why don't you believe me?" Then she added, "We could try again on our own, if you want."

Morton swung his arms around Ettie, pulled her so close that a pain shot up her back, and kissed her hard on the lips. "You're mine, you know. You're my wife, and I want you back with me. Please forgive me for making you sad—I'll try harder, I promise." He reached down and lifted Collette into the air. "We'll all be together now, my sweetheart."

Collette laughed and kissed Morton, then reached out to Ettie and hugged her.

Ettie shivered, at once terrified by the threat Morton had made and by her own concession for peace. She wished she could believe him that things would change. But she couldn't stop wondering how serious he'd been in his threat. Did he truly think her sister's husband, Jake, was the reason for their unhappiness? Would Morton really try to kill him if he imagined something going on between them? *Morton learned to use weapons in the army,* she realized with a chill. *He has a bad temper, and he's already assaulted Jake.* Yes, this was the only solution, she was sure. She would join Morton and would try to keep him and her family apart, despite the loneliness it would cause her.

On a cool day in September, 1935, Ettie and Morton prepared to move into two rooms they'd rented in the house of a middle-aged widow on Logan Street, a long walk from Roberts Street. When Ettie looked out the window of her parents' home, she was relieved that there was no rain, despite the fast-moving clouds and wind. This would be a short journey, moving her few belongings and leaving behind the comfort of familiarity. Fifteen years had passed since the escape from Skvira and the harrowing journey to a new land, to what they were sure would be a better life. Now, at age twenty-four, Ettie wished she could still feel optimism about the future. But she had closed too many doors.

Collette was dancing and singing for her grandparents, twirling around as she repeated, "We're going to be with Daddy now, with my daddy now."

"Come, let's comb your hair and get ready," Ettie said wearily as she lifted Collette from the floor. She walked over to a large mirror so Collette could watch her run the brush through her black curls.

Glancing up from her work to peer at her daughter's big, playful eyes in the mirror, Ettie noticed how gaunt she'd become. *I'm thinner than I've ever been since arriving in Pittsburgh,* she thought, studying her image with anxious eyes. The bit of rouge on her wide cheeks was the only color on her face.

She squared her shoulders, determined to be strong, to do what was necessary so she could protect her daughter and her family. After all, hadn't her mother suffered far greater hardships all of those years in Skvira, after her father left for America? Surely she could try to be a good wife to her husband. It was up to her—it was her mission.

Bennie and his friend had offered to help Ettie move into the two rented rooms. Morton liked Bennie better than anyone else in the family, and he planned to meet them at the apartment to help move their belongings up the two flights of stairs. Not that there were many belongings.

Ettie still had the sheets, towels, and tablecloths they had received as wedding gifts from Morton's brothers. She also had a set of dishes, a few pots and pans, and a set of stainless steel flatware others had given them. The best gift Ettie brought with her was the silver tableware given by Sophie Weiss and her husband, the people in whose home she had first met Morton. After four years of marriage, the gift had never been used. Their furniture consisted of odd pieces that Shmulek and Franya no longer needed and an old bed they'd purchased at a secondhand shop, plus a couple of things Sophie Weiss didn't need any longer. All she took from her parents' home were her clothes, her wedding gifts, the crib for Collette, a broom, a mop, and a bucket. Sarah gave her a bag of vegetables and freshly baked pastry.

When they arrived, Morton's clothing was already in place.

Ettie knew when she arranged to rent the rooms that the place was old and neglected. The first things anyone noticed were the stale odor and the torn wallpaper, several layers deep. The landlady's son had slept in one of the rooms before getting married and moving to another part of the city. The other room was a tiny kitchen with one cupboard, a small sink that made loud noises every time the water was turned on, an old gas stove, and a small icebox. They had to share a bathroom with the landlady and her other two boarders. The rent was low enough that they hoped to manage on their combined earnings.

The rooms were filthy, especially the floor near the icebox, where leaking water had made permanent marks in the cracked linoleum. Ettie immediately began scrubbing everything in the kitchen before she would put anything away. The icebox was stained so badly, no scrubbing with cleanser could get it clean. She noticed old nails poking from several places along the top of the chipped wooden frame around the door, and checked to make sure there were no nails near the bottom, where Collette might get hurt.

* * *

Ettie continued to work at Frank & Seder's, rising before six each morning so she could take Collette to Roberts Street, where Libby continued to look after her. Now that Ettie and Collette had moved out, Libby, Jake, and their infant son Danny had more space and seemed content, even though they still shared the house with a boarder or two.

Sarah continued to worry about Ettie and her granddaughter, but convinced herself that Ettie had done the right thing to go back to a man from such a good family and avoid bringing shame on them all with a divorce. Yitzhac never mentioned Morton's name when he saw Ettie. He loved Collette, and as soon as she arrived each morning, he hugged her and began clapping as a cue for her to dance for him.

Despite both Ettie and Morton contributing to their meager income, there were some months when they didn't have the full rent money. Their landlady responded with threats to evict them if the money wasn't paid in a few days. Each time this happened, Morton miraculously showed up in a day or two with the rent money. Ettie was convinced he must have asked his brothers for help.

Ettie understood that the landlady was having trouble paying her own bills, but that didn't excuse her for trying to manage her finances by cutting back on heat and water. The rooms were so cold that winter that everyone had to wear heavy underwear and sweaters most of the time. Hot water was available for baths only once a week. Lingering in the tub was out of the question because the cold made everyone's teeth chatter before they could dry themselves. Ettie worried that Collette would catch a cold or even the flu.

When summer came, the place was like an oven. The only relief came from a small porch where they could sit outside. By then things were so tense about finances that the landlady forbade Collette from playing on the porch with her dolls and toy dishes. "She's putting water into the toy teapot and cups," the old woman complained, "and that's a waste of water."

Sarah and Bennie were their only visitors, and Morton didn't object to seeing either of them if he happened to come home early. Ettie was grateful that her mother realized how isolated she was, and welcomed her visits whenever she was home alone with Collette. Sarah never came empty-handed, always bringing whatever food she had just made, whether a bag filled with challah and cookies or a jar of homemade soup or gefilte fish. Hoping she could help ease the tension between Morton and the rest of the family, she would whisper to Ettie, "Tell Morton I made this special for him."

Ettie found pleasure when she could get away from the rooms, especially when a cousin got married. She attended the showers before the weddings and then the big events, always without Morton, who was neither welcome nor interested in attending. It was as if he no longer existed. No one mentioned his name, and nobody in the family, other than Sarah or Bennie, ever asked about him.

Ettie took Collette with her to these family events, always letting Morton know where they were going and assuring him that they would return early. Even though Morton never said as much, she knew he timed her return. She stayed for the ceremony, for Collette to hug and kiss all of her relatives, to dance one or two kazutskis, and to have a few refreshments. But she always had to leave before the real excitement started. Each time she returned home, she found Morton reading or playing solitaire. He didn't look up when they entered, and never asked if she had a good time or anything else about the event. There were no more threats or recriminations because Ettie made sure that she did not test the limits of his patience.

They lived this way for a year, struggling each month to pay the rent and buy food with the few dollars Ettie earned and the fewer dollars Morton could manage as he peddled goods in the small surrounding towns. When he planned to be back in Pittsburgh, Morton expected Ettie to have dinner prepared for him. This added tension to their relationship because Ettie never knew for sure if he would make it home for dinner or not, and what time that might be. His old car broke down somewhere almost every week. At times he could fix it and get to the next place without a big delay, but other times he had to flag down help. A large portion of the money he earned went into car maintenance.

After all of her dreams of life with an intelligent man from a good family, the irony of the situation was not lost on Ettie. Her life was not unlike what her mother's had been, always waiting for Yitzhac to return with his horse and buggy, wondering if he had made the trip safely, and knowing he was spending much of his time and money on the horse.

One night Morton did not come home, even though he'd given Ettie an exact time to expect him. She had his dinner waiting and eventually had to wrap it and put it in the icebox, wondering how she would keep it fresh for him or prevent it from spoiling. Ettie assumed he'd had more car trouble and that he was stranded in a small town, waiting for the repairs. He didn't come home the second night, either, and sent no word. She used the telephone in her family's home to call Morton's brother Isaac the next day.

"I'll try to locate him," Isaac promised when she asked if he knew where Morton was. "I just pray that Morton isn't hurt, or in any trouble."

Isaac contacted her a few days later. "I called the police to inquire about any automobile accidents," he told her, then hurried to add, "there were none that involved Morton. And," he drawled as if he'd been reluctant to do so, "I also called some other business people I know, who might have had contact with Morton."

"And?" Ettie prompted.

"And nothing."

After two weeks, with the rent more than a month overdue, the landlady told Ettie she had to leave. Bennie and his friend again helped with the move, this time back to Roberts Street. Nobody had any idea where Morton was.

After two more weeks passed, Morton's younger brother, Sam, visited Ettie. "How much do you need in order to pay the back rent owed to your former landlady?" he asked. Ettie stared at him in surprise, and he explained, "My brothers and I discussed the situation at one of our regular meetings. We don't want people to talk, don't want anyone to say we don't pay our debts." He wrote out a check and gave her an additional twenty dollars in cash for herself and Collette.

Ettie felt numb. Here she was, again deserted by the man who had pleaded with her to stay with him. Here were his brothers, helping her and expressing concern about the family's reputation. She wondered what had happened to Morton, hoped he was not hurt, but part of her wished that he would just vanish and not cause her any more heartache. Shame washed over her with the thought.

When Morton finally reappeared six weeks later, Ettie found out about it through a note he left for her at the drugstore, telling her where to meet him the next day. He gave no clear explanation of where he had been, except to tell Ettie that he had not returned because, she read, *I expected you to contact my brothers, and I knew they would make sure that you and Collette didn't starve. Isaac has invited us to spend some time at his home in Vandergrift until we can figure out what to do next.*

So Morton's brothers understood that Morton loved her and Collette, despite his erratic behavior. *They probably hope to convince me to continue to be patient with him,* she thought bitterly. *They don't have to worry—I'll never leave him and risk him harming anyone in my family because of his temper.* She no longer believed he was capable of deliberately killing anyone, but she feared what might happen if he had an outburst.

Ettie told her boss that a family emergency had come up and she would have to be away for a week. She and Collette then made the trip by bus to Isaac's home. Morton was still away on his latest selling trip so she felt ill at ease there, but safe.

The second evening, while she was helping Isaac's wife prepare dinner, Isaac walked into the kitchen and cleared his throat. "Can we talk business?" he asked Ettie.

Heart racing, she wondered, *What kind of business discussion could he possibly want with me?* But she smiled, nodded, and followed him into the sitting room.

Isaac began talking as soon as she'd sat down. He spoke quickly, with an air of absolute authority. "My brothers and I have agreed to pursue a new business opportunity that could also solve Morton's problems—but it depends on you." He paused and looked intently at her. When she said nothing, he continued. "We are prepared to buy another store that has come up for sale in a town not far from Vandergrift. This store could be for Morton."

This time, feeling some response was required, Ettie lifted her eyebrows. That seemed to be enough. Isaac rose and paced, head down. He cleared his throat and continued.

"We all know from past experience that Morton is not reliable enough to handle it on his own. And you probably know that he resents our interference. If you agree to work side by side with him in the store, drawing on your retail experience and your friendly way with people, there is a good chance it will work. You could also serve as a cashier." He stopped and looked at her. "We wanted to ask you first before discussing it with Morton. Would you be prepared to leave your family and your job in Pittsburgh and make this commitment? The store is in a small mill town so you would have to adjust to living in a community without other Jewish people nearby—there is only one other business family there, and they are much older than any of us."

For Ettie the new business seemed like an answer to her prayers, and she agreed immediately, brushing aside how difficult it might be to live so far from her family and friends.

When Morton heard about it, he saw the offer as an opportunity to show his brothers that his business instincts were sharper than theirs.

Isaac found them a place to live on the second floor of an old house located within walking distance of the store—two small rooms plus a big kitchen and small porch and, best of all, their own bathroom. He also found a local woman willing to look after Collette whenever Ettie had to work. It would be easy for Ettie to walk home to have lunch with her daughter.

Ettie was optimistic when the store opened, despite the isolation she felt when away from the store. She enjoyed her work as cashier and took pride in her ability to calculate the change quickly and accurately. Her responsibilities gave her a chance to talk with the store's clerks without competing with them for sales, and to say a few words to the customers, who were also her new neighbors. She enjoyed her responsibility in the business and her contribution to the store's success. Morton was proud of her, and treated her with more and more respect and tenderness.

This was compensation enough for Ettie as she tried to adjust to the drab town and its inhabitants, who kept to themselves and said hello only if she greeted them first. Most of them had lived in the town all their lives, had gone to the same church every Sunday, and were suspicious of strangers. They respected the Burin family as fair in business, but still considered them all to be rich Jews and not "our kind of people." There were no friendly kosher butcher shops or fresh fish stores where Ettie might stop by for a chat as she bought something for the evening meal. Increasingly, she missed the excitement of being with her noisy family, of screaming to be heard when everyone talked at the same time, and listening to her cousins' jokes during their weekend visits. She missed her mother's visits and the familiar food.

Sometimes Ettie brought Collette to the store, and the clerks fussed over the friendly little girl as she sang and danced for them. They also found Ettie's self-deprecating jokes amusing, but they never considered her a friend and had no interest in contact away from the store. They maintained their distance from Morton, finding his brooding manner off-putting.

Morton's brothers and their wives lived in neighboring Vandergrift, a fifteen-minute drive. The visits with them when they congregated for weekly dinners at Isaac's home were uncomfortable for Ettie, despite the good meals Isaac's wife served. She always felt like the poor relative, never forgetting how financially dependent she and Morton were on his brothers. She was painfully aware that their American-born wives were more educated and sophisticated than she would ever be, and she believed that they looked down on her and her family's rough edges. She couldn't help but notice how they tried to avoid speaking directly with Morton. When he was out of earshot, they spoke of him to her as if he were her child and she was responsible for ensuring that he didn't cause his brothers any further anxiety or expense.

Despite her loneliness, Ettie was determined to make the arrangement work. Then she became pregnant. Morning sickness began almost immediately, and the doctor told her to stay off her feet as much as possible and to stop working immediately. Morton was delighted that another baby was on the way, but when Isaac heard the news, he just stared at Ettie as if she had betrayed him.

Without consulting Morton about how they might manage best without Ettie, Isaac went directly to one of the clerks whose family he knew to be honest and asked her to serve as the cashier and assistant manager. He also began visiting the store more frequently, to keep a close watch on how Morton was running things and to check all the records. Morton's feelings of confidence gave way to anxiety, defensiveness, and anger.

A few weeks before her due date, Ettie returned to Pittsburgh to give birth at the Passavant Hospital, not far from where her family lived. She was alone again, her mother and sister at home looking after Collette and Libby's son, Danny. When Morton learned that they had another girl, he once again decided the baby's name. This daughter would be Rachel, the name of his sister who had died of consumption and malnutrition while still in her teens.

Morton's brothers, trying to hide their disappointment that Ettie would now be tied down with another child, told her how happy they were to have such a pretty baby join the family, someone who would carry the name of their beloved sister.

Ettie, Collette, and Rachel remained at Roberts Street until Rachel was a month old. Collette was thrilled to have a baby sister and immediately took responsibility as her mother's little helper. She was as kind to her baby sister as all her loving relatives had been to her.

When Ettie and her two daughters returned to Morton, she was again surprised by the attention he showered on his new daughter. But it didn't take long to recognize that the business arrangement was doomed. With two children to look after, one an infant still nursing, Ettie's involvement was minimal at best. Morton resented the fact that the woman serving as assistant manager was more concerned about gaining Isaac's favor than his, and he soon became morose. Things came to a head the day Morton noticed a glaring error in the sales receipts. He accused the assistant manager of stealing and fired her. Shortly thereafter her brothers came to the store, threatening that they would kill Morton if he didn't retract the accusations.

The minute Morton walked into their home after work, Ettie sensed trouble. She began crying after he recounted the incident. "Morton, no, you've made a terrible mistake," she sobbed in dismay.

Morton pounded the table, his face dark with fury. "I cannot continue if you turn against me too," he shouted, and suddenly picked up the dishes Ettie had put on the table for their dinner and hurled them against the wall.

Ettie managed to grab Collette and the new baby, and locked herself into the bathroom. They huddled there, both children crying, for what seemed an eternity.

When she heard the front door slam, Ettie emerged cautiously from the bathroom. Morton was gone. Quickly, fearful that he'd come back while she was without a locked door between them, she wrapped the baby in a blanket, took Collette's hand, and left the apartment. She walked as fast as she could toward the town's drugstore, where she called Isaac on a pay phone. "Please, come at once," she asked him. "You have to help Morton."

She knew she could not remain in this town with her children if someone had threatened to physically harm Morton. Her next call was to Pittsburgh, and she was relieved when Bennie answered. "Bennie, I need you to come and help me," she said, her voice quavering despite her effort at calm.

"What's wrong?" Bennie asked, immediately concerned.

"Morton's been threatened. I need to get out of this town."

She returned to the flat, found Morton still gone, locked the door, and started gathering the things she would need to take with her. It didn't take Isaac and Sam long to arrive. She sagged against the door in relief when she heard their voices respond to her "Who is it?" and let them in to wait for Morton's return.

Morton came through the door an hour later, apparently calmer. He quickly agreed that it was not safe for him or his family to remain in the town.

"Bennie's on his way," Ettie said, more to Isaac and Sam than Morton. "We'll go with him." She didn't specify who the "we" were, and was relieved when Isaac nodded and told Morton to come with him.

Sam waited with Ettie, who spoke quietly to Collette and Rachel, trying to keep them calm. Bennie arrived just before midnight in a small delivery truck his new boss had agreed he could use. He spoke briefly with Sam, piled Ettie's suitcases and few belongings into the truck, then helped Ettie, Collette, and Rachel into the cab.

"So tell me what happened," Bennie said as he began the drive along dark country roads toward Pittsburgh.

Ettie recounted the events in a brief monotone, struggling to hold back tears so she wouldn't frighten her daughters. When she finished Bennie glanced at her glistening eyes, nodded, and returned his gaze to the road, not pressing for further details.

When they arrived at the house on Roberts Street, Sarah tried to comfort Ettie with the hope that Morton would apologize to the people in the town and they could put the latest outburst behind them. "We won't tell anyone what happened," she said brightly. "Let everyone think you're here for a visit."

Ettie said nothing. *She's more concerned about what others think than what I'm suffering,* she thought bitterly.

Yitzhac joined them, smiled at his granddaughters, asked Collette to dance for him, and asked Ettie what the troublemaker had done this time. "I told you that man would bring you heartache," he stated when she finished.

It didn't take long for Libby and Jake to come to the kitchen to find out what had happened. "Did Morton hurt you?" Libby asked, her brows puckered in concern "The kids?"

Ettie waved her hand and touched a finger to her lips as a signal for Libby to watch her words. She didn't want her daughters to hear bad things about their father.

Later, when the girls were both sleeping in the living room and the kitchen door was shut, she explained that Morton had not only smashed dishes against the wall, he had also made serious enemies in the town.

"Now he'll have to find work here in Pittsburgh so he can take care of his family," Libby said, her face tight with anxiety. "Don't worry; we'll make space for you and the girls until you can work things out." Ettie wondered exactly what Libby meant, but it was clear to her that this would not be a refuge for long. To underscore that, Libby added, "I hope he doesn't think he can live here. I don't care if I never see him again."

Jake waited until everyone had left the room before he questioned Ettie. "Are you sure you're all right, kid? Is there anything I can do to help?"

Ettie sighed. "Jake, I appreciate your offer," she replied, her voice heavy with resignation, "but you know you're the last person in the world who could help things between Morton and me." She wondered if he had forgiven Morton for attacking him, or if he had simply dismissed it as having no further significance. She knew he was sincere, and appreciated his kindness. *How can he not hold a grudge?* she wondered with a surge of admiration.

A few days later, Isaac came to see Ettie.

"We gave the assistant manager her job back and promised her a raise," he told her. "Naturally, we had to get Morton out of the town before someone harmed him. We found an apartment for him here in

Pittsburgh, and I've convinced an acquaintance of ours, a respected businessman, to give Morton a job in his men's clothing store on Fifth Avenue."

Isaac hesitated. "My brothers and I hope you'll join Morton and keep the family together. Surely you don't want to suffer through the humiliation of a divorce?"

"Divorce is the last thing on my mind," Ettie assured him. She did not tell him about the vow she had made to herself: *I can never leave Morton and risk the consequences of his anger. Besides, I have two daughters now, how can I look after them on my own?*

So it was time for another move, this time to a white wooden house on its triangular lot near the corner of Lombard and Dinwiddie Streets.

* * *

The fifth day of shiva was winding down even though it wasn't yet nine o'clock on Saturday night. Collette was saying goodbye to her friends, David was pacing the room, and Rachel was looking at her watch.

As soon as the visitors left, Rachel moved to sit beside her mother. She studied her hands for a moment as if trying to make a decision. Then she looked up, the skin between her eyebrows still creased with uncertainty. "One thing I never understood, Mother . . . Didn't anyone ever think that they should get Dad to see a psychiatrist? Didn't they realize something was wrong, that he wasn't just a troublemaker?"

Ettie laughed nervously. "Rachel, what're you talking about? Who ever thought that way back then? Any mention of someone needing a psychiatrist meant that person must really be crazy." She shrugged. "Who knows, maybe I was afraid to think such a thing. It was too hard to imagine how a smart man like Morton could be crazy. What did we know about such things? Sure, your father's behavior was unpredictable, even frightening. But I thought he was just moody, short-tempered, depressed, a loner, who knows what else. But crazy? No, that was unthinkable, even if my father did call him a meshuganer. My father had a disparaging name for lots of people." She flicked her wrist with a dismissive gesture.

"Even if someone thought Morton needed help, who could afford a psychiatrist?" Ettie shook her head. "It would have been out of the question. And your dad's family . . . they didn't want him to keep embarrassing them, disgracing their family name. I don't have any idea what they were thinking. How could they admit they had a crazy man in the family? It was not something anybody wanted to talk about."

"You've got to remember the time period we're talking about," Stanley added. "It was before the war, when so little was known about mental illness. There were all kinds of stereotypes in the movies—like a person thinking he was Napoleon or George Washington, or not being able to carry on a normal conversation, or being completely violent and uncontrollable all the time, screaming or laughing hysterically. It's no big surprise that nobody took action to get him to a psychiatrist—nobody thought there was real help available."

Ettie nodded. "And we all know that they were right about that."

Dreams, Screams, and Prayers

"Mother, will you share more details of what happened while I was a toddler?" Rachel asked. "There are so many things I have no memory of. You've told me that I was pretty and didn't cry much, but I haven't heard too many stories."

"Oh yes, a pretty baby," Ettie confirmed, smiling fondly. "Such rosy cheeks, and a chubby face surrounded by all that blond hair."

"I was still quite young, but I do have a few memories of living on Dinwiddie Street," Rachel prompted.

"Oy, that place was *such* a mansion!" Ettie exclaimed, then curled her lip in disgust. "It should have been condemned. You got the whooping cough when we lived there because there was never enough heat in winter. I worried so much."

"Mostly I remember standing in the yard waiting for Collette to come home from school." Rachel turned to Collette. "I missed you so much when you were away. And that yard was all concrete, with a high wooden fence that I couldn't see over—I had to peek through a crack. I longed to be with you all the time because you played all those little games with me and made up great stories."

Collette smiled. "You were a sweet little girl, Rachel, and I enjoyed your company."

"You didn't treat me like a baby," Rachel continued. "You always shared with me everything that the teacher had said, and what you and your friends did. I loved being with you, and wanted to go to school with you. I must have been such a pest."

Collette lifted her brows. "You were never a pest. Why do you think that?"

Ettie remembered those years clearly. *The calm before the storm. Morton's new boss appreciated his hard work and quick mind. Collette loved school after she learned how to read, and especially when she received those gold stars her teacher glued to the top of a page she'd completed! I was so pleased when she brought those home.* When Ettie took her kids with her to shop for groceries, people stopped to tell her what lovely girls she had. *That made me proud. Most of all, I was happy to be back in Pittsburgh.*

* * *

Ettie was glad that she and the kids could spend time each weekend with her growing extended family at Roberts Street, where they congregated to visit and play cards. Once in a while Morton actually walked with her and their daughters to the front of the house, then continued on his way to the Wylie Avenue Library. He never went inside the house, but did wave when he saw anyone near the door or porch. Ettie appreciated the appearance of civility.

When Morton was in a good mood, Ettie found his company stimulating. He talked about the books he was reading, the terrible events taking place in Europe, and the political reactions in Washington. Sometimes after a radio broadcast reported the growing dangers, Ettie asked Morton to explain why the government made certain decisions. Morton would become very intense as he explained that he thought the Nazi invasion of Poland would be the final blow for its Jewish population. He was furious that the United States did not join England in its response. He talked about the isolationist elements in the United States, fearful that if the Americans didn't help England take a stand against the Nazis, Jews in the United States would not be safe. When Roosevelt and Churchill worked out the lend-lease agreement, Morton was relieved, convinced that this would eventually lead the United States to help defend freedom in Europe.

As Morton analyzed international events, he seemed less focused on his own anxieties and resentments. He wasn't alone, everybody was worried about what was happening in Europe those days. Ettie's family worried about what was in store for family members who remained in Skvira or Pogrebischte. The newspapers were filled with speculation about whether America would go to war. Ettie now realized that she understood what was happening more clearly than most of the others in her family, and she was sure that was because of her discussions with Morton.

It was during this time that Ettie's Uncle Nachum, her mother's half-brother, began visiting her home. Ettie told him of Morton's views about the war, and Nachum asked if he could visit on Sunday morning to discuss things with him.

Morton welcomed the visit and greeted Nachum warmly, almost as if he had no idea why the rest of the family had been staying away. They spent the morning eating the pickled herring and brown bread Nachum had brought and talked about politics and the looming war. These visits continued for several years.

Ettie and Morton's rented rooms on Dinwiddie Street were only marginally better than those they'd had on Logan Street before Morton's disappearance. They were cramped and shabby, cold in winter, and unbearably hot in summer. Two families plus another boarder shared the lone bathroom, and the bossy landlady put limits on hot water usage, permitting baths only once a week.

After more than a year of this, Morton saw an announcement in the paper heralding a new government program of subsidized housing, aimed at providing apartments for low-income citizens. He couldn't contain his excitement as he showed the article to Ettie, and he was among the first to put his family's name on the application list. There was no guarantee that they would qualify for an apartment, and it would be more than a year before any of the apartments would be ready. In the meantime, the government began investigating applicants' backgrounds, income, and current living arrangements. They told Morton that if they found everything to be acceptable, his family would be among the first to move in.

Morton studied the diagrams illustrating what the neighborhood would look like, especially the level of privacy within the apartments and the play space for children outdoors. He liked the promise of a few playgrounds equipped with swings and slides scattered throughout the project, grass between each building broken up by a concrete square where children could play games, and the hillside with the magnificent view of the Monongahela River.

He showed the floor plans to Ettie and pointed out that each three-story building would have three hallways with six apartments off each hallway. Ettie preferred the second floor because the windows were not so close to the ground that a burglar could enter, and yet there were not too many steps to climb up to get to the front door. The laundry facilities planned for every few buildings excited her—all with up-to-date wringer washing machines and large contraptions with built-in electric coils and bars for hanging and drying clothes indoors.

The best part of the project was the interior design of the apartments. The two-bedroom unit Morton had applied for had a kitchen with a new refrigerator and stove, built-in cabinets for dishes, and enough space for a table and chairs and a food cabinet. While Ettie admired that, Morton liked the idea of the front door opening into a living room, even though they didn't have any living room furniture, just Ettie's hope chest and a radio. Each of the two bedrooms had a separate clothes closet. Best of all, each apartment had its own tiled bathroom and a linen closet outside the bathroom. Radiators in every room would provide warmth in winter, and the casement windows, when opened, would let in air during the summer.

"Finally," Morton said, "my family will not have to suffer in stuffy, dilapidated rooms with bossy owners telling us when we can take a bath and how much heat we're entitled to."

Ettie put her arms around him and held him close, expressing genuine joy at the news.

* * *

Hard to believe how hopeful everything was back then, Ettie thought as she looked up at her three adult children, each one now considerably older than the young mother she had been when she and Morton were preparing to move into Terrace Village. "You know, when we talked about moving into that new apartment, that was the happiest time of my marriage."

Rachel was biting her lip. Now she jumped in, anxious to share one of her early memories. "Do you remember, Collette, that day Dad took us both for a walk before the buildings were finished? I was so small, but I still remember him telling us to look around, that as soon as we were able to live here, our world would never be the same. Everything would be wonderful. Remember?"

Collette nodded. "I remember walking with Dad several times when he was assessing how much longer it might be before we could move in. We always imagined how happy we would be."

"I never heard any of this before," David said, sounding surprised. "I always thought you considered the move to a housing project as an embarrassment."

"Not at all, not at first," Ettie replied. "In fact, I couldn't believe it when we finally got there. I thought I was in a palace. I don't care what anyone says about Terrace Village, those were nice apartments, nicer than anyplace I'd ever lived before. But I couldn't believe it when the cockroaches started coming through the pipes. Then the bedbug infestation! The management had to send in fumigators, and we all got sick from that. It didn't take long for me to find out how awful some of our new neighbors turned out to be too. You couldn't trust a lot of those people. Remember Mrs. Gabrone upstairs?" she asked Rachel.

Rachel wrinkled her nose. "Who could forget those people?"

Ettie raised her finger and lowered her voice as if they'd stepped back to that time, and she didn't want to be overheard. "She stole my milk for a long time. The milkman would leave it by our door early in the morning, and when I'd go out to get it a little later, it'd be gone. I had no idea who could be taking it. Then one time when her daughter was sick, I offered to come up and stay with the kid while Mrs. Gabrone went shopping. I opened the refrigerator to get something for the little girl, and there I saw it—several bottles of *my* milk, on a shelf in her refrigerator. I was stunned, but I didn't want to start a fight. I don't think I ever said anything to her about it, but the stealing did stop. I guess she got embarrassed."

"You never told us anything about that," Collette said.

"I didn't want to start anything by repeating the story," Ettie answered. Before anyone else could comment, she returned to the earlier subject, her tone animated. "When we moved in, none of us knew what we were getting into; everyone was thrilled to be there. President Roosevelt even came to the official opening to make a speech and have his picture taken while surrounded by crowds of people. I was shocked to see him wearing those leg braces, and his aides helping him to stand up for just a minute. The public never knew how crippled he was. Back then we all thought he was a god. Bubbe Sarah even hung his picture in her bedroom, right up next to the one of Zayde Moishe. Anyhow, the whole day was unbelievable. The president made a special presentation of a key to the people who lived downstairs from us and gave them all new furniture as part of the official launch of public housing in Pittsburgh." She sneered. "Too bad he gave it to that bunch—the father was a big drunk. In less than a year the furniture was all ruined and broken to bits, a big mess."

"I know how excited you must have been when we first moved to Terrace Village because of what you did for my fourth birthday," Rachel said. "July, 1941—you made a big party and invited all the cousins. I was so excited when you put balloons near the ceiling all around the living room. You baked a big cake, and served ice cream too. We all played games and had fun." She looked at her sister, smiling at the memory. "Collette, I remember you were always the one to organize the games. That was the happiest birthday I remember during my whole childhood, and the only time I remember all of our relatives coming to our place to visit when I was a kid. Nothing seemed bad then."

Ettie raised her eyebrows, remembering all of the years she had been afraid to invite her relatives to visit. But this had been different. Even though Morton didn't hang around to participate in the birthday party, instead leaving before anyone arrived to go to a movie, he was so happy to be living in a nice apartment, he encouraged Ettie to invite everyone. "Back then, your father thought all our troubles were over," she said. "He tried hard to make friends with our neighbors—we even went out to a nightclub once, with two other couples. They were big drinkers, and your dad wanted to fit in, so he ordered drinks for himself and me." She threw up her hands. "Phooey! It was awful, and I couldn't take more than a sip. And that club had a stand-up comedian whose jokes were filthy. I couldn't believe some of the awful things he was saying, but I pretended I was enjoying myself."

She shrugged and rolled her eyes toward the ceiling. "Your dad seemed so happy to have friends. Other times he even went out drinking with some of those guys—and he was not a drinker. Who knows what else they were doing?" Ettie waved that away, muttering, "Oh well. We got to know lots of people. There were even some Jewish families in the project. They didn't live in the same building as we did, but somehow we got to know them." She looked at Collette. "Remember that time—it was 1942, I think—your dad invited three families to a seder at our place?"

Collette had been sitting quietly. Ettie didn't know if the pained expression on her face came from her grief or her illness. Now her eyes brightened, and she answered with childlike enthusiasm, "That's what I was talking about the other day—it was the best seder ever. Dad knew all of the prayers and songs without having to read them, and he explained everything so clearly that I never forgot their meaning, to this day. I was so proud of him. I've been to lots of seders since then, but none can compare. Do you remember, Rachel? That was when you found the afikomen, the dessert matzo, so you could get the reward."

Rachel nodded at the familiar story. "That was fun. I was so surprised that I found it—maybe everybody let me find it. After the holiday Dad gave me my reward, that beautiful doll with the blond braids and the overalls. I loved that doll. But it didn't take long for that awful Gabrone boy to destroy it." Her expression soured. "He grabbed it from me and stomped on it in the mud. He broke all my toys, whatever he could grab out of my hands."

David frowned at Rachel, shaking his head. "How come you always dwell on things that were negative?"

"I don't think I'm saying anything wrong," Rachel insisted. "Mother was talking about what it was like in Terrace Village. Most of my memories of that place are negative, especially how the other kids bothered me. I hated living there because the kids were rough, and I didn't have any friends. Don't tell me you liked it there, because I remember you crying a lot."

"Come on, you two," Ettie sighed, "don't start at each other the way you used to do. We're talking about the seder, and it was a good one, all right. Your dad sure knew his stuff. But I had to do all of the cooking, serving, and cleaning, all by myself. None of those women we invited lifted a finger to help me—not like at my mother's place, where everybody helped. And it wouldn't have made any difference if it wasn't a seder. Your dad never helped with anything around the house."

Collette rose and walked over to pat Ettie's arm, then leaned down to kiss her forehead. "You always worked hard and tried to do the right thing. You had so many disappointments, Mother. I was always amazed at how strong you were, during all those rough times."

Ettie nodded. "That's what everyone always said about me, that I had strong shoulders so I could carry all the troubles God gave me. Believe me, it would have been better not to have such strong shoulders.

I wish I had had more confidence in myself. But I did see something special in your dad. And he did something special—he gave me you kids." Ettie blinked back sudden tears.

"Mother, you were right to see something special in him," Collette soothed. "How could you know he would get sick? Even when I was a little girl, I knew he was special, very intelligent. He could explain everything so clearly, and he loved to talk with me about the world. He taught me to read, prepared all those cards with letters and sounds . . . today they are part of the educational materials supplied to teachers, but not then. He made his own set. He never got impatient with me. He didn't just teach me to read, he made me love it."

Finally letting the tears flow, Ettie stood up and kissed her daughter. Collette also began to cry. "Don't you think I knew that, honey? I always knew how much you loved your father. Believe me, I tried my best. When he was well and happy, we were all happy. He tried so hard to be successful and to make us proud, but nothing seemed to work." She paused to fish a couple of tissues out of her pocket, and handed one to Collette. "You weren't the only one who learned from him—I did too. So did Uncle Nachum and even a couple of our friends who lived in the other buildings. When he explained what was going on in the world, especially after Pearl Harbor, it was as if someone turned on a light."

As Collette returned to her chair, Ettie looked around the room. David was sitting with his eyes closed. "Hey David, whatsa matter?" she asked, "Are we putting you to sleep?"

David opened his eyes and grimaced. "Nah. What d'ya expect me to say? I wasn't there. Go ahead, talk."

"Okay, I guess it's good to get it out," Ettie conceded, and settled back into the couch, then paused to gather her thoughts. "Let me tell you," she said finally, "your dad never felt good about himself, never felt people respected him, and couldn't just let things be. It was sad to watch how hard he tried to make friends with those jerks living in Terrace Village. It was even sadder to see him trying to prove he was worthy of his brothers' respect. After our country entered the war, he found out that other men were working in the steel mills and making more money than he was at the clothing store. So he quit his job and got a job in the mill. He told me he could do better on his own, didn't need his brothers to get him a job."

She shook her head sadly. "That was a terrible mistake. He was smaller than the other guys, and not used to that kind of work. Then they started teasing him, even muttering anti-Semitic insults. He got more and more depressed."

It was painful for Ettie to tell her children about those days. She remembered Morton coming home from work, dirty and agitated, hungry for his dinner, angry if the food wasn't ready the minute he arrived and angrier still if it was cold. He was too impatient to talk to anyone. Other times, his temper was frightening, and once when Ettie disagreed with something he said, he threw his plate across the room to smash against the wall. *I never knew what mood he might be in,* she thought, feeling again the tension she'd felt then. *I was always shooing Collette and Rachel outside before I thought he'd arrive, so they wouldn't have to witness his outbursts.*

* * *

Morton was having trouble sleeping most nights, and Ettie thought his impatience might be the result of exhaustion. Exhausted or not, he was often sexually aroused when they were in bed together, and he would reach for Ettie even after one of his angry outbursts. Usually she pretended to be asleep, or she told him she wasn't in the mood, but when he told her that the only way he could get some rest was if they had sex, she complied, always insisting that he use protection so she wouldn't get pregnant. When he told her he had been seeing their family doctor, Dr. Silverstein, about something that would help him feel calmer and sleep better, Ettie thought in relief, *Maybe our home life will calm down.*

Then the unbelievable happened.

On a bright Sunday morning, Collette and Rachel were walking toward their doorway after an early morning outing to one of the project's playgrounds when Rachel paused to play hopscotch with another girl. As they played, Collette talked with the Gabrone girl—until her younger brother ran by and pushed his sister to the ground. After a moment of shock, she began to cry.

"Look what you've done," she sobbed to her brother. "My Sunday dress is dirty now, and Mom and Dad will be mad."

Her brother held up a threatening fist. "You'd better not get me in trouble by telling them," he warned, and she cringed.

Summoned by the commotion, their parents came outside, and Mrs. Gabrone demanded, "What's going on here? What happened?"

After a fearful glance at her brother, the girl pointed at Collette and accused, "She pushed me into the dirt!"

The girl's mother whirled on Collette. "You dirty Jew," she screamed, "You have no business touching my daughter, especially before we go to church!"

Mr. Gabrone stomped up the stairs to the second floor and pounded on the apartment door. When Ettie answered it, he pushed past her and wagged a threatening finger at Morton. "You punish your daughter!" he shouted, then sneered, "She's clearly not the little angel you always make her out to be."

Ettie watched from the top of the stairs as Morton went outside. He insisted that Collette apologize. When Collette tried to explain that she had not pushed the girl, Morton became furious. "Don't you lie!" he hollered. "Get into our apartment *now*."

A dejected Collette climbed the stairs, followed by Morton with Rachel trailing behind. As they came through the door, Ettie began to cry and pulled Collette behind her, trying to shield her from Morton's fury.

"I didn't push her," Collette repeated over and over in the face of Morton's accusations. "I'm not a liar—I'm not lying!"

Rachel sidled up beside Ettie and whispered, "Collette didn't push her. The Gabrone kids are the liars."

Distracted, Ettie told Rachel, "Go back outside—quickly."

As Rachel ran toward the door, Morton grabbed Collette's arm, his face a mask of fury. His expression frightened Ettie. "Morton, no!" she screamed at him, following as he pulled Collette into the bedroom. "Stop it!"

Morton ignored her pleas and Collette's terrified sobs. Still holding her arm, he took off his belt and slapped the strap across Collette's buttocks, shouting at her, "No daughter of mine is a liar!"

Ettie felt the pain herself. How could Morton be assaulting his beloved, good-natured daughter, the little girl who adored him? "Morton, no! Stop, please stop!" she shrieked, and tried to put herself between them, but Morton pushed her out of the room and shut the door.

"Stop, Morton! Please stop!" Ettie continued shrieking again and again over Collette's screams—not screams of pain, but pleas for her father to believe her, that she was not a liar.

Finally everything became quiet. Ettie entered the bedroom and snatched the belt from Morton's limp hand. He stood facing the wall. Ettie left him there. She took Collette's hand and led her out of the bedroom and into the bedroom Collette shared with Rachel. Cooing words of comfort, Ettie hugged her, checked to see how badly bruised she was, then lay down on the bed with her and pulled the blankets up to her shoulders, holding Collette close.

Collette sniffled and looked up at Ettie. "Mummy, I am not a liar. Do you believe me?"

Ettie looked into her daughter's eyes and kissed her forehead. "Of course you're not a liar. I don't know what came over him, to hurt you like that. He knows better. He is not well, or he would never hurt you."

Morton remained in his room with the door shut, moaning softly. When Collette fell asleep, Ettie rose, careful not to wake her, and went out to call Rachel into the house. When her younger daughter entered, Ettie bent and hugged her. "Go and stay with your sister," she said softly.

Rachel looked earnestly into her eyes. "Collette never pushed that girl," she said, "I'm sure of it!"

"I know, honey," Ettie sighed. "Your father didn't know what he was doing."

Morton did not come out of the bedroom for the rest of the day. Finally, near sundown, Ettie knocked on the door and called, "Morton. Do you want something to eat?" When no answer came, she turned the knob and pushed the door open far enough to stick her head inside.

Morton was seated on the edge of the bed, shoulders slumped, head hanging. He looked up at her, his expression totally defeated, and said, "I hope God will forgive me for being evil. How could I hurt my wonderful daughter? I'm rotten and worthless."

* * *

"That's so sad," David whispered, and rose to sit beside Collette. "You must have been horrified."

Collette's eyes were downcast. "Even when he was hitting me, I knew he was sick or he would not be trying to hurt me," she said softly. "My tears were as much for him as they were for myself."

"It was unpleasant outside too," Rachel added, her voice also quiet. "A few neighbors were standing around, and they could hear the screams. I couldn't believe it when I heard one woman whisper to another, 'It's good that somebody put those Jews in their place.'"

* * *

A few weeks after Morton's outburst, Dr. Silverstein left a message with the neighbors whose phone Ettie used when necessary. *It's urgent that you call me*, the message read, followed by a phone number. When she returned the call, he told her that he couldn't help Morton any longer.

"Morton is depressed," he said, "and only a psychiatrist can help him. Mrs. Burin," he continued, his voice insistent, "I'm worried Morton will do real harm to somebody—or, more likely, to himself. It's urgent that you to get Morton to a psychiatrist."

Ettie clutched the telephone receiver tightly, struggling to pay attention as he gave her the name of a psychiatrist. But the room seemed to close in on her, and she fought panic as the darkness of the unknown began erasing everything she understood. *It's really no surprise,* a rational part of her mind said over and over; *why else would he have done that to Collette?*

When Ettie got back to their apartment, she sat in stunned silence, her head resting on her arms, folded on top of the kitchen table. She remembered the talk when she was a little girl living in Skvira, about a man they all knew to be a meshuganer, and how her mother told her to stay away from that house. She also remembered all the times her father had referred to Morton as a meshuganer. *Well, it seems Papa was right all along,* she thought. *The threats against Jake were terrifying enough, but he can't be in his right mind, to have done what he did to Collette, the person he loves more than anyone in the world. Maybe a psychiatrist* can *help.*

When Morton arrived home from work, Ettie asked Collette to take Rachel with her to the grocery store to buy a loaf of bread, knowing it would take the girls fifteen minutes to walk each way. Then she turned to Morton. "We have to talk."

As soon as she repeated what Dr. Silverstein said, Morton's reaction stunned and frightened her. "Don't you ever repeat this to anyone," he hissed. "This is a black mark against my family. Nobody must ever know the doctor said that. I'm counting on you—*do not ruin my family's name*. You must promise me."

Ettie said nothing more about it for the next two weeks. Morton began spending more time in the bedroom, door closed, talking aloud to himself as if he were talking with his brothers, praying and pacing. Ettie knew she had to do something. Finally, when she was out shopping for groceries one day, she called Isaac from the local pay phone and shared with him what the doctor had advised.

The next day Isaac and his three younger brothers arrived at Ettie's home to try to convince Morton that he should go to the psychiatrist. They argued all day, and finally the men went for a walk. Upon their return, Morton pointed at Ettie. "If you tell me to see the psychiatrist and if you go with me, I will."

* * *

Ettie stopped talking, replaying, as she often did, the doctor's visit in her mind. She remembered vividly sitting alone on an overstuffed chair when Morton first went in, and then the door opening later and the doctor waving for her to enter.

Morton had stood with his eyes glued to the floor as the doctor's unemotional voice explained that Morton was depressed and in need of a few shock treatments. "After a few treatments," the doctor proclaimed with an air of professional certainty, "Morton will be ready to return home, better than ever."

"I believed the doctor and thought he knew what he was talking about," Ettie said after relaying this to her children. "Your dad was admitted. Next time I saw him, after those treatments, it was horrifying. His brother Sam came with me, and there was Morton, sitting all tied up in a big chair, staring out at us with a blank face. His first words were, 'How could you do this to me?' Those treatments made him worse, and he was never the same person again."

Ettie noticed the pained expressions on her children's faces. She rubbed her eyes. "Do you want me to go on?"

Rachel was first to answer. "If it's not too hard for you to talk about, Mother." David nodded.

Ettie drew a quavering breath. "It was a nightmare. He wouldn't talk to me, just kept moaning and spitting on the floor, telling me that he was no good. I brought him sandwiches and he'd eat one, then throw the others across the floor." She shuddered as memories surged back. "I heard people yelling in the hallways. I couldn't wait to get out of there."

"Did the doctor or anyone else talk with you about us, or your own well-being?" Rachel asked.

Ettie suppressed sudden anger. "What did they care about any of that? They were just there to give the shock treatments." She looked at Collette. "Do you remember how you begged me to let you visit your dad? I knew it was a bad idea. But the doctor said you could come at the end of the first month."

Collette nodded. " I was eleven years old, but it might have been yesterday. It was so sad, when he came through the door and saw me standing there. At first he said, 'Ah, Collette,' and put his arms around me. Then he swung away and began yelling, 'Don't look at me. I'm disgusting. Spit at me—go ahead, spit at me. I'm worthless. I'm not your father. Forget you ever had a father.' I tried to tell him I loved him, and I was happy to see him. But he just got more upset and told me not to look at him. Somebody came over and told me it would be best if I left. I cried and cried that day."

Rachel, who was only five when Morton entered the hospital in the winter of 1942, recounted her one memory of the hospital. "I remember that time we waved . . . I could barely see him, just an outline of someone, but I saw a hand waving. I didn't understand what was wrong with him. I was surprised he could stand at a window and wave if he was so sick that he had to be in a hospital."

Ettie nodded, recalling her side of that memory. Children Rachel's age were not permitted to visit hospital patients. Rachel hadn't understood what kind of an illness her father had and kept asking when he would be coming home. "I tried to explain to you that he had become very nervous and the doctors were trying to help him to calm down. Then, a few weeks later, I arranged for you to remain in the waiting room with Collette while I visited Morton, and I got someone to take him to a window where he could wave to you before we left. He was calm enough that day to be compliant." Although the wave had not been painful, simply unfulfilling, the memory had remained forever with Rachel.

David began to pace the room, stopping occasionally to stare out the window. Ettie watched him, wondering when he would ask how he fit into all of this. She and his sisters had never before gone into this kind of detail about their shared anguish. *His pain came later,* she thought. *It was different from theirs. He had no memory of Morton.*

David turned to face them and she prepared for the first question, but all he said was, "I think we'd better call it a night and get going."

PART SIX

WALL OF SILENCE

People say they have a screw
loose, their brain like a barn door
hanging off its hinges, swinging in the wind,
and no matter how they shut it, the fit
is not right, and the brain pours out.

Like a dead soldier's intestines
that will not stuff back in. They are
edible food: crackers, bananas,
flakey, nutty as fruitcake, barmy as a crumpet . . .

. . . They say they're off their rocker,
doolally, off their trolley, haywire, short-
circuited and stopped in the middle of the road—
the conductor out to lunch while they
are round the bend—there but not there,
like peek-a-boo games with babies.
They call them cuckoos, daft birds
with goofy calls who abandon their eggs
in the nests of others . . .

—"The Unhinged" by Margo Button

The Telegram

Sunday would be the sixth and next to last day of shiva. David had become increasingly agitated, the silence on how he came to be a part of this family more and more troubling. He had no memory of his father until he was over eleven years old, when Collette and Stanley arranged a visit. His strongest memory of that visit was one of overriding embarrassment coupled with the fear that he would turn out to be the same as his father, a "chip off the old block."

Listening to the old stories about his mother's early life and his sisters' memories of their childhoods brought back the feeling he always had as a child, that he was on the outside looking in. He was still afraid of delving into the past too much, but he'd decided he wouldn't leave Pittsburgh without trying to get some answers.

He looked at his mother. "I want to know something. Almost everything you've been talking about happened before I was born. But one thing I never could figure out . . . if my father was mentally ill, having shock treatments, why didn't you do anything to make sure you didn't become pregnant at such a time? Did you think having another baby was going to help the situation?"

Ettie looked as if he had slapped her across the face. She opened her mouth several times, only to shut it again, her expression uncertain. Finally she sighed and sagged back against the cushions of the couch. "Maybe now is the time to open up, even if it's unpleasant," she said, looking at David with apologetic eyes. "You're right. Bringing another child into the world at that time was the last thing I would have planned."

* * *

Ettie received a visit from her eighty-year-old father-in-law just before Morton's discharge from the hospital. He was still working as an assistant rabbi at the only Orthodox synagogue in Braddock, on the outskirts of Pittsburgh, where he'd been for most of the twenty years since his arrival in the United States. He lived frugally, always seeming out of place in the competitive and materialistic world in which he now lived, happy to be surrounded by his religious books and the freedom to practice his religion without disturbance. Wherever he went, he brought an otherworldly calm and kindness with him.

This spirituality and gentleness filled Ettie with awe and respect while at the same time making her feel unworthy, even guilty, now that he had begun to make regular visits to their apartment in Terrace Village, usually early on Sunday afternoons. He traveled by streetcar, always appearing distinguished and scholarly in his dark suit, with his white hair and neatly trimmed beard and the black umbrella he carried regardless of the weather.

As soon as he settled into a chair at her kitchen table, Ettie offered him a glass of tea. He would pull a cloth pouch from his pocket and extract three sugar cubes, offering one to each granddaughter and dunking the third in his tea before putting it to his lips. He was always delighted to see his granddaughters. After kissing them and completing the sugar ritual, he asked each in Yiddish what she was learning in school, and if she was being helpful to her mother. Smiling and patting them on their heads, he listened as they responded in English.

During each visit he spoke quietly with Ettie, thanking her for her loyalty, praising her for the way she took care of her children, never criticizing anything she did. Despite that voiced approval, she never felt quite worthy to be in his family, always believing she had to strive to do better for his sake. It hurt her that Morton's problems had caused this pious man so much pain and embarrassment.

He always moved the conversation to the past, repeating parts of a story Ettie had heard before, as if he believed that by repeating the details, he might find proof that Morton's illness was not a stain on the family. "Morton was a normal child who only began to get moody when he was a teenager—after his mother's death," her father-in-law explained, then shook his head and added somberly, "and particularly when we didn't have enough to eat." Then he drew himself up. "Morton was the most outstanding scholar the town had ever produced, but he became easily distracted and no longer concentrated on his studies. Soon he began spending time with unruly boys who questioned the Torah and the old ways, boys who wanted to move to Palestine."

His voice fell. "When Morton and the boys wrote out their challenges to the synagogue in a letter and posted it on the wall of the synagogue, imagine how embarrassing it was for a respected rabbi to face the townspeople, with his son part of such an outrage. But what could I do but love him still?" He shook his head again. "It's hard to believe that someone with such a good mind could have mental problems."

On the visit just before Morton's discharge from the hospital, something changed in her father-in-law's tone. He cleared his throat and asked Ettie if he could discuss something privately with her. She immediately asked Collette to take Rachel for a walk.

He began hesitantly. "Please forgive me for having to discuss something very intimate, dear daughter-in-law. I hope you will understand that what I have to say is in the spirit of trying to help you, Morton, and the family."

Ettie became immediately uncomfortable, even frightened, because she knew she could never refuse anything this revered man might ask of her.

"I hope you will not only forgive me, but also be able to forgive Morton, despite the problems you have." He paused and cleared his throat many times before finally getting to the point. "You know, my child, some things are different for men than they are for women. Sometimes men have physical needs that must be fulfilled, and if they are denied, it will affect how they think and react to everything. I plead with you to try to be a good wife to Morton in every sense of the word. The most important duty a wife has is to respond to her husband physically when he needs her. Promise me you won't deny him, even if he finds it difficult to use protection so you can avoid pregnancy."

Ettie was stunned that this holy man was giving her such advice. She was also hurt—after all the problems this man's family had experienced with Morton, he was suggesting that their sex life might be the root of Morton's unstable behavior. *He has been widowed for many years,* she thought. *Maybe he believes this because he himself longs for a woman's touch. Or did Morton say something to his father that made him conclude such a thing? That's what probably happened.*

Nevertheless, she had thought that he, of all people, was more enlightened than the old-timers from Skvira and elsewhere in the old country. She had heard all the stories about how marriages were arranged with no concern for the feelings the boy and girl had for one another. Women were expected to do their wifely duty, even if they found the men physically repulsive. But this was 1942 in America, and this was a more enlightened man talking.

"Don't worry, father-in-law," she managed to reply. "I understand what you mean. I will always do my duty."

He sighed, tears filling his eyes. "Thank you. You are a good person, and I knew I could count on you to do your best for Morton and our family."

* * *

Ettie paused and looked at David, hoping the conversation she'd just related didn't cause him too much pain.

"So you let an old religious man control you," he said, his voice cracking. He shook his head. "I never got to know him. I just have a vague memory of seeing him when I was about five years old, that time we all went to Uncle Isaac's to say goodbye to him, just before he left to live in Israel. I guess I should have thanked him."

At first Ettie sat silently, staring at her son. Then she rose and walked to the front door to look out its small window while she marshaled her emotions. When Collette and Stanley had first moved to this suburban development in the late 1950s, Ettie couldn't hide her disappointment that it would be impossible to drop by to visit her daughter without first finding someone with a car who could drive her there. Even after close to forty years, she continued to think of the neighborhood, a twenty-minute ride from her apartment, as being far away.

She turned and looked around the room before returning to her seat. The combined living-dining room was long and narrow, small but bright. The high cathedral ceiling made it seem more spacious than it was. Light poured in from the large picture window that faced a partially treed field. Ettie wondered how her daughter ever got used to living in a place so far from the buzz of shops and people.

On one wall in the dining room hung a picture of Morton's

grandfather, a rabbi and a respected scholar. Nobody knew the exact date the picture was taken, but it must have been before the turn of the century. There he sat, a man with a flowing white beard, leaning over a table on which were piled large books, an oil lamp to one side. *Morton treasured that photograph,* she remembered. *He hung it in the apartment in Terrace Village, the only thing that ever decorated the walls there.* Now it was a part of her daughter's life, a symbol of the scholarly and religious family heritage.

Clearing her throat, Ettie resumed her story. "Your father seemed so well when he first got out of the hospital, I thought the treatment had done the trick." Morton had returned to his old job selling men's clothes on Fifth Avenue. The owner of the store liked him and wanted to help the family. "Morton wanted to be a good father to you kids, you know."

Rachel nodded. "I remember how he liked tucking us in at bedtime, how he used to sing to us."

Collette began to sing and hum "In a Little Spanish Town."

Rachel touched her forehead in thought, then blurted, "And that other one—'Bye, Bye, Blackbird.'"

"He took us to the park and to the movies," Collette added. "I enjoyed the stories he made up, full of happy children living in a magical world." She looked at her brother. "It's too bad he got sick before you were old enough to know him, David."

Ettie would not spoil these few happy memories her kids had by repeating what actually happened when she was alone in bed with Morton—how he told her that the only thing that made him feel good was her loving him, and how he insisted on sex without any artificial material that would take away the sensation. Of course she went along with it—whatever it took to keep him so positive.

"Well, we had a couple of good months," she agreed. "Then his condition got worse than ever, and there was no doubt that he was a sick man. I used to worry that he might do something to cause trouble." She thought about how fearful she'd been, each time he decided to take Collette and Rachel to the park or to the movies, how she worried whether he would bring them home safely.

It was around this time that she noticed a new habit: he would spit in the street when he passed people, mutter to himself, and sometimes wring his hands. She knew the neighbors were staring at him, making quiet jokes about him, and she prayed that he would not hear them and become angry. Sometimes he pulled the blinds down on all the windows so nobody could see him, convinced they were planning to do harm to him or his family. Then he would begin to pace the length of the living room and kitchen, chanting Hebrew prayers.

It was a shock to others in the family when Ettie became pregnant a few months after Morton's discharge. She told Libby about it before she told Morton. It reignited Libby's anger at Morton, and she told Ettie how sorry she felt for her, living with a man who had to have his own way about everything. "Well, I don't know what you're gonna do now," she declared. "I hope he gets some sense in his head and helps you with things."

Ettie knew this was a crisis she would have to handle on her own. Her family no longer lived nearby. The Hill District had been changing during the past few years. Most of the Jewish immigrants were moving away, while increasing numbers of African-Americans were arriving. Ettie's parents and Libby and Jake and their two children had moved to a quiet street in Pittsburgh's East End, where they rented a nicer but much smaller house than the one on Roberts Street. With Sarah and Yitzhac using one of the three bedrooms, Libby and Jake the second one, and their Uncle Nachum renting the only other full bedroom, they were crowded. Their children were squeezed into tiny spaces, Danny in a corner of the kitchen on a folding bed and his sister Susan in a tiny room not much bigger than a closet. No, Ettie could no longer go running home to her parents if things got worse. Besides, Ettie loved her apartment in Terrace Village, despite the unpleasantness of some of the neighbors.

It was a relief to realize she could get adequate medical care at the Montefiore Hospital clinic set up for poor people. But how could she possibly manage to look after a little baby and her daughters, given the way Morton was behaving? What if he couldn't hold onto his job? He'd told her that people at work didn't appreciate what he did, and he would probably be fired soon. Ettie wasn't sure whether this was true or if his suspicions were part of his deteriorating condition. Now she couldn't even consider going back to work.

* * *

As Ettie talked with her children about how she coped with the unplanned pregnancy, she kept one episode a secret. Before she'd told Morton, she confided in Jeanette, one of her Terrace Village neighbors who had become a close friend. The advice she received startled her. Jeanette advised Ettie to let her arrange for an abortion. The doctor who would do it was Jeanette's relative, a fully licensed doctor who had a separate practice, but secretly performed abortions because he believed women should have that option and also because it gave him a chance to earn extra money. Ettie would not have to tell Morton about the pregnancy. It could all be done very quietly in a room the doctor kept in the attic of his house. Ettie would have to find the money to pay for it, but Jeanette offered to arrange a loan.

It was hard for Ettie to sleep after Jeanette put that solution into her head. She thought of how her own baby sister had died at the age of two in Skvira. She had visions of all the babies clinging to their mothers as they ran or hid from the soldiers. If her mother and the other women had been strong enough to try to protect their children, she would be too. She decided overnight that an abortion was out of the question.

She looked at David, and tried to return her focus to his question about how she could have brought him into the world when his father was in the midst of a mental breakdown. "Your dad was thrilled to hear we were having another baby. For weeks he actually seemed well again. I was dumb enough to think it might work out okay. Then it all started again, this time with the kosher stuff and the constant praying."

When she first met Morton, he was a religious cynic. He had studied all of the texts and cared deeply about the Jewish people, but he doubted the existence of God and sneered at some of the Orthodox practices regarding food and diet. Now he became obsessed with absolute adherence to the dietary laws and strict observance of the Sabbath. Up to that time Ettie never questioned the need to keep a kosher home and did so just as her mother had done. She bought meats from a kosher butcher shop, kept two sets of dishes, and never mixed meat and dairy in her meals. However, now Morton became overbearing, checking every can and package Ettie brought into the house, insisting that she throw away anything with a questionable ingredient. If one of the children accidentally let a spoon or fork meant for dairy fall into the drawer with the meat flatware, he insisted that Ettie boil that utensil.

"Do you remember how he ruined all that good silverware with his boiling?" she asked Collette and Rachel. "He would put on his *yarmulke*, *tallis*, and *tefillin* and start the *davenen*, praying and pacing from one end of the apartment to the other. It was hard to be in the same house with him."

Rachel shook her head sadly, remembering. Collette just closed her eyes. Ettie knew it had been hard for them, too. He forbade his children from writing or riding a bus or using money on the Sabbath, telling them that God would punish them severely if they did not keep the Sabbath holy. Saturday movies with the cousins were forbidden.

Rachel looked at her sister. "Did I tell you about this? I used to hide in my closet on Saturdays, playing teacher to my imaginary class of pupils, writing on sheets of paper or coloring pictures in my coloring book. I don't know why I did it, when I knew how angry he would get if he caught me—I was so terrified that I would get spanked, but I kept on playing school." She turned to Ettie. "You saw me doing it once, and you put your finger to your lips to keep me quiet. Then you shut the door and told Dad that I was taking a nap."

Collette shifted the subject. "Well, David, you wanted to know about what it was like when you came along, and I want to tell you. I was so thrilled to hear that Mother and Dad were having a baby. I remember how excited Dad was when you were born. He bragged to everyone that now he had a son. He came to Miller School late one morning to tell Rachel and me that we had a new brother. First he told our teachers and managed to get them excited, too." She smiled at David. "The first time I saw you, you were so gorgeous. I loved you immediately. I was so proud to take you for walks in the buggy and show you off to my friends."

Ettie looked at her oldest daughter with pride and disbelief. "I don't know what I would have done without you, all those years. You were such a help to me. I know it was hard for you, and I leaned on you too much. And somehow you managed to excel in school while all of this was going on. How did you do it? Everybody loved you, and your teachers said you were the best. You gave me the strength to go on." She sighed and looked at Rachel and David, adding, "All of my children did."

Rachel laughed. "I'm not so sure we *all* did. I was a real problem back then, wasn't I? Crying for Collette to take me with her and her friends whenever they went anywhere. Not wanting to go to bed at night. And then getting sick all the time."

Ettie lifted her eyebrows in surprise. "It was hard for you, but you were a sweet little girl. I was so stressed out that I didn't have any time to spend with you. Sometimes I didn't know how I could get through another day. Collette was helping me a lot with David, but you were only five years old when David was born. Maybe you felt abandoned."

"Well, I always thought it was my fault Dad ended up leaving. It took me years to get over it. It was all because of that birthday party I wanted you to take me to; I knew all my cousins would be there and we'd play games, and I always liked the birthday cake and ice cream. You kept saying no, because you knew Dad had hidden a small packed suitcase, and you were worried he was planning to leave. I cried and cried that I wanted to go to the party, and finally you said okay. You got David ready and took us to the party. I think David was about six months old. I don't remember where Collette was that day, maybe at the IKS. When we got home from the party, you went from room to room calling, 'Morton, Morton,' but he was gone. You kept saying that you knew he was planning to leave and that's why you didn't want to go to the party. You said now you didn't know what to do. I was sure it was all my fault that he disappeared."

"I never blamed you. I realized if he hadn't gone that day, it would have been the next. I never knew before now that you blamed yourself," Ettie said, her voice heavy with regret. She hadn't thought of Rachel, only remembered her feelings of total despair.

* * *

Morton had gone without leaving any message about where he was going or for how long. He had not yet been paid for that month's work. They had food to last for only a day or two. And there she was with her three kids. Her first thought was that maybe he would come home that night, the next day, or in a few days. After all, hadn't he disappeared in the past? Still, it was hard to erase from her mind what he had been saying for the past few days—that he didn't deserve to be alive, that he didn't deserve to be in America when the Nazis were killing Jews all over Europe. What if he tried to harm himself?

Like a sleepwalker, she nursed David, washed him, and put him to bed. As she prepared dinner for Rachel and Collette, she tried to hide her panic, but when Rachel began asking where her daddy had gone, Ettie broke down and cried. Rachel picked at her food, said she wasn't hungry, and went into the bedroom to play with her paper dolls. Collette remained in the kitchen, trying to comfort her mother.

Finally, after two days went by with no word, Ettie called Isaac to let him and his brothers know that Morton had disappeared again. Isaac didn't sound surprised. "We'll come and see you tomorrow. We want to help you."

"I'll be okay for now," Ettie assured him. She had already learned from Jeanette how to apply for welfare, and had decided to contact the administrator of the housing project to let him know that she would not be able to pay the full amount of rent they were assessed based on Morton's earnings. She didn't want to take more charity from her brothers-in-law.

It was the fall of 1943. The news on the radio focused on the horrors of soldiers being killed by the Japanese and people being uprooted in countries she had never heard about. The Nazis had overrun most of Europe, and Jews were disappearing. American cities ran air raid drills to prepare in case of enemy attack, and they were frequent in Pittsburgh, one of the country's centers of manufacturing. Morton had been concerned that they all learn what to do during those drills. He had instructed Collette and Rachel to get into the apartment immediately if the sirens began.

Ettie couldn't help wondering if her children would end up having the same kind of childhood she had: living without their father, hiding from soldiers, and witnessing the aftermath of their rampages. She wasn't sure if she would be able to protect them as well as her mother had. *No, that won't happen,* she convinced herself. *America is safe, a good place to live where our children can go outdoors and play without fearing for their lives.*

After Morton's disappearance, Ettie appreciated Collette's offers to take David for walks in his stroller. She would glance out the kitchen window as they walked down the street toward the benched area on the little hill behind the administration building, Rachel walking alongside, holding onto the stroller's handle. Rachel would return smiling and excited, repeating the stories Collette made up for her, imitating the different voices Collette had used for each character.

One of those days, after Ettie saw them walk toward the benches, a pounding on the door startled her. None of her neighbors announced themselves that way—they were usually very tentative and sometimes called out while they knocked.

She opened the door to a deliveryman holding a telegram sent from a New York City hospital. It provided a telephone number for her to call and the name of a contact person. The telegram message read: *Morton Burin admitted September 5. Call for further details.* Ettie's heart began to pound as her mind raced. What was he doing in New York? Had he been injured in an accident? Had he become ill?

She didn't have a telephone and had to ask her neighbor if she could use their phone to make a long distance call. They hesitated because of the expense, but she said she would try to call person-to-person and reverse the charges. It worked. They all hovered in the kitchen near the phone while she made the call.

After she got connected to the name on the telegram and announced who she was, she listened, saying almost nothing other than answering yes or no and asking one-word questions— "Where?" or "When?" Her last question was, "What should I do now?"

The information stunned and horrified Ettie. Morton had taken a train to New York, had somehow spent a few nights wandering in the city, sleeping who knows where, and had finally made his way to the shipping docks, where he pleaded to be put on a boat to Poland. He told them that he didn't deserve to be an American citizen, didn't deserve to live, and should be sent to a concentration camp to die with his people. He made quite a scene, and the police were called to take him away. They drove him immediately to the psychiatric ward of a city hospital. As soon as the doctors at the hospital were able to break through his resistance and get his address, they'd sent the telegram.

Ettie's knowledge that Morton was suffering with mental problems did not help her grasp the extent to which he had lost touch with reality. As much as she had been through with Morton, she couldn't conceive of anyone wanting to be put into the torturous situations beginning to leak out about concentration camps. What could he have been thinking? Hadn't she done everything anyone could expect to adapt to his moods? They were blessed with lovely children and had a chance to make a go of it. Even though she had been trying hard to be a good wife and mother, he was anxious to throw his life away. She felt like a total failure. And once again she felt humiliated by this man. How could he turn his back on her like this?

She hung up and thanked her neighbors, hoping they hadn't figured out what she was talking about. Then, telegram in hand, she started down the hill to find her children.

Collette was well into a funny story, and Rachel was looking at her adoringly, laughing. Collette stopped in mid-sentence when she saw her mother approaching with a paper in her hand. Ettie was almost out of breath, but she said, "Now we know where your father is."

"Oh, boy! Where is he, did he send us a letter?" Rachel asked.

Ettie handed Collette the telegram. "He's in a hospital in New York, Rachel, and they're sending him back to a hospital in Pittsburgh. There's a telephone number here, and I've already called it." Anticipating the question concerning what was wrong with him, Ettie explained, "He got very nervous and confused and didn't know where he was. They were afraid he would be hurt. When he comes back here, they'll try to find out what his problems are and help him calm down." Ettie didn't know what else to say without terrifying her daughters. She averted her eyes and went over to the stroller to check David and wipe drool from his chin. She couldn't tell them the shocking truth about his request to be sent to Poland.

"When they find out what his problems are, will he come home again?" Rachel asked.

Ettie thought the kindest answer was one that gave her hope of a normal family life. "Of course, honey, once the doctors know what's the matter, they can make him better." Ettie knew better, though she yearned to convince herself that it was possible.

Collette looked at her mother with great sadness and understanding in her eyes. Now that Ettie had chosen this approach, it would be difficult to turn back. Ettie knew she had to pretend to Rachel and later to David that the doctors would find a way to cure Morton. Nothing more had to be said to Collette, who understood that this was the most comfortable explanation, even though she recognized the depth of her father's severe anguish.

They walked back up the hill together toward their apartment, the bright sun and blue sky no competition for the darkness of Ettie's mood.

From that day on, Ettie tried to keep the myth of Morton's expected cure alive. The first time David was old enough to ask for his daddy, Ettie was able to answer without telling a lie. Morton had fallen—or was he knocked over?—and broken his leg. It was in a cast for two months. Even after the cast came off, Ettie didn't change her story, continually reassuring David that when his father was able to walk, he would come home. After several months, Morton developed back pains and the hospital began testing to determine if the problem could be alleviated. That gave Ettie another easy story to tell David, that his father's leg was better but now he had something wrong with his back. Over the years it seemed that his father managed to contract one physical ailment or disability after another, and Ettie continued to explain to David that all of these required continued hospitalization.

Ettie and Collette agreed that it was best not to discuss Morton's mental illness with people who didn't already know. This included teachers, neighbors, and new acquaintances. Ettie was afraid that people would look down on, or even shun, her children if they found out about their father. She feared that when Collette and Rachel were old enough to go on dates, boys would not want to take them out and no family would want their child to marry a person whose father was in an insane asylum.

Collette was convinced that there would be jokes about her father if people who didn't know him heard about his illness. She even pretended to laugh herself, hiding the hurt inside, when kids made jokes about anyone who was in "the looney bin" or was a "nut case." She would come home subdued after hearing teachers use disparaging phrases when scolding kids who misbehaved. Like Ettie, she believed that as long as people didn't know the details, they would still respect her father.

Ettie and Collette both explained to Rachel that if anyone asked about her father, the best answer would be to say, "He's in a hospital and the doctors are trying to find out what is wrong with him." This response, they agreed, was what David should give, once he grew older. Ettie knew that someday she'd have to explain the situation to her son, but not until he was old enough to understand.

Several years went by, and David only knew that his mother's visits to the hospital upset her, especially when he asked if his father was getting better. After a few years, he stopped asking if the doctors had discovered the problem or when he might be coming home. He longed for a father he could play games with or talk to, but whenever he asked his sisters anything about the situation, they always said they didn't know and changed the subject. Learning it was a topic best ignored, he gradually avoided the subject.

* * *

As this sixth day of shiva continued and they sat around Collette's living room talking with friends and relatives who dropped by, Ettie understood how differently Morton's death was affecting each of them. Collette's early love and close bond with her dad had never weakened, even though the nature of the relationship had changed drastically. Rachel felt very little connection to the man who had just died; in her mind, the father she knew had died years earlier, when hope for his cure and return disappeared. David's loss and his sadness over that loss also happened long ago, but he felt more pain because others in the family had kept the truth from him for so long.

Ettie's loss was more complicated. She felt little to bond her with the person Morton had become, but his existence was a constant reminder of her disappointment, pain, embarrassment, and anger at both him and herself. *I should have known better than to marry him . . . should've found the strength to get out of the situation before it was too late . . . should've handled things differently when he became ill . . . should've done more to protect the children from the fear of how people would react to a mentally ill father.* Now she had to face up to the fact that she'd misled people living in her apartment building by pretending to already be a widow. Performing the rituals of a newly widowed woman made her feel guilty, given that she saw herself as merely going through the motions. She knew it wasn't Morton's fault, but that didn't change how she felt about him, and herself. No matter that other people admired her strength and courage through the years—*I'm just a big dummy.*

It was difficult to witness Collette crying softly to one of her cousins, explaining how much she would be missing her visits with her father. Rachel joined the conversation, adding, "For many years after he went into the hospital, I prayed he would get better. Every year when I blew out the candles on my birthday cakes, my only wish was for my dad to get better and come home. My prayers were never answered."

David looked from Rachel to Ettie, then stared at the ceiling, murmuring to himself, "All those years, I didn't know what I was supposed to be wishing or praying for. I believed a big lie."

Rachel continued before anyone could respond to David. "The few times they sent him home, promising he was better, just resulted in another disappointment. For many years I didn't see him, and when I finally did, he didn't seem like my father. He knew he had a daughter named Rachel, but he didn't know I was that person. I never connected with the man I saw after all those years. I should have tried harder, I guess, but he seemed like a stranger."

Collette's face fell. "I'm so sorry you felt that way, Rachel, because he loved you very much when you were a little girl, was very proud of how pretty and smart you were. His illness was never cured, but he became loveable in different ways, and we were able to have many happy times together. It was almost as if my relationship with him was divided into two parts, both with great meaning to me. I wish it could have been the same for you."

Collette looked at her husband for confirmation. Stanley crossed the room to them. "I was always happy that Collette still had a father who could be part of her life," he said, "even if it was only through our visits and local excursions with him, when we took him on a pass from the hospital. My father died when I was a teenager, and I always missed having him with me. The visits with Collette's dad filled a void for me too. We would bring him a suit to change into and then go for a ride, usually to a coffee shop somewhere in Mount Lebanon. We all had lunch or snacks, and it just seemed like any family outing, very pleasant, and nobody in the coffee shop would have guessed that he was from Mayview. "

Ettie looked at Stanley in disbelief, then quickly looked away, turning her gaze to Rachel, who was on the verge of saying something. Instead she put her hands in the air, palms up, as if to say "go figure." Ettie leaned over and whispered to Rachel, "He sure never went through what I did with that man."

The Visits

Not long after Ettie learned that Morton was in the New York hospital and would soon be transferred to one in Pittsburgh, she put in her application for public assistance. It was processed quickly enough to enable Ettie to cover most of her immediate expenses. The day after she told her family about the call, Libby and Jake dropped by to talk with her and brought a shopping bag full of food that Sarah had prepared for her. Jake hugged Rachel and Collette, gave them chocolate bars, and put his arm around Ettie's shoulders. "Don't worry, kiddo, we're here for you. Just let us know how we can help."

Ettie looked at the floor and sighed. She was grateful for the visit and knew the offer was genuine. But she didn't know how she'd cope with such an overwhelming predicament. The tears began to flow. "Yeah, I know. But what can anybody do? It's no use."

Later in the day, Bennie dropped by to make sure his sister was okay. He had been married for three years and already had two children of his own. Ettie knew he was working long hours and barely making a living delivering groceries. She wouldn't dream of adding to his burden.

Morton's brothers, Isaac and Sam, arrived a few days later. They explained that they had been in touch with the doctors at the Western State Psychiatric Hospital where Morton would be transferred and had arranged for a meeting. They wanted her to attend with them after Morton's arrival.

"This is a modern hospital, aware of the latest treatments," Sam assured her.

Isaac also sounded optimistic: "It's not a place where they just dump people and forget about them. If there's anything that can be done to help Morton, the doctors in this hospital will know about it."

Then Sam put words to what Ettie had been thinking. "You know, as awful as it is, what Morton did, it's lucky he didn't try to harm you or the kids."

Before they left, Isaac gave Ettie fifty dollars to help her manage the household.

Ettie didn't waste time thinking about what to do next. She was on her own, and she knew that her children must come first. Even though her marriage had been a big mistake and failure, she had to make sure that nobody could accuse her of not doing her duty as a mother. She would always put the physical needs of her children above her own. It was her responsibility to make sure that they were cared for so they wouldn't get sick, never went hungry, were neat and clean, and behaved in a way that would bring them respect in the world. It was important that Morton's family must never be ashamed of them.

She was also determined to ensure that her children could rise above what she felt was the disgrace of their father's illness. Maybe she had been denied an education that might have protected her from her current state of dependency, but that would never happen to her children. Collette was already excelling in school, and Rachel was learning quickly, so it was possible to hope for success for them. With luck, maybe David would turn out the same. They would have to do better than other kids to earn people's respect and convince people that they were capable. And if her children turned out well, despite the obstacles already in their way, people would know that she was not to blame for what had happened to Morton.

Good things were happening for Collette. She was in the sixth grade at Miller School, an exuberant student who loved to read, especially poetry, and who typically earned straight A's on her report cards. The teachers were effusive in their praise when Ettie visited the school on parents' nights. Ettie felt a surge of pride when one teacher commented loud enough for other parents to hear, "If all of my pupils were as smart and dependable as Collette, I wouldn't have any problems ever."

It was still difficult for Ettie to understand how Collette managed to be so cheerful and enthusiastic despite all the strain at home. She joined the school choir, performed in school plays, volunteered as a student safety officer, and even took ballet lessons at the IKS where Ettie and Libby had met so many of their friends when they were girls. Collette liked to sit and talk with Ettie each evening, repeating all the details about her school day. Although Ettie enjoyed the attention, she was uncomfortable with how much she was leaning on her oldest child. The more they talked about Collette's success in school and other activities, the more Ettie became annoyed with herself for her own deficiencies, and she would often end the conversation by telling Collette that she was wasting time and should focus more on her homework.

It was no surprise that Rachel liked school more and more, always trying to do as well as Collette. The first-grade teacher praised her good work. Not only was she obedient, but Collette had taught her to read a year earlier, and she learned all the new things faster than the other children did. Still, Ettie worried about Rachel, who had become shy and high-strung, and who often became irritated with other children who didn't follow the rules of the games they played. It seemed that Rachel preferred to spend hours playing alone, reading, coloring, making up games, and talking to imaginary people.

The older David got, the more needy Rachel became of Ettie's attention. She picked at her food, cried about the clothes she had to wear, and was afraid of the dark. When she tried to play with David, she was too serious for the energetic boy, and he would grab her toys and make her cry. She also got sick more often now than when she was younger, frequently developing coughs, fevers, and sore throats. When she went outside to play, she usually returned with scraped, bloody knees. She argued when it was bedtime, not wanting to go to bed until Collette could join her in their shared room. Ettie scolded her, warning her of the consequences to her health, but the tension seldom lifted.

Rachel adored Collette and wanted to be with her constantly, even when Collette spent time with her friends. It was a real treat when Collette took her to the library or to the movies, especially the Saturdays when they met their cousins at the Enright Theater in East Liberty. Ettie was grateful that Collette never complained and actually seemed to enjoy her role as big sister. The two sisters had grown attached to each other, enjoying the long talks and the games they made up before bedtime. Rachel listened intently whenever Collette told her about her activities or conversations with friends. It took a burden off Ettie, whose nerves were on edge as she tried to adjust to her new life.

The biggest worry was David. Would she be able to raise a little boy without a father? Everyone said he was precocious and handsome, with his huge, long-lashed brown eyes and infectious smile, and she loved holding him close. But he was a handful—big for his age, hard to carry around, and rambunctious. His crying as an infant upset her, especially when she was in the middle of cooking or doing housework. After he learned to walk at nine months, his energy and curiosity took him into every room, every cabinet, and every drawer in the apartment. Trying to keep up with him—ensuring that he did not hurt himself and cleaning up after him when he spread things over the floor or broke anything breakable within reach—exhausted her. When she tried to take dangerous things away from him, he cried and kicked. She hoped he would not develop a temper like his father's. Much as she tried not to think about it, she could not suppress the fear that he might turn out like Morton.

Looking after her young son and two daughters was tiring enough. What got Ettie down the most was the self-imposed expectation that she should show love and understanding to Morton as the doctors tried to determine whether there was anything they could do to help him. They tried psychoanalysis and more shock treatments. They told Ettie that he was suffering from paranoid schizophrenia, that he had created a complex arrangement in his mind regarding plots against him—who was on his side and who was against him. He suspected that everyone except Ettie was weaving a web to harm him, his brothers and the doctors being the main schemers plotting against him. The doctors told her that it was important for her to keep his trust so they could find ways to break through. Not one of the doctors, or even the social worker, asked her how things were going at home, how she had explained the situation to her children, or whether she or her kids needed help.

Ettie managed to visit Morton once a week, despite her increasing dread of the ordeal. Although Western State Psychiatric Hospital was a short bus ride through Terrace Village to Oakland, she had to find someone to look after David until she returned. She also had to time the visits so that she could first serve lunch to her daughters and be back home before their return at the end of the school day. She was sometimes able to find a neighbor she could trust to look after David, but she preferred it when her mother was able to come and help for a few hours. Although it was difficult for Sarah to keep up with the active boy, David grew to enjoy his bubbe's visits, especially because she was indulgent, laughed, and gave him whatever he wanted. By the time Ettie returned, Sarah always seemed exhausted and eager to get back to her home.

The visits with Morton were something else. Those times when he concentrated on how much he hated the hospital food and pleaded with her to bring him deli sandwiches and pastries, she didn't feel so bad. Other times he started out friendly, almost normal, asking her how she was, or how the children were. Then, before she could finish answering, his eyes darting to the window or the door, he'd begin muttering, "They have spies everywhere, you know—the doctors, my brothers. They're plotting—always plotting ways to get even with me."

If she tried to point out that they only wanted to help him, he would accuse her of siding with the rest of them. He would look at the way her arms rested on her lap, and suggest that she was giving signals to the "others" in their plots against him. After half an hour, he might start pacing, behaving as if nobody was in the room.

The worst visits started with no questions at all, just a demand for the food as soon as he entered, then complaints that it wasn't what he was expecting, and no conversation until she decided it was time to leave. During those visits Ettie was unsure whether Morton differentiated between her and the hospital staff.

As soon as Collette turned twelve, she was permitted to visit her father regularly on weekends, and she couldn't wait. Each time Morton saw her in the room with Ettie, his first reaction was usually a hug and a kiss. Sometimes the entire visit went well, and they talked about her activities at school. She had a calming influence on him, but this did not prevent him from frequently turning away from her, telling her how ashamed he was for her to see him in a place like this, or asking her to leave and not come back. It was heartbreaking for Ettie to witness these encounters without becoming angry with Morton. On the way home Collette would defend her father: "I know he's ill, Mother, and I'm not hurt by what he said. Please, don't let it hurt you, either."

Ettie continued to try to protect Rachel and David from the truth. So far, David was too young to even wonder. Rachel already understood on one level, but always got anxious on the visiting days. She would run toward her mother as soon as Ettie returned from each visit, and begin questioning her: how did he look, what did they talk about, did he ask about her, and was he getting better? Ettie made up conversations, assuring Rachel that her father always asked how she was, whether she was doing well in school, and that he wanted her to know that he missed her. "He told me how much he wants to be here to play with David, too," she'd add.

Rachel's questions about whether the doctors thought he would be better soon were harder to answer, and Ettie's usual response was, "We have to wait and see." Sometimes Rachel made little greeting cards for him, hoping he would send one back with a special note for her. None ever came, and over the course of the next year, Ettie noticed that Rachel asked fewer and fewer questions.

The Routine

Life began to settle into a routine for Ettie, a welcome relief from the constant fear she'd felt when Morton was home. Her top priority each day was preparing meals for her children and getting Collette and Rachel off to school on time. She adhered religiously to a regular schedule of household chores in the hours between the meals. Her only breaks from the routine were the visits from her neighbors, when she offered them a cup of coffee and discussed whatever they had on their minds.

Monday was laundry day, the hardest day for Ettie. It meant carrying baskets of laundry to the laundry room in a basement three buildings away, no matter what the weather, rushing home once the clothes were in the machines, and returning regularly to check on the clothes to make sure nobody stole anything. When each load was washed, she had to compete with the other women to use one of the six electrically heated racks for drying. In order to get a head start, she woke each Monday at five in the morning before her children were awake, so she could be first to arrive and secure two washing machines.

Once the clothes were in the machines, she could return home in time to awaken Collette and Rachel and help them get ready for school. She prepared their breakfast, brushed and braided their hair, saw them off, and got David dressed so she could take him with her back to the laundry room where she had to hang the remaining clothes and bring home what was dry. Two or three more trips to the laundry room during the day would usually be enough for her to finish the week's laundry and end the day feeling totally exhausted.

Tuesday was the day for ironing clothes, a task Ettie found somewhat relaxing because she could stay in the apartment and listen to the radio for the latest news or the old songs she used to dance to, and sometimes even sing along. In the summer she could listen to radio broadcasts of

Pittsburgh Pirate baseball games, which she had begun to enjoy. When she finished the ironing, she scrubbed the bathroom.

Wednesday was the time for dusting the furniture, mopping the painted concrete floors and the kitchen linoleum, and cleaning the stove and refrigerator. This was another exhausting day. She also had to find time to wash her windows every few weeks, and to take her turn every six weeks mopping the hallway and cleaning the large garbage bins in front of the building. These tasks were supposed to be shared by the six households who used each hallway, but most of the families ignored the responsibility, and it was usually a filthy job by the time Ettie's turn arrived.

Thursday or Friday was shopping day, depending on when she visited Morton. Friday was also the day she usually made chicken soup for the Sabbath, even though Ettie stopped observing serious religious traditions connected with the Sabbath when Morton was hospitalized. But chicken soup was healthy for her children, and her family had become accustomed to it on Friday nights. Once it was cooked, she could reheat it on Saturday and serve the cold chicken in sandwiches.

Ettie looked forward to Friday afternoons, when Libby and Jake dropped by with the gefilte fish, challah, coffee cake, and poppy seed cookies that Sarah made each week. If they brought their daughter Susan with them, Rachel enjoyed playing with her. The visits usually lasted less than an hour, but it was good to hear all the family news and joke around with Jake. Sometimes Libby would invite Ettie to join them for a movie they were planning to see with some of their friends during the weekend. They were never surprised when Ettie declined the invitation.

Occasionally Jake would stop by on his own for a few minutes during the week, taking time out of his work as a bill collector as he drove from home to home in the neighborhood surrounding Terrace Village. He tried to time his visits for when Collette would be home so he could discuss her activities with her or what she wanted to be when she grew up. Rachel liked to be home when Uncle Jake dropped by because he always had a big hug and took the time to ask her questions about things she was doing too. Mostly she liked his visits because he made Ettie laugh. When David got a little older, Jake delighted him by twirling him around in the air.

At first, Ettie's Saturdays tended to be more relaxing than other days, assuming that was not the day she decided to visit Morton. But increasingly, she was taking Rachel to see a doctor at the Montefiore Hospital Clinic as Rachel's health deteriorated. Collette would stay home looking after David for the full morning during those clinic visits. Ettie would sit in the waiting room trying to occupy Rachel's attention but constantly agitated by the doctor's late arrival or by the unruly children who ran around making noise as they and their families waited to be called.

On Sundays Ettie relaxed with the Sunday *Pittsburgh Press*, reading all the sections in the paper. Sometimes she baked a chocolate cake, and she usually did some household chore not finished during the week. Sunday evenings, she began sorting her clothes for the Monday laundry.

Not only was it an exhausting routine, it was totally boring except for the family visits and baking the chocolate cake. Her kids loved that cake. Ettie tried not to think about the girl she was once, the girl who loved to dance, who dreamed of an education and having a career. When she looked into the mirror, she saw sad eyes and thick, dark hair pulled off a weary, round face and held in place with numerous bobby pins. She wore no makeup, and her loose-fitting cotton housedresses covered a body that was becoming flabby. *No man would be attracted to me now,* she thought, *even if I was single and interested in starting again.* Which was the last thing on her mind.

Although Ettie was only thirty when David was born and still an attractive woman, she had no desire for any man. She wished the doctors could find a way for Morton to get better, but she knew that if he did, it would never be what she had dreamed of before she married him. What she longed for now more than anything was company, friendship, and help in bringing up the kids.

As time went on, Libby and Jake did everything they could to include Ettie and her family in their lives. It wasn't just the short visits to bring the Sabbath foods. Summer weekends, when all of the cousins gathered for picnics at North Park on the outskirts of Pittsburgh, Jake went out of his way to pick up Collette and Rachel, squeeze them into the car, and ensure that they had a fun day with their cousins. He always asked Ettie to come along and bring David, but she knew there was no room in the small car, even though Jake would have found a way to squeeze her in by putting all of the kids on the grown-ups' laps. Mostly, though, Ettie realized that if she saw all of her cousins enjoying a happy outing with their husbands and kids, it would just deepen her sense of aloneness.

Nobody's Business

Ettie paused to wipe her glasses and blow her nose. "Yeah, those were hard times. I don't know how I got through it all."

Rachel shifted forward, her expression signaling that what she was about to share was a painful memory of her own. "I'll always remember that time when I was in the second grade . . . Collette was already in the seventh grade at Fifth Avenue Junior High so she ate lunch there in the cafeteria, but I still came home for lunch. Dad had been in the hospital a year or so. When I walked into the apartment, you were waiting for me, Mother, to tell me there was a surprise for me in the bedroom. I was so shocked when I opened the bedroom door and saw Dad sitting on the bed! He was pulling on his socks. When he saw me, he broke into a wide smile, and said, 'Rachel, come here and give me a hug.' I was so thrilled; I hugged him, and he held me in his arms. I thought he was better and had come home to stay."

Ettie scowled. "Oh yeah, really better! I was terrified. The hospital called me on our neighbor's phone before he arrived to tell me your dad had escaped out the window in a second-floor office while getting dental work done. They suspected that he would head home, and they warned me to keep him calm until they arrived to take him back. They said I should act as if everything was okay, that I was happy to see him." Her voice cracked as she repeated the instructions she'd received. "'He mustn't have any suspicion that we're on our way to get him,' they said, 'or he might run again, or get violent.'" She shook her head. "Awful."

David looked from Ettie to Rachel. "Where was I when this was happening?"

"You were two years old, so I guess you were in the house. I don't remember." Ettie felt her cheeks heat with embarrassment, and she looked away.

"I was so happy to see Dad," Rachel continued, "and I wanted to stay there with him. But Mother, you told me I had to eat lunch quickly and go back to school. You said you had to get some medicine for him. I wanted to believe you, but I knew something was strange. I was so scared. Then someone from the hospital knocked on the door, and you hurried me out of the apartment, telling me to go to school."

"Well, they had warned me that there could be a bad scene," Ettie replied.

"I didn't go to school, though," Rachel admitted. "I went outside and hid behind the bushes. I saw the whole thing—Dad being carried out on a stretcher. I didn't realize it then, but he must have been in a straitjacket. What did they do, sedate him?"

Ettie nodded. "It was terrible."

Rachel spoke more slowly. "I watched them put the stretcher in the ambulance and drive away. I wondered why he was on a stretcher when shortly before, he'd been sitting on the bed, hugging me. I remained very still behind those shrubs. Then I remembered that you told me to go right to school, so I began running. I was always early for school, so when I heard the late bell ringing just as I got close to the door, I was too terrified to go inside. The teacher always got mad when kids were late. She would scream at them, ask them in front of everybody why they were late, and tell them they needed a note from home. For me, that was worse than missing an afternoon. So I walked back home, hid behind the bushes again, then finally came into our apartment and told you I came back home because I wanted to know what was going on."

"I explained it all to you, didn't I? That he had run away from the hospital and had to go back?" Ettie began to cry. "But I couldn't tell you that I didn't want you there in case he got violent when they came in to get him. I just told you that I didn't want you to cry because your daddy had to go back to the hospital."

"Mother, please understand, I was never upset with you," Rachel said softly, touching her mother's arm. "But I never fully understood what was happening, how he could be there smiling at me and hugging me one minute, then on a stretcher going into an ambulance the next." She sat up straight, and her voice hardened. "And I've never understood why the doctors didn't show more interest in how you and our family were coping with everything. They were never concerned at all about any of us."

"Nothing mattered to them except to get him back in the hospital," Ettie agreed. " That's the way it was in those days."

"Now I want to know the rest of what went on," David insisted, then hesitated. "About the lobotomies and all."

Ettie sat back in her chair. "Well, I guess it's up to me to finish the story, then." She cleared her throat. "Some story!

"When they took your father away, they didn't know what to do with him. So they sent him to Mayview State Hospital, way out in the South Hills, beyond Mount Lebanon. Visiting him involved a fifteen minute bus ride downtown, where I transferred to another bus to Mayview. The trip on that second bus took close to an hour each way. Still, I tried to visit him as often as possible, when I could find somebody to stay with you kids. I would pack a shopping bag full of his favorite foods and hope that would cheer him up."

Ettie tipped her head to one side and squeezed her lips together, remembering. "That place was terrible. You could hear people screaming from the windows as you approached. Even though the buildings were spread out and there was some greenery here and there, it didn't fool anyone—it was a mental institution. I had to wait in a shabby waiting room with all the other visitors, all of us at long wooden tables on hard, old chairs—we were usually at different tables, but there was still no privacy.

"I used to see one woman all the time, waiting for her son. When the attendant brought him in to see her, she would try to hug him, and he would begin to yell and swear at her to leave. Sometimes he would physically push her away. Many times I saw her leave after a few minutes. I always felt so sorry for her, to have a child in a place like that, acting so mean to her. That must have been the worst." Ettie paused to think about that for a moment.

"Sometimes your dad was glad to see me, but most of the time he was only interested in what I had in the bag. I would ask him what he did in the past week, and he would say 'nothing' or 'played checkers.' Sometimes he would tell me the names of different doctors he believed were scheming against him with his brothers. I tried to interest him in conversation by talking about current politics, but usually after half an hour he would start squirming and looking over his shoulder or at other patients with visitors, and I knew the visit was over." She sighed. "It seemed to me he was getting worse and worse.

"Then one day I got a letter from Western State Psychiatric Hospital—that first hospital he was in, the one in Oakland—asking me to come in for a meeting. There was a treatment they were having a lot of success with, and they wanted to discuss it with me. I didn't know what to expect. I called your Uncle Isaac to come with me."

"I didn't know his brothers were so involved," Rachel said.

"Oh, yes . . . We met at the hospital, and after a short wait, we got called into the office to find three doctors and a social worker sitting around a table. The walls were lined with books, and there were lots of framed degrees hanging here and there. The main doctor, Dr. Solokoff, began talking about a great breakthrough in curing mental illness. The others just sat there nodding in agreement. He said it was an operation where they make a very small incision in the side of the head to get to the area in the brain that is causing the trouble. Once there, they can make some alterations to eliminate the emotional outbursts. He had a chart showing the parts of the brain and pointed to where they make the incision. It was a lot of gobbledy-gook to me. He said they had performed the operation on several people recently, and most were back in the community quickly, and functioning well. Although they couldn't guarantee anything, it was the only possibility for a cure, he said—to get Morton out of the state hospital."

David shook his head in wordless disbelief, then asked, "Didn't they tell you anything about the side effects of lobotomies, about how they could change a person's entire personality?"

Ettie shook her head. "All they told us was that it would calm him down, they never said anything else. Who knows if they even knew about side effects? They wanted him to have the surgery, that was clear, and they only talked about how it might help."

"How did Uncle Isaac react?" Collette asked.

"Well, Uncle Isaac seemed very encouraged. He told the doctors that Morton's family were all hard-working business people and good citizens, that they cared about other people, and it was their strongest wish to have their brother well and able to enjoy life as much as they did. To him, this sounded like an answer to their prayers, if it worked.

"I did ask them if anything could go wrong, what the dangers were.

It scared me, this cutting into Morton's brain. They glanced at each other and got all fidgety. I always wondered what they were hiding from us," she mused, then continued. "But the main doctor got out all these notes and started reading a lot of technical stuff about other cases where people got better. Then he suggested that we think it over, call them if we had anymore questions, and let him know by the end of the week, so he could schedule the surgeries he would be doing. What he never told us was that they were still doing research to test the surgery's long-term outcomes.

"Isaac went back and discussed it with his other brothers, then Isaac and Sam came to visit me and asked me what I thought. I told them I wasn't sure. I didn't understand the whole thing, but cutting into the brain scared me. Yet, if it was the only possibility of a cure that the doctors could offer, maybe it was the only thing we could do. Otherwise, Morton would be left in Mayview to rot for the rest of his life, because he was getting worse, not better.

"Isaac told me that they were in favor of the surgery. They'd found out that the doctor was tops in his profession, and Morton would have the best care. Isaac and I both signed the papers. The doctor was very optimistic, but warned us again that there was no guarantee." Ettie put her head back and stared at the ceiling. "That was it—your father had the lobotomy."

"So what happened next?" David asked, his voice agitated.

After a few seconds, Rachel answered. "I remember. They thought he was better at first. They sent him home and he seemed better. He still had a bandage around his head, the first time I saw him. I don't remember too much else about how he spent his time, or what he did. I think I was about eight years old by that time." She glanced at Ettie for confirmation.

"Yeah, that's right," Ettie agreed. "Remember that little grocery store his brothers bought for him on Carson Street in the South Side?" Rachel and Collette nodded. "It wasn't long after the war ended, and they thought there would be a big demand for food, with all the new families starting up. They convinced Bennie to get involved, actually gave him a share in ownership of the store. Bennie was easygoing and your dad got along with him, so we thought it might work out. Bennie would bring your dad home each night when they closed the store.

They asked me to work there too, as many hours a week as I could manage, so I could make sure things were okay. David, you were old enough to go to nursery school at the IKS by then. Collette looked after Rachel each day after school until I picked you up, and we both walked home."

"It must have been hard for everyone," David said sadly. "I don't remember any of this."

"Everything went along fine for a few months," Ettie said, "although the store was not making money because it had to compete with some of the new supermarkets. When people got their paychecks, they went to the supermarkets to get food, but when they were short of money, they came to our store and bought on credit. Many of them were heavy drinkers, too, so they didn't have any money left to pay their bills after they got drunk."

She sighed. "But that was only part of our worries. Soon whatever improvement your dad had shown began to fade away. He started believing that people were talking about him and planning to do something to him. He swore at some of the customers—spit to the side when he saw them, then chased them out of the store. Once he started doing that, we had to call the hospital, and they took him back fast. They claimed they had not made the correction in exactly the right spot on the brain, that they would make another adjustment, and he would be fine."

"That's horrible," David said.

"We hired another cousin temporarily to help keep the store going. I was working more hours than before, and Collette had her hands full, trying to look after everything at home when I wasn't there. Rachel, remember how unhappy you were with the situation?"

Rachel shifted uncomfortably. "I'm embarrassed when I think about it. I wasn't very helpful, was I? I didn't like having Collette boss me around, and I used to call you at the store, crying and saying that I'd always thought Collette was my friend, but now she was scolding me a lot." Rachel looked over at her sister. "Collette, I don't know how you handled all of that. I do remember a very scary story you told me once, about how I would be punished by secret swordsmen who would come into the room through a crack in the plaster if I misbehaved. I was terrified." Rachel laughed. "That was pretty clever of you, and you can imagine the images it conjured!"

"I didn't know about that," Ettie said. "I knew it was a bad arrangement, but I couldn't quit. I was earning a salary, and if your father got better this time, he needed a way to make a living. By now your Uncle Bennie was depending on the store for a living too. But the whole thing was becoming a totally losing proposition. Phooey!" She threw up her hands.

"They sent your father home a second time, and he seemed much better. I was really hopeful. It was around this time that you started to get real sick, Rachel. We didn't know what was wrong, but you developed one sore throat after another, and began losing weight. First they removed your tonsils, but it didn't help. They said you had a childhood condition that made you twitch a lot. You needed lots of rest, and they decided to put you in the hospital. They were worried about you getting a rheumatic heart."

"I remember some of that," David said, "everyone worrying about Rachel's health."

Rachel grimaced. "That hospital was disgusting. I was put into a ward with about six children, all of us in one big room. I was afraid to say anything to those other kids because they swore a lot and were always shouting for the nurse. Then Dad came to visit me. He brought me a handful of get well cards, some real funny ones. I thought we had a wonderful visit, and I didn't want him to leave. As soon as he left, some of the other kids laughed and told me that I had a crazy father and that he belonged in the "looney bin." I didn't know why they said that because they didn't know he had been in the hospital, and he didn't do anything during the visit that seemed strange to me. I started to cry, and they called me a big baby. When the nurse came in, I told her that the other kids were saying mean things to me."

Rachel paused, her expression growing even more sour. "The nurse's response was shocking. She said, 'You stop making up stories about these nice children, you dirty Jew. Who do you think you are!'" She looked to Ettie. "I told you about it when you visited me, and you must have said something to the head nurse, because the next day they moved me into another room with fewer people until I went home. And after that the mean nurse acted as sweet as could be."

"Such ignorance." David shook his head. "I never knew any of these details. Sometimes I wonder how I could be in the dark about so many things going on in our family."

"You were a little boy, how could you know?" Ettie told him.

David shrugged. "Let's go back to the lobotomies—what happened?"

"Well," Ettie replied, "the second correction lasted longer than the first one, but it didn't work in the end. Your dad went out for a walk, and the next thing I knew, the police came to the door to tell me he had been in a fight and they had to lock him up. Remember, Rachel? You and David came with me in the police car to get your dad out of jail. He had a black eye and bruises all over his face."

Rachel scowled. "Yeah, I remember. It was creepy."

"After that the doctors wanted him to go back to the hospital for a third adjustment. Their expert opinion was that the living arrangements did not offer the right environment for his rehabilitation, that Morton should try to live somewhere away from us, out of the city in a quiet place, with no pressure. So your uncles arranged for him to live on a farm on the outskirts of Pittsburgh. Their father agreed to move in with him. Can you believe it, such a religious and observant man, a rabbi, leaving the rooms he had next to the synagogue and all his rabbinical duties, just to devote himself to helping his sick son recuperate at a dirty farm? We went to visit them a few times. It was very strange. Morton was helping do odd chores around the farm, but he had never done anything like that before and didn't have a clue what was expected. He seemed very dull . . . " Ettie rubbed her forehead, as if it would soothe the memory.

David asked, "What happened next?"

"The inevitable happened, that's what. Someone from the town called him a crazy Jew, he punched the guy in the face, they called the police, and Morton was back in the hospital. The experiment on him was a failure, and he was back in Mayview State Hospital. They had nothing else they could do for him. That was the end of the line.

"It was clear each time I visited him after the last surgery that he was totally changed. Maybe they started giving him drugs. I don't know what new drugs they had by that time, but when he entered the visiting room, he shuffled in, all stooped over. Then he stared into space for the whole visit, or laughed continuously when nothing was said. He gulped down the food I brought him and answered questions with one-word answers, slurring his words. He was totally uninterested in any topic I brought up. The only positive change was that he was no longer angry. The lobotomies had placated him. I knew it was a hopeless situation."

Collette spoke up. "I visited him a lot after that. He never told me to leave or to not look at him. He seemed happy to have company. Years later, after I met Stanley and we visited him together, he liked to sit and play checkers with us, take a walk, or go for a ride. He had a different personality, but we had pleasant visits. I guess he had become more like a child than a father."

"It was years after the surgeries that I found out what was wrong," David said to Ettie. "It's still hard for me to believe that you didn't tell me what was going on, that you let me find out the way I did."

Ettie became defensive. "You were not even three years old when he had the first surgery! He was home some of the time on and off that year, but you say you have no memory of that. By the time he went back to Mayview, you were still so little—what could I tell you? Believe me, it was on my mind all the time."

"Maybe not right then, but at least by the time I was six, you should have told me the truth," David insisted.

Rachel nodded her agreement. "It was always a strain to keep the truth from him. I can't believe that none of the social workers from the hospital recognized that it was something you might need help with, Mother."

Ettie felt the old anger rise. *That anyone associated with the hospital would ever offer any help or advice—hah!* "Are you kidding?" she said, her voice rising with the anger. "Maybe they didn't have time, or maybe they didn't give a damn, but what it boiled down to was that nobody from the hospital ever approached me with an offer to help me figure out how to make it easier to help my family. Your dad's brothers did what they could so we could get along financially. Uncle Sam dropped by for an hour or so and talked with me whenever he came into the city on a business trip. He tried to be helpful. And Rachel, when he and Aunt Patty offered to take you into their home for a year to help you recover from your recurring illness, that was something extra-special.

But nobody who had any professional training ever offered to help me. Nobody!"

Stanley cleared his throat. "Maybe I shouldn't be saying this, but I never understood why the social workers didn't intervene in a more helpful way. They realized that one child in the family had been affected physically by all of the stress and disruption, but they were content to have her go to live with relatives. They should have tried to find a way to add supports so she could remain with her family."

Ettie flashed a look of surprise at Stanley. "I was worried everyone would think I was a bad mother. I thought that Sam and Patty might want to adopt Rachel."

"Oh no, that would not have happened," Rachel said without hesitation. "The year I spent with Uncle Sam and Aunt Patty was helpful, and I always had a lot of affection for them. They were very kind to me, and I enjoyed living in a nice house and having pretty clothes, but I missed my family a lot. It was strange in many ways, and I don't think they ever saw it as more than a temporary thing. Even when I was there, I got the feeling that I shouldn't talk about Dad, and I know Uncle Sam and Dad's other brothers tried to avoid mentioning his name, even when strangers saw me and wanted to know how I was related." After a pause, Rachel added, "It was wonderful that they treated me so well. They did help me get better, and I always felt I had a special connection with them. It was more fun later on, when they invited Collette and me to spend part of our summer vacations there."

After a quick glance at David, Rachel shifted the subject back to the fact that the truth had been kept from him for so long. "It truly upset me that I had to keep such a big secret from you, David. I was terrified that if I let it slip out, something terrible would happen. I'm not sure, maybe I was scared that you would get hysterical if you found out, or maybe I believed that if anyone outside of the family learned the truth, they wouldn't want to have anything to do with us. It was on my mind all of the time when I met new people, fearing that they'd ask what my father did or where he was. Sometimes they did ask, and I just fumbled around, saying he'd been sick for a long time and the doctors didn't know what to do. I don't think it should have been such a big secret."

Collette shook her head. "I don't agree with you at all, Rachel. We didn't have to tell anybody. It was nobody's business. Why should we have given people something to gossip about? If they were curious, well, that was just their tough luck."

Rachel's expression made it clear that she disagreed. "Somebody should have told David that Dad had a nervous breakdown or something, even if he didn't understand what it meant. We should have told anybody who asked. Besides, now we know it was no secret to anyone, we just thought it was. I was really shocked when some of my high school friends told me once that they'd known all along, and wondered why I never said anything about my father."

* * *

David never fully recovered from the traumatic way he learned the truth about his father. He was ten years old, walking home from school, arguing with one of his friends, Manny, about who had the best hook shot in basketball. There should have been nothing to argue about. David was taller, stronger, and far more athletic than most of the boys in his class. But he was unsure of himself, and their teasing upset him. He tried to poke fun back, calling the considerably shorter Manny "a pip-squeak."

Manny ran ahead, then turned back to yell, "Yeah, but your father's in the nuthouse."

"He is not!" David retorted, but Manny repeated the taunt until David was blinking back tears.

"What are you arguing about?" Manny sneered. "We all know your father is in the looney bin! Cuckoo, cuckoo—ha!"

David ran the rest of the way home. His sisters were sitting in the living room when he pushed open the front door, and when they saw him sobbing, they ran to the door to see if he was injured. Ettie rushed out of the kitchen, rubbing her hands on the bib apron she wore.

David screamed through his sobs, "Tell me it isn't true! Tell me, tell me—it can't be true. Manny said my father is crazy."

Rachel jumped to her feet and waved her arms in the air. "I told you not to lie to him!" she screamed. "I knew it would be bad—now look what's happened!" She ran from the room, and a moment later her bedroom door slammed.

David threw himself on the floor, where he writhed, looking up at Ettie. "How can it be true?" he moaned. "Why didn't you tell me?"

Collette knelt beside David, trying with Ettie to soothe him, but soon both she and Ettie were crying along with David as they tried to explain what had happened to Morton.

"Mother didn't lie when she told you that Dad had a broken leg," Collette told him. "That was true the first time you asked. When you asked the next time, she told you he had back trouble and that was true too. Then she told you the same thing she told Rachel the day the telegram arrived—that Dad was sick and the doctors were trying to figure out what his problems were so they could find the right medicine to help him."

Ettie nodded urgently, stroking the hair from David's forehead. "How could I tell you the truth when you were so small? How can you tell a little boy something like that? I hoped maybe your dad would get better and I wouldn't have to tell you, especially when they decided to do the surgery. He was home for a little while after the operation—you were two or three years old. I just hoped it would all work out. I didn't want people to know because they don't understand about mental illness. I was afraid they might say mean things to you." She dropped her hand and sat back on her heels. "Then you stopped asking, and I hoped the right time would come, but I couldn't get the nerve to tell you. I was trying to protect you."

"Well, you didn't protect me, did you?" David shouted. "What just happened is worse, isn't it? They knew all the time, and now I feel like a dumb jerk. It seems that people in the neighborhood aren't the only ones who think it's something to be ashamed of—you're ashamed too, if you didn't have the nerve to tell me. Now the other kids don't just think I'm a liar, they think I'm a stupid fool." He sat up and gestured angrily at Collette, at the closed bedroom door, sobbing. "And why do Collette and Rachel know everything, but you never tell me? That's what I'd like to know!"

It didn't matter to David when Ettie explained that his sisters knew because they were there when it happened, that she loved him and thought she was doing the right thing. He couldn't get over the pain of realizing that they had all participated in such a deception.

"I thought I was helping to protect all of you." Ettie's voice cracked. "I guess I've been wrong."

* * *

David frowned as if determined not to accept a repeat of all the excuses he had heard on that painful day so long ago. "I remember Rachel went ballistic when I repeated what Manny said to me. And by the time Collette and Stanley arranged a visit so I could meet my father, I was eleven by then!"

Now, after all these years, discussing these painful memories was exhausting for Ettie. She wished David could understand better what she had gone through and why she'd tried to protect him by not sharing how hopeless the situation seemed to her. She wished he didn't feel that she had betrayed him. And she wondered how Collette could have remained so devoted to her father all these years. *I hope Morton's death doesn't bring Collette more suffering, she's ill enough already. And Rachel—* She had never realized that Rachel felt so much guilt about something totally beyond her control.

Collette turned to Ettie. "It's hard to imagine what you were going through, Mother. I think we were right to try to avoid talking about it, even though I agree that it was hard for David, finding out the way he did."

Rachel tried to change the subject. "You continued working for a while after Dad went back to the hospital, didn't you?"

Ettie nodded, relieved to focus on something other than the lie. "At first Uncle Bennie tried to run the grocery store on his own. I managed to help him for a year or so, for a few days each week. The store wasn't making any money, and they ended up getting rid of it. I think everybody lost money in the end."

Rachel shifted the conversation again. "Mother, wasn't it during that time that you almost had a boyfriend? Remember, that guy who used to drive you home?"

David's eyebrows rose. "What's this? Another secret?"

"Him?" Ettie snorted. "Get out of here—he was no boyfriend! He liked me okay, and he was fun to talk with. He worked for a company that supplied some of the dairy products for the store. Every time he came in, he *kibitzed* around, real silly stuff. Then once he arrived near the end of the day, when we were getting ready to close up, and I told him I had to catch a streetcar, so he offered me a ride home. After that, he timed his appointments so he could drive me home each time he came. Sure, it was nice to get a ride—I was so exhausted! But then he started asking me to go out with him. What did I need him for? I told him I already had a husband and didn't need anybody to fool around with. I think he expected me to change my mind, because he kept trying, but after a while, he disappeared. I'm sure he was only interested in one thing. *Feh!*"

"Well, I thought he was nice," Rachel said. "He was friendly to me when he dropped you off, and I used to hope that he would be your boyfriend. He even brought me a coloring book once. I wanted him to take us for a ride in his car."

Collette looked annoyed. "Why are you talking about him, Rachel? He was a very coarse man. He couldn't hold a candle to Dad. I could never have accepted him if Mother got involved with him."

Ettie looked askance at Collette and nodded to herself, thinking, *See, I was right.* David looked at Collette, then at his mother, and opened his mouth as if to comment. Then he closed it and looked away. Ettie was glad he chose not to pursue it.

Making the Marks

Wanting to conclude the topic of the grocery store, Ettie said, "After your father's brothers and Uncle Bennie realized the store was not succeeding, they put it up for sale. I think they took a beating, but they got rid of it, and Uncle Bennie returned to his old job as a deliveryman. Your Uncle Isaac told me that he and his brothers had decided at a meeting that they didn't want me to go back on welfare, so they would send us a check each month to cover the rent in Terrace Village and enough extra for necessities. As time went on, once in a while they sent you kids some clothes from their store."

"Those were nice," Rachel said, nodding. Then she grimaced. "But mostly I remember wearing hand-me-downs from everybody in the family. Aunt Libby would drop off a shopping bag full of clothes that other people had outgrown or got tired of, and we'd each see what we could use. Nothing ever fit me right, I was so skinny, but you would sew a tuck here and there, and that was that."

"Believe me, we never went hungry," Ettie said, "and I didn't have to leave you alone anymore to go out to work. I was grateful. Clothes weren't so important."

"No, that's for sure." Rachel laughed. "What counted was getting high marks in school." She looked at her sister and added, "The teachers were always nice to me, telling me that if I was half as good as you, Collette, they knew everything would be fine. I used to try to get even better marks than you did. You were sure a hard act to follow!"

"How do you think I felt?" David interjected. "With two sisters always excelling in school, it was almost too much to handle."

The years after Morton's permanent hospitalization were not easy for Ettie, but they were more predictable and less stressful than before. Life went from uncertainty to drudgery, alleviated by Collette's cheerfulness and Ettie's pride in her achievements. Rachel's health was always a concern, but she did excel in school and would likely be able to achieve success if she could only stay well and not squabble so much with David. They seemed to irritate each other constantly. He was noisy in the games he played, and she constantly scolded him to be quiet while she read or studied. This routine typically ended with Ettie trying to intervene amidst accusations and tears from both her son and her daughter.

The truth was that Ettie hadn't known how to relate to David. He was always a big boy for his age, full of energy and difficult to restrain. His teachers reported that he was highly intelligent but at the same time not motivated. The fact that he eventually found a way to excel in an academic setting was beyond Ettie's wildest dreams at the time, and vindication after years of worry.

"You must have been so lonely all of those years, Mother," Rachel said, "especially before we had TV. I don't remember you ever getting out much unless there was a family wedding or bar mitzvah." She smiled impishly as she added, "*Then* you danced and were the life of the party. But what did you do for enjoyment or relaxation the rest of the time? Besides seeing us do well in school, what brought you pleasure while we were growing up?"

Ettie slowly shook her head. "Nothing."

Everyone was quiet until David spoke. "I know you enjoyed visits from Aunt Libby and Uncle Jake. When Uncle Jake came to visit and bring the food for Friday nights, I used to put a towel around my shoulders, pretend I was Superman, and start jumping from the chairs. I wanted him to come in and play with me. Sometimes he did."

Rachel laughed. "I remember as he came in the door, he would yell out, 'Enta, Tilla Benta!' and you would start to laugh. I liked his visits because you laughed more when he was there."

Ettie nodded, smiling at the memory. "Yeah, those visits helped some."

"By the time Dad went back to Mayview State, you had a lot of friends in Terrace Village too, didn't you?" Rachel added.

Again, Ettie nodded slowly. "Yeah, I guess so. A lot of the people who caused trouble when we first moved in had moved away, and nicer people replaced them after the war, some young couples. I liked to sit and talk with them."

Most were people Ettie might not have had contact with if she had been living in another environment. They included second-generation couples from among Pittsburgh's many ethnic groups, some unmarried mothers, some women married to abusive husbands, and a few Jewish families living on the father's pay from menial jobs. One woman with five children had a husband serving several years in prison for stealing jewels. Most of her neighbors were drawn to Ettie because she was both comforting and willing to give honest advice. They shared their personal problems and fears, and Ettie understood their dilemmas because of her own experiences.

Ettie thought about the neighbors who had been such a big a part of her life. "I really liked the Ambrosia couple, across the hall. They both were going to night school, and she would tell me about the books she was reading. Her husband was studying to be an engineer.

"I felt sorry for Rose Ann Marvin—her husband was a drunk and wife-beater. He was a truck driver—he'd spend his paycheck drinking, then he'd come home, they'd argue about money, and he'd beat her black and blue. They had three pretty little girls . . . She was a talented artist, but that didn't help them pay the bills. He'd end up breaking things in their apartment. I wish she could have left him . . . I think she did, many years later."

Ettie chuckled as she remembered another woman. "And Nellie Stanton was funny. I didn't approve of how she lived her life, but she made me laugh. Remember when she used to come into our place in the morning after some guy left, telling me how her two hind cheeks hurt? What a character she was!"

They all laughed. "Yeah, you were the community social worker," Collette added.

Ettie broke into a big smile, her mood definitely lifting. Her apartment *had* been the destination for neighbors who wanted companionship. She always knew she was well liked and respected. "Jeanette Stein did a lot of favors for me. She knew I was interested in politics and liked the Democrats. During one election she told someone in the Democratic office about me, and they asked me if I'd like to help. I got paid ten dollars to go around knocking on doors, trying to convince people to come out and vote. And I got a chance to help count the votes after the polls closed. I loved that."

That was the same Jeanette who had advised Ettie to get an abortion. She remained Ettie's closest friend, especially since she had a son close to David's age. Jeanette's husband earned a modest salary selling insurance, and Ettie often wondered if they had somehow lied to the management about their situation in order to be accepted for public housing. Jeanette had been training to be a classical singer, and had confided to Ettie that she'd had an affair with her teacher, even though her husband was devoted to her. Sophisticated in her dress and speech, Jeanette constantly urged Ettie to wear more stylish clothes, use makeup, and have her thick black hair styled into something more becoming. Ettie's response was always the same: "What for? Who am I trying to impress? I already have a husband, and he's not around. I sure don't need any other man to give me heartache." Then she'd admit the real reason. "Besides, I can't afford it."

Ettie smiled at a memory that ran throughout all of the others. "You want to know what gave me pleasure? I got the most pleasure listening to you kids when you were telling me what you were doing in school—the books you were reading and what you were learning, especially about history."

Collette chuckled. "That's nice to hear. I used to worry that I was boring you."

Ettie lifted her eyebrows. "How could you have thought that? I learned a lot from all of you. And of course, I knew if you got high marks and could go to college, you would have a career, and then people would respect you. It became my main ambition. When you were in high school, Collette, it gave me so much pleasure that you were an outstanding student. I loved it when you got to be editor of your school newspaper."

"Did you like it when she became a cheerleader?" David asked, and they all laughed, remembering the arguments when Ettie had to grant permission for that. At the time Ettie thought it was a frivolous activity that would not help her daughter get high marks or get into a college, and might even get her in with the wrong crowd. But the school principal called Ettie and convinced her it would be good for the school and for Collette.

Rachel reminded them of another source of disagreement when Collette was in high school. "Hey Mother, remember when Collette used to go to the apartment downstairs to ask Richard Stanton for help with geometry?"

David looked at Collette. "What did you do that for? I didn't think you needed help from any other students."

Rachel answered for her. "He was some kind of mathematical genius, but Mother didn't want her getting involved with Nellie Stanton's son. She thought he would get her in trouble because his mother brought strange men home. After Collette had been there for ten minutes, Mother would send me downstairs to tell her to come home." More laughter.

"I knew I was right about that, though," Ettie added.

"I knew I had to do well in school," Collette explained. "I wanted to go to college and we couldn't afford it, so I was determined to get a scholarship and make it happen. That meant I had to get the highest marks, even in geometry. I worked so hard at it. If I couldn't figure it out on my own, I tried to get help. If I didn't get a high mark, you got mad at me, Mother. Sometimes you would holler at me for not studying enough. That upset me, because I was working so hard."

"Oh, I was such a mean mother," Ettie teased, but they all knew why theirs was never a calm or peaceful household. Often the stress got to be too much for Ettie, and she lost her temper. She often looked exhausted or upset, though at the time the kids didn't know why. But this was not the time to focus on those episodes.

"Well, I always knew you gave Rachel more chocolate cake than you gave me," David quipped, and they laughed, breaking the tension.

"I'll tell you this, Collette," Ettie said, recalling a particularly rich pleasure from the past with the same thrill of pride she'd felt then, "that day you called to tell me you'd won the honor scholarship to go to the University of Pittsburgh was the happiest day of my life. And sitting in the audience at your graduation, when you were valedictorian, and the whole family was there—what a thrill!"

She looked at Rachel and David and added, "Rachel, when you got all your scholarships, —that was also up there among my happiest days. You got your tuition and even all of your books paid for; you were amazing! And David, when you became a professor, can you imagine how proud I was?"

David responded with a hint of sarcasm. "I guess you would be, after that high school English teacher was always complaining about me not doing my homework, or falling asleep in her class. And that awful guidance counselor," David paused, frowning as he tried to conjure a name, "Mr. Anderson—he thought I would never amount to anything. He discouraged me from even thinking about college."

"But you scored so high on those entrance exams, they couldn't stop you," Ettie said gleefully.

David grinned. "Yeah. That's when Uncle Sam and Uncle Sol told me they would help me with my tuition, too—that I was like an investment to them." The grin sagged a bit. "It would have been nice to hear that they cared about me. I suppose they did, but I didn't know it then. I'm glad I had money saved from my summer jobs so I didn't have to take very much from them." He paused and shook his head, his expression rueful. "Then different trouble started when I protested against the Vietnam War. Everyone must have thought I would be a bum, or worse."

Ettie looked at her watch. "Well, all of you know the rest of the story."

* * *

When Rachel was ready for high school, Morton's brothers decided to make it possible for Ettie and her family to move to a nicer neighborhood, closer to where Libby and Jake were living. Collette was already in her sophomore year at the University of Pittsburgh, but they hoped that Rachel and David would benefit from attending better schools.

They bought a small apartment building near Friendship Avenue and expected Ettie to serve as the property manager—to collect the rents, vacuum the hallways, and call repairmen when something broke down. They put her on their business payroll with a small salary, enough to pay the rent and buy food and other necessities. The main advantage was that she could contribute to Social Security, thus assuring some financial protection as she got older.

What a dump, Ettie thought when she first saw the building. *I'm glad they don't expect us to live in one of the apartments—"efficiency," ha! Tiny, more like it.* She realized that the brothers' business plan made good sense, but as time went on, she hated the job more and more. She always felt like a janitor and found it aggravating to take calls from the tenants every time something broke down. Those calls came only when people were upset—sometimes crying, and often yelling at her, if the repairs didn't happen immediately. Isaac expected her to get three bids before finalizing arrangements with repairmen, and he was meticulous in reviewing the bills and trying to keep costs down.

"I was happy that we could move to a better neighborhood, and David and Rachel got to go to better schools," Ettie said. "That's what was important. And it was nice, living closer to the rest of my family. My mother used to visit me several times a week. But the apartment we moved into in that big, old house wasn't nearly as nice as the apartment in Terrace Village!"

"I'm with you," David agreed. "I had to leave some good friends when we moved there."

Rachel shook her head. "I couldn't stand Terrace Village, and going to Fifth Avenue Junior High School in 1950 with those rough kids. I don't know what I would have done if I'd had to continue going to high school there." She shuddered. "The teachers were always screaming at the class because they didn't pay attention and were unprepared—most of the kids just sat there falling asleep. Someone was always stealing my lunch money. Kids were always pushing in the halls. I had no real friends, I wasn't learning anything, and I hated it," she concluded, her voice adamant. She looked at Ettie. "The teachers even told you to try to get me out of there. That's why I wrote to Uncle Sam, to tell him how bad it was. I was hoping he would find a way for us to move to a nicer neighborhood."

"Well, I guess Uncle Sam and the others were more concerned about you than anybody else, because that's what they did," David said, emotion deepening his voice. He looked at his mother. "How did you feel about Dad's family? Did it bother you to be so dependent on them?"

This was a touchy subject, and Ettie didn't want to delve into her feelings about it. She often wondered how she would have managed without their help, if she could have found the energy to get a job she liked, if she could have arranged her time so her family would not be neglected. She was pretty sure she would have had to stay on welfare indefinitely.

David was waiting for an answer. "Oh, don't start on that," she said, waving the subject away with one hand. "What would we have done without them? They're good people. I'm pretty sure your grandfather encouraged them to help us before he left for Israel in 1948. But they didn't have to keep coming to our rescue, didn't have to take care of us. They had small businesses and their own families. They lived a comfortable life, but they were never rich. I can't complain about anything with them.

"I was determined to raise you kids so they would be proud of you and would know that everything they did for us was worth it. I never really felt like I was a part of their family, but you kids are a part of their family, and I wanted them to be proud of you. And it all worked out, didn't it?"

"So that was it," David said, shaking his head. "I always wondered why you didn't defend me when Uncle Sam came to tell me to stop protesting the Vietnam War, claiming I was shaming the family name because I was shown on TV in the evening news. Even Rachel took my side on that one, but you were afraid to disagree with him. Now I get it."

Ettie began to cry. "Don't bring that up. I knew you were right, but I was afraid to argue with Uncle Sam. He and his brothers did so much to help us. Years later he finally told me he realized you were right to oppose the war."

Stanley had been listening quietly as he walked in and out of the room. Now he joined the discussion. "You should try to see it from their point of view, David. They were businessmen, the only Jews in a small town. They felt they had to avoid controversy at all costs, especially anything to do with patriotism. They had lived the first part of their lives worrying about staying alive in a Christian country. Then they achieved some success in a small town in America, and lived their lives struggling to fit in, to be accepted by the church people and Lions Club members. They thought a war resister in the family would endanger their good name and the respect their customers had for them."

Unconvinced, David shrugged and said, his tone bitter, "All I can say is that they should have cared more about what was right before they criticized me. If I had been one of their sons, they would have been more supportive."

PART SEVEN

THE UNVEILING

Pack up all my care and woe
Here I go, singing low
Bye bye blackbird.

—"Bye Bye Blackbird" by Mort Dixon/Ray Henderson

Goodbyes

The week of shiva was drawing to a close. This was the last morning that Ettie would spend time with Rachel and David. When past visits came to a close, Ettie was sad to say goodbye, but this time she was happily anticipating the return to her usual routine and the activities at the Forward-Shady seniors' building. She was anxious to take her daily walks around the parking lot, do her own shopping, and cook and eat whenever it suited her.

She was grateful that none of her neighbors had commented about her deception, pretending she had been a widow for thirty years. *Who knows, maybe my kids are right, maybe I wasn't kidding anybody all that time,* she thought. *But at least I don't have to explain to my neighbors why I lied to* them. She caught herself and sighed. *What's the matter with me, anyway? Why do I always care so much whether people know the truth?*

She was sorry that her need to hide the truth had created problems for David and Rachel, and she wondered if it was too late to turn over a new leaf. She had found the week exhausting, talking so much about the past, especially since she did most of the talking, but it was good that almost everything was out on the table. Now she didn't want to dwell on it anymore. *My kids turned out the way I hoped, and my life is pleasant now. That's enough.* Her grandchildren still had to find their way, and she worried about them, but they were not her primary responsibility.

Her big worry was Collette, the one person Ettie knew she could always lean on. It wasn't fair that Collette was plagued with bad health. *It's a blessing that Collette has Stanley, and the two of them have a special bond.* Ettie remembered when Collette first met Stanley. *They were both still in high school—I was so thrilled that she'd found a kind-hearted boyfriend.* During Collette's first year at Pitt she dated other young men from good families—*A couple of them liked her a lot.* Ettie paused in thought. *I was wrong to think that Morton's illness would interfere with the kids' relationships.*

But what an adjustment it was to let go, to let Collette lead her own life! Ettie thought, remembering when Collette and Stanley were first married. Then she felt her face flush with embarrassment. *I actually resented Stanley. I was annoyed when Collette focused on satisfying his wishes and needs more than those of the rest of the family.* Now, though, she was grateful, not only for Stanley's devotion to Collette, but for his unselfishness in helping all of them whenever a need arose.

Ettie got ready early and was waiting outside on the bench near the front door of her building when David and Rachel pulled into the driveway off Forward Avenue. Ettie rose, waved to Sonya Friedman as she walked away from the building, then quickly slipped into the car. "Well, let's get going," she said briskly after greeting her kids. "I'll bet you guys'll be happy to get home."

Rachel nodded. "It's been an intense week for all of us. I hope it wasn't too much for you, Mother."

"You know, I could've done without it, but maybe it was time for everyone to get things out on the table. I am glad it's almost over, though."

After a short period of silence, Ettie asked David if he had heard anymore from home about how his wife and kids were. David seemed worried when he responded. "I'm anxious to get home," he admitted. "It's been a hard week for Sandy."

The morning at Collette's passed quietly, with only one visitor, Collette's childhood friend, Kay. They had remained close through the years, even though their lives had gone in different directions. She understood the suffering the family had endured and embraced each one with genuine warmth. She and Collette talked about their days in elementary school together for a while, then Kay got up to leave. She put her arm around Ettie's shoulders. "Well, Mrs. Burin, you should be very proud of your children."

"You're darn tootin' I am," Ettie exclaimed, sudden tears welling in her eyes. She smiled at them all. "What's not to be proud of?"

After Kay left, Ettie and her children gathered around the kitchen table to eat a light lunch during this last hour of shiva. "Kay was right,"

Ettie said to them. "I'm very proud of all of you, and I hope you're happy. And," she added, "I hope I didn't push you *too* much to do well in school."

"I always loved school, from the time Dad taught me how to read," Collette said. "I admired most of my teachers, and enjoyed the friends I made there." She paused and looked over at Stanley, who smiled. "I worked hard, and I must admit that there were times I felt bad because I didn't get as high a mark on an exam as you expected, but I always knew you wanted us to achieve success so we could have a good life. You devoted your life to us, you loved us so much and wanted to make sure we got the education you missed. I always felt sad that you had so many disappointments in life, and I wanted to succeed and make you happy. When I was on the stage as valedictorian of my high school graduating class, the main thing I saw from the stage was your big smile."

Ettie smiled now, blinking back tears.

"I was always happiest when I was in school, too," Rachel said, then grinned at her sister as she added, "Part of it for me was trying to be just like Collette. But I liked it when the teachers praised me. I was shy, so the attention I got when I got the highest mark on an exam pleased me."

"You studied all the time," David said to her. "I thought you were silly."

Rachel shrugged. "I guess I worried about my marks more than I should have in high school. I was always concerned about being able to afford to attend college and realized I would need a scholarship, just like Collette. Even in the 1950s, a lot of people thought it was a waste of money to give a girl a higher education." She looked at Ettie. "You're the one who convinced me of the importance of getting an education. You always made it clear that it was essential for a girl to have a career and be financially independent, even if she married a successful person. Thank you for that inspiration, Mother." She glanced at David. "After I got those scholarships, I relaxed and enjoyed school even more at Pitt."

Rachel turned her gaze back to Ettie. "And later, when I became a widow with two little kids, you were the one to encourage me to go to graduate school. You knew how much I wanted to, and you didn't hesitate to take care of my kids so I could do that. It wouldn't have happened without your help and love. So that explains my successful career."

Ettie smiled again. "Well, that last part wasn't easy, that's for sure, but I knew how important it was for you. And I always loved spending time with your kids." She turned to David. "What about you? You're quiet. What made you a scholar after so much turmoil in high school?"

"Ah, now it's my turn." David grinned and dragged his fingers through his hair. Then his grin faded. "I have to admit that I felt angry and betrayed that you all lied to me about Dad. I hope you know that I got over it long ago, Mother. I hope you know how much I love you."

Ettie felt tears well in her eyes and spill over to stream down her face. This was what she had been praying she might hear someday.

"Once I knew the truth about Dad and realized how the other kids could embarrass and taunt me about having a father in a mental institution, I found it very uncomfortable in school." He squinted, as if peering a great distance into the past. "I'll never forget the time that Neil Caplan tried to bully me, in high school. Just as I was about to retaliate he said, 'Don't fuck with me, Burin, or I'll tell everyone about your father!'"

Ettie gasped. "You never told me that story! I didn't know."

"What was the point? It would've hurt you, and what could you have done about it? But that made me wish I didn't have to go to school and be around those guys. And the guidance counselor and school principal were almost as bad. Once I was called to the principal's office, and he said he wanted to talk with my father. He asked what my father did for a living. I began to sob and couldn't stop for a long time. Finally I left without discussing anything with him."

"I didn't know that happened, either," Ettie mumbled, her pleasure evaporated.

"I'm sorry you didn't have anyone in the family you could confide in like I did," Rachel said gently. "I shared all my worries and disappointments with Collette and Mother. They tried to help me think things through. It must have been very lonely for you, being the only guy in a family with three women."

David nodded. "Yeah, and I was afraid that I would turn out like my father, that I'd be 'a chip off the old block.'" He looked at Stanley. "When you brought Dad to my bar mitzvah, I felt as if everybody was comparing me to him, and wondering if that's what I would become."

"A lot of people thought you looked like him when he was younger, when I first met him," Ettie said. "That's why they were looking at both of you. None of my family had seen him for over ten years. They weren't prepared for how much his looks had changed."

"That's all in the past now." David leaned back in his chair as if distancing himself from that subject. "I've often wondered how I got through the rough times and found the path I'm on. I guess it didn't hurt that I was pretty intelligent and good at sports." He laughed, then grew serious. "It helped that there were people who believed in me and helped me to believe in myself. One was Uncle Bennie. He used to take me golfing with him, and he made me feel that he cared about me and respected me for who I was. My first supervisor when I was on a student field placement—the psychiatrist, Dr. Schwartz—helped me to have faith in myself. The love and support of my wife was a big help too. But I think more than anything else, it was that love in my early childhood that mattered the most, the love you showed me, Mother, and you too, Collette. That was the foundation." David paused and grinned at Rachel. "I guess you and I got closer later, but you too."

David leaned forward again, eyes on his steepled fingers, intent on his thought. "One more thing. You know what I think? We are all resilient." He looked up at Ettie. "You and Bubbe Sarah were able to overcome so much in your life and still find joy with your kids and grandkids, with your relatives, and even your neighbors. You like to read, you like music, politics, and even sports. I think you passed on that resilience to us."

He leaned back and dropped his hands palm down on the table. "It doesn't make sense to dwell on the pain of the past. It wasn't anybody's fault that Dad got sick. Everyone did their best, and you tried to protect and encourage us when we were growing up."

Ettie looked around the table. "I'm really lucky to have all of you." She wanted to say more, but emotion closed her throat.

She and her children finished their sandwiches and kissed goodbye, tears now flowing freely down their faces. As David and Rachel prepared to leave, Ettie called out, "Take care of yourselves, you two. I love you. I hope we'll be together soon, at a happier time."

Rachel glanced back from the car and saw her mother standing outside the front door, looking very old, tears still streaming down her face as she waved and blew kisses.

Requests

The morning following the end of shiva, the distant ringing of the phone woke Ettie. She had tossed and turned for over an hour the night before and had finally taken a sleeping pill. Now, groggy and disoriented, she mumbled, "One of the kids can get it," and rolled over, hoping to sleep a little longer. She wasn't in the mood to talk with anybody.

It continued to ring. Finally she remembered where she was and what day it was. "All right already, I'm coming," she muttered, pushing herself out of bed. Almost tripping over her slippers, she stumbled to the phone and lifted the receiver.

"Ettie, it's Bea."

Ettie cheered up when she heard her cousin's voice. "Bea! It's nice of you to call."

"Are you okay? I've been worried about you. That was a lot for you to go through."

Ettie sighed. "What's the point of complaining?"

"I'm taking a walk today, and I want to stop by. I have something for you. When's a good time?"

The fog in Ettie's head was clearing. She found Bea's company soothing, and Bea herself refined and upbeat, someone who made Ettie feel good about herself. She smiled as she replied, "Come in about an hour, if that's good for you. We can have a cup of tea together."

Bea arrived with a bag of cookies in her hand. She put her arms around Ettie, whispering that she understood what an ordeal the past week had been. Then she held Ettie at arms' length and declared, "You know, Ettie, you always did everything you could to help Mort. And you raised three wonderful children. You should be very proud of what you've accomplished. I wish people realized what it was like for you to raise a family with that kind of shadow hovering over it."

"Well, I certainly don't wish my suffering on anyone, but it wasn't Mort's fault that he got sick. Besides, he did give me my kids." Ettie led the way into the kitchen and indicated a chair at the table as she turned away to get the cups.

"Mort was a smart man," Bea said as she put the bag of cookies on the counter, then pulled out a chair and settled into it. "That's what attracted you."

"That's true." Ettie piled the cookies on a plate, poured boiling water into the cups and twirled the teabags in the water, then turned to the table with one of the cups and the plate of cookies.

Bea nodded her thanks as Ettie slid the cup across the table to her. "Too bad nobody knew how to help him. We all tried to show our love for you and your family, but we always knew it wasn't enough. We were all afraid to talk about what happened to Mort. It must have been so lonely for you, to feel uncomfortable about talking about your husband."

"Yeah, but I had plenty to keep me occupied. And all of you had your own families and worries," Ettie said as she retrieved the second cup and sat down across from Bea.

Bea leaned forward in her chair. "There's something I've been wanting to discuss with you, Ettie. I think people have a lot to learn from you. I have neighbors—a young family with a new baby, and the mother is suffering from depression. Her mother-in-law came to help her recently and told me about it. The young woman is having a rough time taking care of the baby, but the family is worried about keeping the depression a secret, and I don't think they're getting her the help she needs." Bea shook her head in disapproval. "They wouldn't do that if she had a heart condition."

"That's really sad, but what can I do about it? It's not the same thing I went through." Ettie pointed to the plate piled with cookies, hoping Bea would take the first one. "Let's talk about something else. How're your grandchildren?"

They talked for about an hour, about different cousins and people they both knew in the neighborhood, before shifting to local politics, then stories of the past. When Bea rose to leave, Ettie smiled and walked with her to the door. "Thanks for dropping by, Bea."

Bea hesitated. "You understand a lot, Ettie, and maybe there's a way you could help people who are going through what you went through. You're a very understanding person. Think about it." Ettie promised she would.

Later, as she washed the cups and spoons they had used, Ettie began to wonder how many families included someone who was mentally ill. *Funny, I always thought nobody else had the same bad luck I did. But what could I do now to help anyone else with such troubles? I'm no psychiatrist.* Nevertheless, she felt concern for the young woman and her baby. *It is something to think about,* she decided.

Ettie awoke the next day with a terrible headache, chills, and a fever. *Well, this is the final insult,* she thought. *Now I'm suffering again because of Mort—going to the funeral and sitting shiva have left me with the flu.* Then she caught herself. *There I go, blaming him again. He's gone, and it's time to put the bitterness aside.*

By the time Collette called to tell her that she and Stanley wanted to visit, Ettie had stopped feeling sorry for herself, but explained that she was ill. "I don't want to expose you to my germs."

"Please take care of yourself, Mother. You know how much you mean to us."

Rachel and David called later in the day to let her know they'd arrived home safely, and two of her grandchildren called as well. She was smiling her contentment as she hung up after the last call, reassured that her family cared about her.

Once again her mind turned to Morton. It was still hard to remember what the good times with him were like. *Or why I fell for him in the first place,* she thought, then acknowledged after a moment, *He needed me. He always had a look about him that he needed to be loved. And he told me I was the only person he trusted.* Up to that time, nobody else in her life had ever made her feel so important. *I thought I could help him.*

Ettie didn't have any sure answers about her actions in the past, but she wondered if there was anything she could say that would help Bea's neighbors to get the help they needed. She wasn't sure exactly what Bea expected of her, so she tried to put it out of her mind. *Why should I get involved with people I don't know? What if I said the wrong thing? I could do more harm than good.* She decided to wait until she felt better, then maybe Bea could explain more about the kind of help the family might need.

Ettie's flu lasted for more than a week. As she sat at her kitchen table going through the pile of mail one of her neighbors had dropped off, she looked a second time at one envelope that she'd first thought was junk mail. It was from the Squirrel Hill Jewish Community Center and had the name of Sharon Gold above the return address. Her neighbors had told her how impressed they were with Mrs. Gold, a new person on staff, who always had time to ask them how they were feeling, and remembered their names after only one meeting. She set the handful of envelopes down and opened that one.

The contents of the letter startled Ettie. Mrs. Gold was heading up a project on how the Jewish Community Center and the old Irene Kaufmann Settlement House had affected the lives of immigrants in Pittsburgh's Jewish community. *You have been identified as someone we should interview to find out what life was like for the Jewish immigrants to Pittsburgh's Hill District, and what the IKS meant to you. I will call you to seek your agreement for an interview*, she wrote. Ettie wondered who had identified her. It had been years since she participated in IKS activities, which she still thought of as the Ikes, the name everyone used when she was younger. She shrugged. It couldn't hurt to meet with Mrs. Gold.

When she received the call, she readily agreed to an interview in a few weeks. *No big deal,* she thought, and didn't bother to tell her kids about it.

The Speech

David called with news that he would be receiving an honor from the University of Pittsburgh's Alumni Association as the recipient of its annual Distinguished Alumnus Award. "I'll receive the award at a ceremony where I'll be giving the keynote address to a crowd of about five hundred people." Members of the faculty will be in attendance along with a large number of the alumni and the student body, he told Ettie. In their shared excitement, he didn't mention what he planned to say.

Ettie was ecstatic. It was one thing that her children had all gone on to get university degrees, with both Rachel and David earning doctorates, but now this public recognition of the child she had worried about the most was more than she had ever dreamed of—surely this proved that she had not failed as a mother.

Ettie, Collette, and Stanley were among the first to arrive on the night of the ceremony. They stood by the door and greeted the other relatives before the event began. David's wife and three children accompanied him to the event, and many of the relatives from both Ettie's and Morton's families also attended. Rachel and her children made the trip, as did Collette's children. They were all delighted to share this honor to recognize David's success and looked forward to celebrating with him at the end of the formal part of the evening—but they also whispered that they were prepared for a long, boring, academic ceremony before that point.

The speaker introduced David, making reference to his many scholarly accomplishments, including writings on schizophrenia and how it often unfairly stigmatized and otherwise harmed families. Then David began his talk as if it would be an academic paper. He summarized the implications of his research for improving the way mental health professionals relate to family members of patients suffering from schizophrenia—a disease that recent research had shown to be largely biological in its nature and causation. He also summarized a litany of research studies stressing the need for mental health professionals to form alliances with family members, support them, and teach them skills for coping with their irrational, sick, and yet beloved parent, spouse, or child.

Most relevant to Ettie and her children, David discussed the need for mental health professionals to help family members overcome the sense of stigma and shame, and especially the unwarranted guilt they might feel. He made it clear that recent research debunked old notions that schizophrenia and other psychotic disorders were caused by faulty family relationships. His words reminded Ettie of the way mental health professionals had made her feel at the time of Morton's diagnosis and treatment, how they seemed insensitive to her feelings and oblivious to the implications for her children.

What he said next shocked both Ettie and his sisters.

"You all might be wondering what drew me to this field of research. To answer that, I have to reveal a family secret. My family is present, and they don't know what I am about to say. They are probably fearing what I'm about to reveal, but I hope it'll help them to realize that there is no need to remain afraid."

Ettie's proud smile vanished. Apprehension stiffened her entire body. As if moving in unison, Collette and Rachel both turned to check on their mother, then made eye contact with each other, their faces pinched with worry. They looked away quickly. Ettie kept her eyes glued to the floor.

David took a deep breath, and his voice quavered when he continued. "My father became mentally ill when I was an infant. He suffered from paranoid schizophrenia and had been hospitalized in Mayview State Hospital ever since he received a lobotomy nearly fifty years ago."

Hearing those words, Ettie began to relax, and she sensed the tension easing in the bodies of her daughters, seated on either side of her. For a moment Ettie sat still, trying to sort out what she was feeling. *Relief.* Relief not unlike how one feels when a painful medical procedure cures a more severe pain. David was lifting the shroud of secrecy and shame that for so long had haunted their family.

David described how hard it was for his family, and thanked all of those who had helped them get through the tough times: his father's brothers for their financial and moral support; his deceased grandmother, Sarah, for her love and encouragement; other relatives for their interest and companionship. "Mostly, however, I thank my mom, who, despite all the hardships she endured, devoted herself to her children and made sure that they understood the value of an education that she herself had wanted so badly but was never able to obtain." Ettie was blinking back tears as he thanked his older sisters for helping his mom take care of him and for believing in him.

Choked up with emotion, David had to stop a few times as he continued his speech. When Ettie glanced around, she noticed hers were not the only tears—all around her, family members were crying. He finished to thunderous applause.

Tears still streaming down her face, Ettie embraced him at the conclusion of the ceremony, and thanked people she didn't recognize who came up to congratulate her for her strength and courage. "I was touched that you mentioned my mother, your Bubbe Sarah," she whispered to him. Sarah had died of heart failure at the age of eighty, when David was twenty-five. "She never lost her confidence that you would make me proud one day, and she was right."

Rachel joined them, and Ettie whispered in her ear, "Well, are you happy, now that your brother has decided to go public?"

"Mother, I'm so proud of him. It was a remarkably candid and emotional speech. I'm amazed he could get through it. It took a lot of courage." Collette put her arms around David and told him how impressed she was that he'd used his honor to share so much without belittling anyone.

A man David's age approached from the audience, smiling proudly. He enthusiastically congratulated David on his award and speech as Ettie watched, wondering who this stranger was. David knew him, though. After hearty greetings, he turned to Ettie and his sisters and said, "It's been almost forty years since I last saw this guy's face, but it's one I'd never forget. Mother, Rachel, Collette, this is Manny, the boy who used to live up the street from us." *The boy who taunted David, saying his father was in the nuthouse,* Ettie remembered.

Afterward, they returned to the hospitality room that David had arranged in his hotel, and Ettie surprised them all.

"Guess what, I might be a celebrity too. I had a call from a lady from the Jewish Community Center who is putting together a book on what the center has meant to families for the past hundred years. Someone told them I would be a good subject to interview to find out what it was like living in the Hill District back when I was a girl, and also when we lived in Terrace Village. They want personal stories on how the IKS helped. I agreed to let them interview me. Now, I think I'll take some lessons from my son when they come to talk to me."

"I'm so happy they asked to interview you," Collette said. "You've had experiences very few people had."

Rachel nodded enthusiastically. "What a great idea. You can help lots of people. Do you think this is part of someone's Ph.D. dissertation?"

"Well, I'll let you know when I find out," Ettie replied. She knew now what she had to do, whatever the purpose of the project was.

* * *

A few weeks later, Ettie sat down for the interview and talked about the dances at the settlement house, about the different ways her daughters used the IKS, and about the nursery school she took David to when she was working in the grocery store on Carson Street. The IKS played a positive role as a place where her children could enjoy various activities, she said.

As soon as she began to talk about Morton's illness, though, Mrs. Gold looked alarmed and tried to change the subject. But Ettie insisted on talking about it. "I praise the IKS for what it did for me and my family, but it's important that the whole story be included," she insisted.

She revealed how she wished there had been people available that she could talk to about what she was going through with a schizophrenic husband, and described the loneliness of losing a husband and not being able to mourn or to share the pain. She touched on the fears of being ostracized because people might think there was something wrong with their family. And she concluded with the hope that there was more help available today for people facing similar tragedies.

When the community book came out, Ettie's story was one of many that described the immigrant experience and, for some, the hardships single mothers experienced, raising children on meager resources. Some of the stories mentioned physical illnesses; Ettie's story was the only one bringing to light the loneliness and perceived stigma associated with mental illness.

When they got their copies of the book, some of Ettie's neighbors called to tell her how impressed they were with her courage. Some told her about people in their families who had been mentally ill. One woman remarked that it had been terrible in the old country, when they locked a crazy person up in a room and pretended he or she didn't exist because everyone thought it was a stain on the family. Another told her that an uncle of hers had killed himself during the Depression, and they'd been unable to bury him inside the Orthodox cemetery. It was then that Ettie decided to call Bea and offer to sit down with her neighbors, to tell them how important it was to seek professional help and not hide from the reality.

Within a few weeks of the book's publication, Ettie received a phone call from Mrs. Gold, inviting her to appear on a panel at the Jewish Community Center. "Me on a panel? You gotta be kidding! I'm no speaker—I'd get so nervous that I'd probably lose my voice. I'm sorry, but that's not for me."

Mrs. Gold backed off for a minute. "Okay, Mrs. Burin, I understand. But maybe you would consider something else? Would you be willing to talk about it again with me, but let us make a video of the conversation so we can use it in our staff development sessions?" Ettie hesitated, but agreed.

She cried a lot during the interview, but she answered each question with honesty. The last question got her to open her heart: "Mrs. Burin, what has been the most difficult challenge in all of this for you?"

She thought a moment, then said quickly, "I can answer that for sure. I don't know how I got through those years, wondering why the doctors couldn't help my husband, knowing how much pain it caused my children, and worrying about how others might make fun of them if they found out their father was schizophrenic." She sighed. Now she had put the dreaded word to it. But she went on. "Nobody wanted to talk about Mort. I think partly they thought they were protecting me by not bringing up his name, and partly they were still angry with him because he didn't fit in. I know my family felt that way, and I think his brothers felt the same. I made up things to tell my son, trying to hide the truth from him. That was a mistake. I wish someone had helped my family face the reality of the situation."

Ettie stared at the interviewer. "And you know, that's why I agreed to do this, because I've been told that other families today need help and advice on how to deal with mental illness."

Ettie declined Mrs. Gold's offer to look at the video after it was edited and ready for use. She was afraid that she would be embarrassed and change her mind about letting them use it. Already she was wondering who might see it and what they would think. But she knew she'd done the right thing.

The Unveiling

In the middle of January Collette and Stanley visited Ettie to discuss the unveiling of the headstone at Morton's gravesite. Collette said that she and Stanley had asked the rabbi what he would suggest in terms of any religious or traditional requirements.

"I'm sure you'd like to invite all the relatives and friends to join us, wouldn't you?" Ettie interjected. "Don't worry, I won't give you a hard time, like I did before the funeral." She looked into her daughter's eyes. "It's okay; I know that's the way you kids want it—no big secrets anymore." Collette looked concerned, but before she could react, Ettie continued. "Since I gave that interview to Mrs. Gold and talked with the neighbors about your father, it's been easier. I don't have to be careful every time I open my mouth. Anyhow, I'm an old lady now—who cares what I say?" She shrugged. "It doesn't matter anymore."

"Mother, give yourself credit," Collette protested. "What you say does matter—you're making a difference to people when you encourage them to get help for emotional problems."

"Maybe you're right, Collette. Maybe I missed my calling—I should've been a social worker." She laughed, then headed into her kitchen. "Would you like some juice? How about you, Stanley?"

When Ettie returned to the living room, she saw Stanley and Collette exchange glances and nod. Before Ettie could satisfy her curiosity, Collette began to speak. "Let me tell you what the rabbi said about the unveiling. I think it will work out well. He said we can handle it any way we want to, at any time, although it's usually held about a year after somebody dies. If we want the rabbi to attend he can, but it isn't required. We can read prayers, or just get together to share some personal thoughts."

"Whatever you kids want to do is fine with me, only don't expect me to make any speeches," Ettie said, then added, "I think the rabbi should be there. I always thought they had to be there. It's only right."

"Mother, nobody will have to make any speeches, it'll be very informal. If anyone wants to speak, they can, no pressure."

"That's good." Ettie nodded.

"I'm glad you agree," Collette said, clearly relieved. "We'll make arrangements with the rabbi and get a date that is good for Rachel and David."

Ettie wasn't surprised when her other two children phoned later in the day. Rachel's call came first. After a few words of greeting, Ettie asked what Rachel thought about the plans for the unveiling.

"Sounds fine to me, Mother, especially if we can keep it informal."

Ettie wasn't so sure. "Tell me the truth, Rachel—do you really think people will have memories they want to share? A lot of them don't even remember your dad."

"So much has happened since the funeral," Rachel said. "In fact, since David gave his speech, I've been able to talk more freely to strangers about Dad and the fact that he was mentally ill. It's been a relief."

"Yeah, maybe for you, but my relatives know how hard I had it. I don't want to talk about the bad times with Morton, and they would think it was silly if I started to share any other memories."

"People won't expect you to speak, Mother," Rachel said, sounding surprised. "Not everyone will be speaking; you can be part of it without speaking. That's why this kind of service is comfortable—there are no expectations. Stop worrying."

"Okay, okay," Ettie sighed. "But I bet you'll try to come up with something to say."

"It's different for me. I want people to realize that before he got sick, Dad could be a very loving father; that's what I want to remember most. He did a lot of nice things with Collette and me when we were kids. He seemed to like our company."

"Yeah, he really did," Ettie admitted. "He liked to take you places. He was very proud of you."

Not too long after they ended their conversation, Ettie received a phone call from David.

"Hey David, how's everything?" she asked cheerfully. "I just got off the phone with Rachel. What do you think about the plans for the unveiling?"

"Everything's cool. I'll be there, and I'll do what I'm supposed to do," David responded calmly.

"Are you going to give another speech?" Ettie teased.

"I'll think of something to say. Something that helps people to realize that my not seeing my father all of those years doesn't take away from his importance in my life."

The conversations with her children left Ettie wondering what good memories she could share about Morton. She wouldn't feel comfortable talking about the early days, and the excitement she once felt in his presence. She would feel foolish talking about his intellect and the promise she once believed of a good life with him. Then she realized what the most important thing was that she should say, and it wasn't about her at all.

* * *

The day of the unveiling was unusually cold and damp for mid-March. The snow and ice that had covered the cemetery had melted a week before, leaving the ground a mush of half-frozen mud. Collette and Stanley and their children were already there when Ettie arrived with David and Rachel and her children, as were Morton's two surviving brothers and two of their sons. Next on the scene were Bennie, Bea, and Libby's son, Danny. A few friends showed up as well—altogether about twenty people.

The rabbi started the service by explaining that he would read a few prayers. "But the main purpose of an unveiling is to share some fond memories of the loved one. After the prayers, I invite anyone who has something to say to do so."

Morton's brother Sol stepped forward to speak first. "You know, we never understood Mort. He was ahead of his time. He had ideas about our business that today are accepted practice, but back then we thought his ideas were too aggressive, out of line with the small-town atmosphere we had in our stores. He was a very smart man."

"I didn't know Uncle Mort until I began visiting him with my dad about ten years ago," Solomon's son, Lenny, said. "I was amazed when

Dad brought a Hebrew prayer book, and Uncle Mort could read it more beautifully than anyone I'd ever heard."

When Collette cleared her throat, everyone looked at her with concern, but she smiled and waved away their worries. "I loved my father very much," she said. "I have loving memories from before he became ill, and also of our visits with him in the hospital. He taught me to read, he took me places, and he told wonderful stories. I was always so proud of him."

"I remember my father coming to tuck Collette and me into bed at night," Rachel added. "He would sing to us. He didn't have a good singing voice, but we were so happy. He loved to sing 'In a Little Spanish Town' and 'Bye, Bye, Blackbird.' Those were the happy times. Then he got sick and had to be hospitalized. I missed him very much."

"I don't have any memories of my father before he became ill," David told those gathered. "I never saw much of him at any time of my life. But a year before he died my family visited him, and he wanted to play checkers with us. He beat all of us!"

Scattered, appreciative laughter, then everyone looked at the rabbi, expecting him to wrap things up. But Ettie stepped forward. "I have something to say."

In a clear voice, she spoke the words she had prepared for this moment. "It's no secret, I had a hard life with Mort. And it was tough on all of us after he got sick. What did we know about mental illness back then? It's a shame that he got sick before they had medication that might have helped him. He couldn't help himself, he tried to get help from doctors, but nothing worked. I don't want to dwell on those rough times. Today I want to share one thing with everyone. Morton loved his children. He couldn't always show it, but I always knew—I knew when each one was born, he was thrilled. He didn't get to enjoy them as they grew up. If he had stayed healthy, they would have brought him much joy and pride. And that is what I want my children to know." Ettie was crying as she finished.

As they walked together toward the cars to head back to the city, Rachel said, "Mother, that was a beautiful thing you said. Thank you."

Ettie wiped her eyes. "I thought about it a lot, whether to speak or not. I couldn't just say anything, it had to be the truth. I wish my life had been easier. But I know how much you kids lost when your dad got sick, each of you in a different way. When anyone thinks about Morton, it is important that they think about you kids. Because of you, his troubled life had special meaning."

Glossary

afikomen – food eaten at the end of the meal. In the Passover seder, it is the piece of matzo hidden for children to hunt for and then the last item eaten

bar mitzvah – an initiation ceremony when a Jewish boy reaches the age of thirteen and becomes responsible for moral and religious duties

Bes Medresh – place of learning, synagogue

beshert – fated, preordained

bris – religious ritual for a circumcision

bubbe – grandmother

bubbe maisse – old wives' tale, grandmother's tale

challah – traditional Jewish white egg bread, eaten on the Sabbath and holidays

chazar – pig

cheder – Hebrew school

chupah – wedding canopy

davenen – pray

droshky – a carriage used, mostly in Russia, for transporting people

ech – a groan, a disparaging exclamation

feh – phooey, it's no good, it stinks

flanken – cut of beef, stewed and served with horseradish

goldene medina – golden country

goy – a gentile, a member of any non-Jewish nation

humantashen – pastries in Ashkenazi Jewish cuisine recognizable for their three-cornered shape; eaten during the Jewish holiday of Purim

kaddish – an important and central prayer in the Jewish prayer service, the central theme being the magnification and sanctification of God's name, said as part of the mourning rituals

kaynahora – spoken to ward off the evil eye

kazutski – lively Russian dance

ketubah – marriage contract

kibitz – look on to offer unwanted or meddlesome advice; chat; converse

kinderleh – children

kopek – Russian unit of currency, coin

kvetch – complain, whine

Litvak – Jewish person from Lithuania

maideleh – little girl

matzo – unleavened bread eaten especially during Passover; a cracker-like flatbread, not allowed to rise before or during baking

mazel tov – congratulations

mensch – a human being; a decent person; an upright, responsible person

meshuganer – crazy, mad, insane man

mikveh – ritual bath

mitzvah – good deed

nachis – pleasure

nu? – so? well?

oy! – Oh!

oy, gevalt – cry of anguish, suffering, frustration

oy vay – Dear Me

payes – earlocks of hair or sidecurls, sidelocks

rebbeh – master, teacher, or mentor, derived from the identical Hebrew word rabbi, mostly referring to the leader of a Hasidic Jewish movement.

schlepped – carried clumsily or with difficulty, lugged

schnapps – clear, alcoholic beverage similar to vodka

seder – "the order," refers to Passover service celebrating freedom through reading the history of the Jews' exodus from slavery in Egypt; recitation of prayers for traditional foods and wine

Shabbas – Shabbat, the Sabbath

shah – be quiet

shaina – pretty

shidech – match, marriage, betrothal

shiva – seven-day mourning period observed by Jewish people after the funeral

shlemiel – a jerk

shmuta – a worthless rag

shtetl – small Jewish village in eastern Europe

shtik drek – piece of human dung, excrement

simcha – celebration or joy, happy event

tallis – prayer shawl

tefillin – phylacteries, a pair of black leather boxes containing scrolls of parchment inscribed with biblical verses to serve as a "sign" and "remembrance." Hand tefillin are worn wrapped around the arm, hand, and fingers; head tefillin placed above the forehead

treyf – unkosher food

tsores – troubles, misery

vay is mir – woe is me

yarmulke – skullcap worn by Jewish men

yenta – a gossip

yeshiva – an educational institution for study of Torah, Talmud, and Rabbinic literature

zayde – grandfather

Bibliography

Ansky, S., *The Dybbuk and Other Writings* (edited by David G. Roskies), New York, Schocken Books, 1992

Button, Margo, *The Unhinging of Wings*, Lantzville, British Columbia, Oolichan Books, 1996

Goldstein, Rebecca, *Mazel*, New York, Viking Penguin Books, 1995

Howe, Irving, *World of Our Fathers*, New York, Harcourt Brace Jovanovich, 1976

Jewish Chronicle of Pittsburgh, *We Are Family . . . Stories of Pittsburgh Families*, Pittsburgh, Pennsylvania, Pittsburgh Jewish Publication and Education Foundation, 2000

Jewish Community Center, *Then and Now:1895–1995*, Pittsburgh, Pennsylvania, 1995

Langley, Lee, *From the Broken Tree,* New York, Thomas Congdon Books, 1978

Lincoln, W. Bruce, *Red Victory: A History of the Russian Civil War,* New York, Simon and Schuster, 1989

Malkin, Carole, *The Journeys of David Toback*, New York, Walker and Company, 1981

Myerhoff, Barbara, *Number Our Days*, New York, Simon and Schuster, 1978

Neugroschel, Joachim, *The Shtetl, A Creative Anthology of Jewish Life in Eastern Europe*, New York, Woodstock, 1989

Pittsburgh Jewish Newspaper Project, Carnegie Mellon University Libraries, Pittsburgh, Pennsylvania

Richmond, Theo, *Konin, A Quest*, London, Random House, 1995

Stryker, Roy and Seidenberg, Mel, *A Pittsburgh Album 1755–1958,* Pittsburgh, Pennsylvania, *Pittsburgh Post-Gazette*, 1959

Vishniak, Roman, *A Vanished World*, New York, Farrar, Straus, & Giroux, 1983

Wiesel, Elie, *Souls on Fire—Portraits and Legends of Hasidic Masters,* New York, Summit Books, 1972

Zborowski, Mark and Herzog, Elizabeth, *Life is with People: The Culture of the Shtetl*, New York, Schocken Books, 1967

About the Author

Leah Rae Lambert has had an extensive career in education, social work, research, and planning. She holds undergraduate and graduate degrees from the University of Pittsburgh and a Ph.D. from the University of Toronto. She grew up in Pittsburgh, and has enjoyed living and working in Toronto for many years.

Breinigsville, PA USA
03 September 2010
244868BV00003B/50/P